LOVE AND WAR™

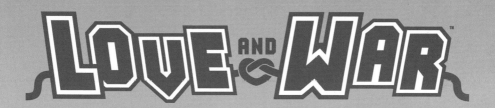

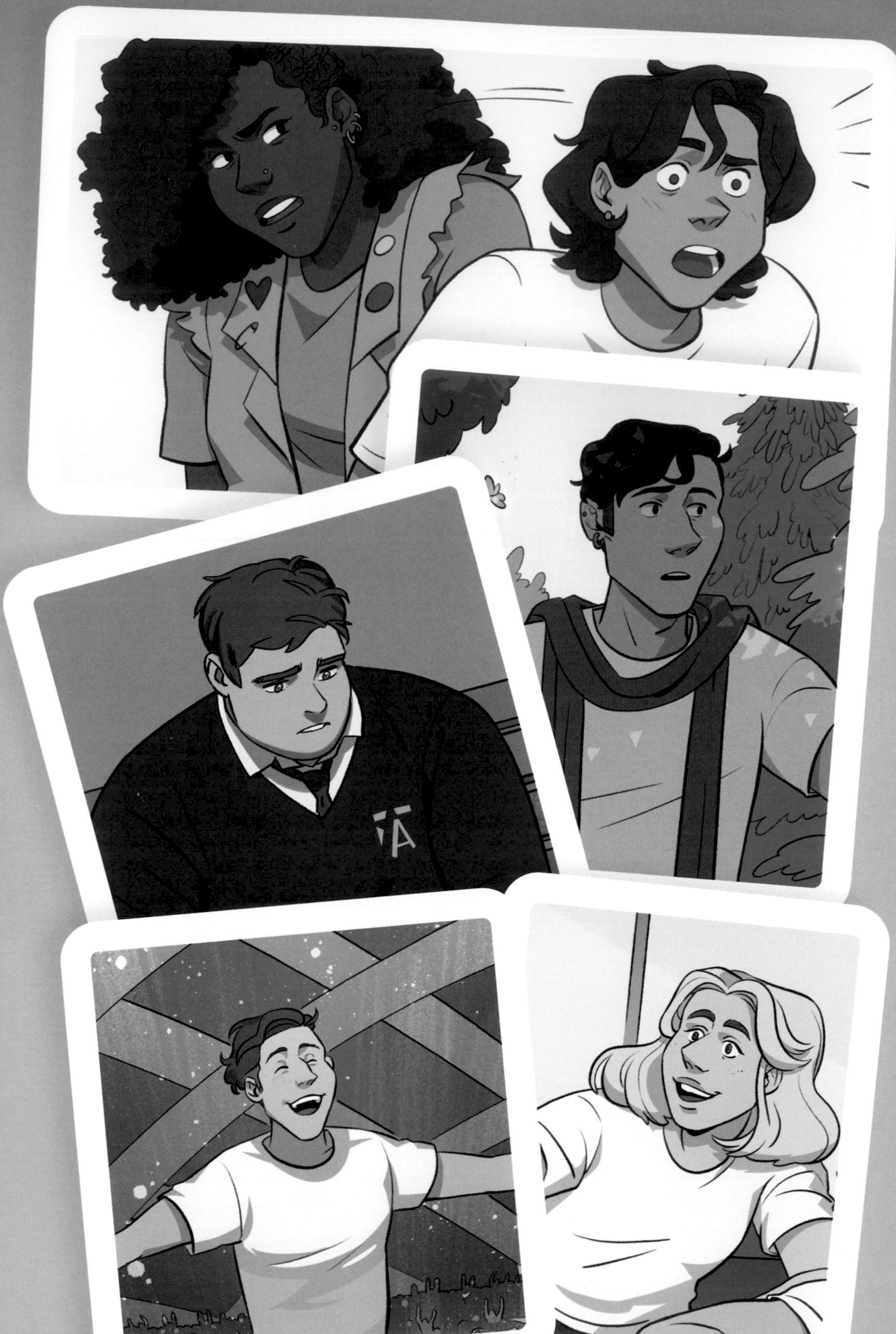

Love and War

WRITTEN BY **ANDREW WHEELER**

ART BY **GUILLERMO SAAVEDRA** (CHAPTERS 3-5)

AND **KILLIAN NG** (CHAPTERS 1-2)

COLORS BY **C.R. CHUA** (CHAPTERS 2-5)

AND **KILLIAN NG** (CHAPTER 1)

LETTERS BY **HASSAN OTSMANE-ELHAOU** (CHAPTERS 2-5)

AND **ADITYA BIDIKAR** (CHAPTER 1)

EDITED BY **ALLISON O'TOOLE**

DESIGN BY **CINDY LEONG**

 DARK HORSE BOOKS

Dark Horse Team

PRESIDENT AND PUBLISHER **MIKE RICHARDSON**
EDITOR **Daniel Chabon**
ASSISTANT EDITORS **CHUCK HOWITT-LEASE** and **MISHA GEHR**
DESIGNER **ANITA MAGAÑA**
DIGITAL ART TECHNICIAN **JASON RICKERD**

Special thanks to David Steinberger, Chip Mosher, and Bryce Gold.

Published by Dark Horse Books
A division of Dark Horse Comics LLC
10956 SE Main Street
Milwaukie, OR 97222

First edition: September 2022
Trade paperback ISBN 978-1-50672-805-6

10 9 8 7 6 5 4 3 2 1
Printed in China

Comic Shop Locator Service: comicshoplocator.com

MIX
Paper from responsible sources
FSC® C169962

CHAPTER

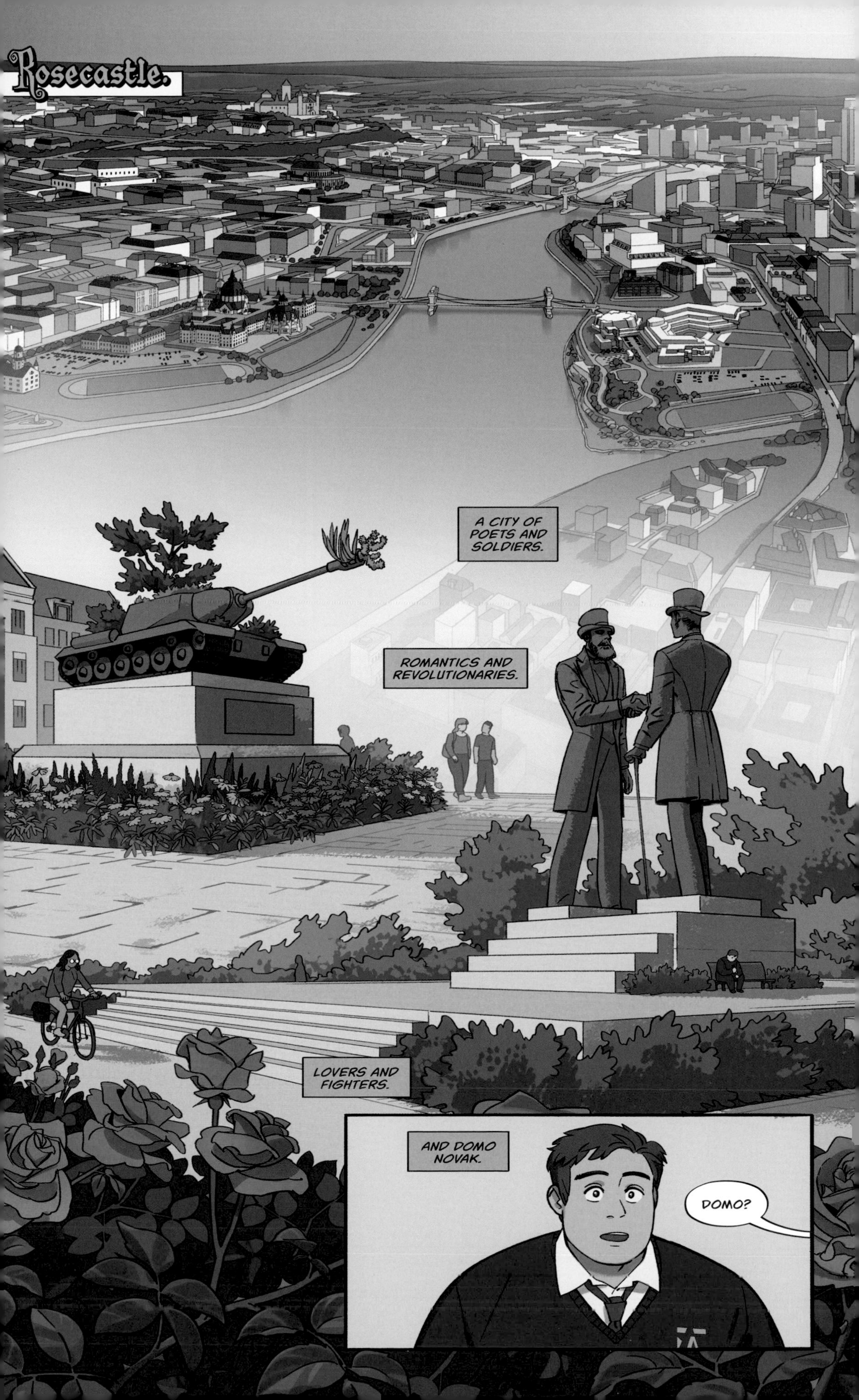
Rosecastle.
A CITY OF POETS AND SOLDIERS.
ROMANTICS AND REVOLUTIONARIES.
LOVERS AND FIGHTERS.
AND DOMO NOVAK.
DOMO?

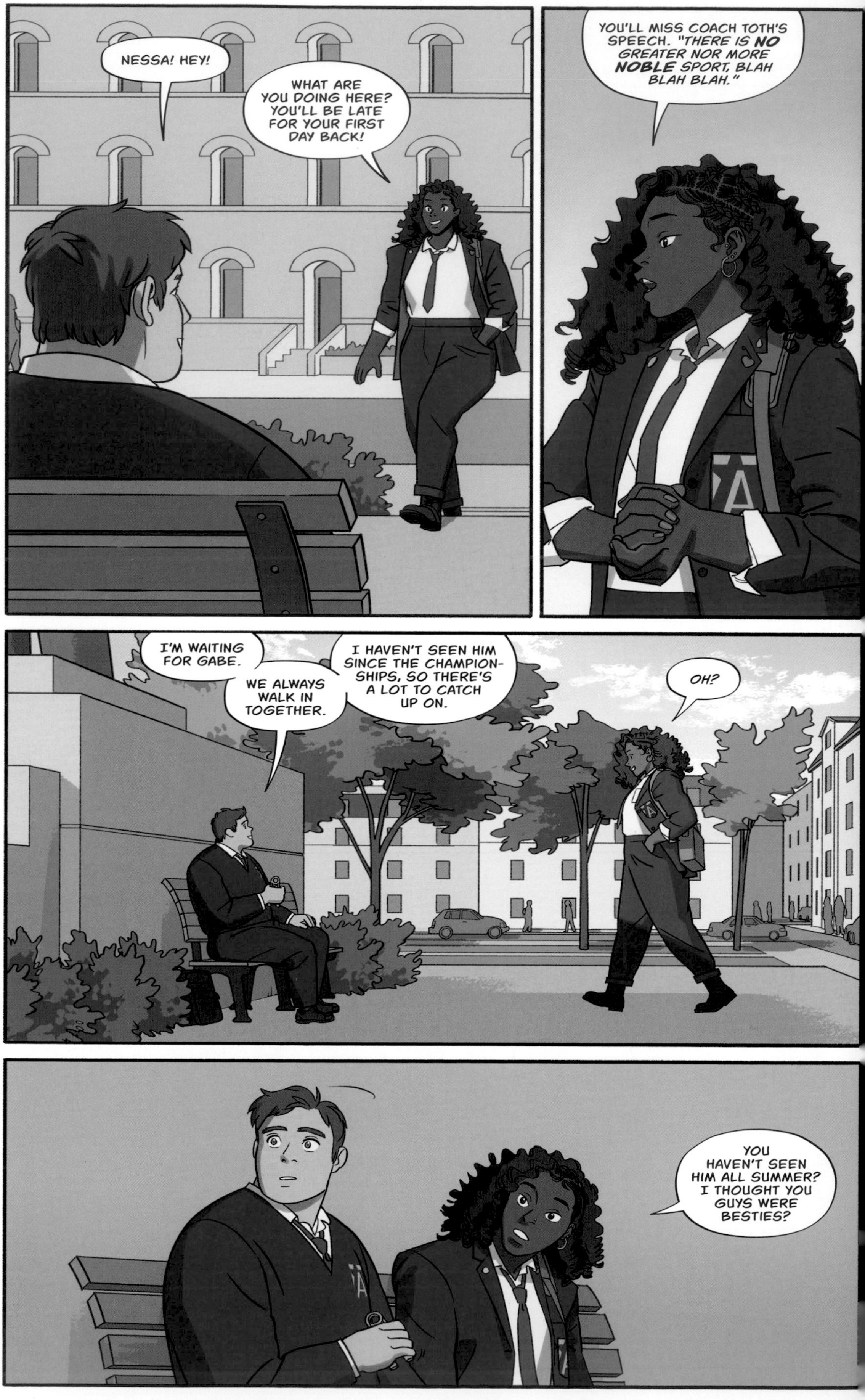
NESSA! HEY!
WHAT ARE YOU DOING HERE? YOU'LL BE LATE FOR YOUR FIRST DAY BACK!
YOU'LL MISS COACH TOTH'S SPEECH. "THERE IS NO GREATER NOR MORE NOBLE SPORT, BLAH BLAH BLAH."
I'M WAITING FOR GABE.
WE ALWAYS WALK IN TOGETHER.
I HAVEN'T SEEN HIM SINCE THE CHAMPION-SHIPS, SO THERE'S A LOT TO CATCH UP ON.
OH?
YOU HAVEN'T SEEN HIM ALL SUMMER? I THOUGHT YOU GUYS WERE BESTIES?

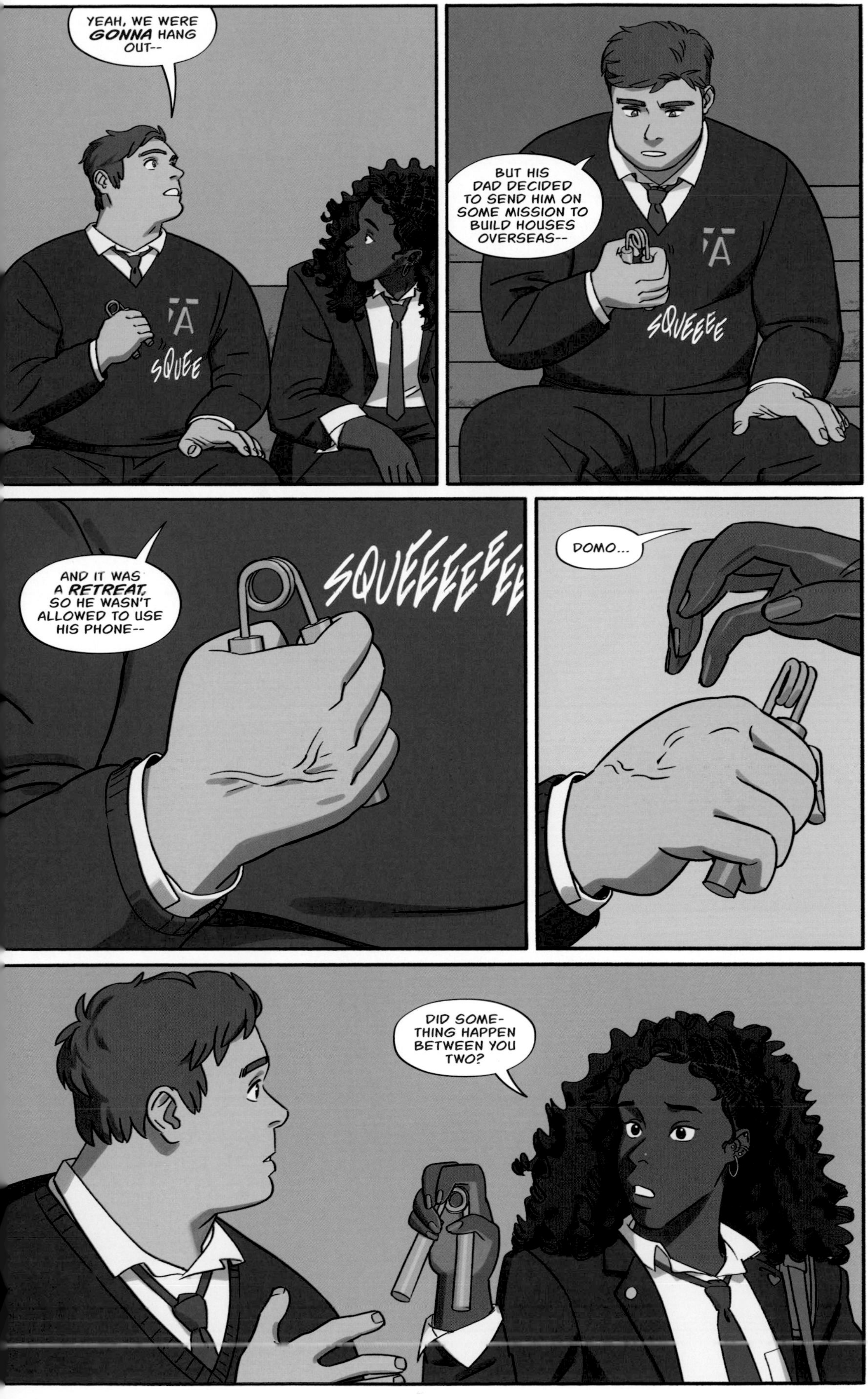
YEAH, WE WERE GONNA HANG OUT--
SQUEE
BUT HIS DAD DECIDED TO SEND HIM ON SOME MISSION TO BUILD HOUSES OVERSEAS--
SQUEEEE
AND IT WAS A RETREAT, SO HE WASN'T ALLOWED TO USE HIS PHONE--
SQUEEEEEEEE
DOMO...
DID SOME-THING HAPPEN BETWEEN YOU TWO?

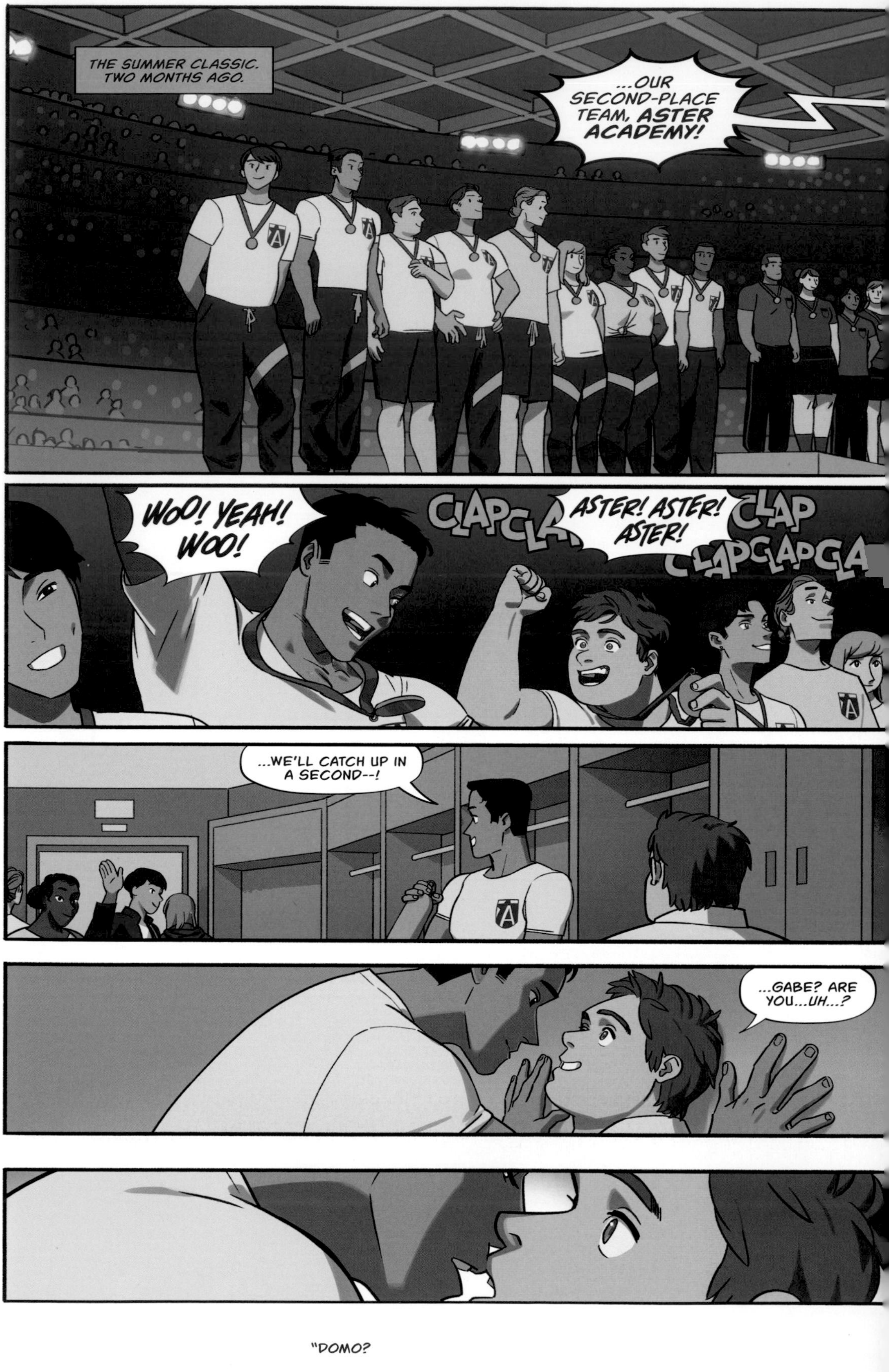
THE SUMMER CLASSIC. TWO MONTHS AGO.
...OUR SECOND-PLACE TEAM, ASTER ACADEMY!
WOO! YEAH! WOO!
ASTER! ASTER! ASTER!
CLAP
...WE'LL CATCH UP IN A SECOND--!
...GABE? ARE YOU...UH...?

"DOMO?

"DID SOMETHING HAPPEN?"

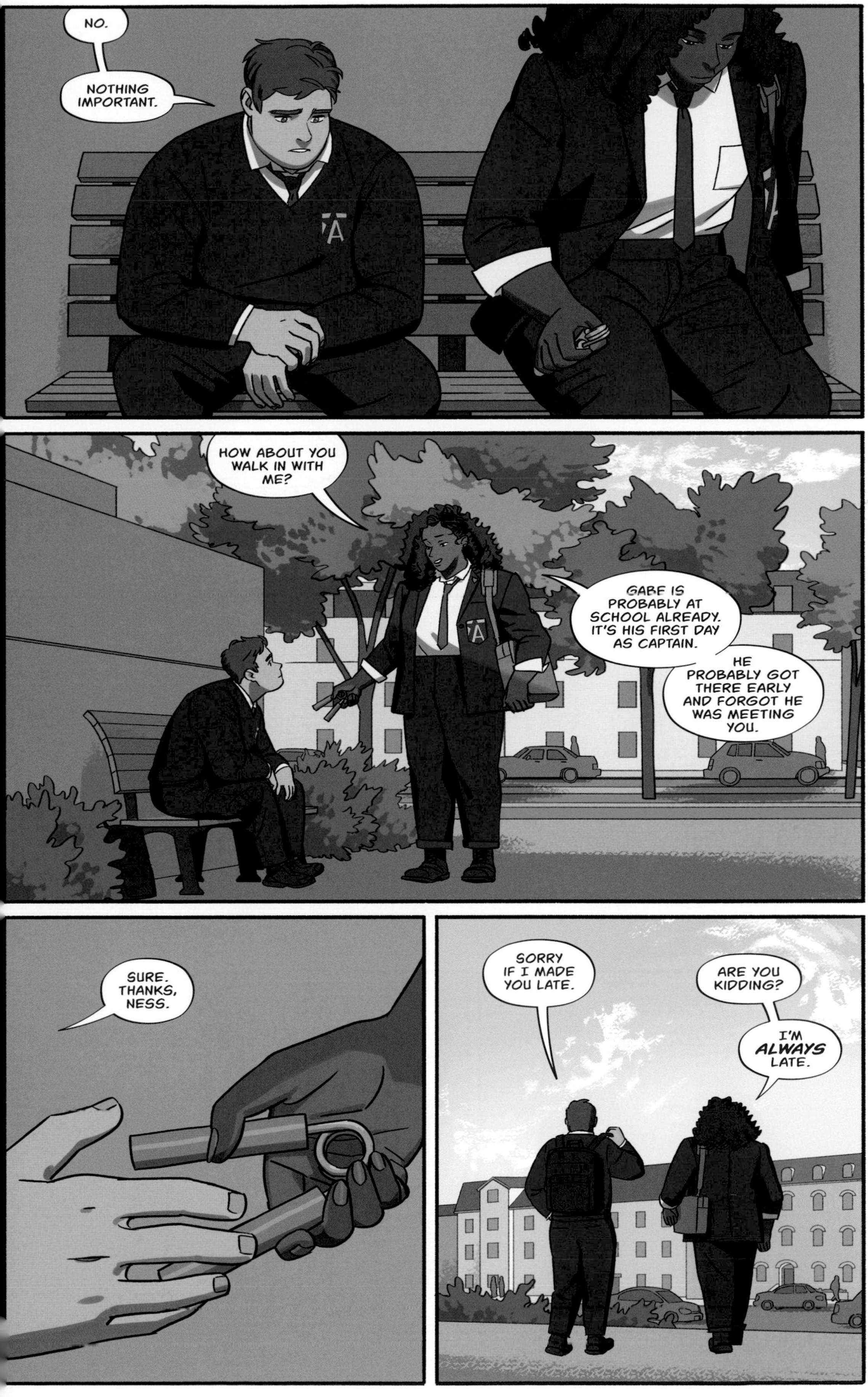
NO.
NOTHING IMPORTANT.
HOW ABOUT YOU WALK IN WITH ME?
GABE IS PROBABLY AT SCHOOL ALREADY. IT'S HIS FIRST DAY AS CAPTAIN.
HE PROBABLY GOT THERE EARLY AND FORGOT HE WAS MEETING YOU.
SURE. THANKS, NESS.
SORRY IF I MADE YOU LATE.
ARE YOU KIDDING?
I'M *ALWAYS* LATE.

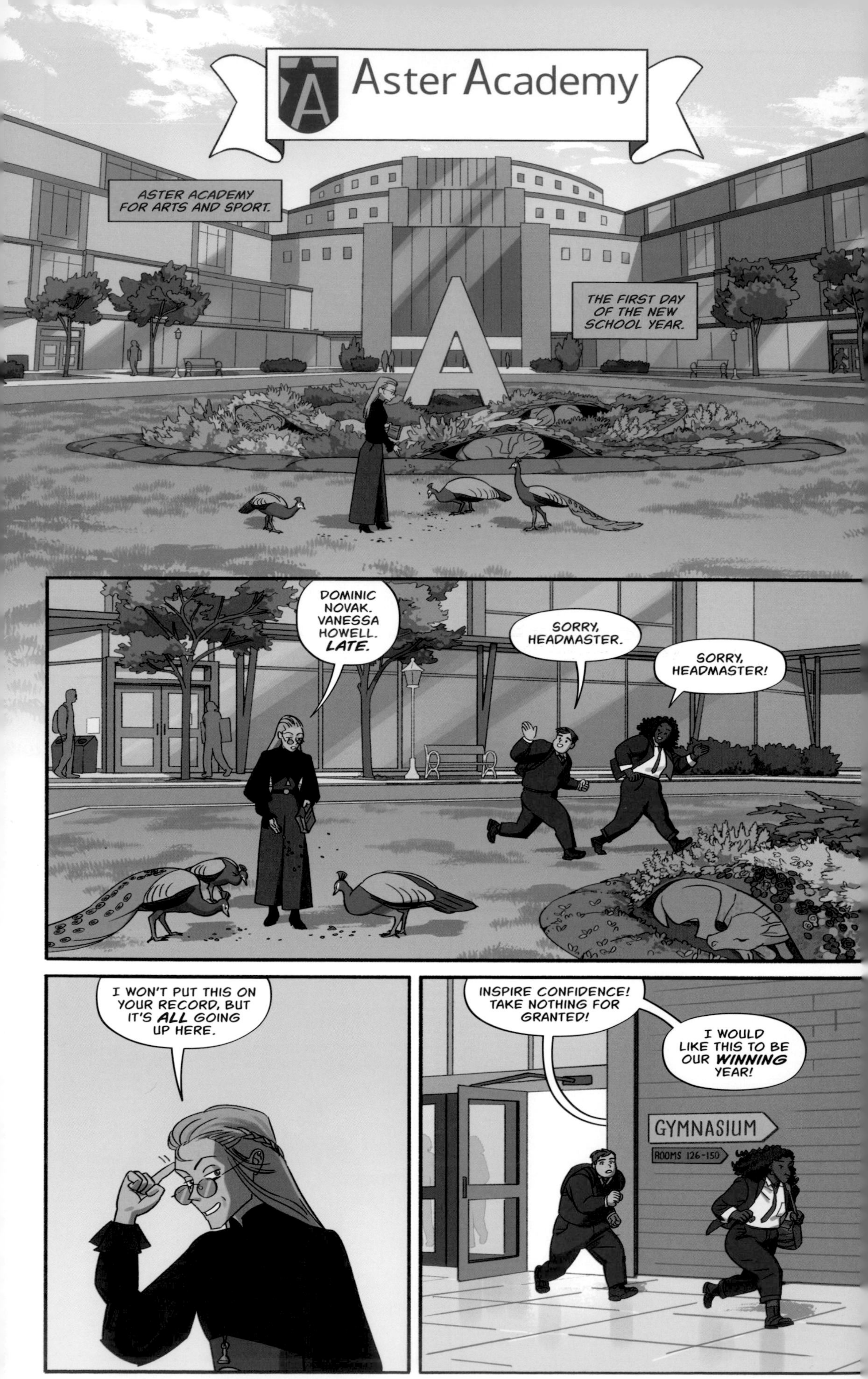

Aster Academy
ASTER ACADEMY FOR ARTS AND SPORT.
THE FIRST DAY OF THE NEW SCHOOL YEAR.
DOMINIC NOVAK. VANESSA HOWELL. LATE.
SORRY, HEADMASTER.
SORRY, HEADMASTER!
I WON'T PUT THIS ON YOUR RECORD, BUT IT'S ALL GOING UP HERE.
INSPIRE CONFIDENCE! TAKE NOTHING FOR GRANTED!
I WOULD LIKE THIS TO BE OUR WINNING YEAR!
GYMNASIUM
ROOMS 126-150

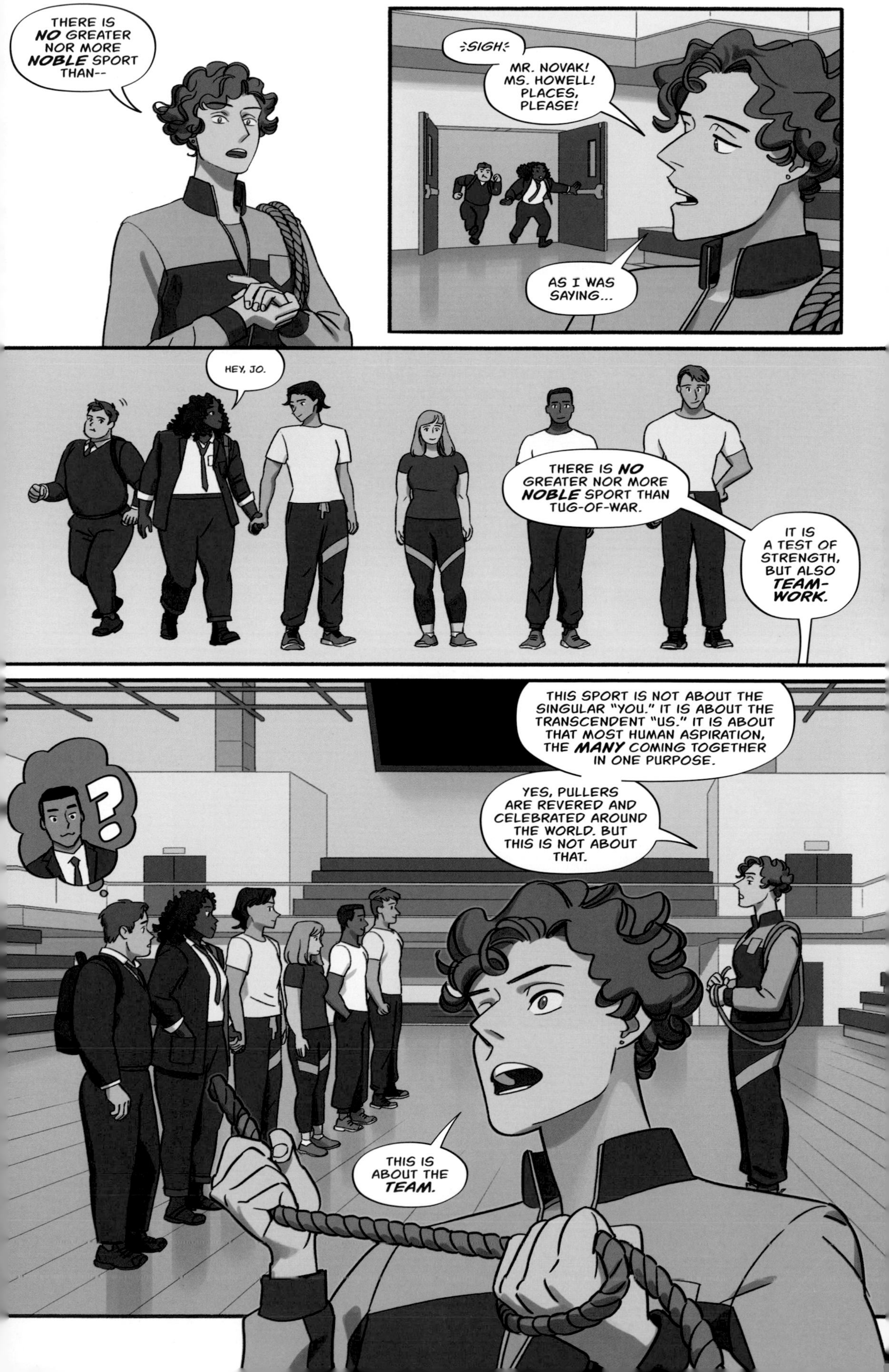
THERE IS *NO* GREATER NOR MORE *NOBLE* SPORT THAN--
SIGH
MR. NOVAK! MS. HOWELL! PLACES, PLEASE!
AS I WAS SAYING...
HEY, JO.
THERE IS *NO* GREATER NOR MORE *NOBLE* SPORT THAN TUG-OF-WAR.
IT IS A TEST OF STRENGTH, BUT ALSO *TEAM-WORK.*
THIS SPORT IS NOT ABOUT THE SINGULAR "YOU." IT IS ABOUT THE TRANSCENDENT "US." IT IS ABOUT THAT MOST HUMAN ASPIRATION, THE *MANY* COMING TOGETHER IN ONE PURPOSE.
?
YES, PULLERS ARE REVERED AND CELEBRATED AROUND THE WORLD. BUT THIS IS NOT ABOUT THAT.
THIS IS ABOUT THE *TEAM.*

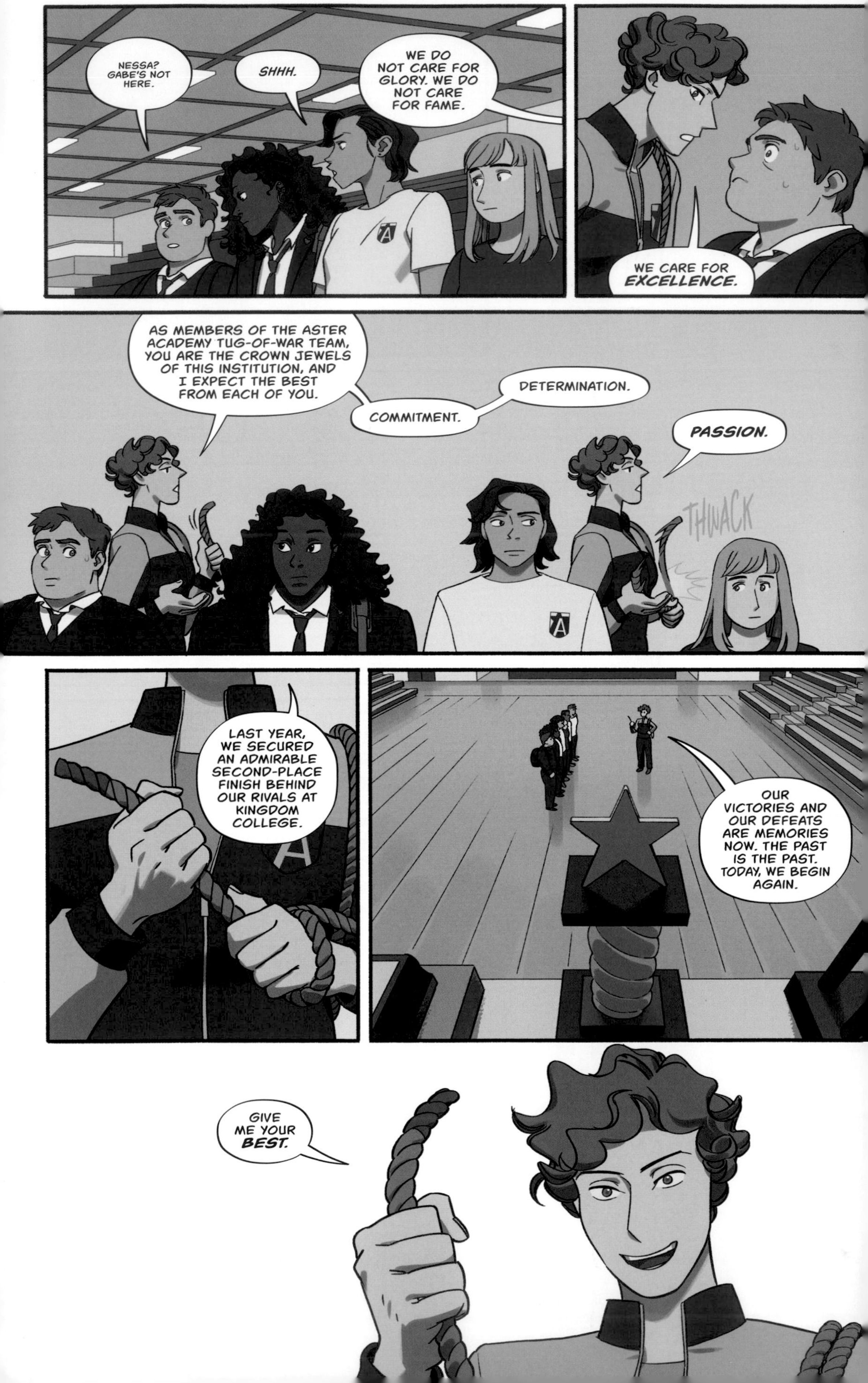
NESSA? GABE'S NOT HERE.
SHHH.
WE DO NOT CARE FOR GLORY. WE DO NOT CARE FOR FAME.
WE CARE FOR EXCELLENCE.
AS MEMBERS OF THE ASTER ACADEMY TUG-OF-WAR TEAM, YOU ARE THE CROWN JEWELS OF THIS INSTITUTION, AND I EXPECT THE BEST FROM EACH OF YOU.
COMMITMENT.
DETERMINATION.
PASSION.
THWACK
LAST YEAR, WE SECURED AN ADMIRABLE SECOND-PLACE FINISH BEHIND OUR RIVALS AT KINGDOM COLLEGE.
OUR VICTORIES AND OUR DEFEATS ARE MEMORIES NOW. THE PAST IS THE PAST. TODAY, WE BEGIN AGAIN.
GIVE ME YOUR BEST.

CAPTAIN?

Domo	Jocasta
Nessa	Byron
Bethany	—
Simon	— ⚓ ?

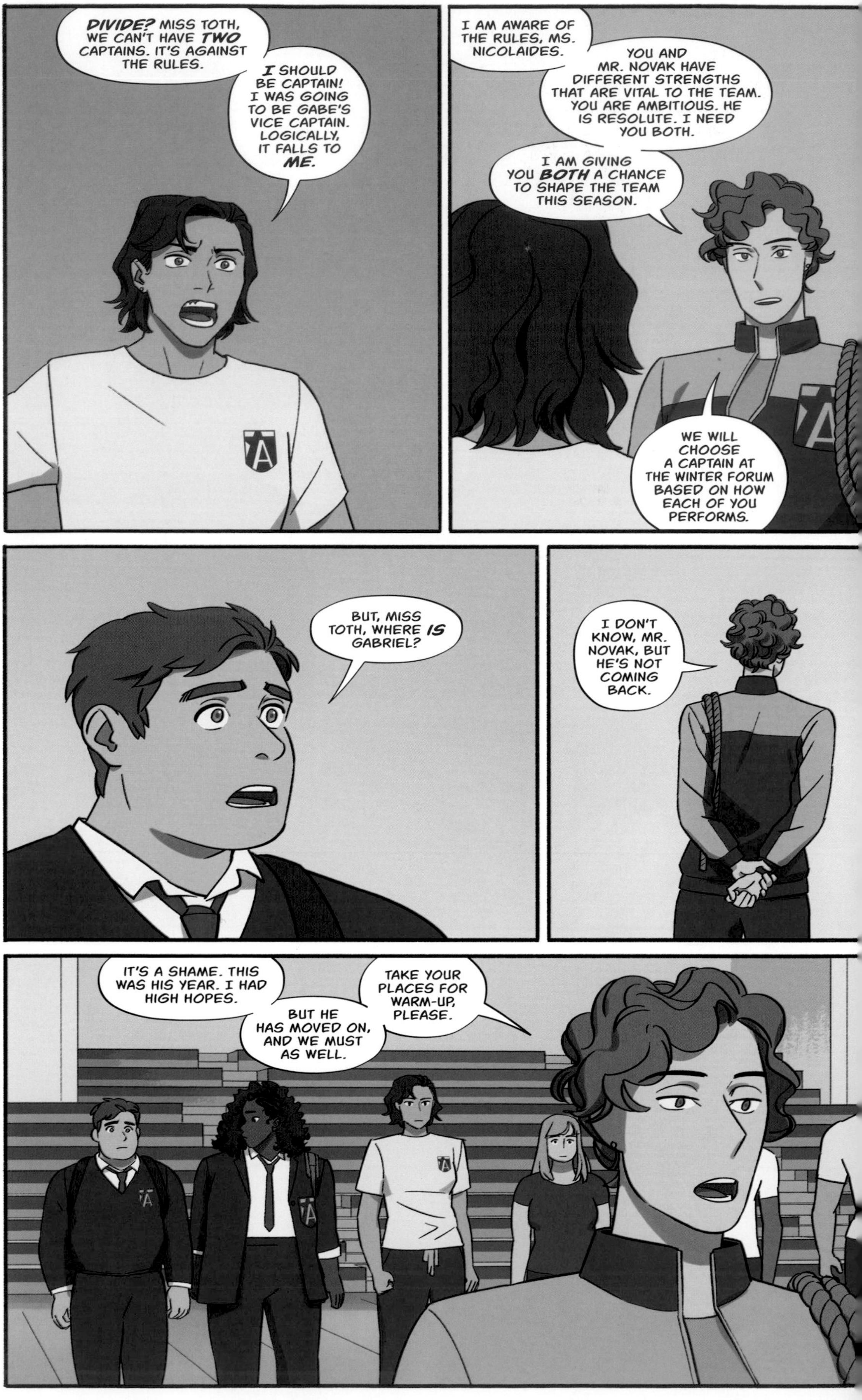
DIVIDE? MISS TOTH, WE CAN'T HAVE TWO CAPTAINS. IT'S AGAINST THE RULES.
I SHOULD BE CAPTAIN! I WAS GOING TO BE GABE'S VICE CAPTAIN. LOGICALLY, IT FALLS TO ME.
I AM AWARE OF THE RULES, MS. NICOLAIDES.
YOU AND MR. NOVAK HAVE DIFFERENT STRENGTHS THAT ARE VITAL TO THE TEAM. YOU ARE AMBITIOUS. HE IS RESOLUTE. I NEED YOU BOTH.
I AM GIVING YOU BOTH A CHANCE TO SHAPE THE TEAM THIS SEASON.
WE WILL CHOOSE A CAPTAIN AT THE WINTER FORUM BASED ON HOW EACH OF YOU PERFORMS.
BUT, MISS TOTH, WHERE IS GABRIEL?
I DON'T KNOW, MR. NOVAK, BUT HE'S NOT COMING BACK.
IT'S A SHAME. THIS WAS HIS YEAR. I HAD HIGH HOPES.
BUT HE HAS MOVED ON, AND WE MUST AS WELL.
TAKE YOUR PLACES FOR WARM-UP, PLEASE.

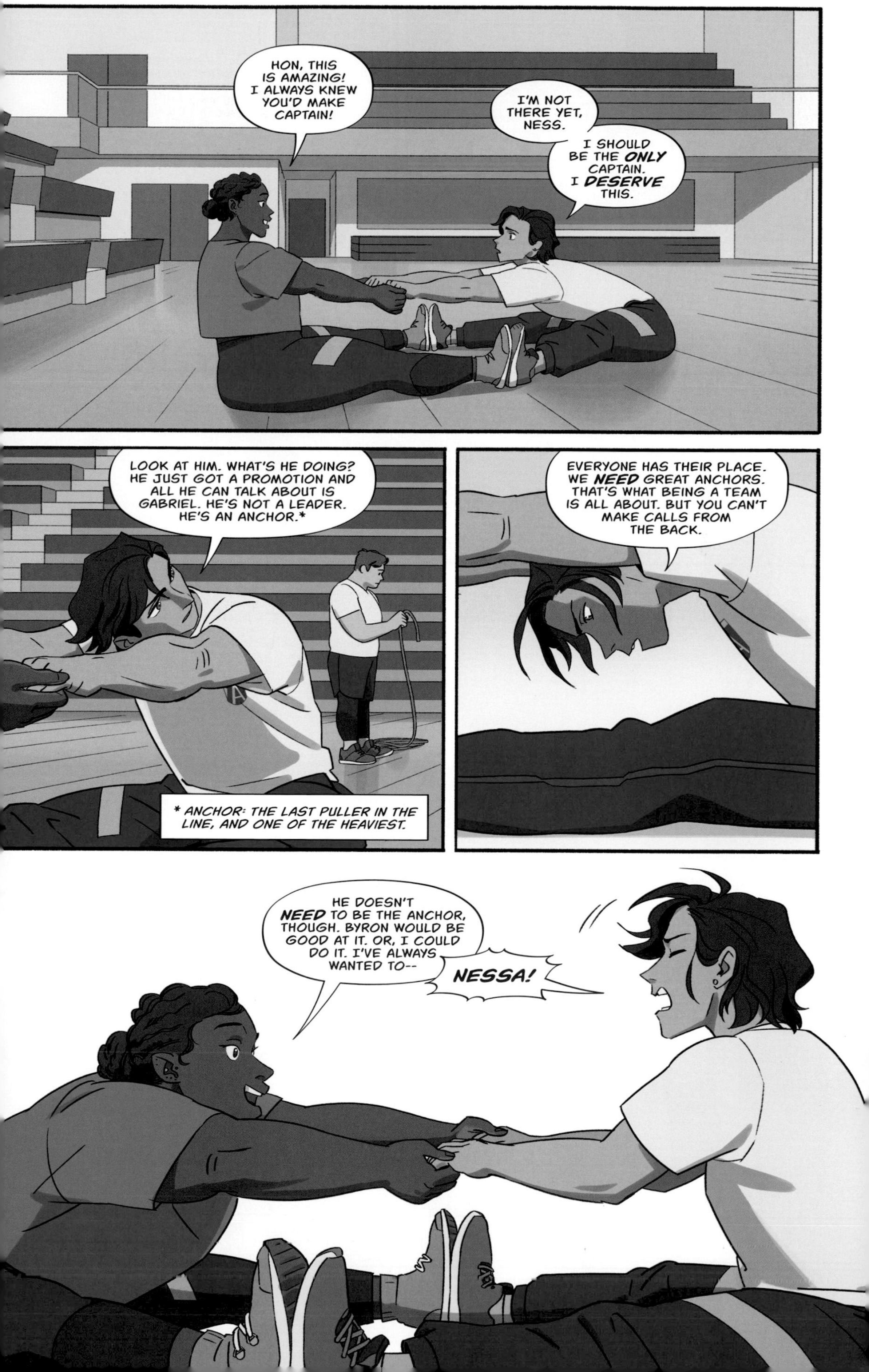
HON, THIS IS AMAZING! I ALWAYS KNEW YOU'D MAKE CAPTAIN!
I'M NOT THERE YET, NESS.
I SHOULD BE THE ONLY CAPTAIN. I DESERVE THIS.
LOOK AT HIM. WHAT'S HE DOING? HE JUST GOT A PROMOTION AND ALL HE CAN TALK ABOUT IS GABRIEL. HE'S NOT A LEADER. HE'S AN ANCHOR.*
* ANCHOR: THE LAST PULLER IN THE LINE, AND ONE OF THE HEAVIEST.
EVERYONE HAS THEIR PLACE. WE NEED GREAT ANCHORS. THAT'S WHAT BEING A TEAM IS ALL ABOUT. BUT YOU CAN'T MAKE CALLS FROM THE BACK.
HE DOESN'T NEED TO BE THE ANCHOR, THOUGH. BYRON WOULD BE GOOD AT IT. OR, I COULD DO IT. I'VE ALWAYS WANTED TO--
NESSA!

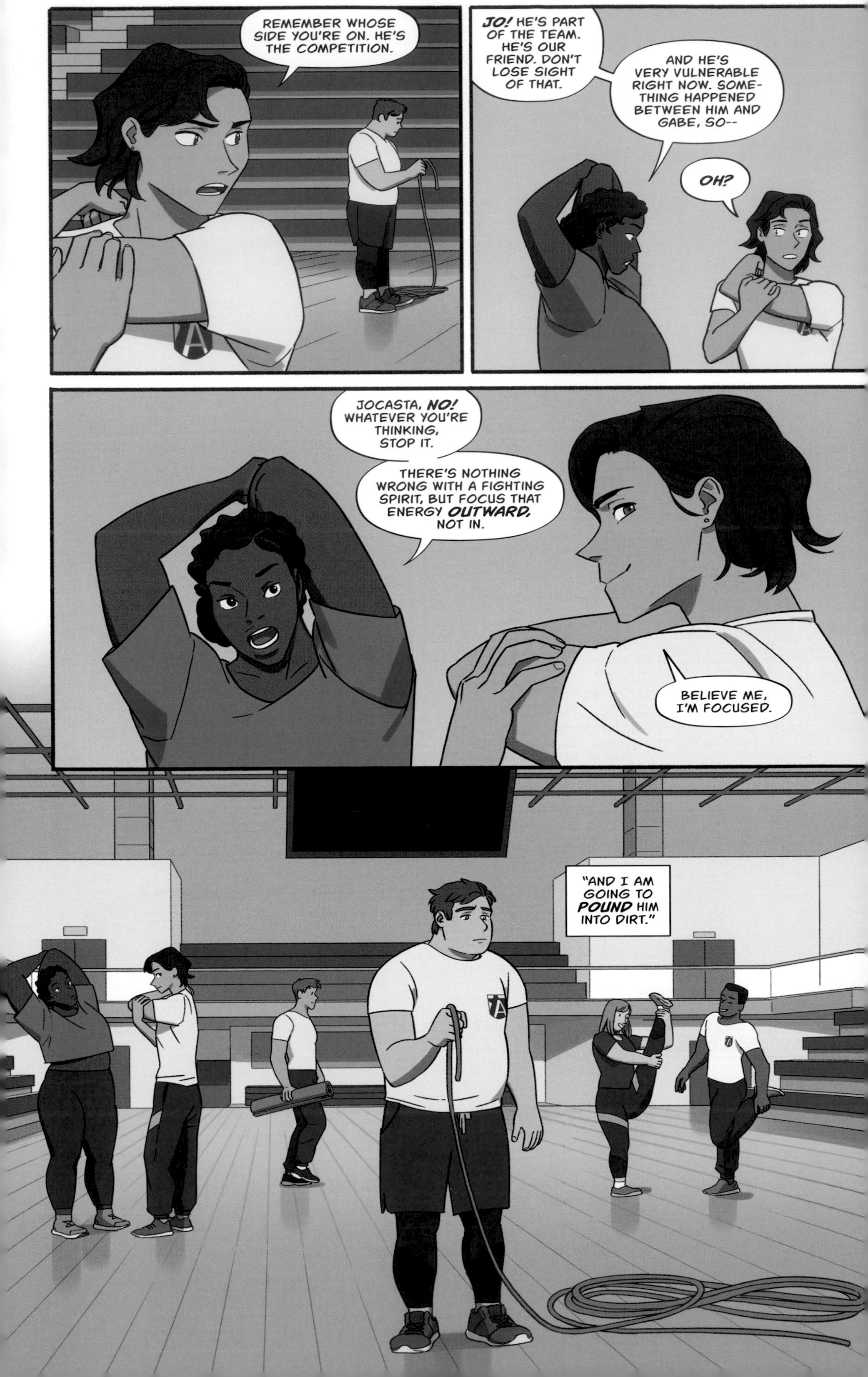
REMEMBER WHOSE SIDE YOU'RE ON. HE'S THE COMPETITION.
JO! HE'S PART OF THE TEAM. HE'S OUR FRIEND. DON'T LOSE SIGHT OF THAT.
AND HE'S VERY VULNERABLE RIGHT NOW. SOMETHING HAPPENED BETWEEN HIM AND GABE, SO--
OH?
JOCASTA, NO! WHATEVER YOU'RE THINKING, STOP IT.
THERE'S NOTHING WRONG WITH A FIGHTING SPIRIT, BUT FOCUS THAT ENERGY OUTWARD, NOT IN.
BELIEVE ME, I'M FOCUSED.
"AND I AM GOING TO POUND HIM INTO DIRT."

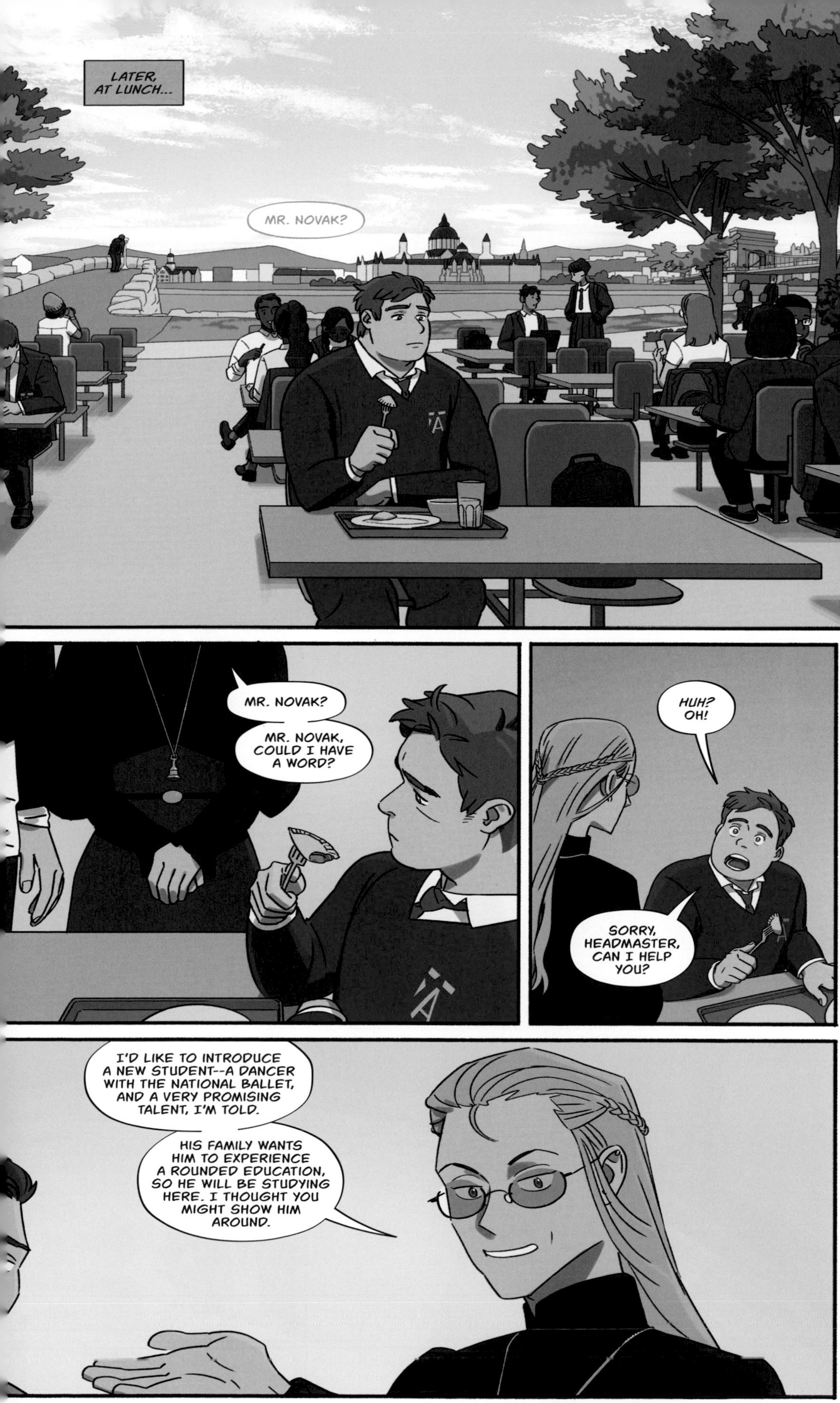
LATER, AT LUNCH...
MR. NOVAK?
MR. NOVAK?
MR. NOVAK, COULD I HAVE A WORD?
HUH? OH!
SORRY, HEADMASTER, CAN I HELP YOU?
I'D LIKE TO INTRODUCE A NEW STUDENT--A DANCER WITH THE NATIONAL BALLET, AND A VERY PROMISING TALENT, I'M TOLD.
HIS FAMILY WANTS HIM TO EXPERIENCE A ROUNDED EDUCATION, SO HE WILL BE STUDYING HERE. I THOUGHT YOU MIGHT SHOW HIM AROUND.

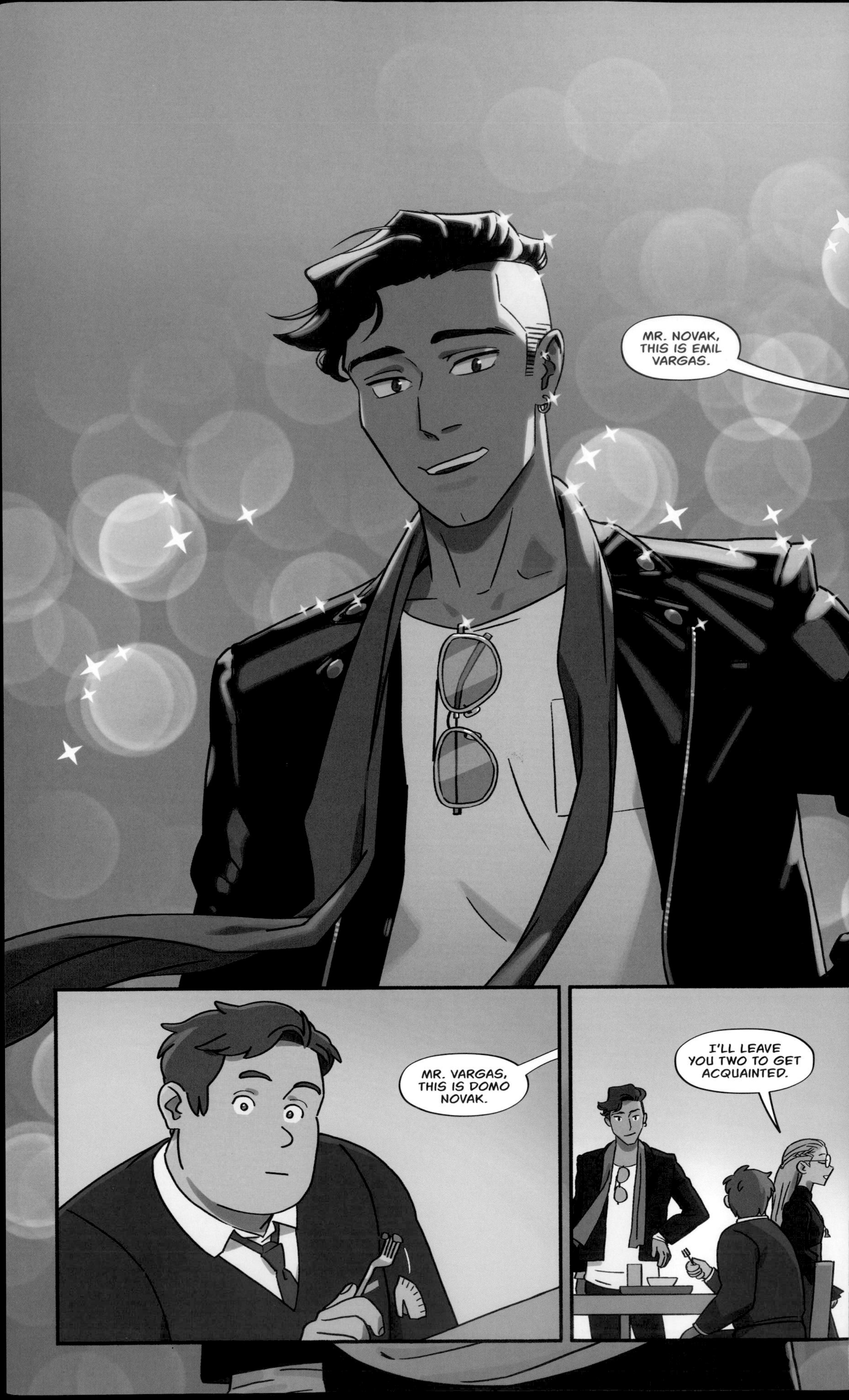
MR. NOVAK, THIS IS EMIL VARGAS.
MR. VARGAS, THIS IS DOMO NOVAK.
I'LL LEAVE YOU TWO TO GET ACQUAINTED.

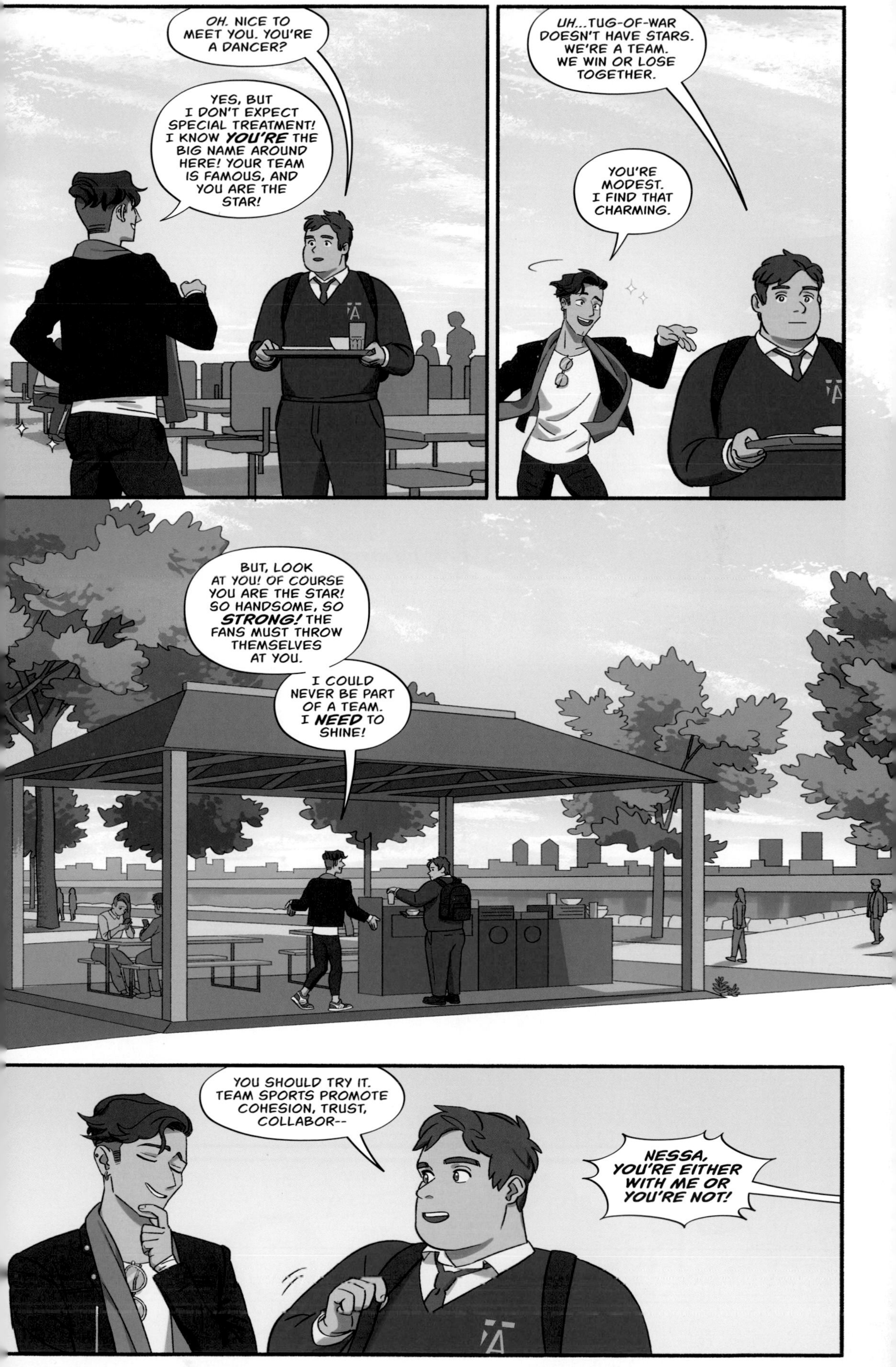
OH. NICE TO MEET YOU. YOU'RE A DANCER?
YES, BUT I DON'T EXPECT SPECIAL TREATMENT! I KNOW YOU'RE THE BIG NAME AROUND HERE! YOUR TEAM IS FAMOUS, AND YOU ARE THE STAR!
UH...TUG-OF-WAR DOESN'T HAVE STARS. WE'RE A TEAM. WE WIN OR LOSE TOGETHER.
YOU'RE MODEST. I FIND THAT CHARMING.
BUT, LOOK AT YOU! OF COURSE YOU ARE THE STAR! SO HANDSOME, SO STRONG! THE FANS MUST THROW THEMSELVES AT YOU.
I COULD NEVER BE PART OF A TEAM. I NEED TO SHINE!
YOU SHOULD TRY IT. TEAM SPORTS PROMOTE COHESION, TRUST, COLLABOR--
NESSA, YOU'RE EITHER WITH ME OR YOU'RE NOT!

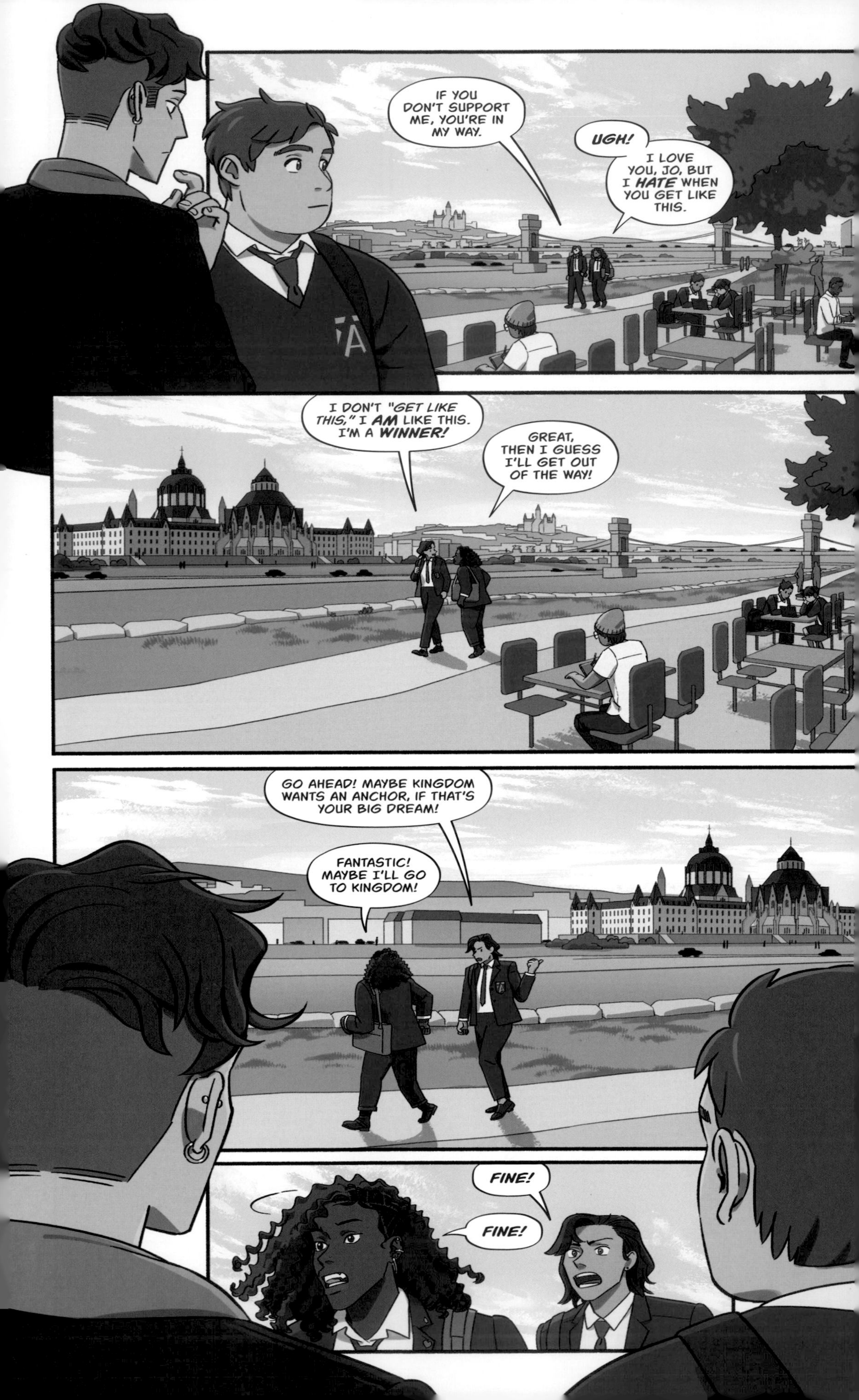

IF YOU DON'T SUPPORT ME, YOU'RE IN MY WAY.
UGH!
I LOVE YOU, JO, BUT I HATE WHEN YOU GET LIKE THIS.
I DON'T "GET LIKE THIS," I AM LIKE THIS. I'M A WINNER!
GREAT, THEN I GUESS I'LL GET OUT OF THE WAY!
GO AHEAD! MAYBE KINGDOM WANTS AN ANCHOR, IF THAT'S YOUR BIG DREAM!
FANTASTIC! MAYBE I'LL GO TO KINGDOM!
FINE!
FINE!

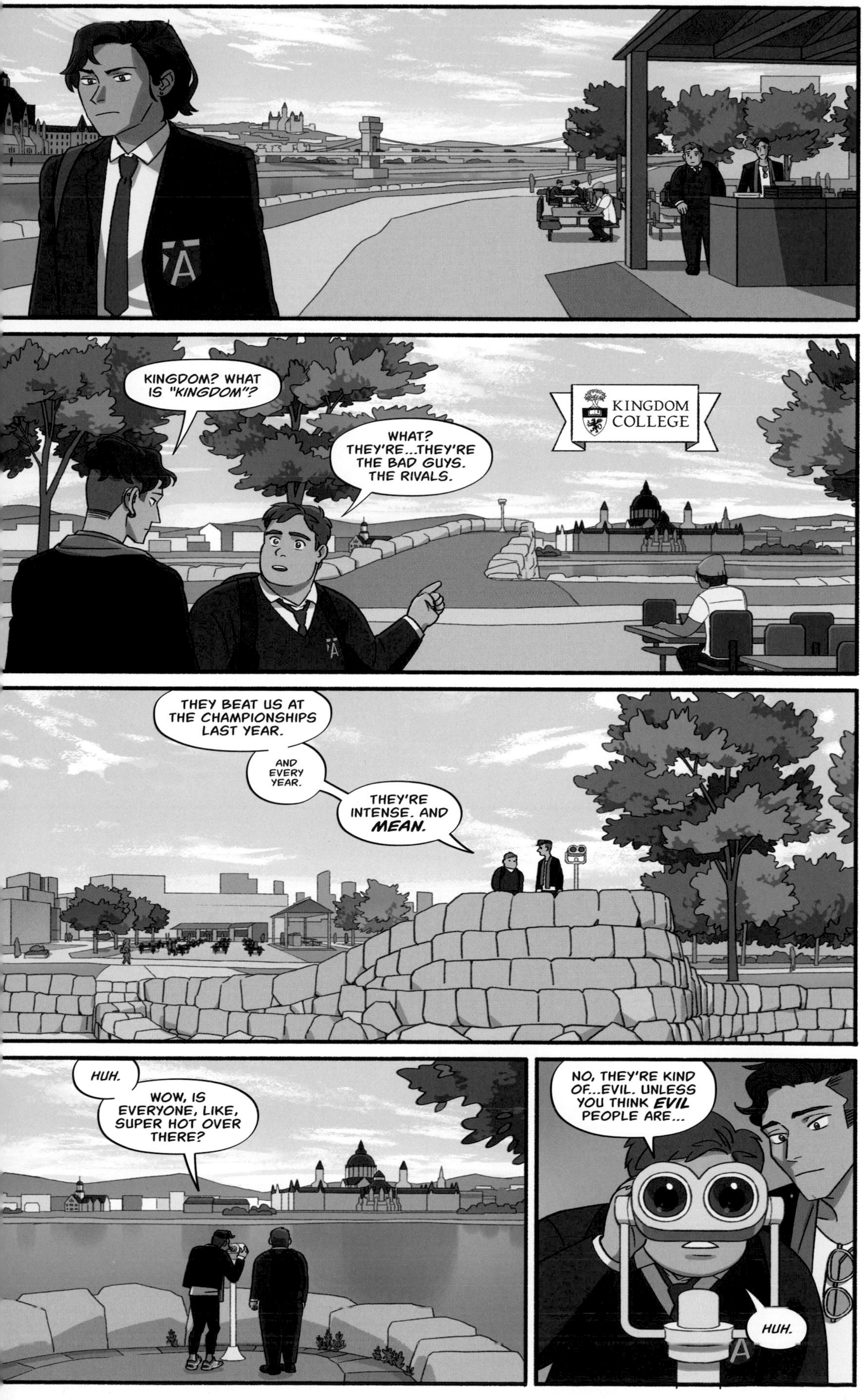
KINGDOM? WHAT IS "KINGDOM"?
KINGDOM COLLEGE
WHAT? THEY'RE...THEY'RE THE BAD GUYS. THE RIVALS.
THEY BEAT US AT THE CHAMPIONSHIPS LAST YEAR.
AND EVERY YEAR.
THEY'RE INTENSE. AND *MEAN.*
HUH.
WOW, IS EVERYONE, LIKE, SUPER HOT OVER THERE?
NO, THEY'RE KIND OF...EVIL. UNLESS YOU THINK *EVIL* PEOPLE ARE...
HUH.

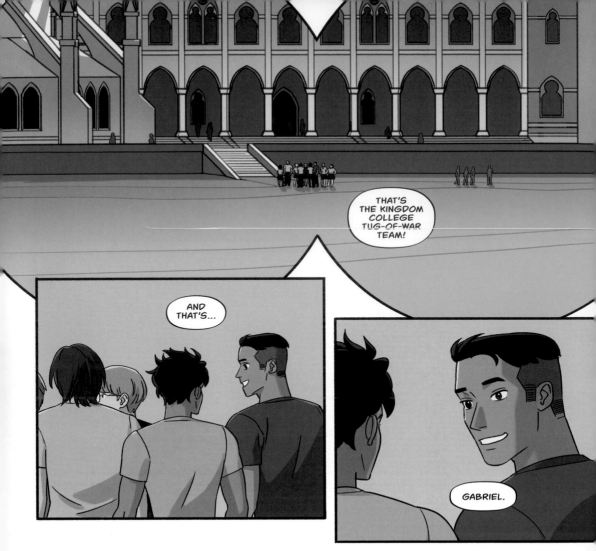

THAT'S THE KINGDOM COLLEGE TUG-OF-WAR TEAM!

AND THAT'S...

GABRIEL.

GABRIEL?

WHO IS GABRIEL?

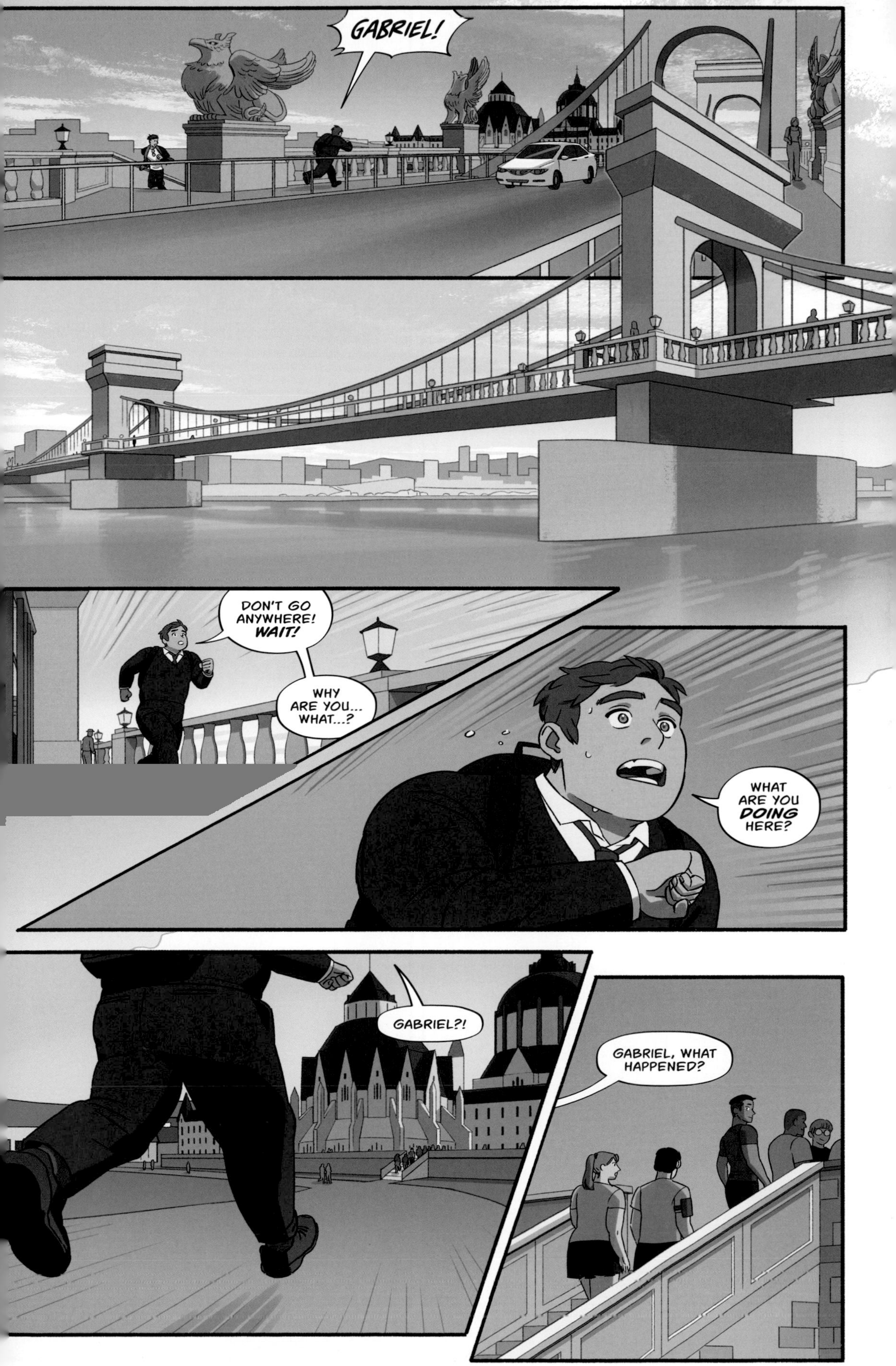
GABRIEL!
DON'T GO ANYWHERE! WAIT!
WHY ARE YOU... WHAT...?
WHAT ARE YOU DOING HERE?
GABRIEL?!
GABRIEL, WHAT HAPPENED?

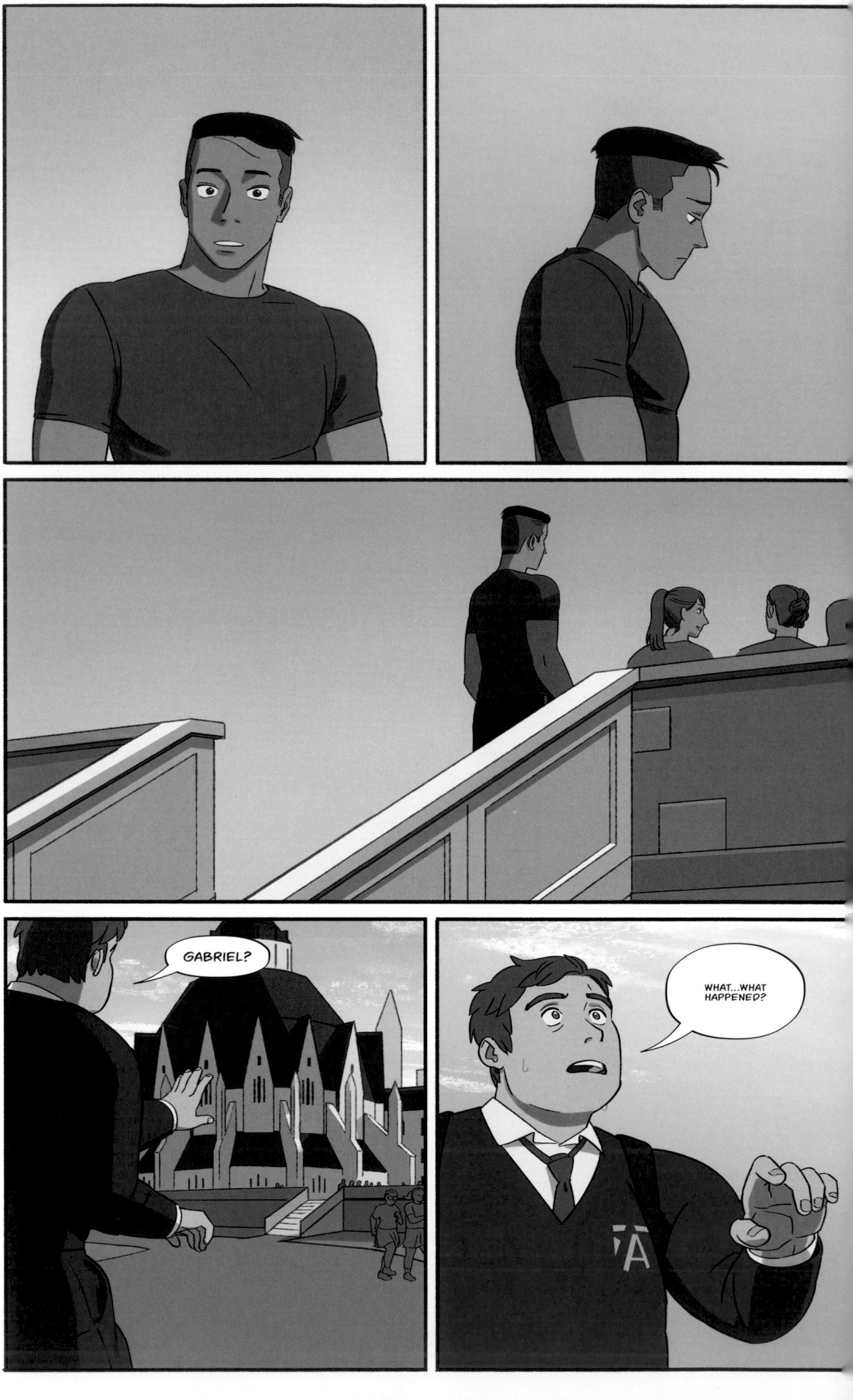
GABRIEL?
WHAT...WHAT HAPPENED?

CHAPTER

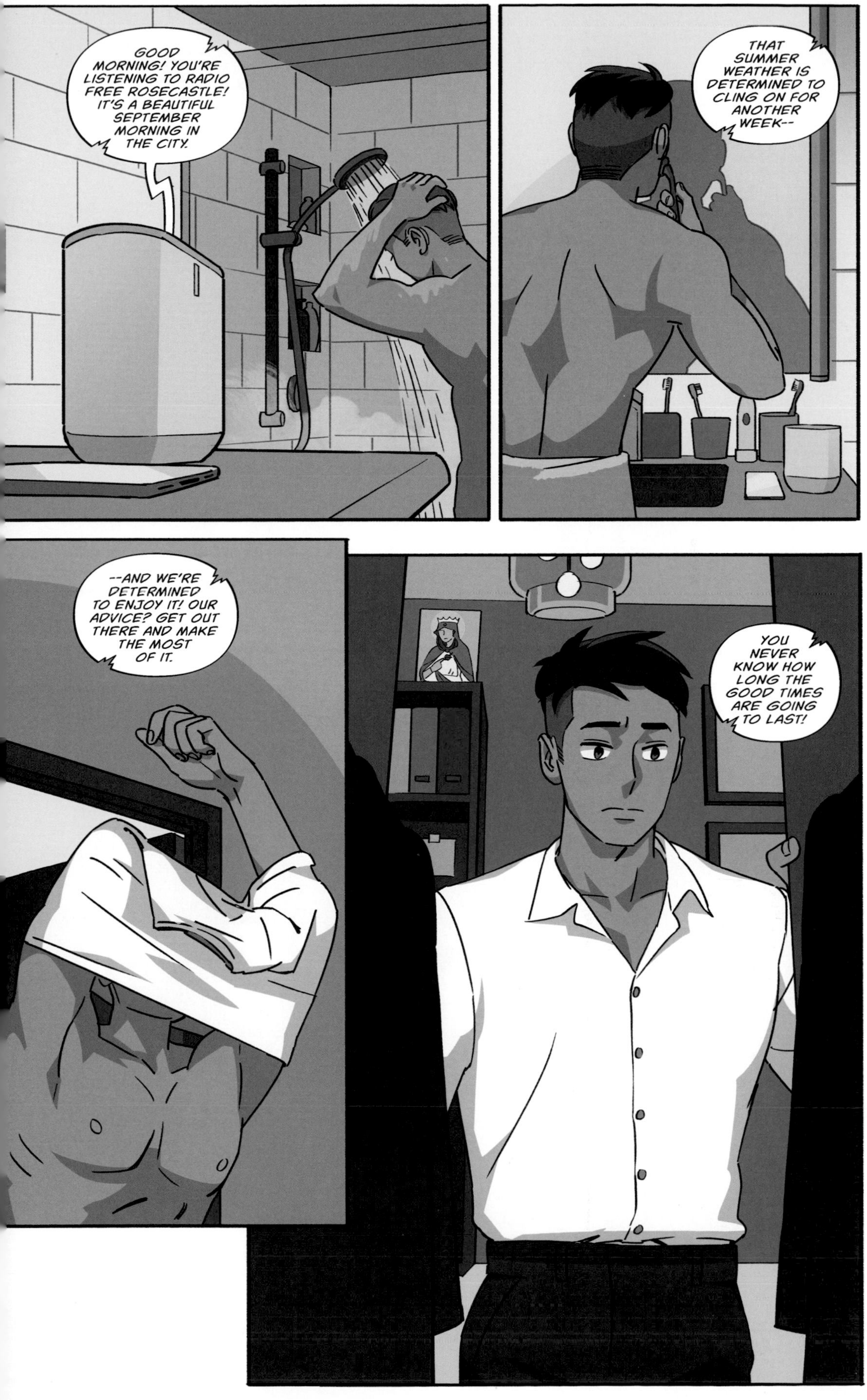
GOOD MORNING! YOU'RE LISTENING TO RADIO FREE ROSECASTLE! IT'S A BEAUTIFUL SEPTEMBER MORNING IN THE CITY.
THAT SUMMER WEATHER IS DETERMINED TO CLING ON FOR ANOTHER WEEK--
--AND WE'RE DETERMINED TO ENJOY IT! OUR ADVICE? GET OUT THERE AND MAKE THE MOST OF IT.
YOU NEVER KNOW HOW LONG THE GOOD TIMES ARE GOING TO LAST!

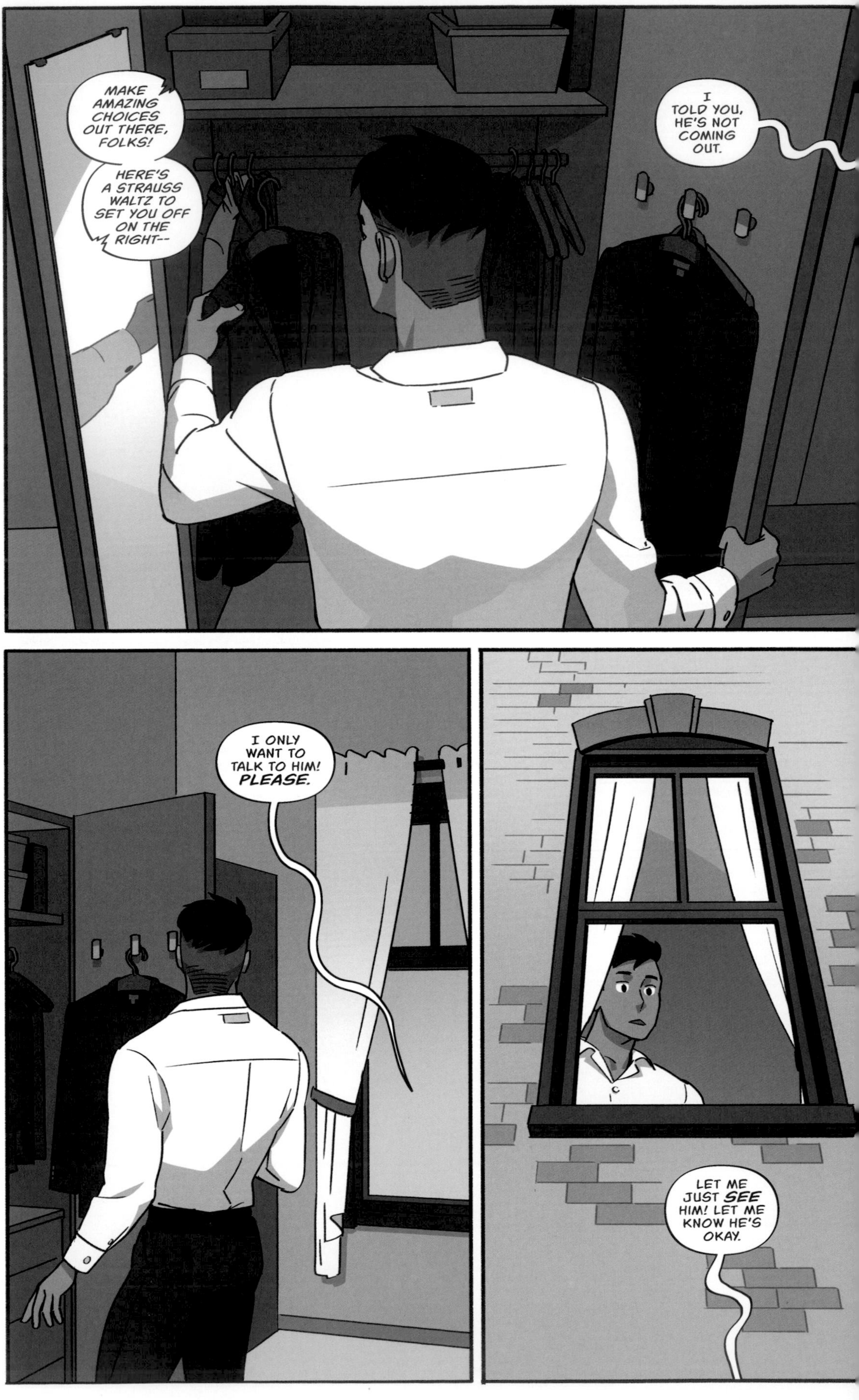
MAKE AMAZING CHOICES OUT THERE, FOLKS!
HERE'S A STRAUSS WALTZ TO SET YOU OFF ON THE RIGHT--
I TOLD YOU, HE'S NOT COMING OUT.
I ONLY WANT TO TALK TO HIM! PLEASE.
LET ME JUST SEE HIM! LET ME KNOW HE'S OKAY.

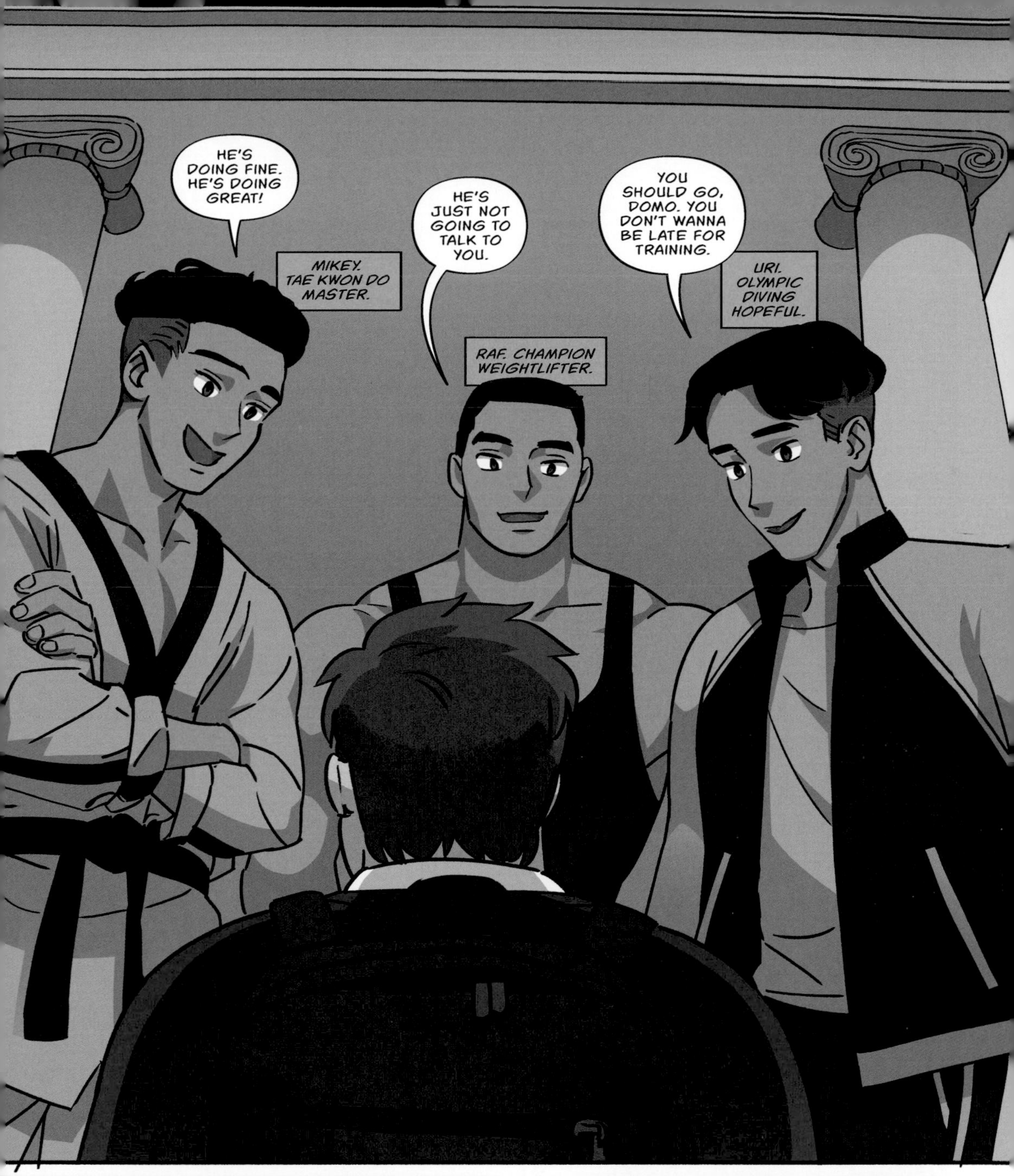
HE'S DOING FINE. HE'S DOING GREAT!
MIKEY. TAE KWON DO MASTER.
HE'S JUST NOT GOING TO TALK TO YOU.
RAF. CHAMPION WEIGHTLIFTER.
YOU SHOULD GO, DOMO. YOU DON'T WANNA BE LATE FOR TRAINING.
URI. OLYMPIC DIVING HOPEFUL.

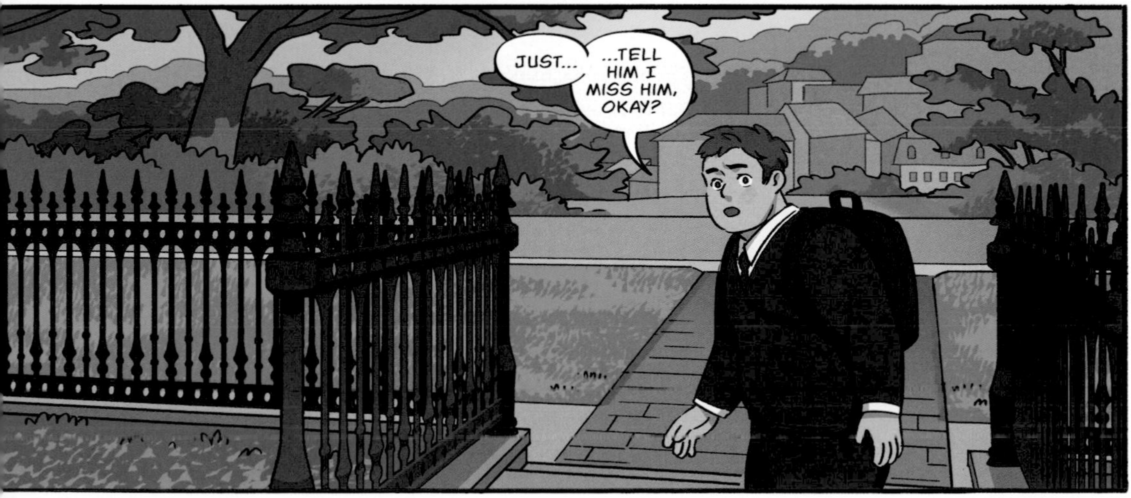
JUST...
...TELL HIM I MISS HIM, OKAY?

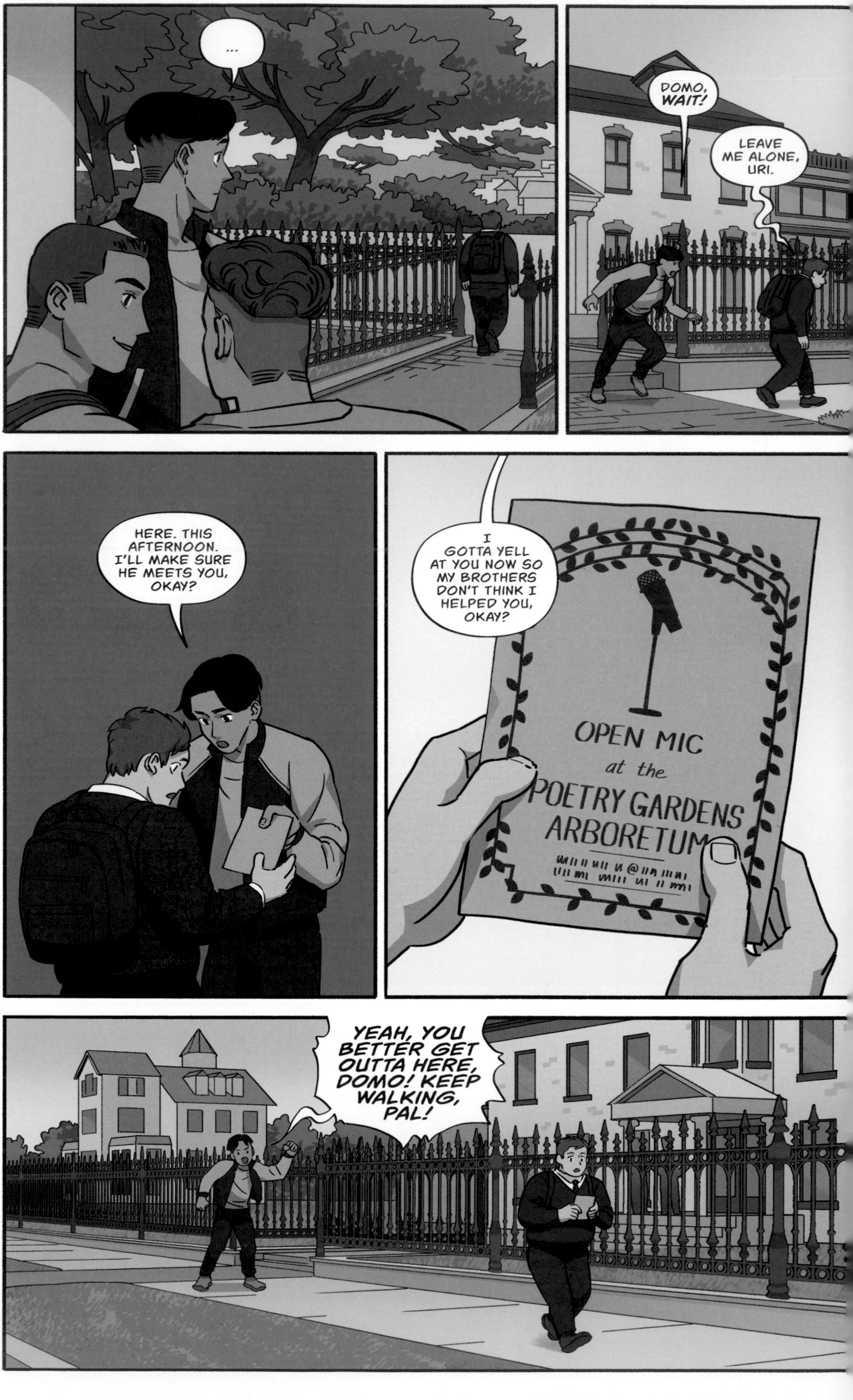
...
DOMO, WAIT!
LEAVE ME ALONE, URI.
HERE. THIS AFTERNOON. I'LL MAKE SURE HE MEETS YOU, OKAY?
I GOTTA YELL AT YOU NOW SO MY BROTHERS DON'T THINK I HELPED YOU, OKAY?
OPEN MIC at the POETRY GARDENS ARBORETUM
YEAH, YOU BETTER GET OUTTA HERE, DOMO! KEEP WALKING, PAL!

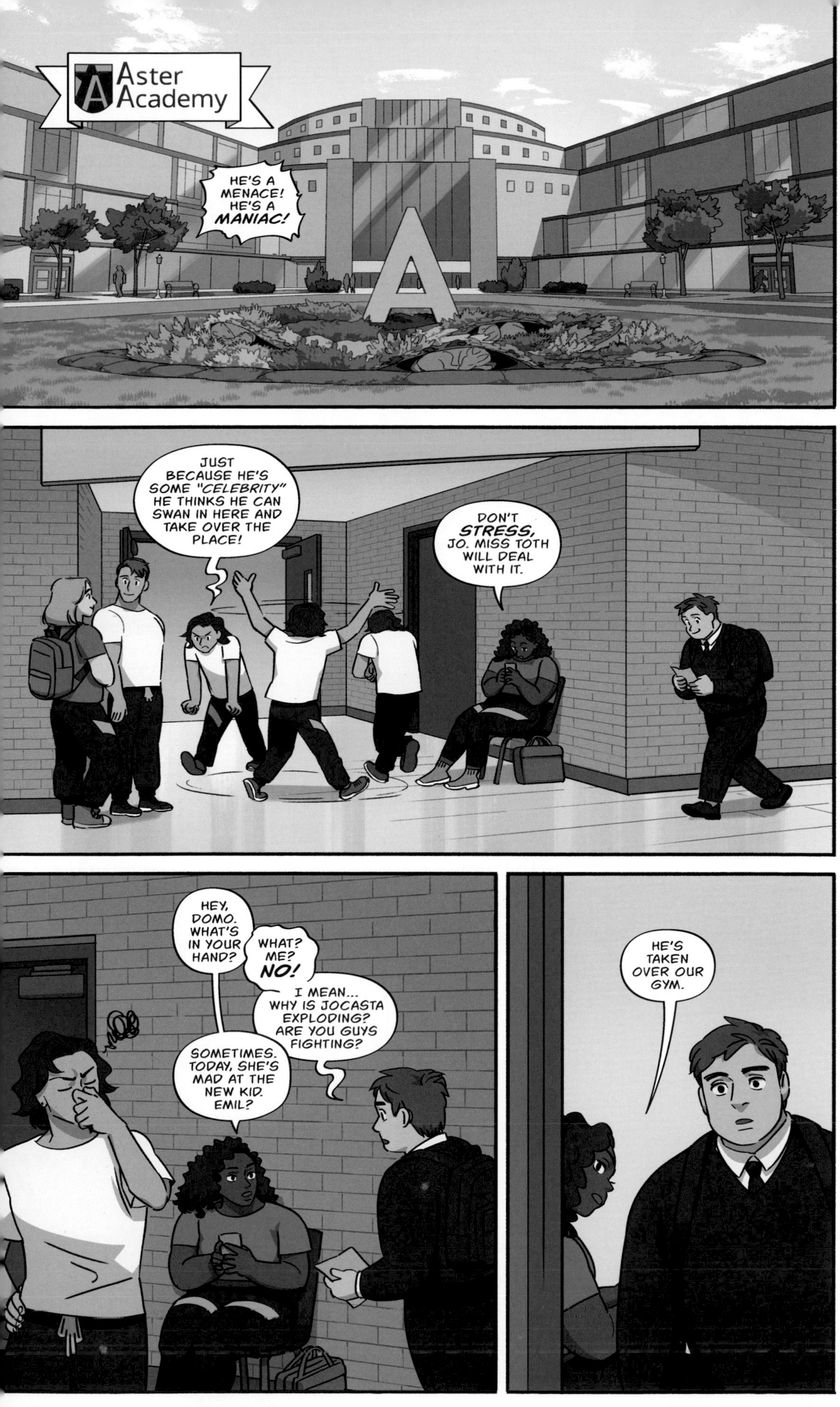
Aster
Academy
HE'S A MENACE! HE'S A MANIAC!
JUST BECAUSE HE'S SOME "CELEBRITY" HE THINKS HE CAN SWAN IN HERE AND TAKE OVER THE PLACE!
DON'T STRESS, JO. MISS TOTH WILL DEAL WITH IT.
HEY, DOMO. WHAT'S IN YOUR HAND?
WHAT? ME? NO!
I MEAN... WHY IS JOCASTA EXPLODING? ARE YOU GUYS FIGHTING?
SOMETIMES. TODAY, SHE'S MAD AT THE NEW KID. EMIL?
HE'S TAKEN OVER OUR GYM.

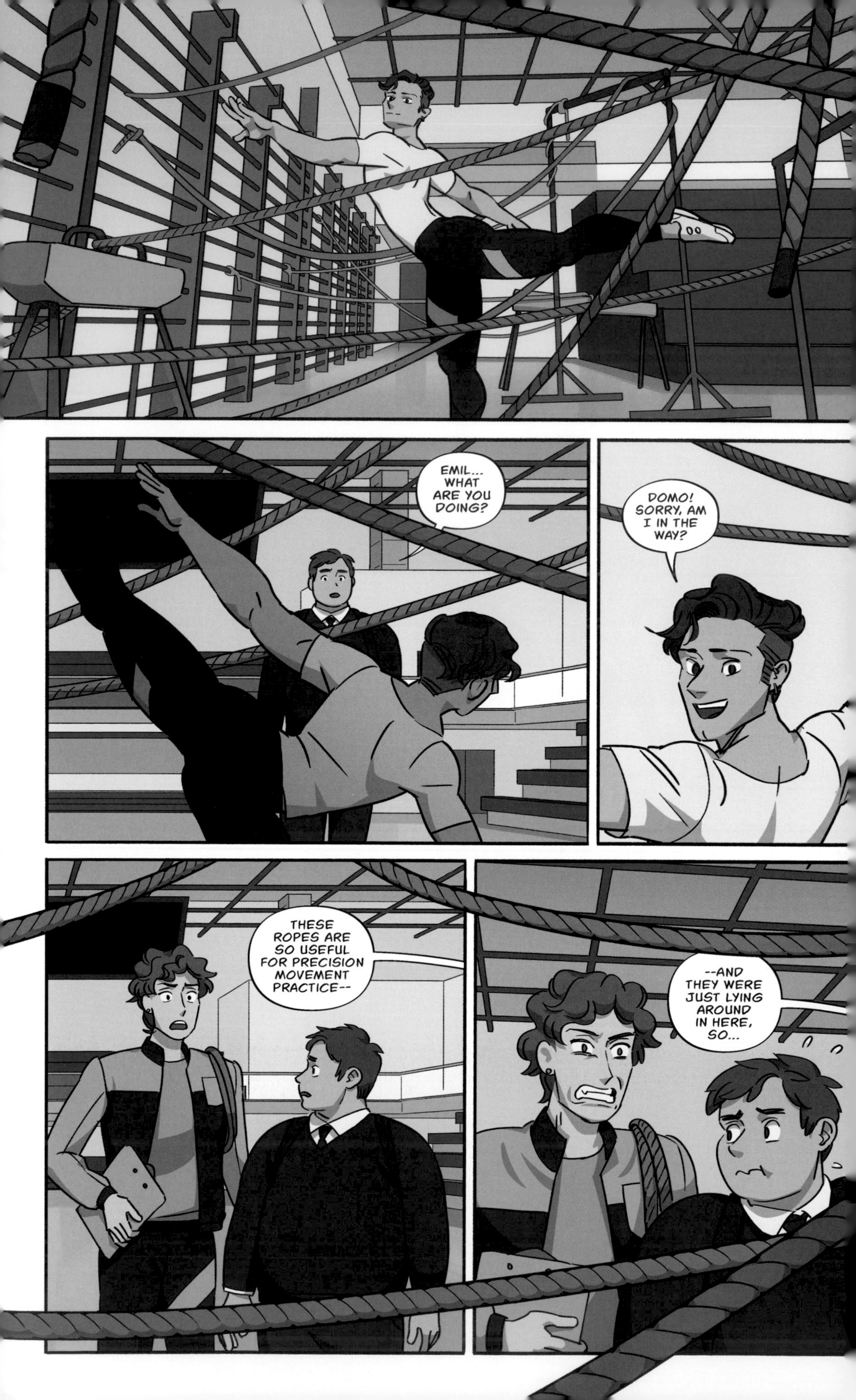
EMIL... WHAT ARE YOU DOING?
DOMO! SORRY, AM I IN THE WAY?
THESE ROPES ARE SO USEFUL FOR PRECISION MOVEMENT PRACTICE--
--AND THEY WERE JUST LYING AROUND IN HERE, SO...

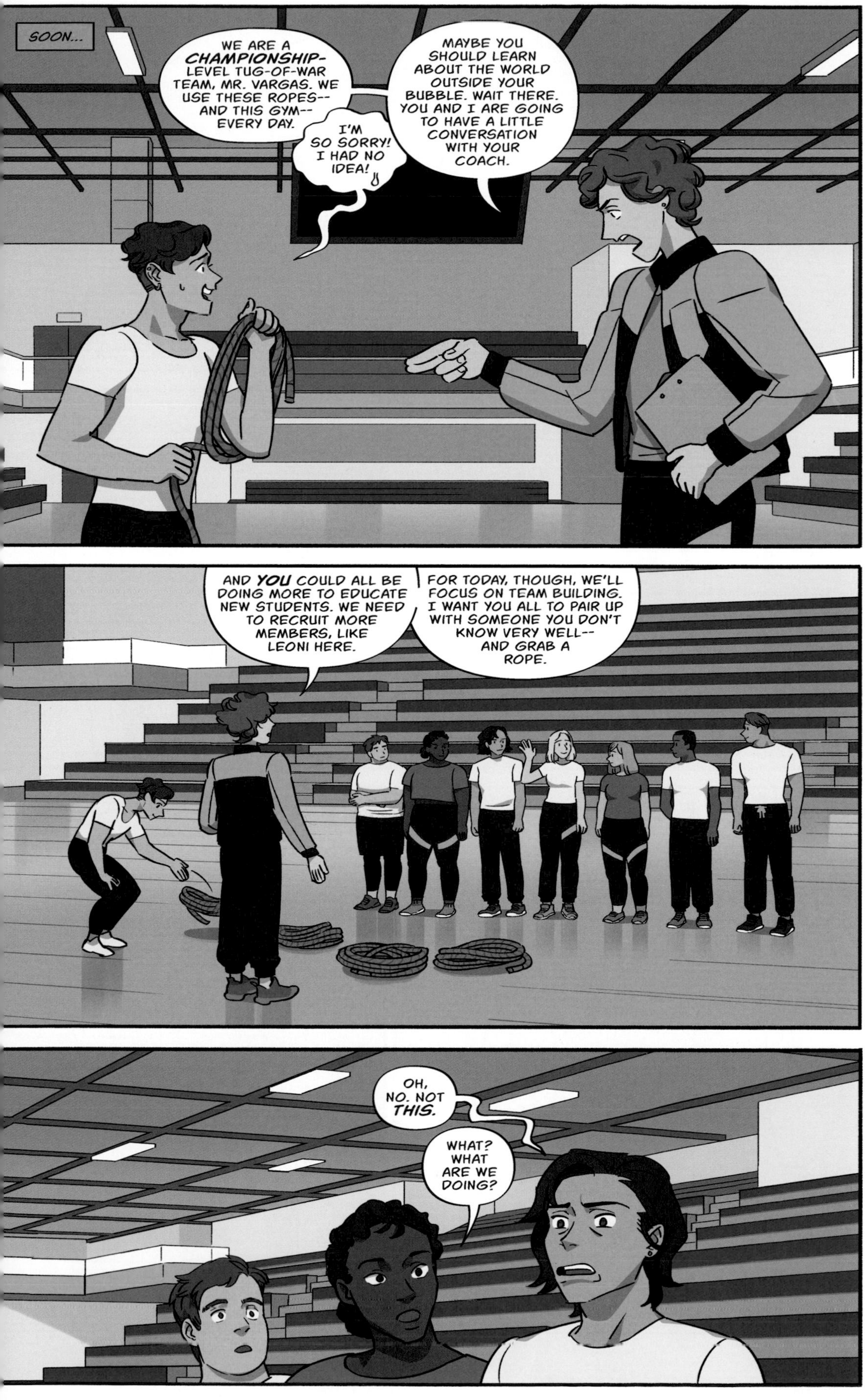
SOON...
WE ARE A CHAMPIONSHIP-LEVEL TUG-OF-WAR TEAM, MR. VARGAS. WE USE THESE ROPES-- AND THIS GYM-- EVERY DAY.
I'M SO SORRY! I HAD NO IDEA!
MAYBE YOU SHOULD LEARN ABOUT THE WORLD OUTSIDE YOUR BUBBLE. WAIT THERE. YOU AND I ARE GOING TO HAVE A LITTLE CONVERSATION WITH YOUR COACH.
AND YOU COULD ALL BE DOING MORE TO EDUCATE NEW STUDENTS. WE NEED TO RECRUIT MORE MEMBERS, LIKE LEONI HERE.
FOR TODAY, THOUGH, WE'LL FOCUS ON TEAM BUILDING. I WANT YOU ALL TO PAIR UP WITH SOMEONE YOU DON'T KNOW VERY WELL-- AND GRAB A ROPE.
OH, NO. NOT THIS.
WHAT? WHAT ARE WE DOING?

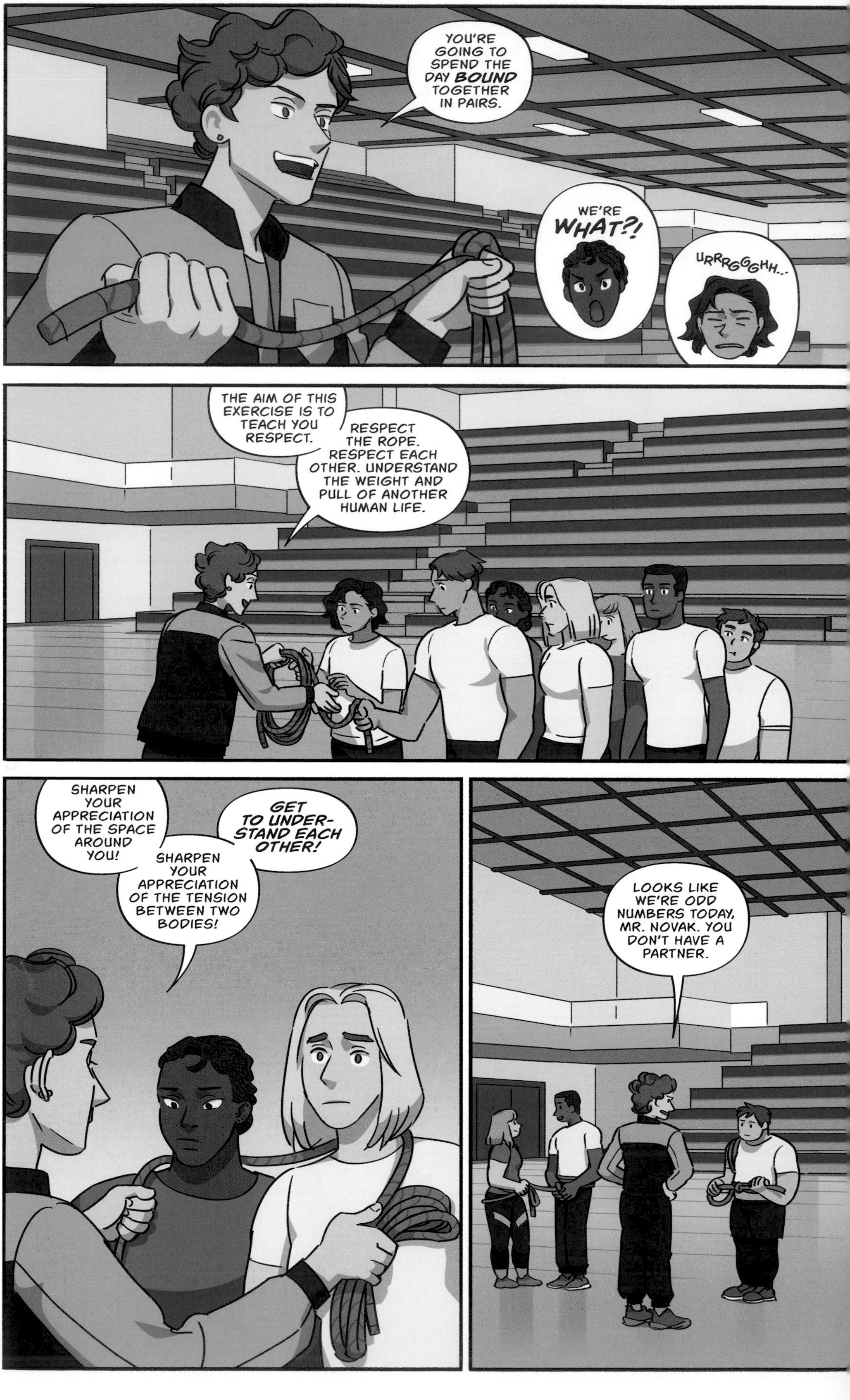
YOU'RE GOING TO SPEND THE DAY **BOUND** TOGETHER IN PAIRS.
WE'RE **WHAT?!**
URRRGGGHH...
THE AIM OF THIS EXERCISE IS TO TEACH YOU RESPECT.
RESPECT THE ROPE. RESPECT EACH OTHER. UNDERSTAND THE WEIGHT AND PULL OF ANOTHER HUMAN LIFE.
SHARPEN YOUR APPRECIATION OF THE SPACE AROUND YOU!
SHARPEN YOUR APPRECIATION OF THE TENSION BETWEEN TWO BODIES!
GET TO UNDER-STAND EACH OTHER!
LOOKS LIKE WE'RE ODD NUMBERS TODAY, MR. NOVAK. YOU DON'T HAVE A PARTNER.

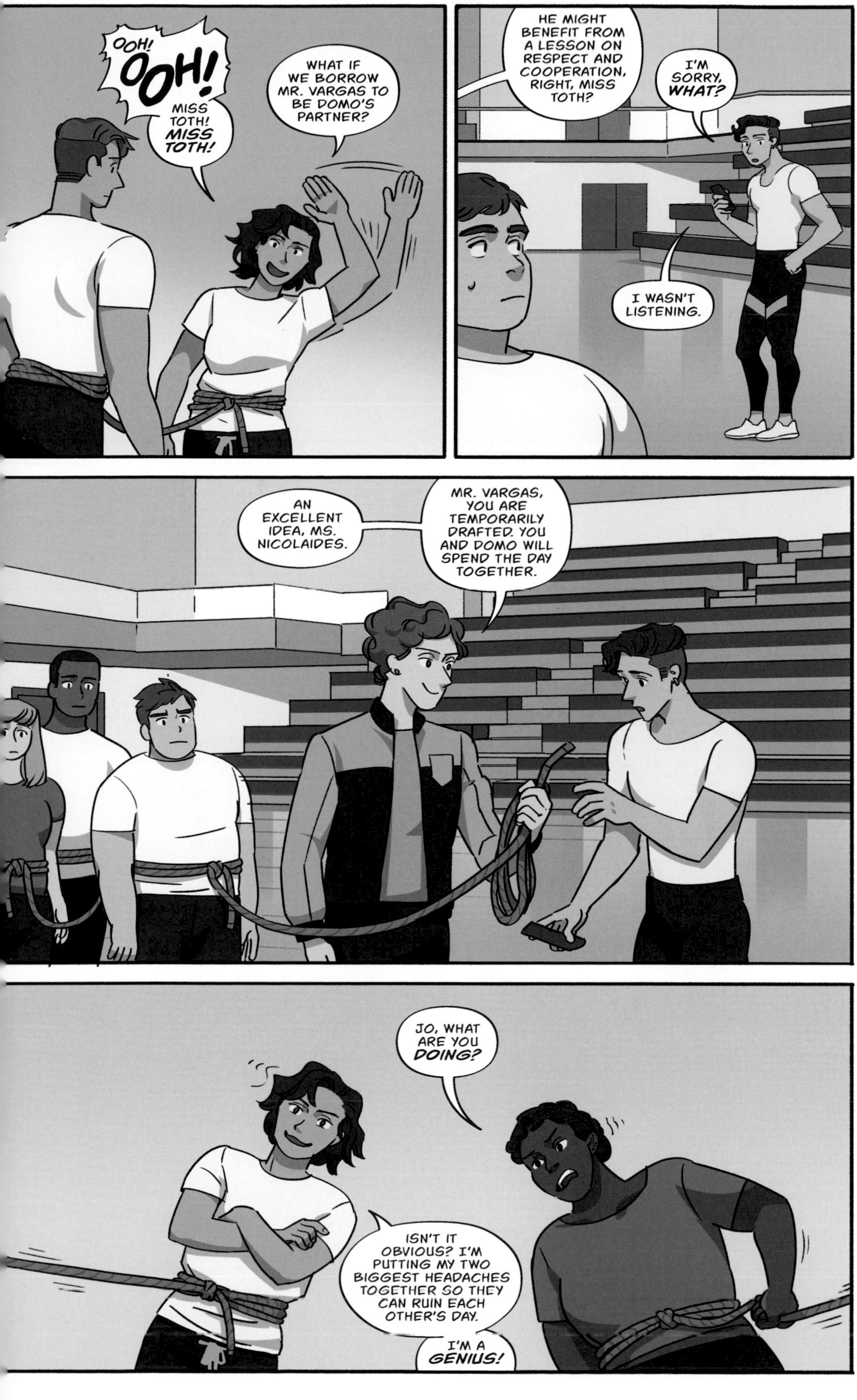
OOH! OOH!
MISS TOTH! MISS TOTH!
WHAT IF WE BORROW MR. VARGAS TO BE DOMO'S PARTNER?
HE MIGHT BENEFIT FROM A LESSON ON RESPECT AND COOPERATION, RIGHT, MISS TOTH?
I'M SORRY, WHAT?
I WASN'T LISTENING.
AN EXCELLENT IDEA, MS. NICOLAIDES.
MR. VARGAS, YOU ARE TEMPORARILY DRAFTED. YOU AND DOMO WILL SPEND THE DAY TOGETHER.
JO, WHAT ARE YOU DOING?
ISN'T IT OBVIOUS? I'M PUTTING MY TWO BIGGEST HEADACHES TOGETHER SO THEY CAN RUIN EACH OTHER'S DAY.
I'M A GENIUS!

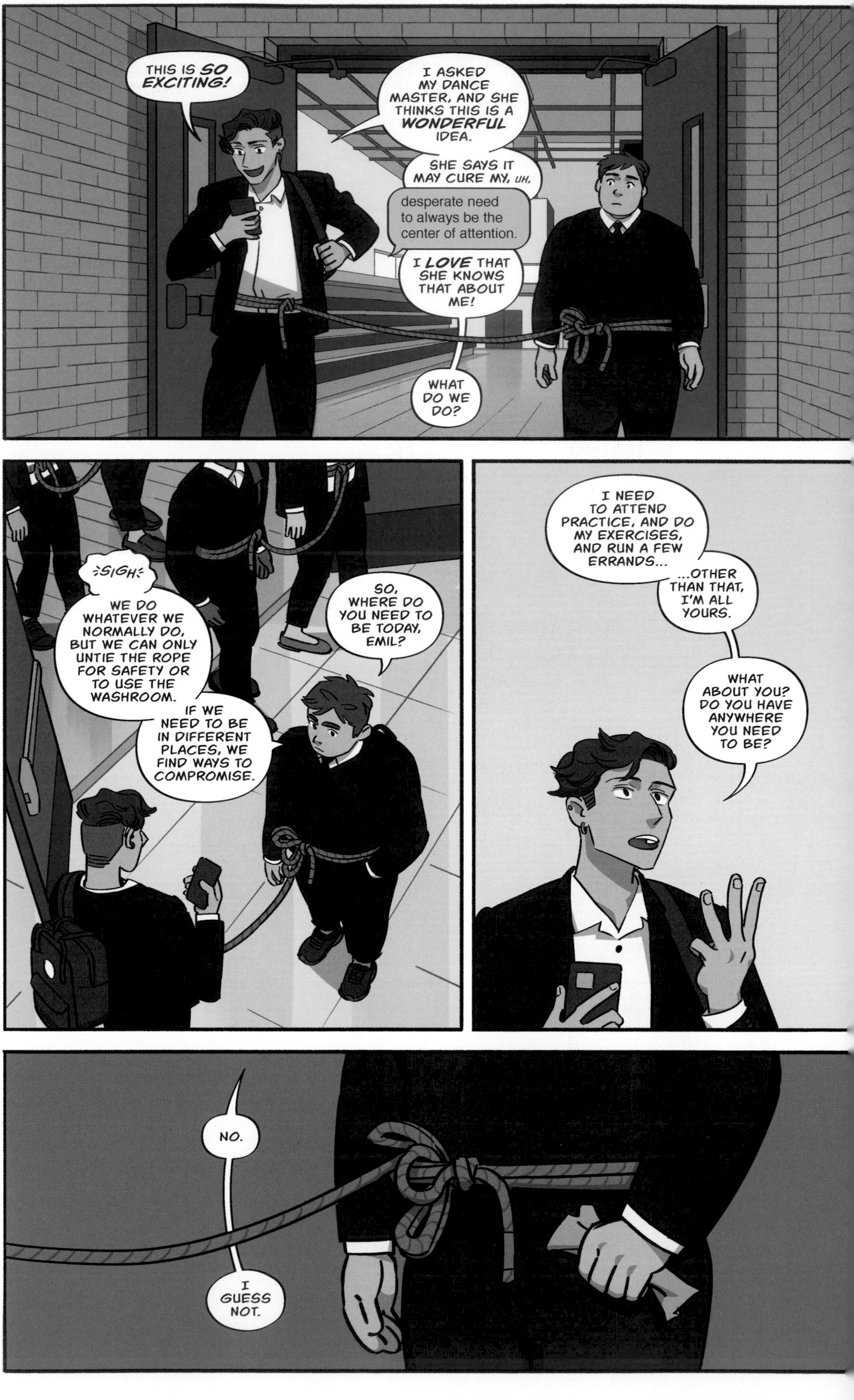
THIS IS SO EXCITING!
I ASKED MY DANCE MASTER, AND SHE THINKS THIS IS A WONDERFUL IDEA.
SHE SAYS IT MAY CURE MY, UH,
desperate need to always be the center of attention.
I LOVE THAT SHE KNOWS THAT ABOUT ME!
WHAT DO WE DO?
SIGH
WE DO WHATEVER WE NORMALLY DO, BUT WE CAN ONLY UNTIE THE ROPE FOR SAFETY OR TO USE THE WASHROOM.
IF WE NEED TO BE IN DIFFERENT PLACES, WE FIND WAYS TO COMPROMISE.
SO, WHERE DO YOU NEED TO BE TODAY, EMIL?
I NEED TO ATTEND PRACTICE, AND DO MY EXERCISES, AND RUN A FEW ERRANDS...
...OTHER THAN THAT, I'M ALL YOURS.
WHAT ABOUT YOU? DO YOU HAVE ANYWHERE YOU NEED TO BE?
NO.
I GUESS NOT.

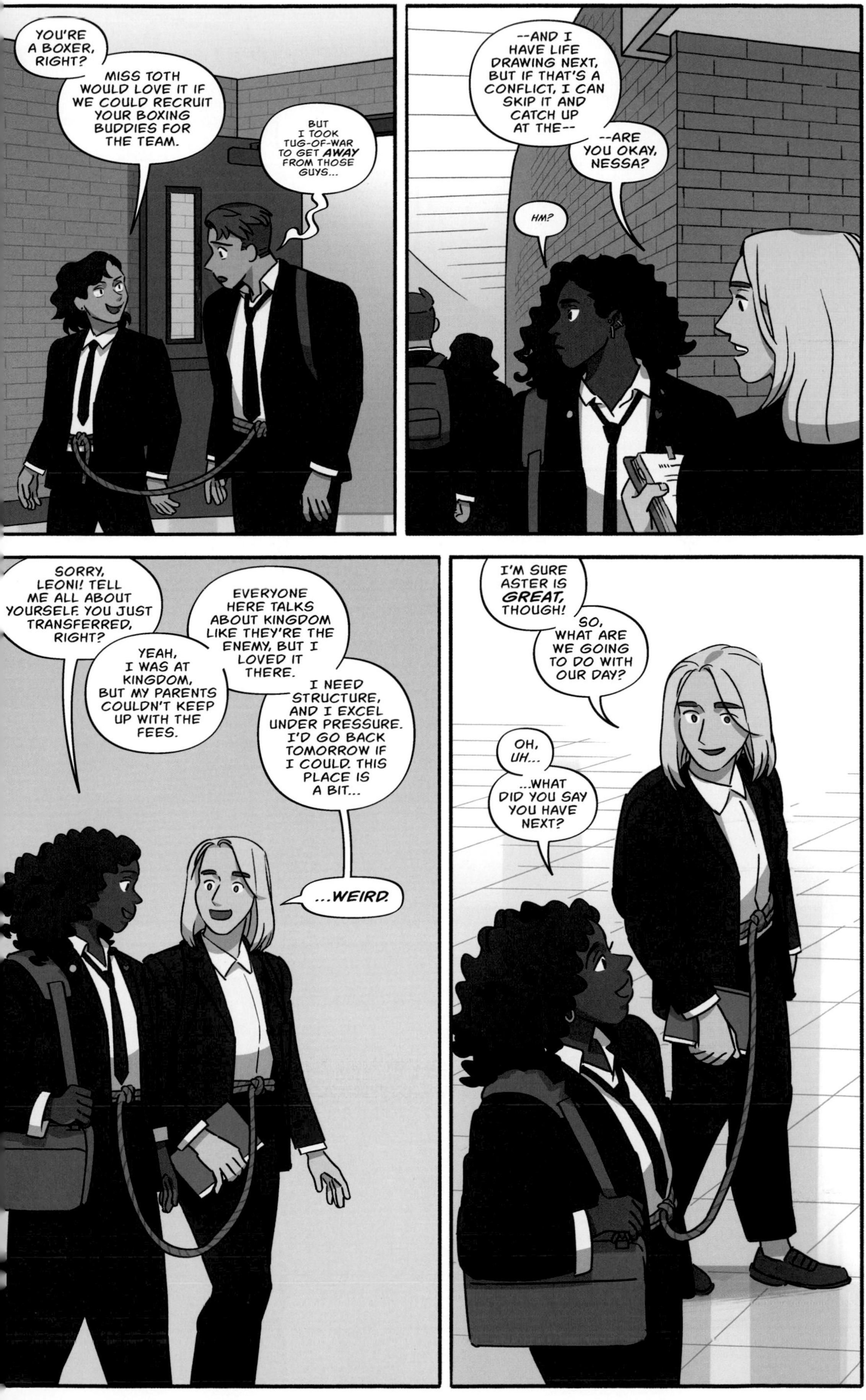
YOU'RE A BOXER, RIGHT?
MISS TOTH WOULD LOVE IT IF WE COULD RECRUIT YOUR BOXING BUDDIES FOR THE TEAM.
BUT I TOOK TUG-OF-WAR TO GET AWAY FROM THOSE GUYS...
--AND I HAVE LIFE DRAWING NEXT, BUT IF THAT'S A CONFLICT, I CAN SKIP IT AND CATCH UP AT THE--
--ARE YOU OKAY, NESSA?
HM?
SORRY, LEONI! TELL ME ALL ABOUT YOURSELF. YOU JUST TRANSFERRED, RIGHT?
YEAH, I WAS AT KINGDOM, BUT MY PARENTS COULDN'T KEEP UP WITH THE FEES.
EVERYONE HERE TALKS ABOUT KINGDOM LIKE THEY'RE THE ENEMY, BUT I LOVED IT THERE.
I NEED STRUCTURE, AND I EXCEL UNDER PRESSURE. I'D GO BACK TOMORROW IF I COULD. THIS PLACE IS A BIT...
...WEIRD.
I'M SURE ASTER IS GREAT, THOUGH!
SO, WHAT ARE WE GOING TO DO WITH OUR DAY?
OH, UH...
...WHAT DID YOU SAY YOU HAVE NEXT?

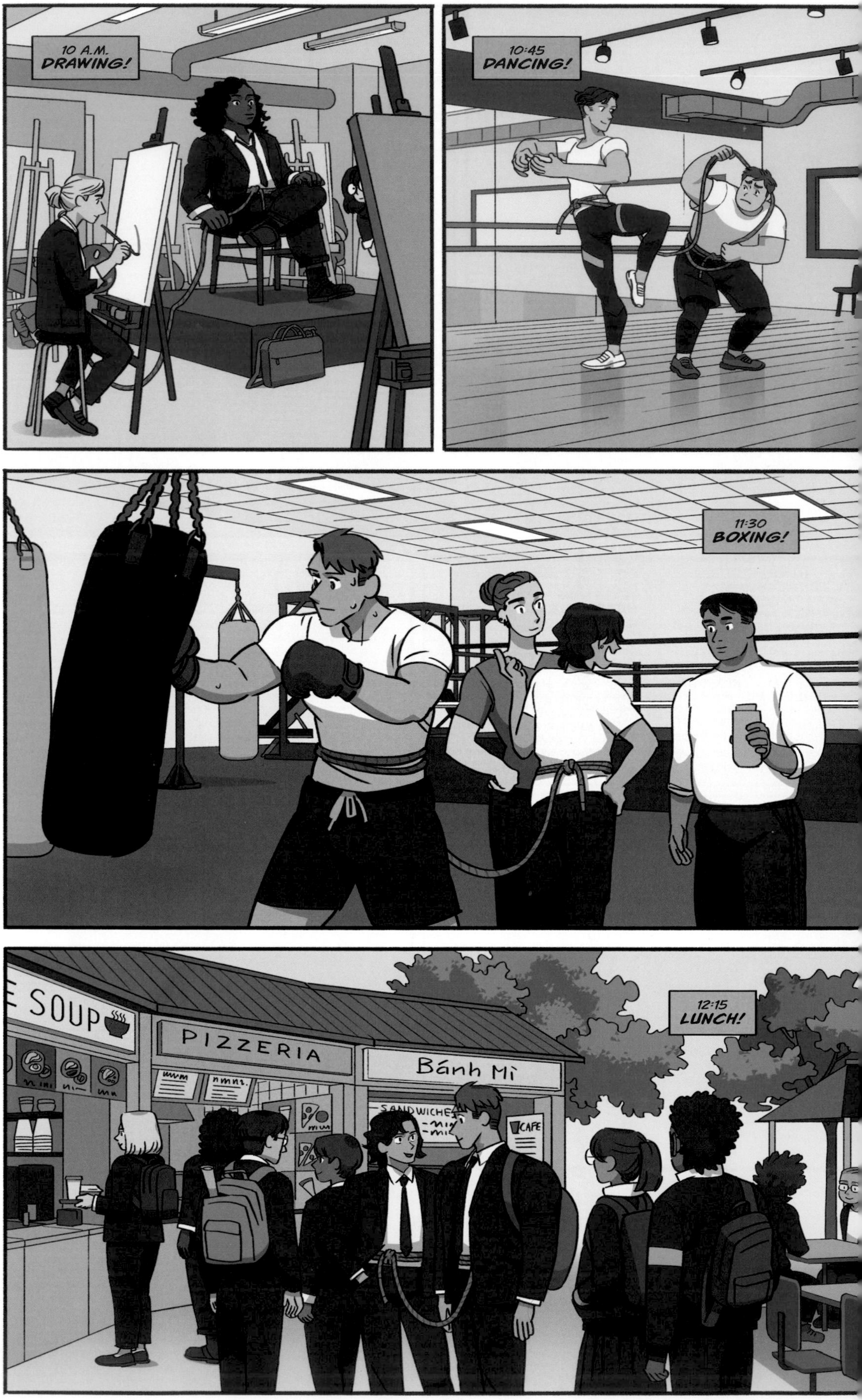
10 A.M.
DRAWING!
10:45
DANCING!
11:30
BOXING!
12:15
LUNCH!
E SOUP
PIZZERIA
Bánh Mì
CAFE

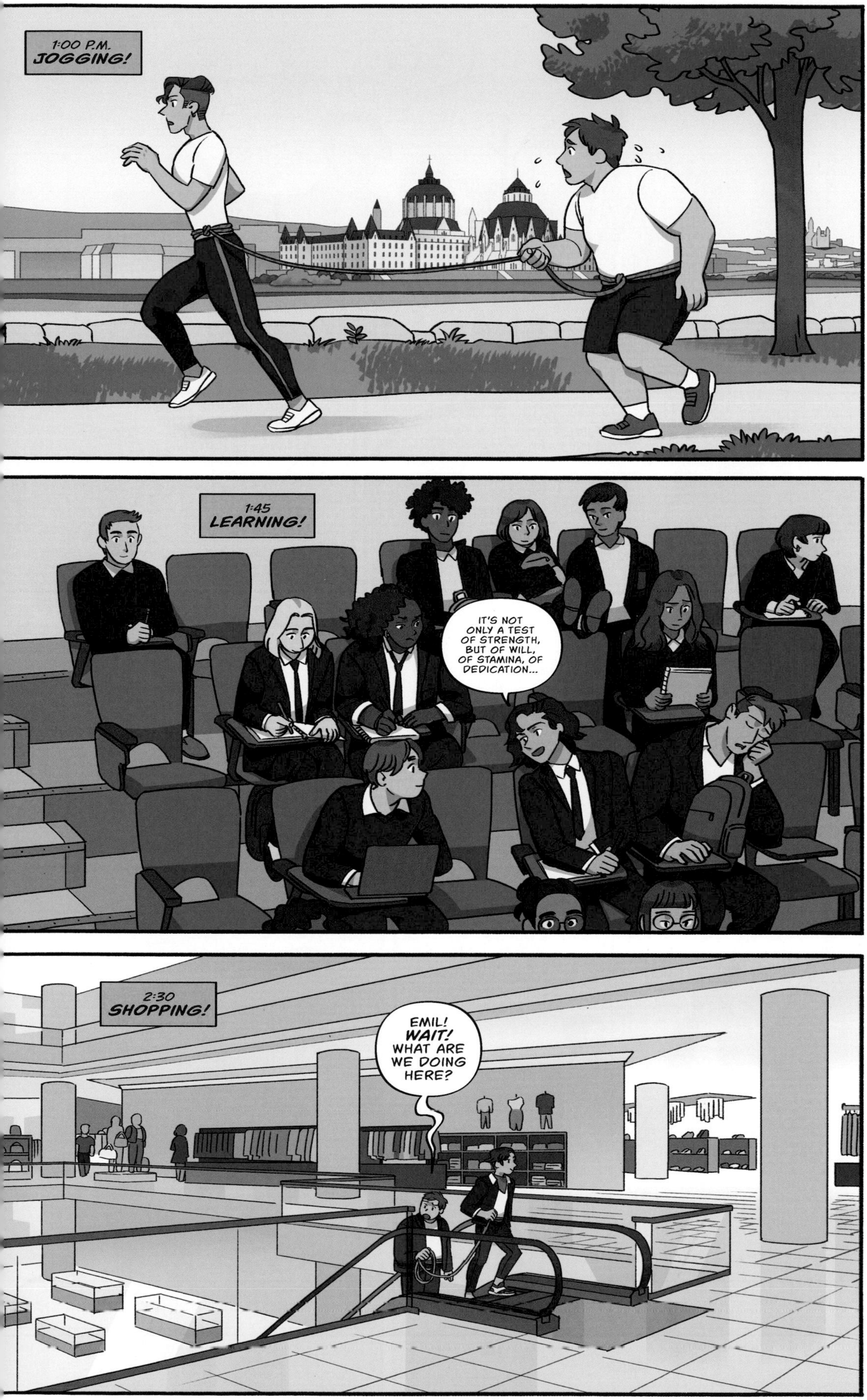
1:00 P.M.
JOGGING!
1:45
LEARNING!
IT'S NOT ONLY A TEST OF STRENGTH, BUT OF WILL, OF STAMINA, OF DEDICATION...
2:30
SHOPPING!
EMIL! WAIT! WHAT ARE WE DOING HERE?

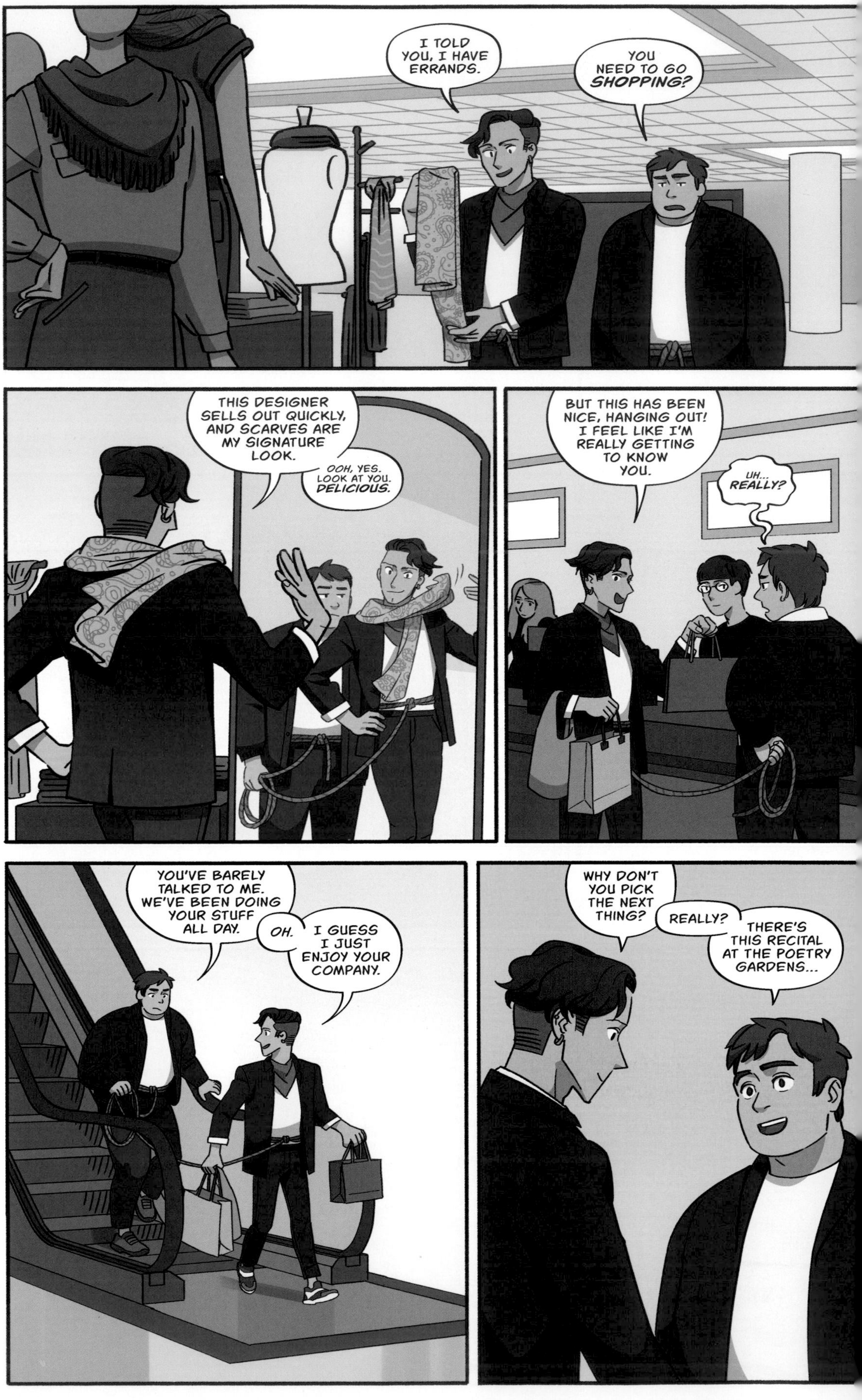
I TOLD YOU, I HAVE ERRANDS.
YOU NEED TO GO SHOPPING?
THIS DESIGNER SELLS OUT QUICKLY, AND SCARVES ARE MY SIGNATURE LOOK.
OOH, YES. LOOK AT YOU. DELICIOUS.
BUT THIS HAS BEEN NICE, HANGING OUT! I FEEL LIKE I'M REALLY GETTING TO KNOW YOU.
UH... REALLY?
YOU'VE BARELY TALKED TO ME. WE'VE BEEN DOING YOUR STUFF ALL DAY.
OH.
I GUESS I JUST ENJOY YOUR COMPANY.
WHY DON'T YOU PICK THE NEXT THING?
REALLY?
THERE'S THIS RECITAL AT THE POETRY GARDENS...

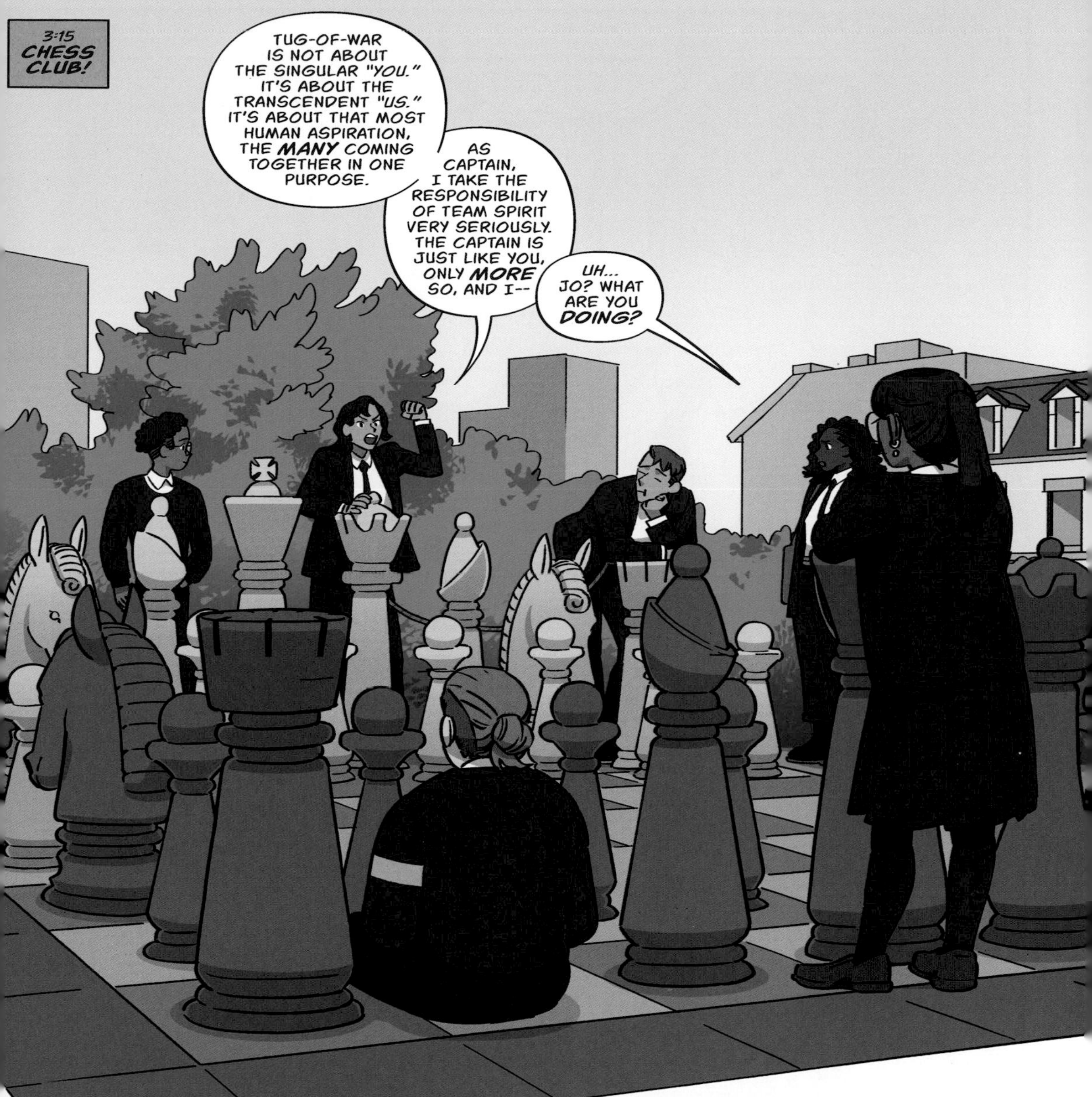
3:15 CHESS CLUB!
TUG-OF-WAR IS NOT ABOUT THE SINGULAR "YOU." IT'S ABOUT THE TRANSCENDENT "US." IT'S ABOUT THAT MOST HUMAN ASPIRATION, THE MANY COMING TOGETHER IN ONE PURPOSE.
AS CAPTAIN, I TAKE THE RESPONSIBILITY OF TEAM SPIRIT VERY SERIOUSLY. THE CAPTAIN IS JUST LIKE YOU, ONLY MORE SO, AND I--
UH... JO? WHAT ARE YOU DOING?

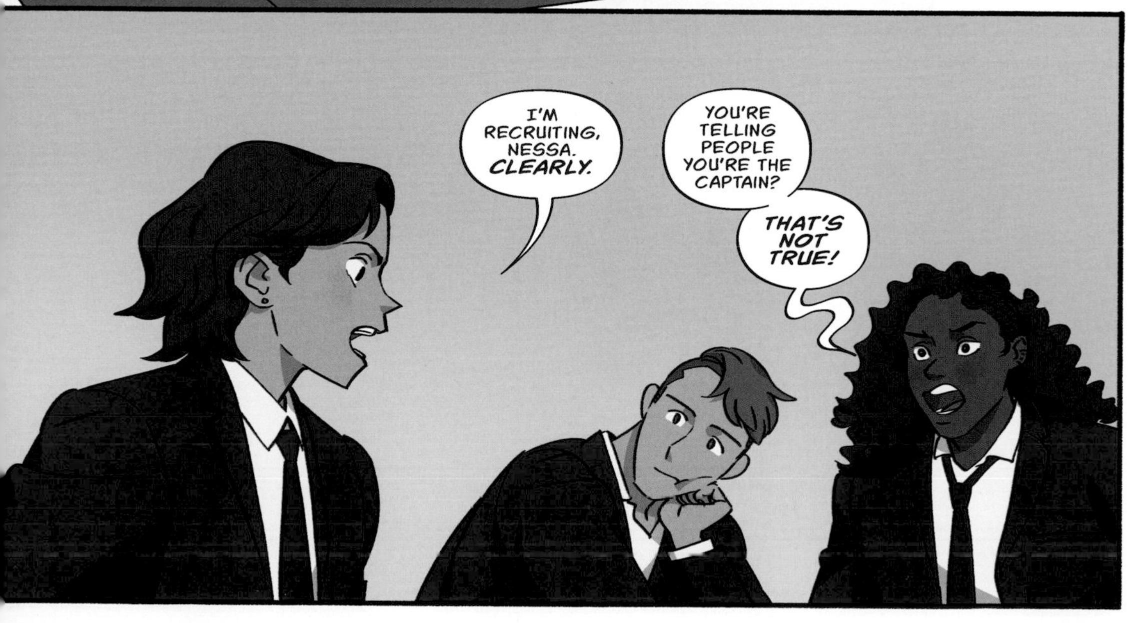
I'M RECRUITING, NESSA. CLEARLY.
YOU'RE TELLING PEOPLE YOU'RE THE CAPTAIN?
THAT'S NOT TRUE!

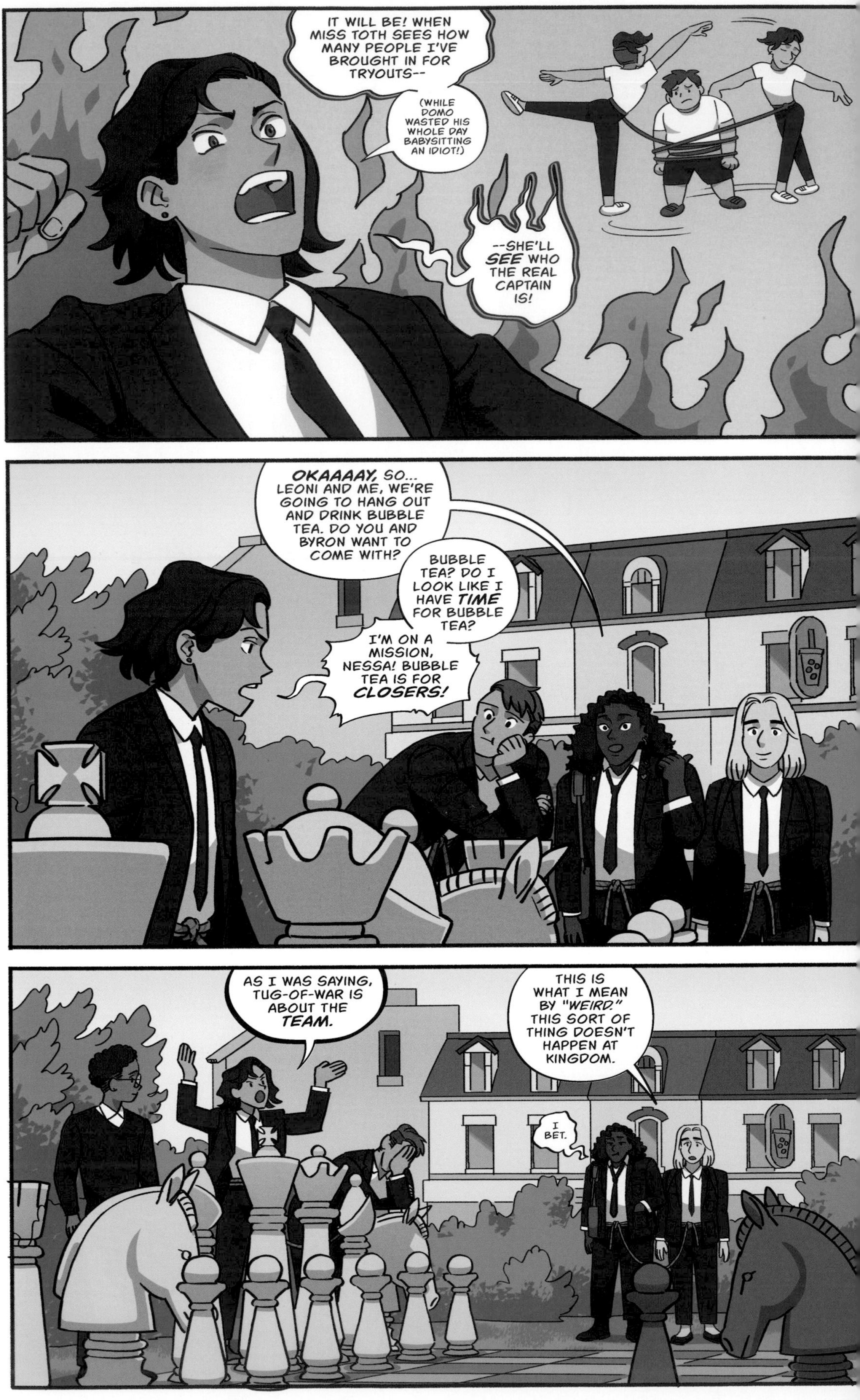
IT WILL BE! WHEN MISS TOTH SEES HOW MANY PEOPLE I'VE BROUGHT IN FOR TRYOUTS--
(WHILE DOMO WASTED HIS WHOLE DAY BABYSITTING AN IDIOT!)
--SHE'LL SEE WHO THE REAL CAPTAIN IS!
OKAAAAY, SO... LEONI AND ME, WE'RE GOING TO HANG OUT AND DRINK BUBBLE TEA. DO YOU AND BYRON WANT TO COME WITH?
BUBBLE TEA? DO I LOOK LIKE I HAVE TIME FOR BUBBLE TEA?
I'M ON A MISSION, NESSA! BUBBLE TEA IS FOR CLOSERS!
AS I WAS SAYING, TUG-OF-WAR IS ABOUT THE TEAM.
THIS IS WHAT I MEAN BY "WEIRD." THIS SORT OF THING DOESN'T HAPPEN AT KINGDOM.
I BET.

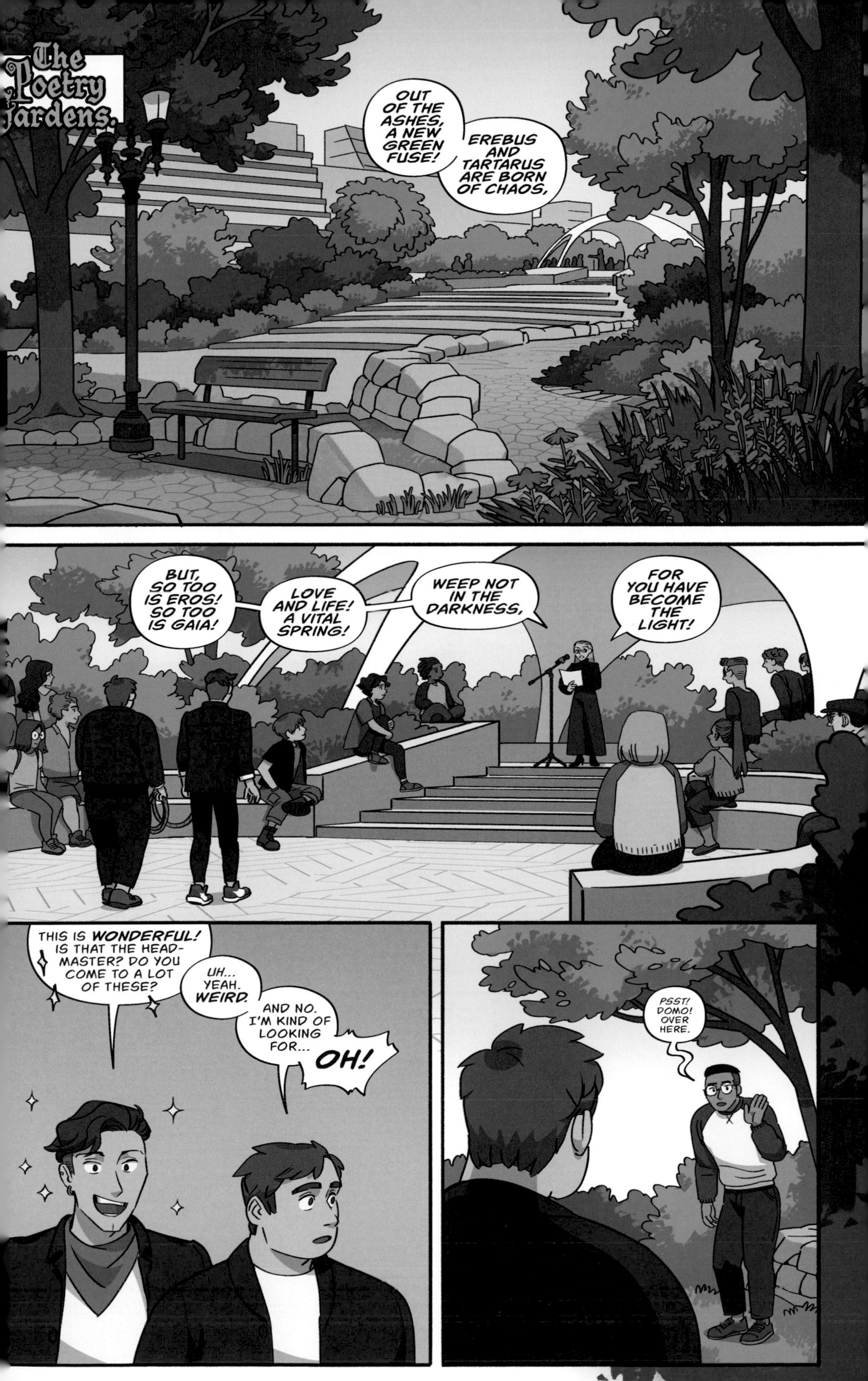
The Poetry Gardens.
OUT OF THE ASHES, A NEW GREEN FUSE!
EREBUS AND TARTARUS ARE BORN OF CHAOS,
BUT, SO TOO IS EROS! SO TOO IS GAIA!
LOVE AND LIFE! A VITAL SPRING!
WEEP NOT IN THE DARKNESS,
FOR YOU HAVE BECOME THE LIGHT!
THIS IS WONDERFUL! IS THAT THE HEAD-MASTER? DO YOU COME TO A LOT OF THESE?
UH... YEAH. WEIRD.
AND NO. I'M KIND OF LOOKING FOR...
OH!
PSST! DOMO! OVER HERE.

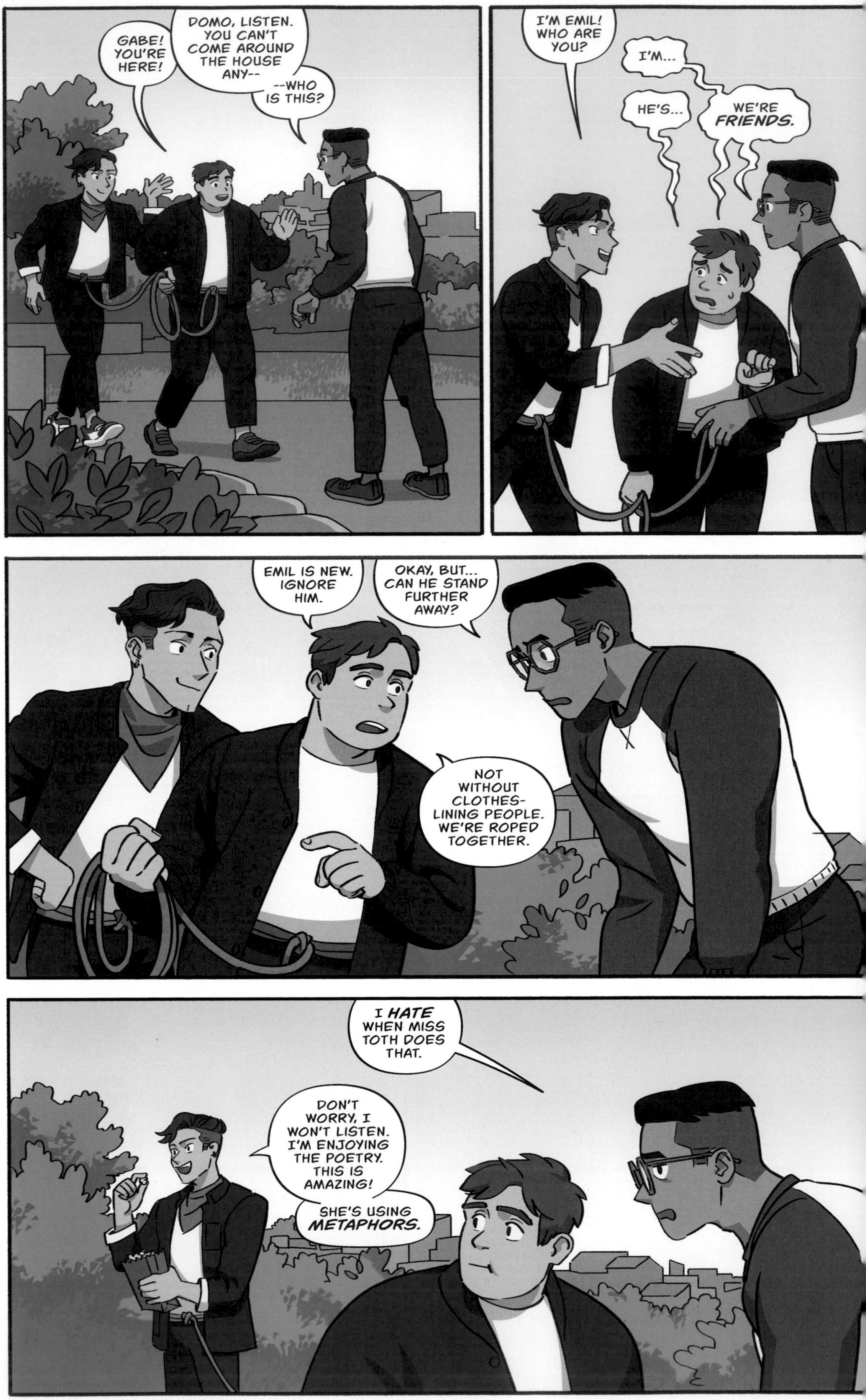
GABE! YOU'RE HERE!
DOMO, LISTEN. YOU CAN'T COME AROUND THE HOUSE ANY--
--WHO IS THIS?
I'M EMIL! WHO ARE YOU?
I'M...
HE'S...
WE'RE FRIENDS.
EMIL IS NEW. IGNORE HIM.
OKAY, BUT... CAN HE STAND FURTHER AWAY?
NOT WITHOUT CLOTHES-LINING PEOPLE. WE'RE ROPED TOGETHER.
I HATE WHEN MISS TOTH DOES THAT.
DON'T WORRY, I WON'T LISTEN. I'M ENJOYING THE POETRY. THIS IS AMAZING!
SHE'S USING METAPHORS.

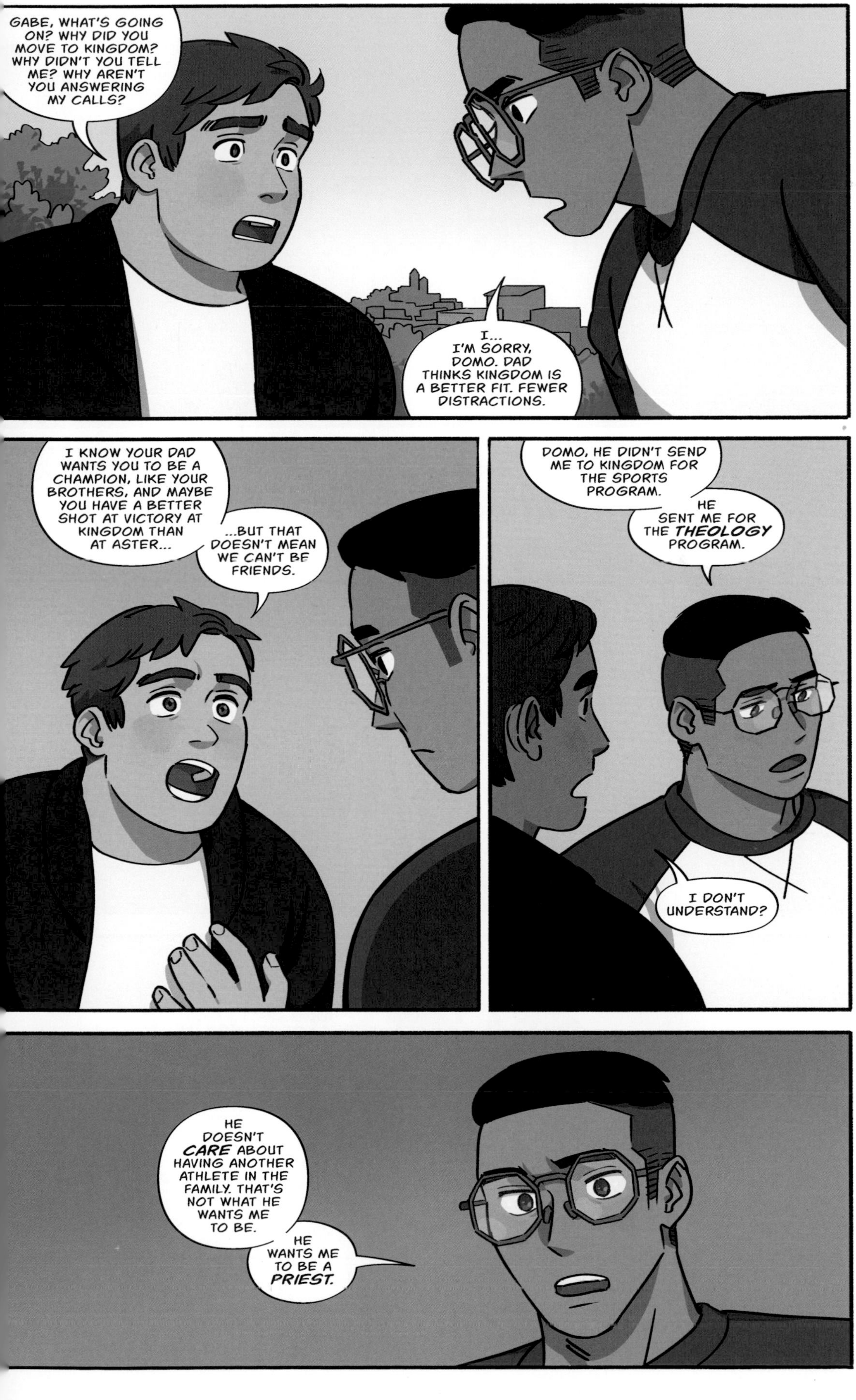
GABE, WHAT'S GOING ON? WHY DID YOU MOVE TO KINGDOM? WHY DIDN'T YOU TELL ME? WHY AREN'T YOU ANSWERING MY CALLS?
I... I'M SORRY, DOMO. DAD THINKS KINGDOM IS A BETTER FIT. FEWER DISTRACTIONS.
I KNOW YOUR DAD WANTS YOU TO BE A CHAMPION, LIKE YOUR BROTHERS, AND MAYBE YOU HAVE A BETTER SHOT AT VICTORY AT KINGDOM THAN AT ASTER...
...BUT THAT DOESN'T MEAN WE CAN'T BE FRIENDS.
DOMO, HE DIDN'T SEND ME TO KINGDOM FOR THE SPORTS PROGRAM.
HE SENT ME FOR THE *THEOLOGY* PROGRAM.
I DON'T UNDERSTAND?
HE DOESN'T *CARE* ABOUT HAVING ANOTHER ATHLETE IN THE FAMILY. THAT'S NOT WHAT HE WANTS ME TO BE.
HE WANTS ME TO BE A *PRIEST*.

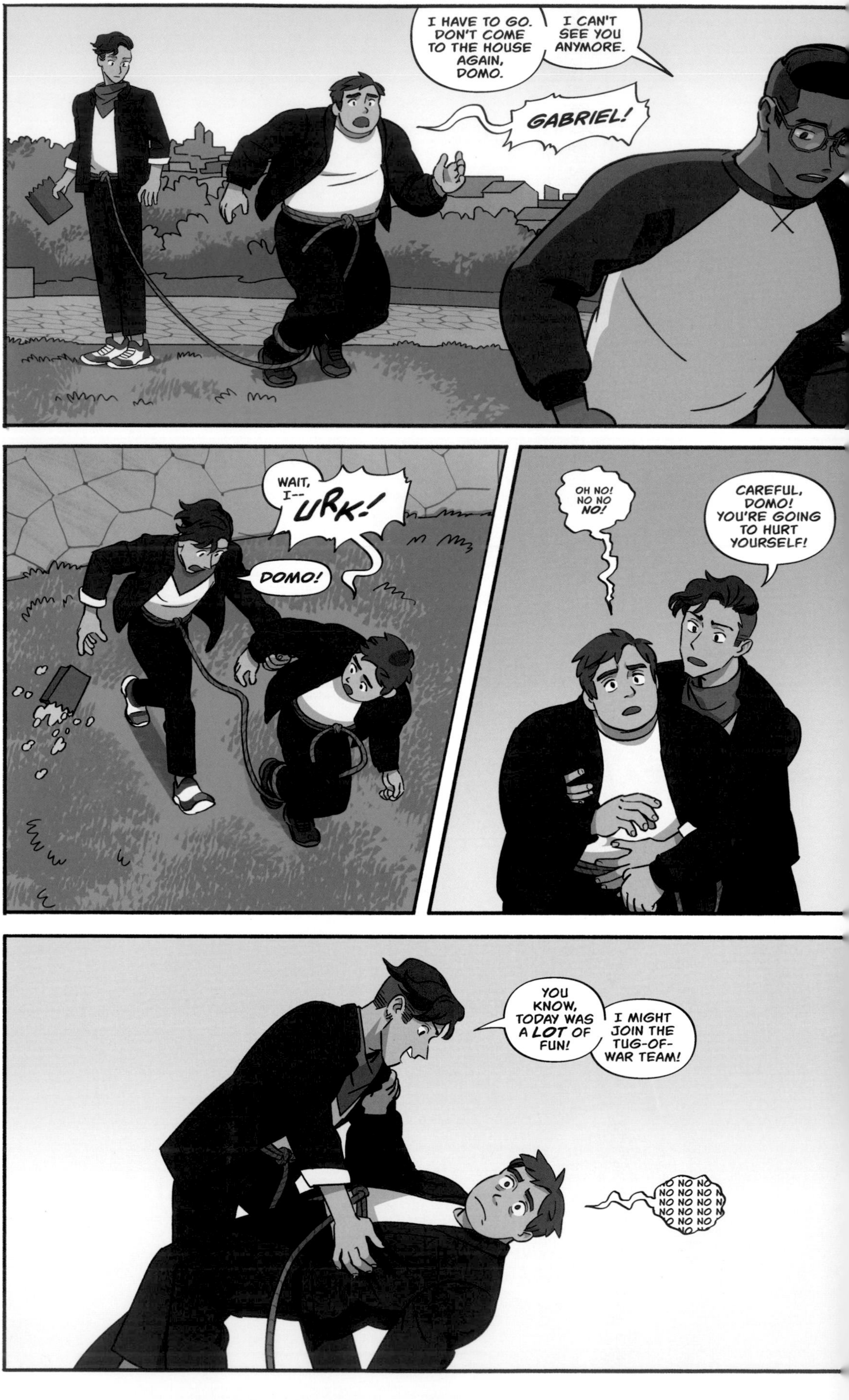
I HAVE TO GO. DON'T COME TO THE HOUSE AGAIN, DOMO.
I CAN'T SEE YOU ANYMORE.
GABRIEL!
WAIT, I--
URK!
DOMO!
OH NO! NO NO NO!
CAREFUL, DOMO! YOU'RE GOING TO HURT YOURSELF!
YOU KNOW, TODAY WAS A LOT OF FUN!
I MIGHT JOIN THE TUG-OF-WAR TEAM!
NO NO NO NO
NO NO NO
NO NO NO
NO NO

CHAPTER

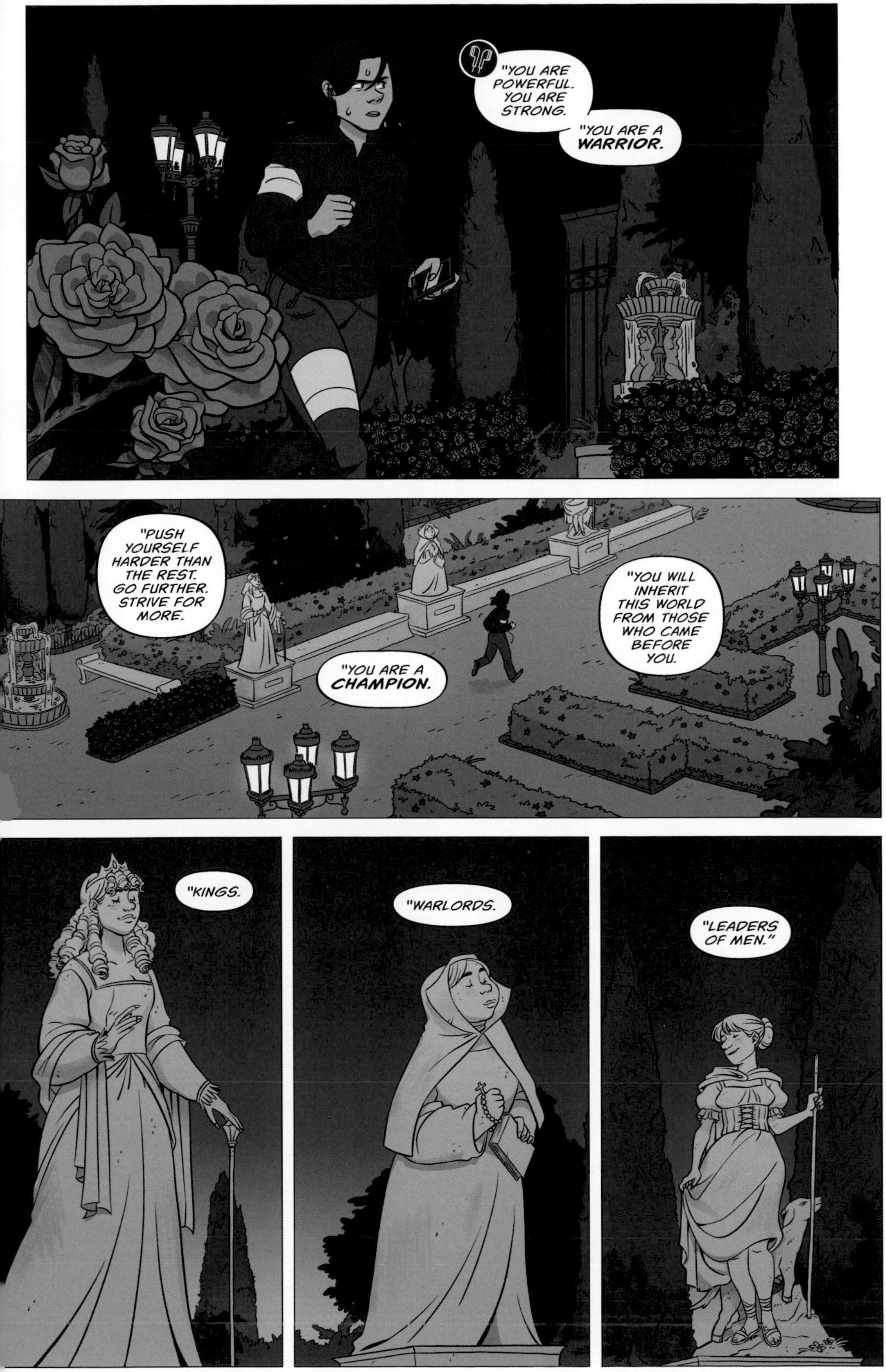
"YOU ARE POWERFUL. YOU ARE STRONG.
"YOU ARE A **WARRIOR.**
"PUSH YOURSELF HARDER THAN THE REST. GO FURTHER. STRIVE FOR MORE.
"YOU ARE A **CHAMPION.**
"YOU WILL INHERIT THIS WORLD FROM THOSE WHO CAME BEFORE YOU.
"KINGS.
"WARLORDS.
"LEADERS OF MEN."

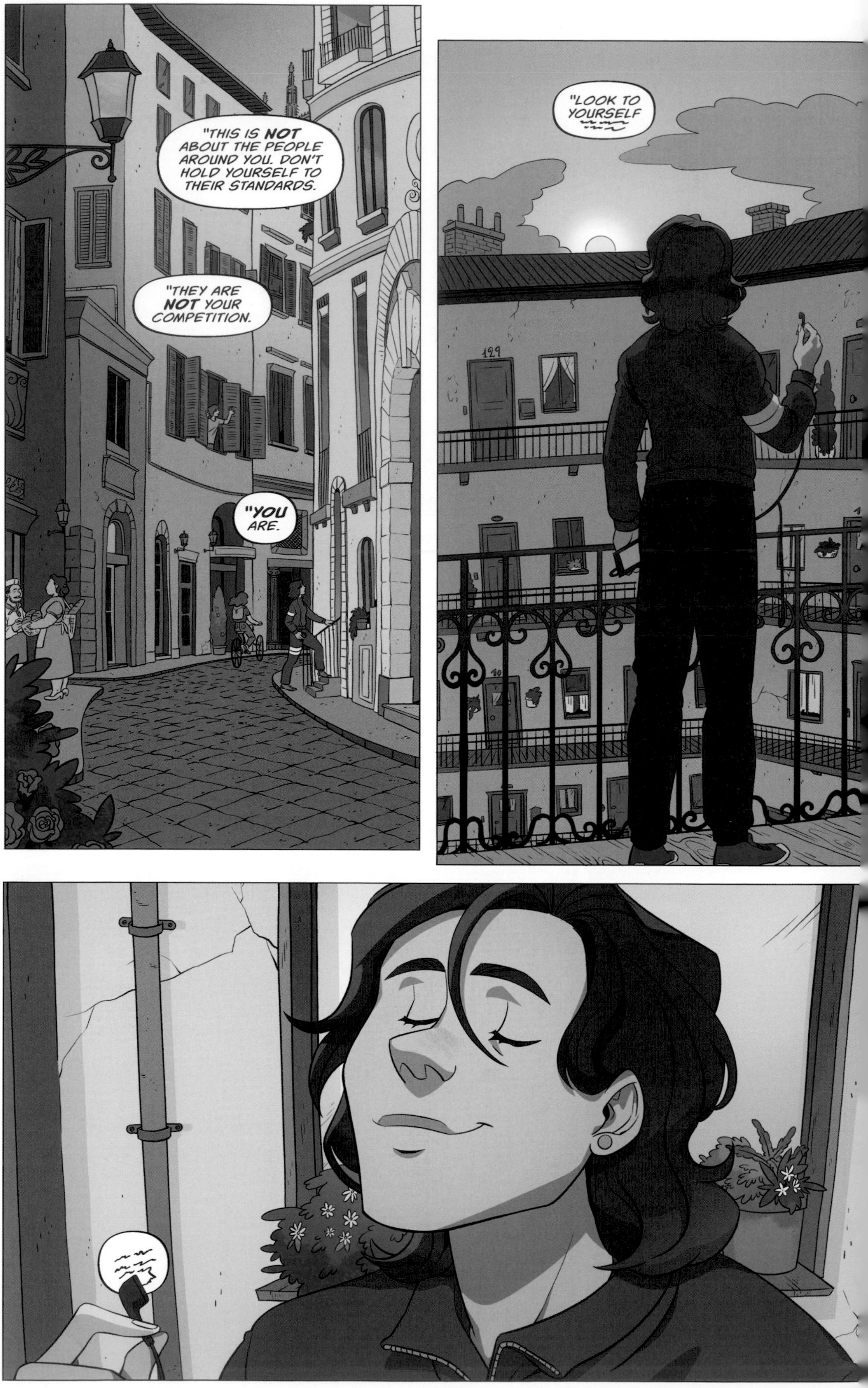
"THIS IS **NOT** ABOUT THE PEOPLE AROUND YOU. DON'T HOLD YOURSELF TO THEIR STANDARDS.
"THEY ARE **NOT** YOUR COMPETITION.
"**YOU** ARE.
"LOOK TO YOURSELF

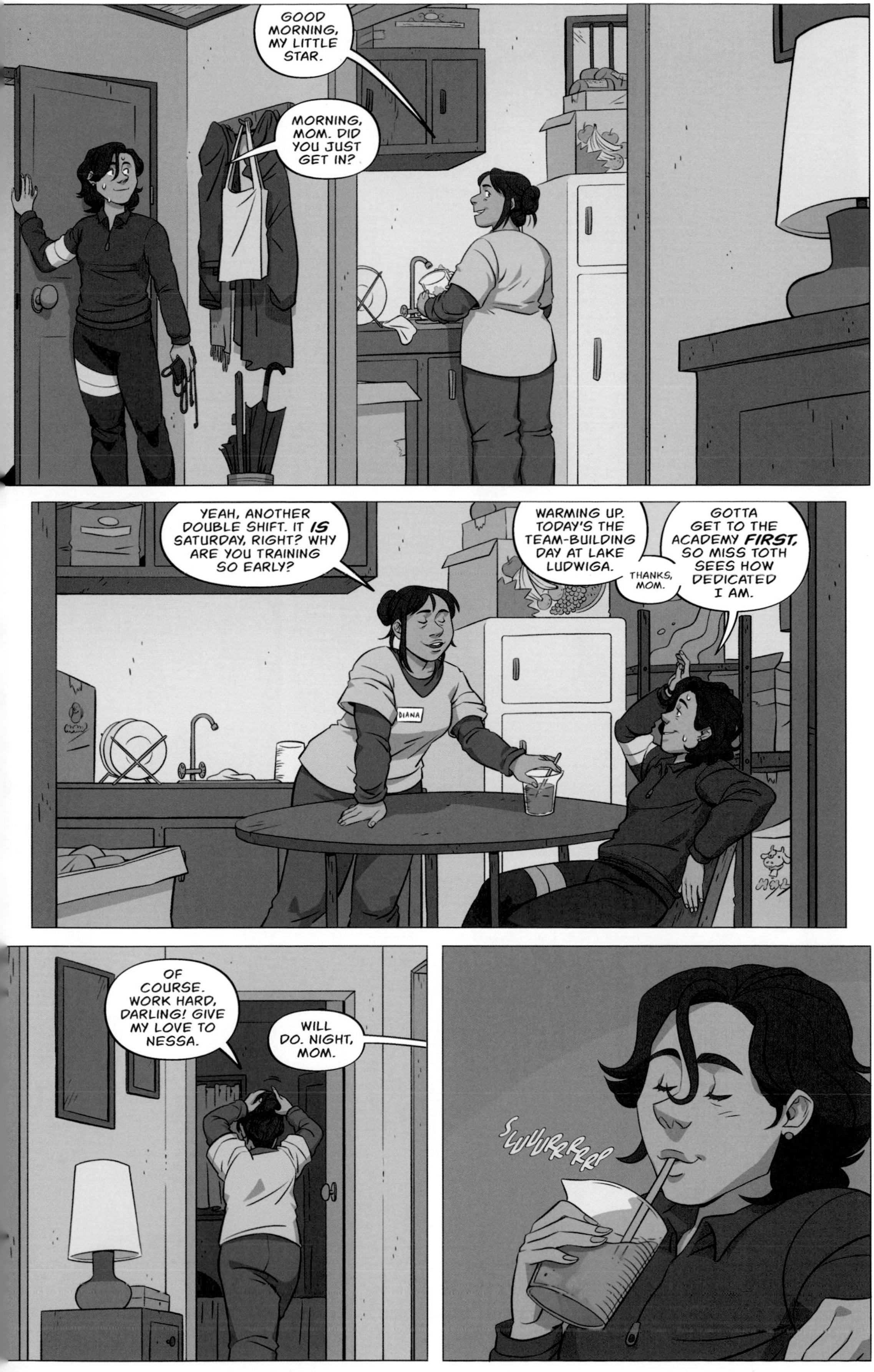
GOOD MORNING, MY LITTLE STAR.
MORNING, MOM. DID YOU JUST GET IN?
YEAH, ANOTHER DOUBLE SHIFT. IT IS SATURDAY, RIGHT? WHY ARE YOU TRAINING SO EARLY?
DIANA
WARMING UP. TODAY'S THE TEAM-BUILDING DAY AT LAKE LUDWIGA.
THANKS, MOM.
GOTTA GET TO THE ACADEMY FIRST, SO MISS TOTH SEES HOW DEDICATED I AM.
OF COURSE. WORK HARD, DARLING! GIVE MY LOVE TO NESSA.
WILL DO. NIGHT, MOM.
SLUUURRRRP

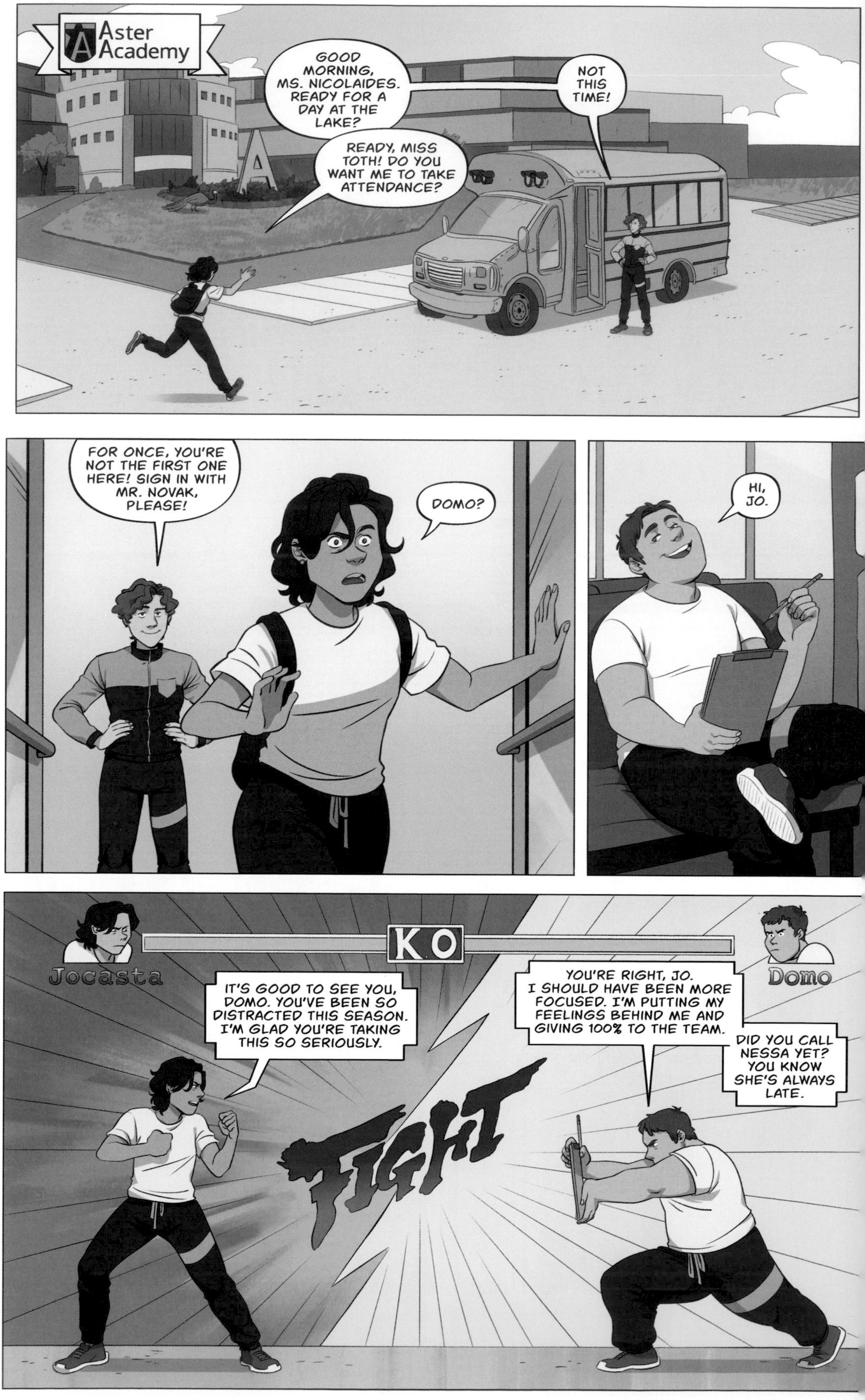
Aster Academy
GOOD MORNING, MS. NICOLAIDES. READY FOR A DAY AT THE LAKE?
NOT THIS TIME!
READY, MISS TOTH! DO YOU WANT ME TO TAKE ATTENDANCE?
FOR ONCE, YOU'RE NOT THE FIRST ONE HERE! SIGN IN WITH MR. NOVAK, PLEASE!
DOMO?
HI, JO.
K.O
Jocasta
Domo
IT'S GOOD TO SEE YOU, DOMO. YOU'VE BEEN SO DISTRACTED THIS SEASON. I'M GLAD YOU'RE TAKING THIS SO SERIOUSLY.
YOU'RE RIGHT, JO. I SHOULD HAVE BEEN MORE FOCUSED. I'M PUTTING MY FEELINGS BEHIND ME AND GIVING 100% TO THE TEAM.
DID YOU CALL NESSA YET? YOU KNOW SHE'S ALWAYS LATE.
FIGHT

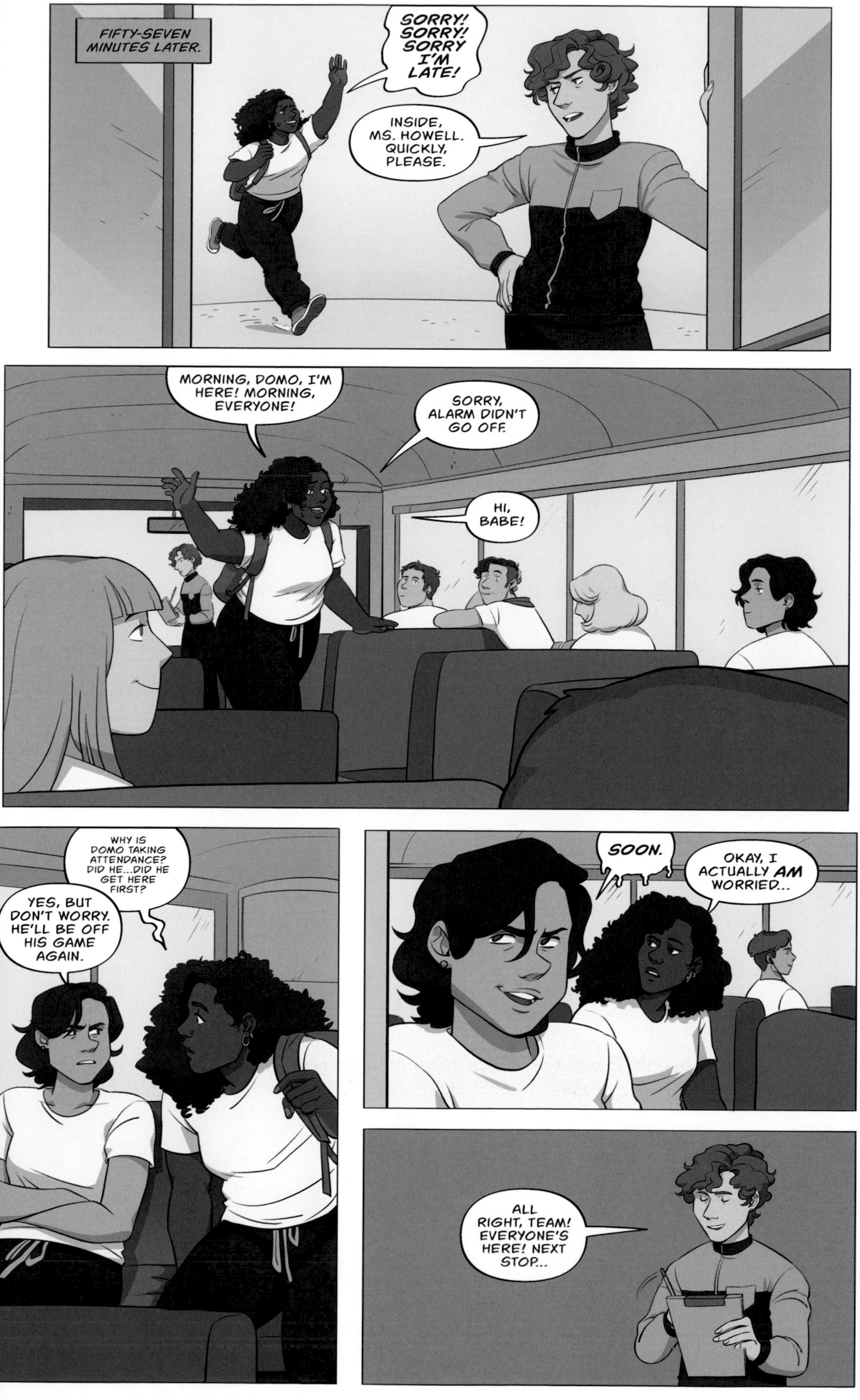
FIFTY-SEVEN MINUTES LATER.
SORRY! SORRY! SORRY I'M LATE!
INSIDE, MS. HOWELL. QUICKLY, PLEASE.
MORNING, DOMO, I'M HERE! MORNING, EVERYONE!
SORRY, ALARM DIDN'T GO OFF.
HI, BABE!
WHY IS DOMO TAKING ATTENDANCE? DID HE...DID HE GET HERE FIRST?
YES, BUT DON'T WORRY. HE'LL BE OFF HIS GAME AGAIN.
SOON.
OKAY, I ACTUALLY AM WORRIED...
ALL RIGHT, TEAM! EVERYONE'S HERE! NEXT STOP...

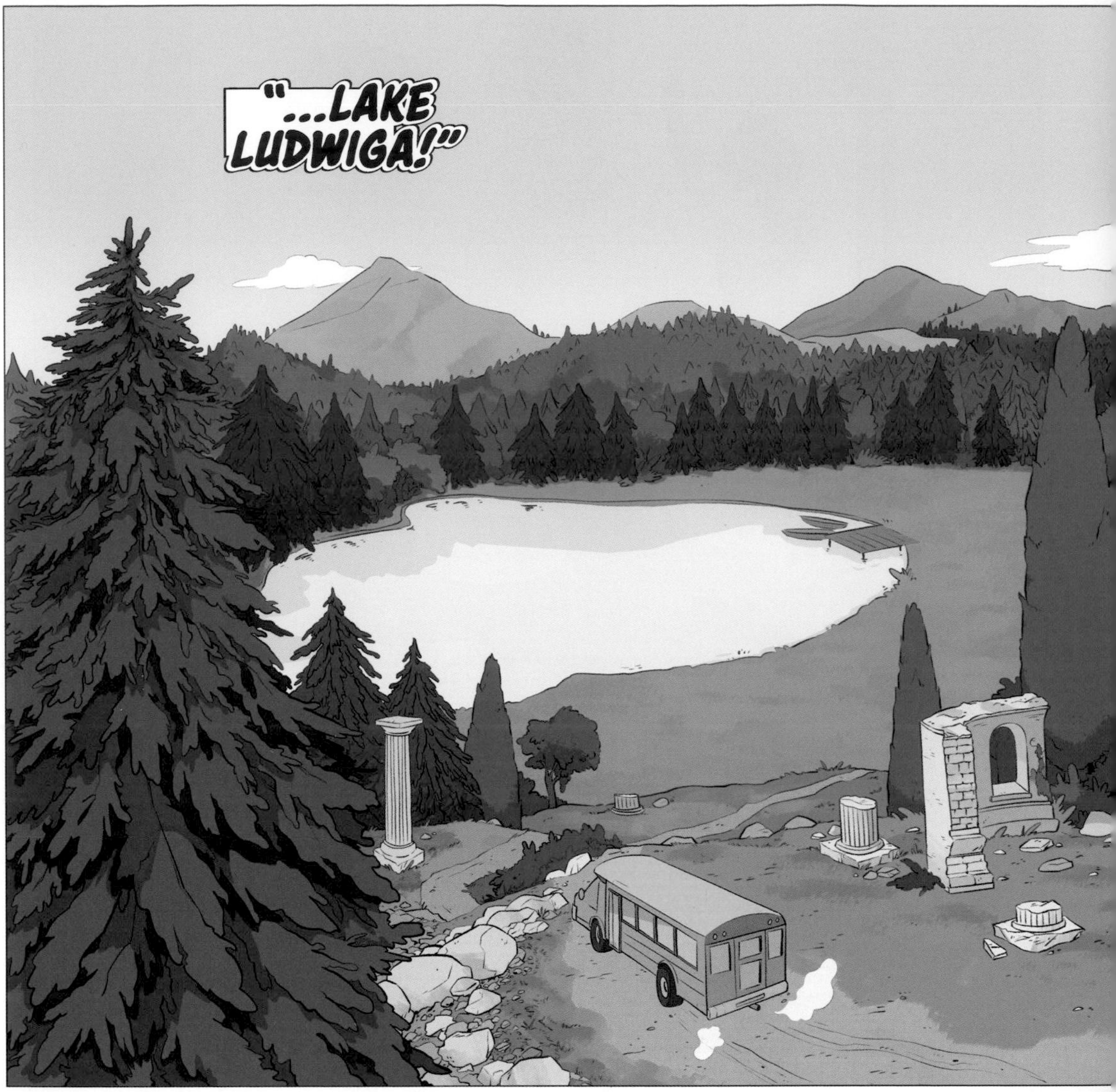
"...LAKE LUDWIGA!"

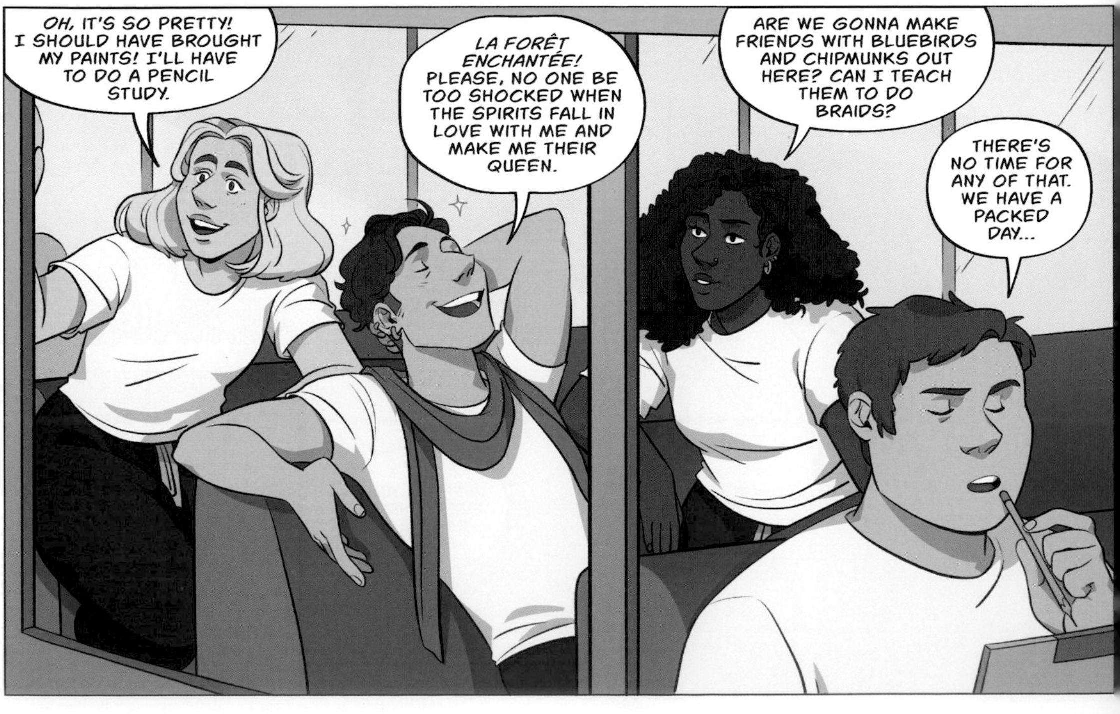
OH, IT'S SO PRETTY! I SHOULD HAVE BROUGHT MY PAINTS! I'LL HAVE TO DO A PENCIL STUDY.
LA FORÊT ENCHANTÉE! PLEASE, NO ONE BE TOO SHOCKED WHEN THE SPIRITS FALL IN LOVE WITH ME AND MAKE ME THEIR QUEEN.
ARE WE GONNA MAKE FRIENDS WITH BLUEBIRDS AND CHIPMUNKS OUT HERE? CAN I TEACH THEM TO DO BRAIDS?
THERE'S NO TIME FOR ANY OF THAT. WE HAVE A PACKED DAY...

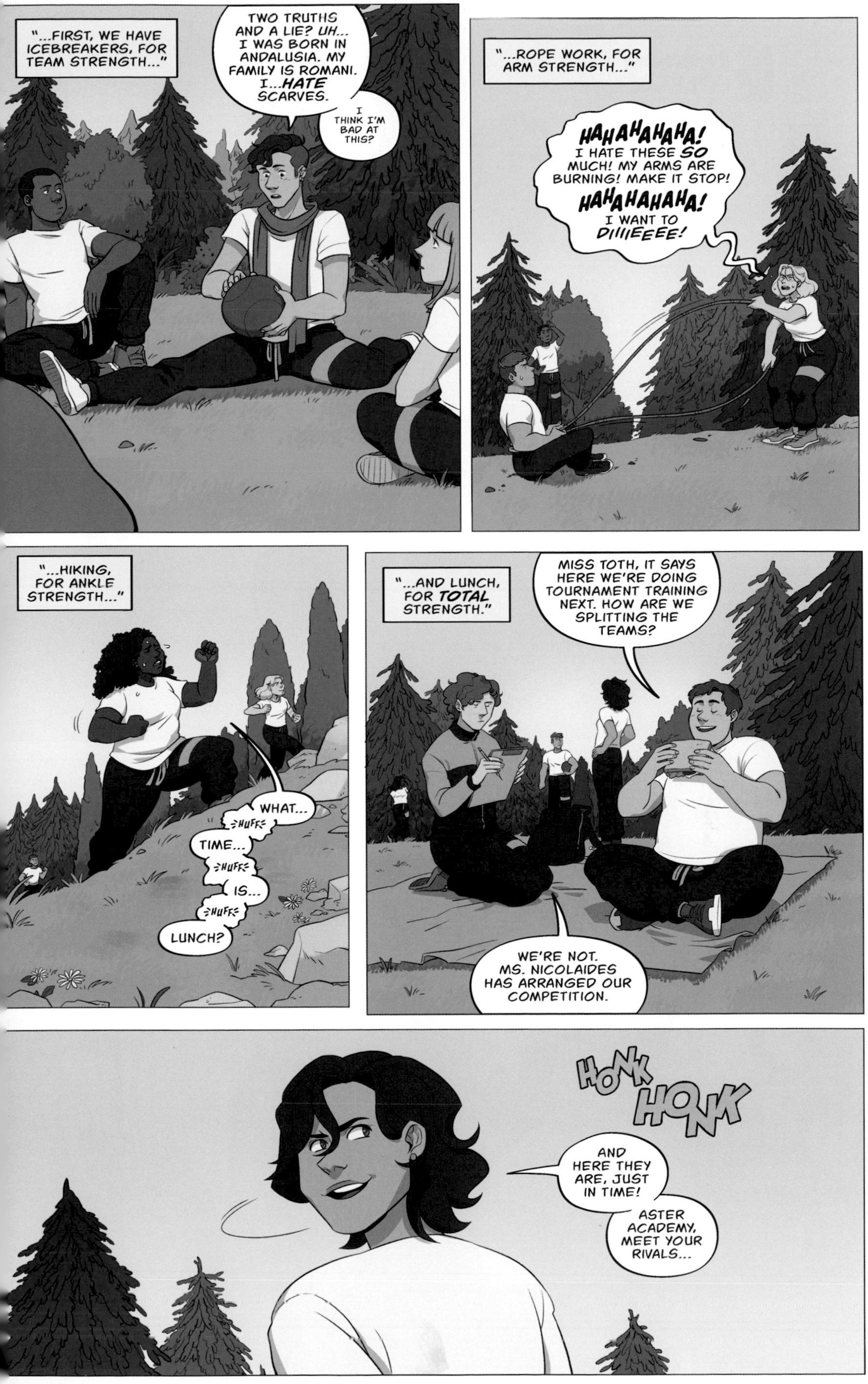
"...FIRST, WE HAVE ICEBREAKERS, FOR TEAM STRENGTH..."
TWO TRUTHS AND A LIE? UH... I WAS BORN IN ANDALUSIA. MY FAMILY IS ROMANI. I...HATE SCARVES.
I THINK I'M BAD AT THIS?
"...ROPE WORK, FOR ARM STRENGTH..."
HAHAHAHAHA! I HATE THESE SO MUCH! MY ARMS ARE BURNING! MAKE IT STOP! HAHAHAHAHA! I WANT TO DIIIIEEEE!
"...HIKING, FOR ANKLE STRENGTH..."
WHAT...
HUFF
TIME...
HUFF
IS...
HUFF
LUNCH?
"...AND LUNCH, FOR TOTAL STRENGTH."
MISS TOTH, IT SAYS HERE WE'RE DOING TOURNAMENT TRAINING NEXT. HOW ARE WE SPLITTING THE TEAMS?
WE'RE NOT. MS. NICOLAIDES HAS ARRANGED OUR COMPETITION.
HONK HONK
AND HERE THEY ARE, JUST IN TIME!
ASTER ACADEMY, MEET YOUR RIVALS...

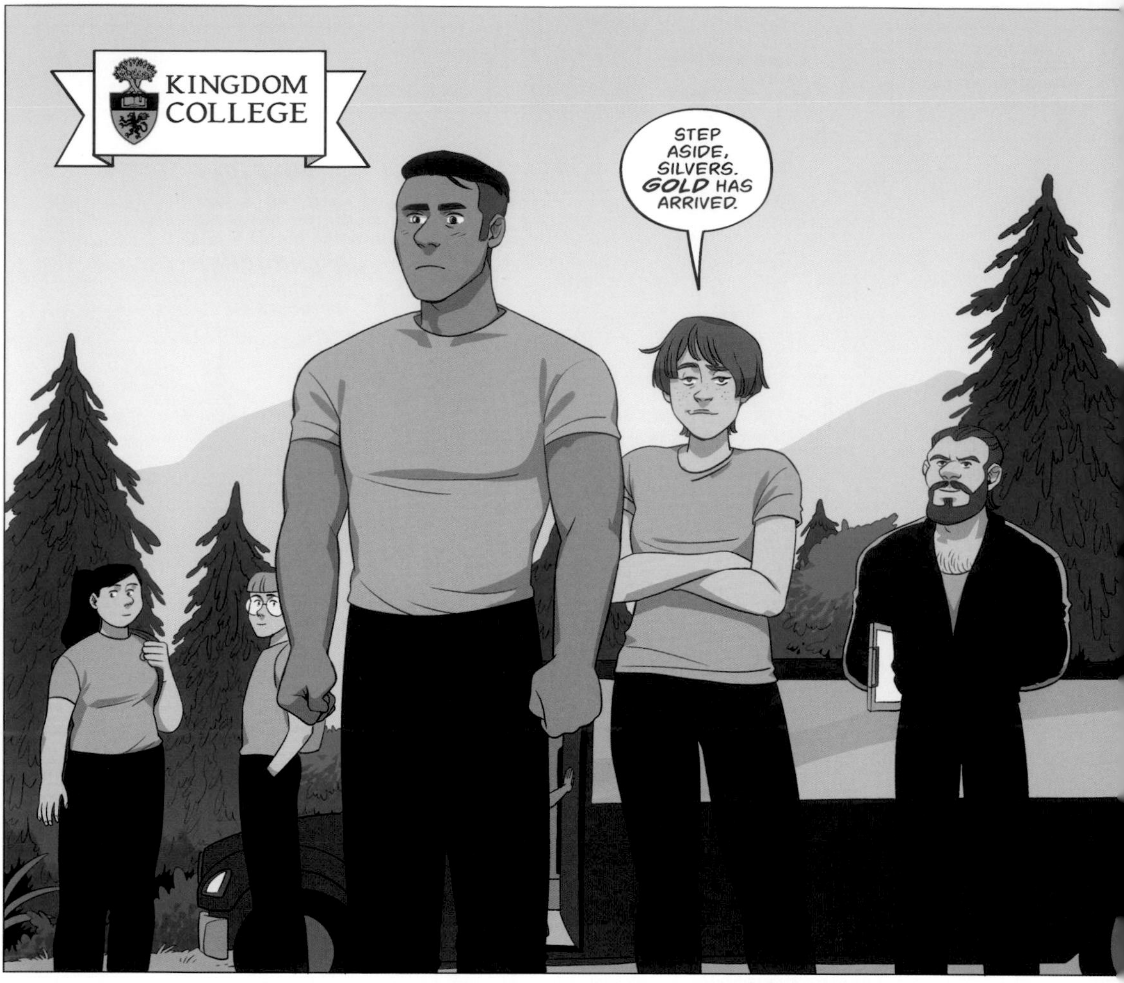
KINGDOM COLLEGE
STEP ASIDE, SILVERS. GOLD HAS ARRIVED.

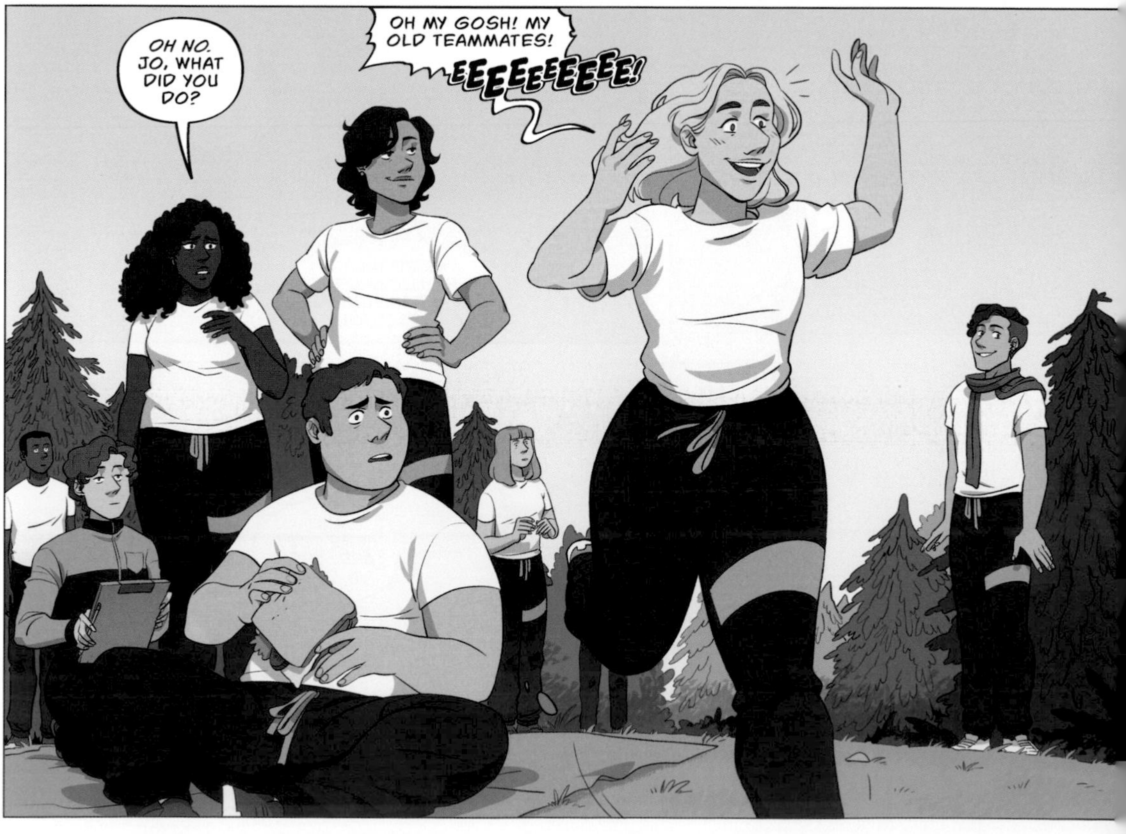
OH NO. JO, WHAT DID YOU DO?
OH MY GOSH! MY OLD TEAMMATES!
EEEEEEEEEE!

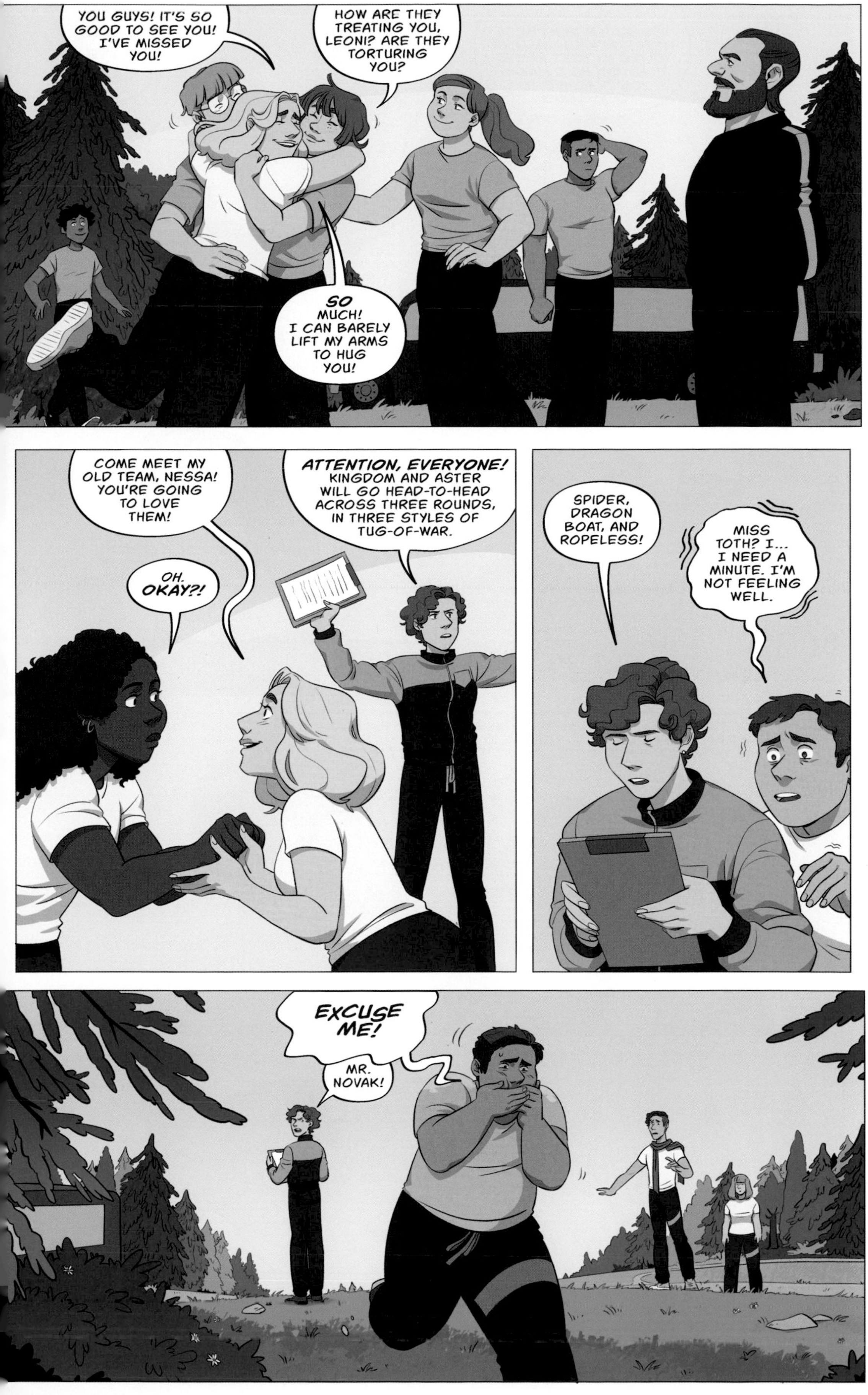
YOU GUYS! IT'S SO GOOD TO SEE YOU! I'VE MISSED YOU!
HOW ARE THEY TREATING YOU, LEONI? ARE THEY TORTURING YOU?
SO MUCH! I CAN BARELY LIFT MY ARMS TO HUG YOU!
COME MEET MY OLD TEAM, NESSA! YOU'RE GOING TO LOVE THEM!
OH. OKAY?!
ATTENTION, EVERYONE! KINGDOM AND ASTER WILL GO HEAD-TO-HEAD ACROSS THREE ROUNDS, IN THREE STYLES OF TUG-OF-WAR.
SPIDER, DRAGON BOAT, AND ROPELESS!
MISS TOTH? I... I NEED A MINUTE. I'M NOT FEELING WELL.
EXCUSE ME!
MR. NOVAK!

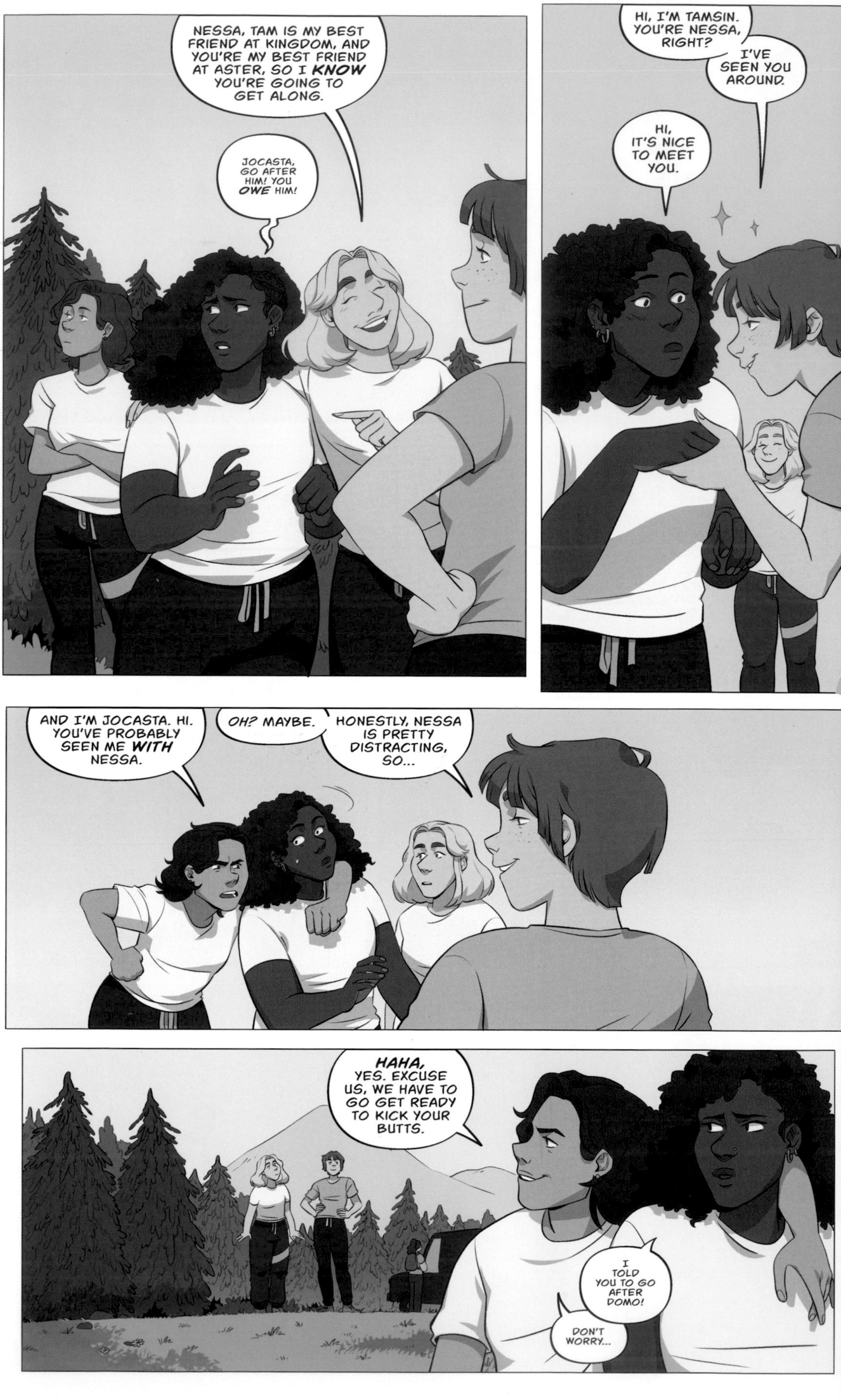
NESSA, TAM IS MY BEST FRIEND AT KINGDOM, AND YOU'RE MY BEST FRIEND AT ASTER, SO I **KNOW** YOU'RE GOING TO GET ALONG.
JOCASTA, GO AFTER HIM! YOU **OWE** HIM!
HI, I'M TAMSIN. YOU'RE NESSA, RIGHT?
I'VE SEEN YOU AROUND.
HI, IT'S NICE TO MEET YOU.
AND I'M JOCASTA. HI. YOU'VE PROBABLY SEEN ME **WITH** NESSA.
OH? MAYBE.
HONESTLY, NESSA IS PRETTY DISTRACTING, SO...
HAHA, YES. EXCUSE US, WE HAVE TO GO GET READY TO KICK YOUR BUTTS.
I TOLD YOU TO GO AFTER DOMO!
DON'T WORRY...

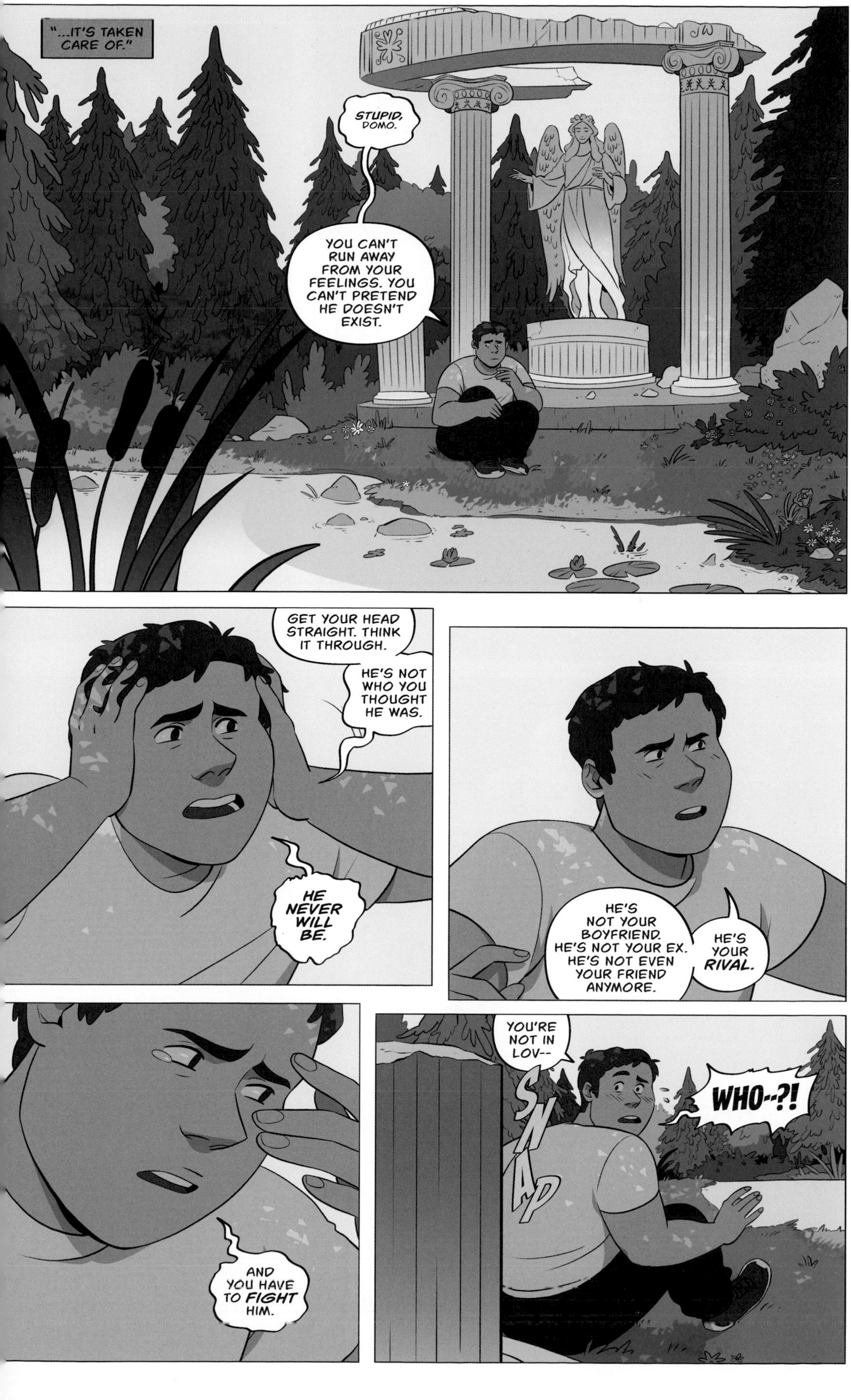
"...IT'S TAKEN CARE OF."
STUPID, DOMO.
YOU CAN'T RUN AWAY FROM YOUR FEELINGS. YOU CAN'T PRETEND HE DOESN'T EXIST.
GET YOUR HEAD STRAIGHT. THINK IT THROUGH.
HE'S NOT WHO YOU THOUGHT HE WAS.
HE NEVER WILL BE.
HE'S NOT YOUR BOYFRIEND. HE'S NOT YOUR EX. HE'S NOT EVEN YOUR FRIEND ANYMORE.
HE'S YOUR RIVAL.
AND YOU HAVE TO FIGHT HIM.
YOU'RE NOT IN LOV--
SNAP
WHO--?!

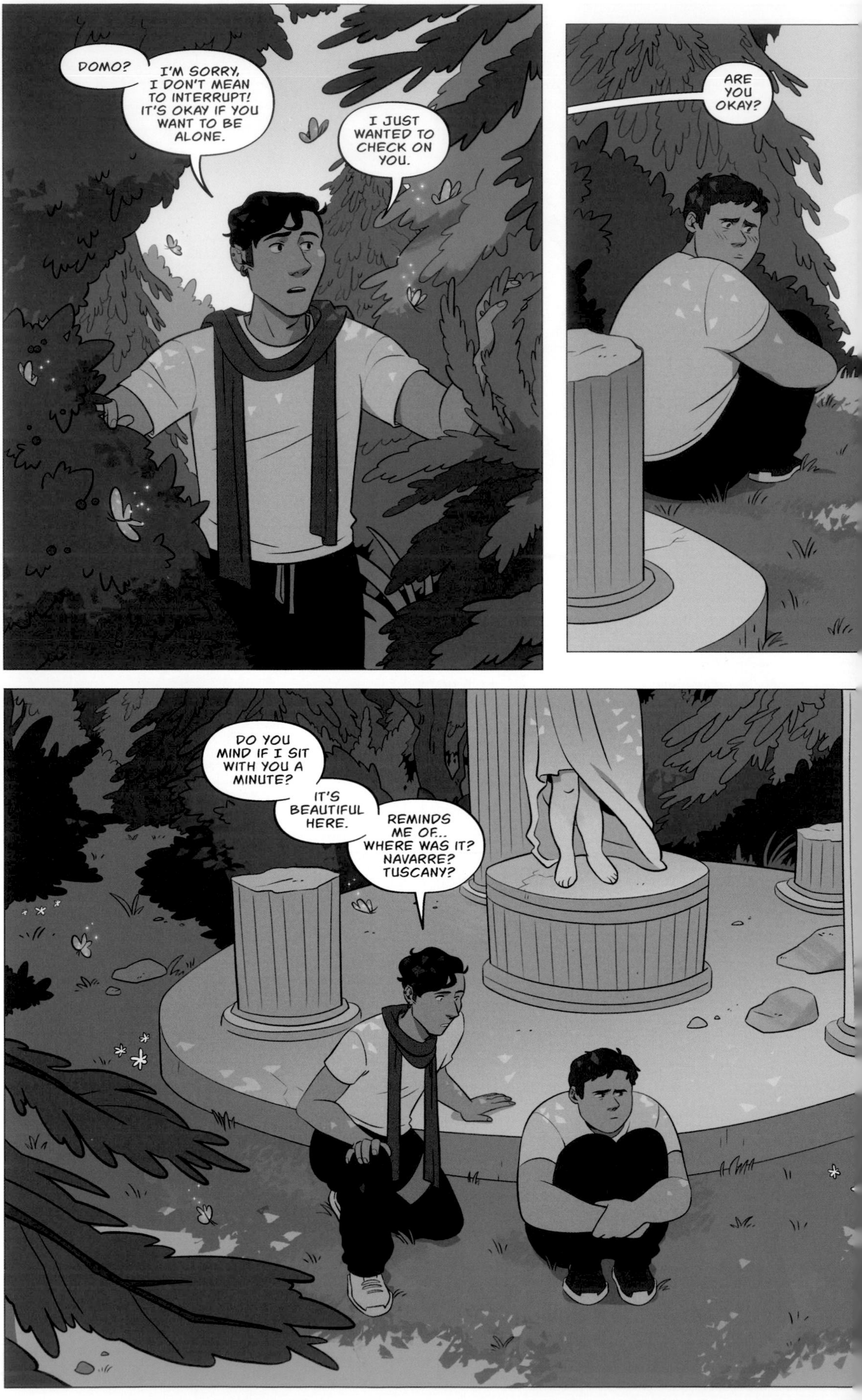
DOMO?
I'M SORRY, I DON'T MEAN TO INTERRUPT! IT'S OKAY IF YOU WANT TO BE ALONE.
I JUST WANTED TO CHECK ON YOU.
ARE YOU OKAY?
DO YOU MIND IF I SIT WITH YOU A MINUTE?
IT'S BEAUTIFUL HERE.
REMINDS ME OF... WHERE WAS IT? NAVARRE? TUSCANY?

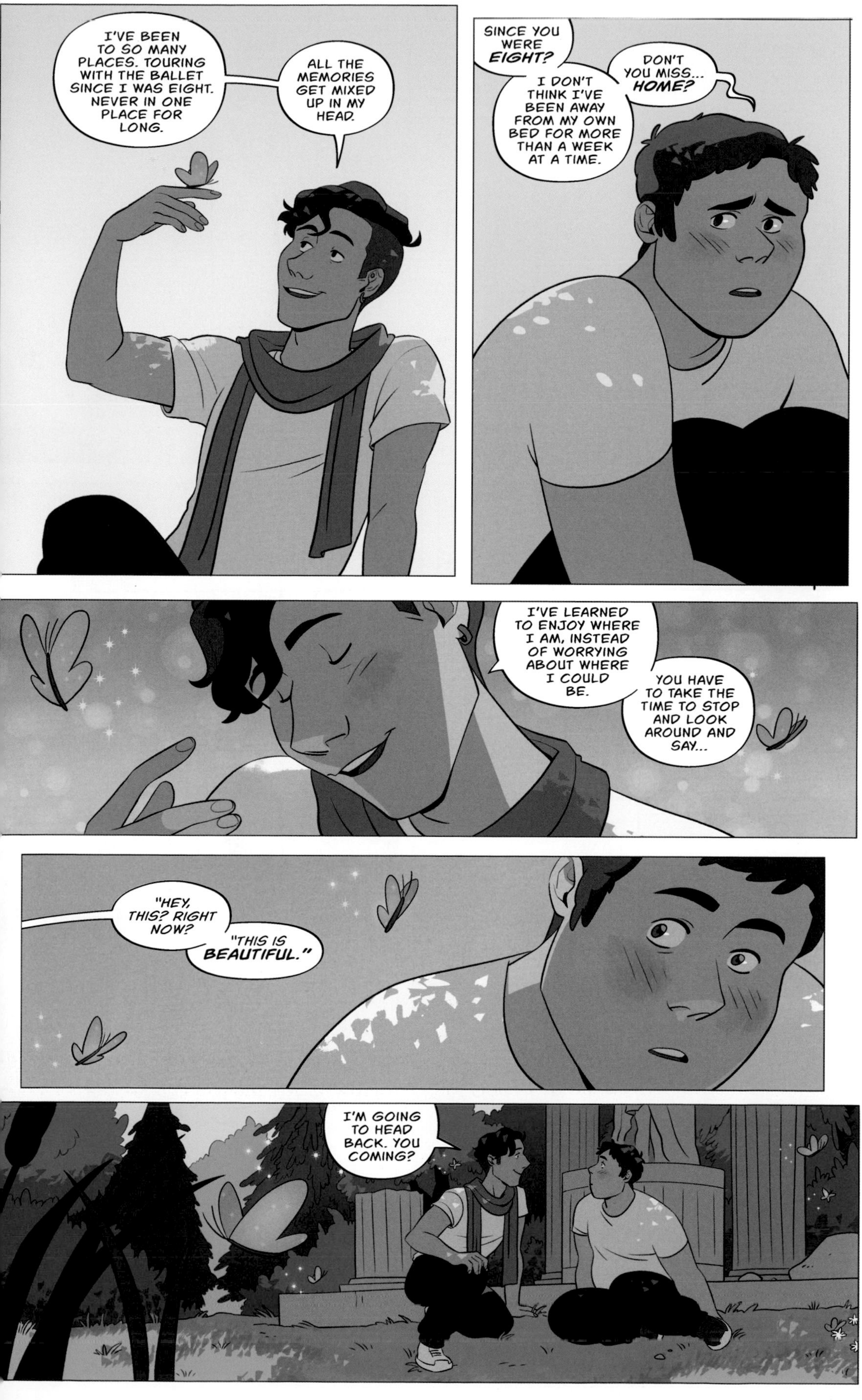
I'VE BEEN TO SO MANY PLACES. TOURING WITH THE BALLET SINCE I WAS EIGHT. NEVER IN ONE PLACE FOR LONG.
ALL THE MEMORIES GET MIXED UP IN MY HEAD.
SINCE YOU WERE **EIGHT?**
I DON'T THINK I'VE BEEN AWAY FROM MY OWN BED FOR MORE THAN A WEEK AT A TIME.
DON'T YOU MISS... **HOME?**
I'VE LEARNED TO ENJOY WHERE I AM, INSTEAD OF WORRYING ABOUT WHERE I COULD BE.
YOU HAVE TO TAKE THE TIME TO STOP AND LOOK AROUND AND SAY...
"HEY, THIS? RIGHT NOW?
"THIS IS **BEAUTIFUL."**
I'M GOING TO HEAD BACK. YOU COMING?

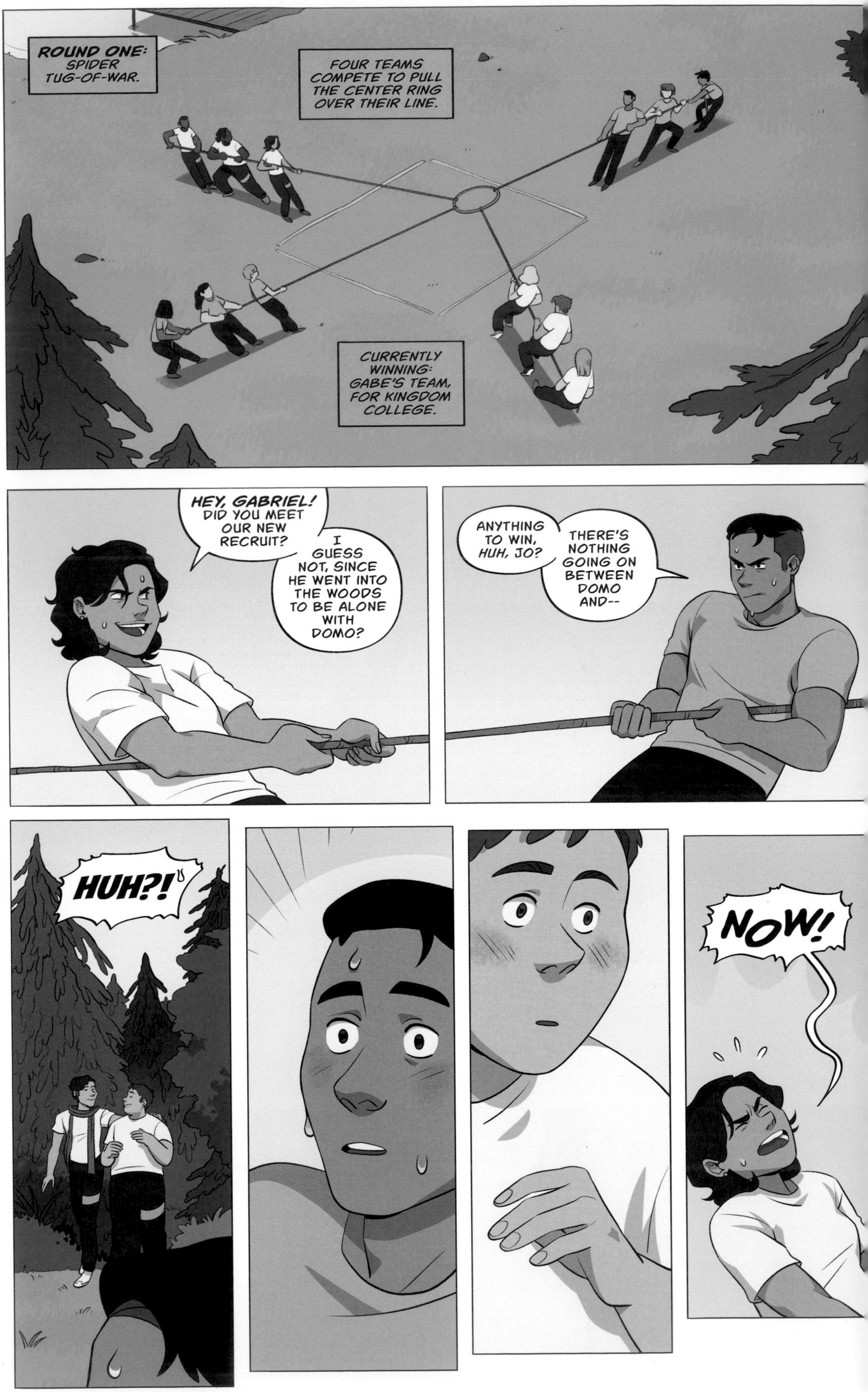
ROUND ONE: SPIDER TUG-OF-WAR.
FOUR TEAMS COMPETE TO PULL THE CENTER RING OVER THEIR LINE.
CURRENTLY WINNING: GABE'S TEAM, FOR KINGDOM COLLEGE.
HEY, GABRIEL! DID YOU MEET OUR NEW RECRUIT?
I GUESS NOT, SINCE HE WENT INTO THE WOODS TO BE ALONE WITH DOMO?
ANYTHING TO WIN, HUH, JO?
THERE'S NOTHING GOING ON BETWEEN DOMO AND--
HUH?!
NOW!

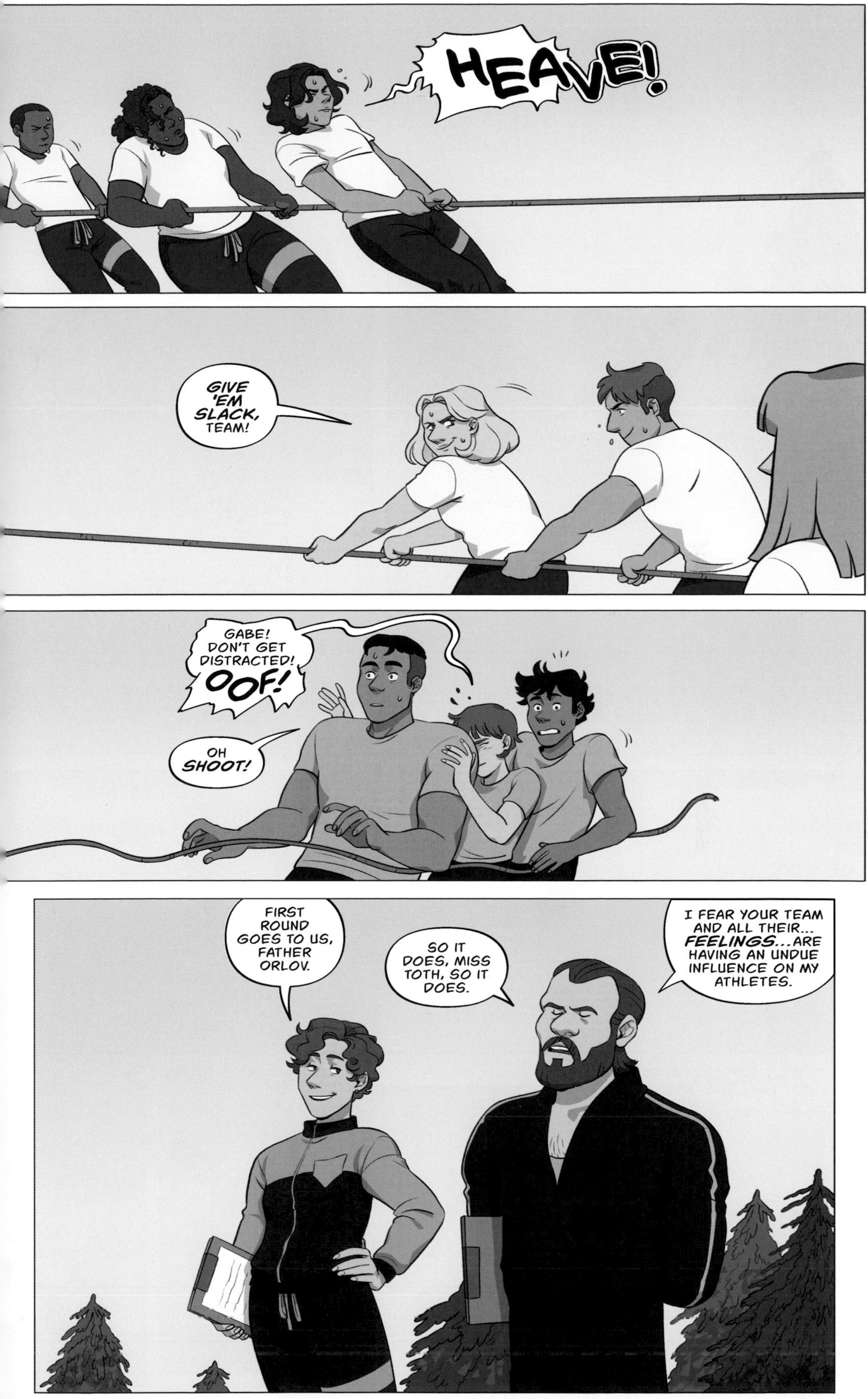
HEAVE!
GIVE 'EM SLACK, TEAM!
GABE! DON'T GET DISTRACTED!
OOF!
OH SHOOT!
FIRST ROUND GOES TO US, FATHER ORLOV.
SO IT DOES, MISS TOTH, SO IT DOES.
I FEAR YOUR TEAM AND ALL THEIR... FEELINGS... ARE HAVING AN UNDUE INFLUENCE ON MY ATHLETES.

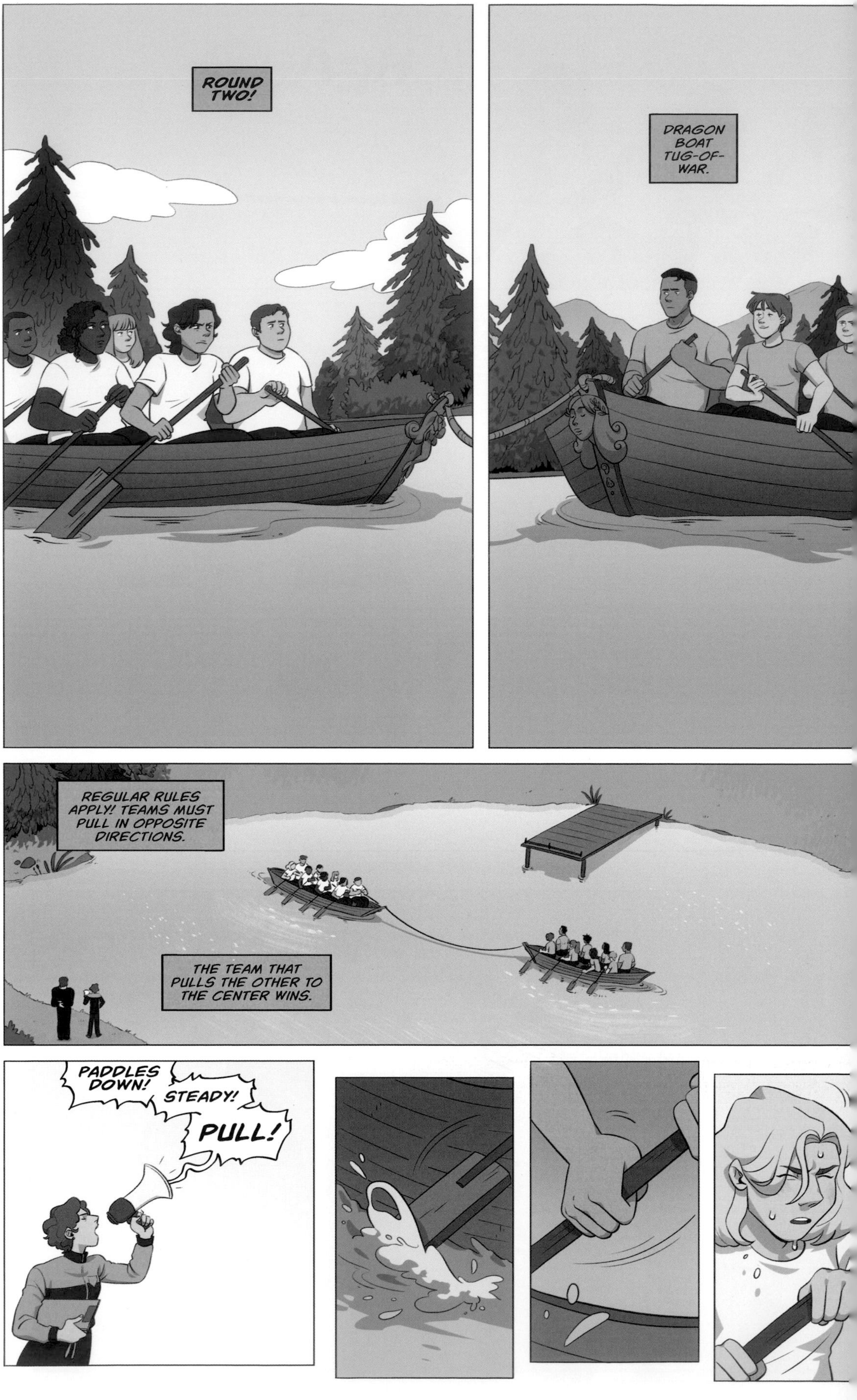

ROUND TWO!
DRAGON BOAT TUG-OF-WAR.
REGULAR RULES APPLY! TEAMS MUST PULL IN OPPOSITE DIRECTIONS.
THE TEAM THAT PULLS THE OTHER TO THE CENTER WINS.
PADDLES DOWN!
STEADY!
PULL!

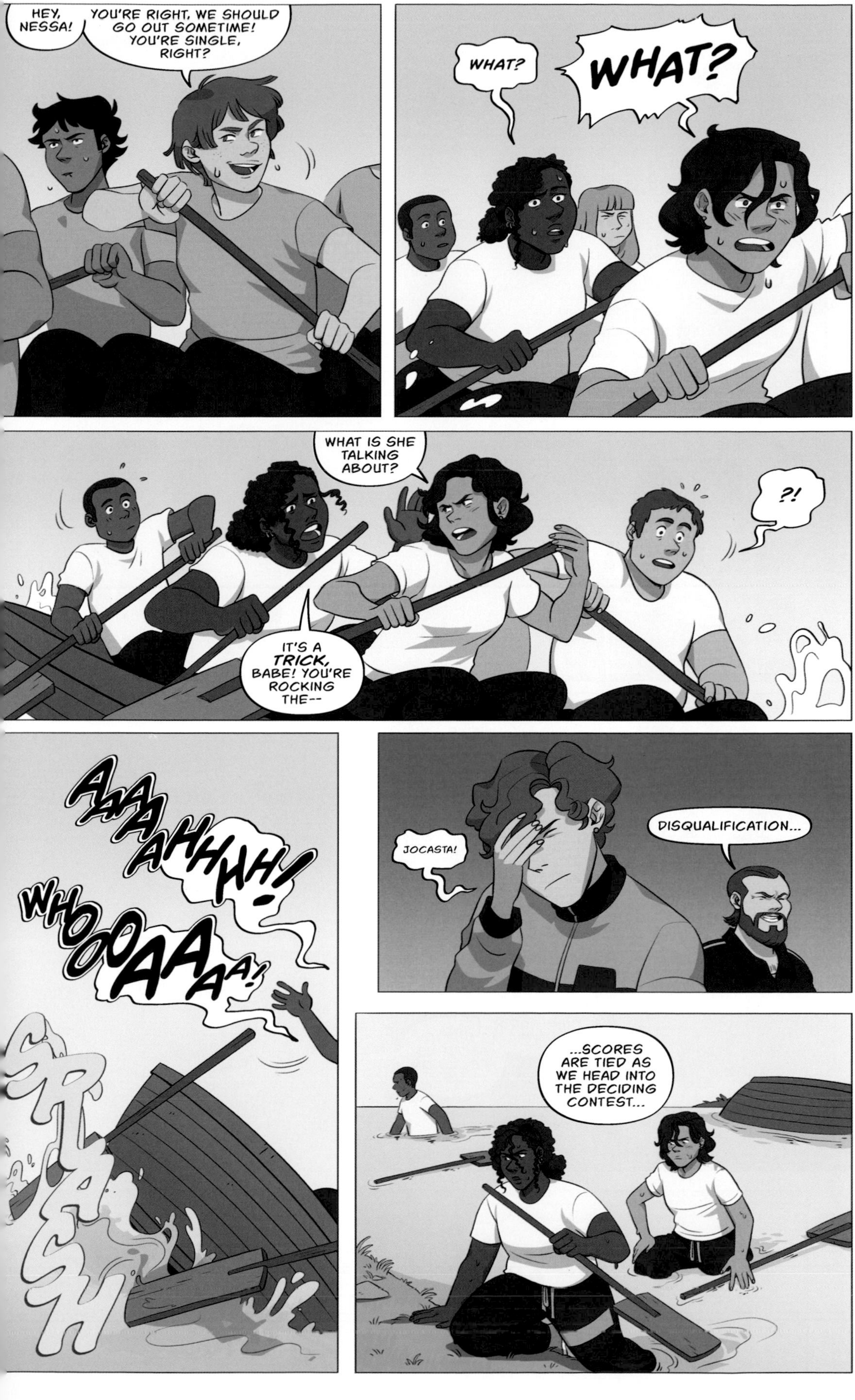
HEY, NESSA!
YOU'RE RIGHT, WE SHOULD GO OUT SOMETIME! YOU'RE SINGLE, RIGHT?
WHAT?
WHAT?
WHAT IS SHE TALKING ABOUT?
?!
IT'S A TRICK, BABE! YOU'RE ROCKING THE--
AAAAAHHHH!
WHOOOAAAA!
SPLASH
JOCASTA!
DISQUALIFICATION...
...SCORES ARE TIED AS WE HEAD INTO THE DECIDING CONTEST...

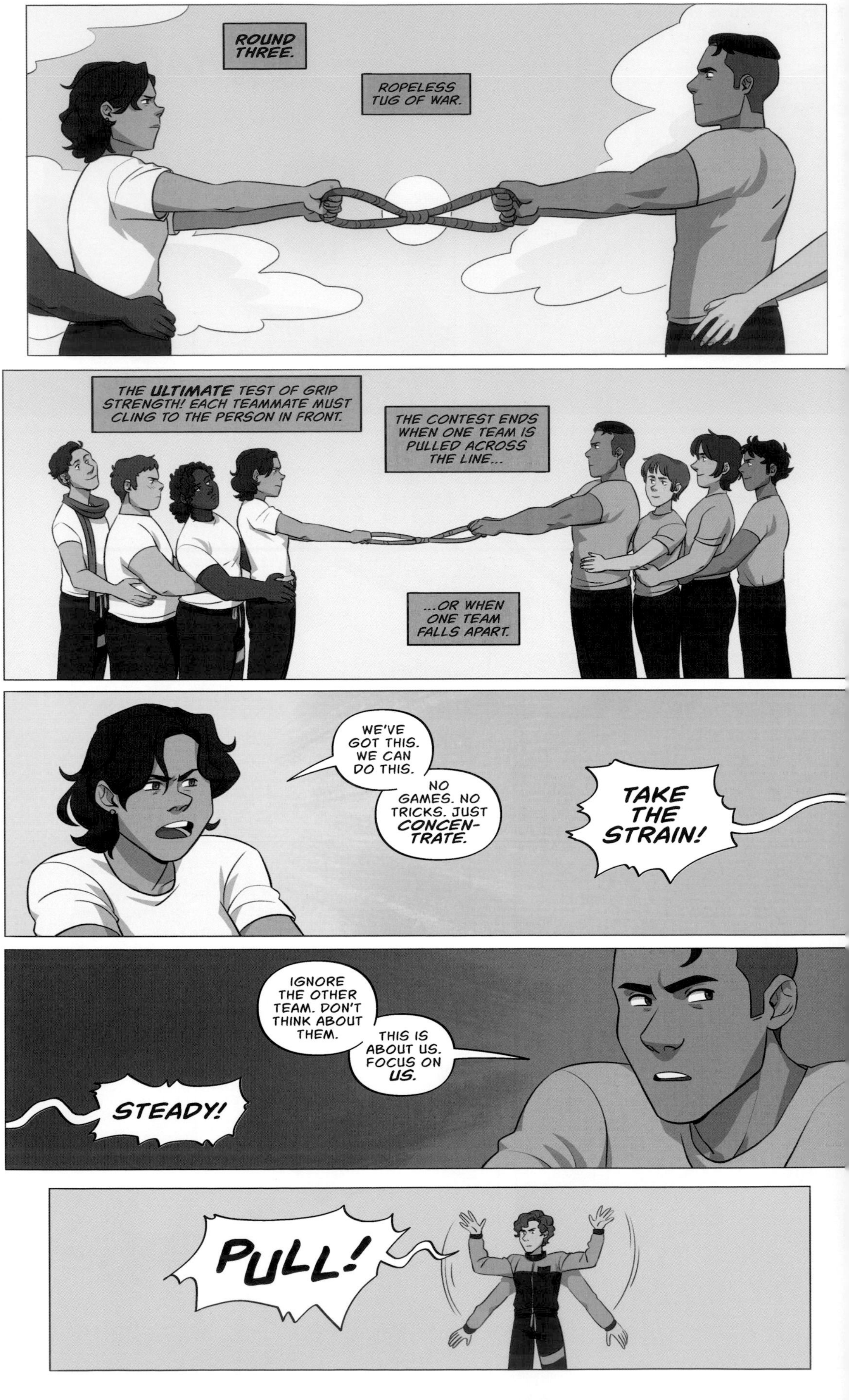
ROUND THREE.
ROPELESS TUG OF WAR.
THE ULTIMATE TEST OF GRIP STRENGTH! EACH TEAMMATE MUST CLING TO THE PERSON IN FRONT.
THE CONTEST ENDS WHEN ONE TEAM IS PULLED ACROSS THE LINE...
...OR WHEN ONE TEAM FALLS APART.
WE'VE GOT THIS. WE CAN DO THIS.
NO GAMES. NO TRICKS. JUST CONCEN-TRATE.
TAKE THE STRAIN!
IGNORE THE OTHER TEAM. DON'T THINK ABOUT THEM.
THIS IS ABOUT US. FOCUS ON US.
STEADY!
PULL!

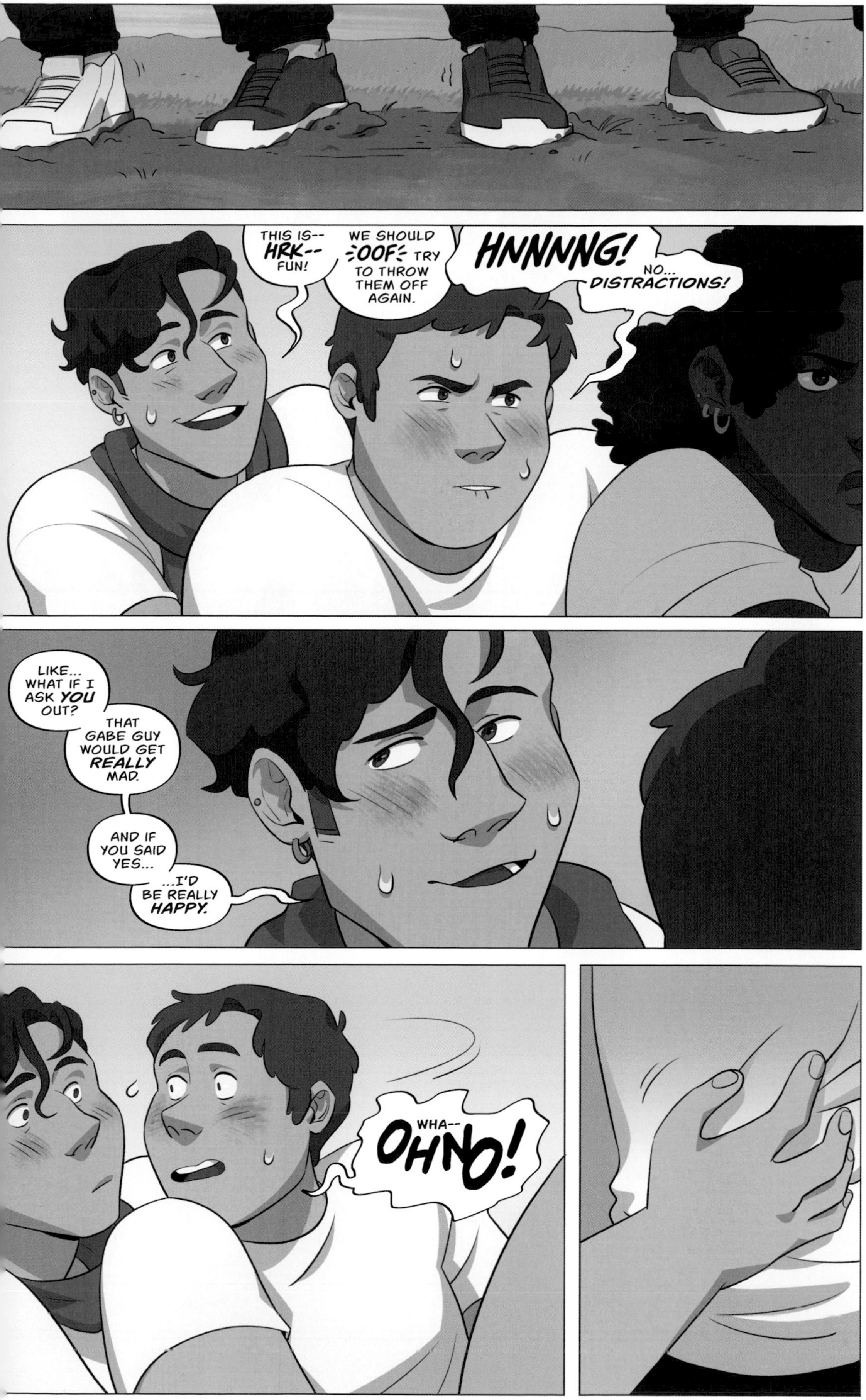
THIS IS-- HRK-- FUN!
WE SHOULD OOF TRY TO THROW THEM OFF AGAIN.
HNNNNG!
NO... DISTRACTIONS!
LIKE... WHAT IF I ASK YOU OUT?
THAT GABE GUY WOULD GET REALLY MAD.
AND IF YOU SAID YES...
...I'D BE REALLY HAPPY.
WHA-- OHNO!

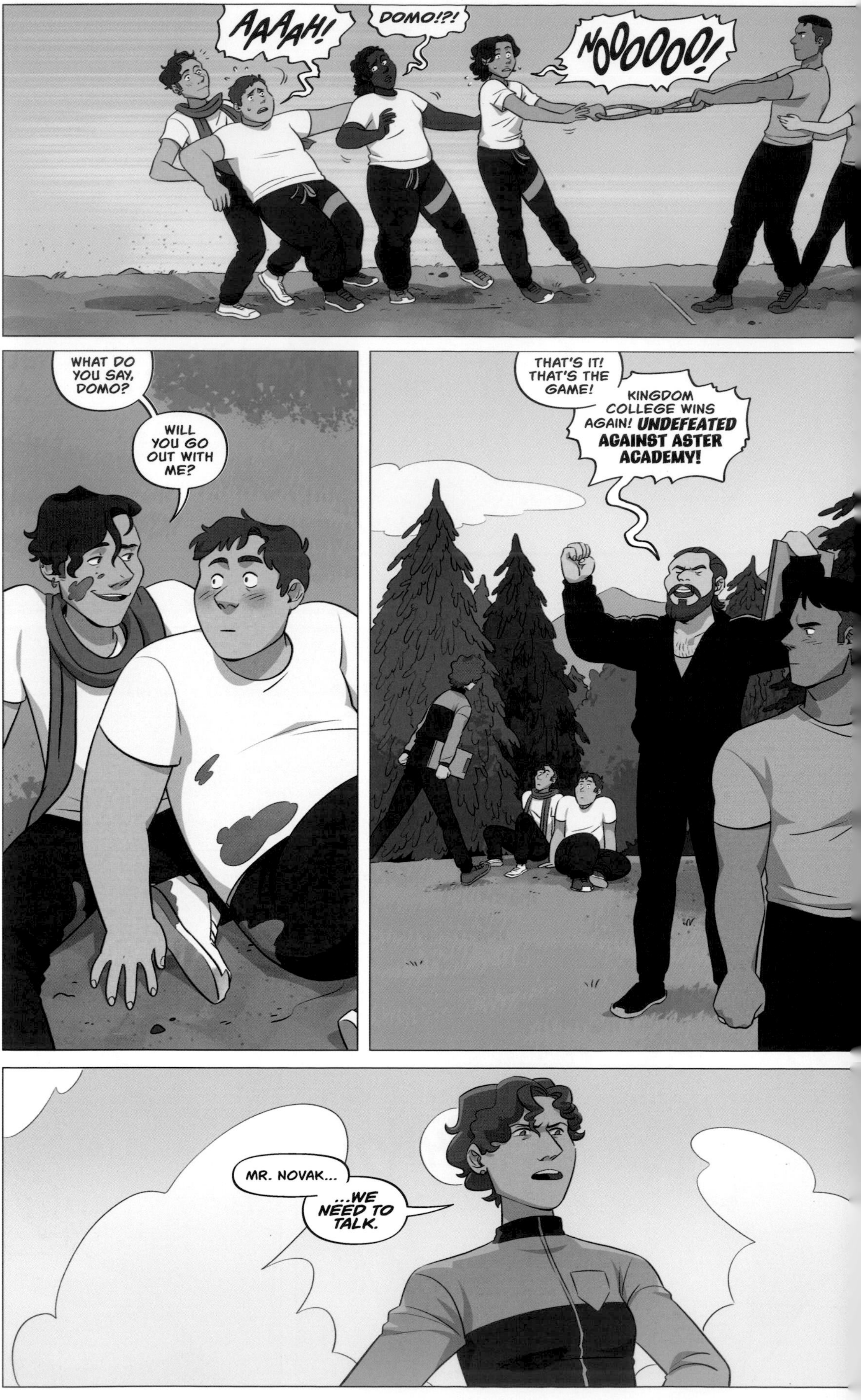
AAAAH!
DOMO!?!
NOOOOOO!
WHAT DO YOU SAY, DOMO?
WILL YOU GO OUT WITH ME?
THAT'S IT! THAT'S THE GAME!
KINGDOM COLLEGE WINS AGAIN! UNDEFEATED AGAINST ASTER ACADEMY!
MR. NOVAK...
...WE NEED TO TALK.

CHAPTER

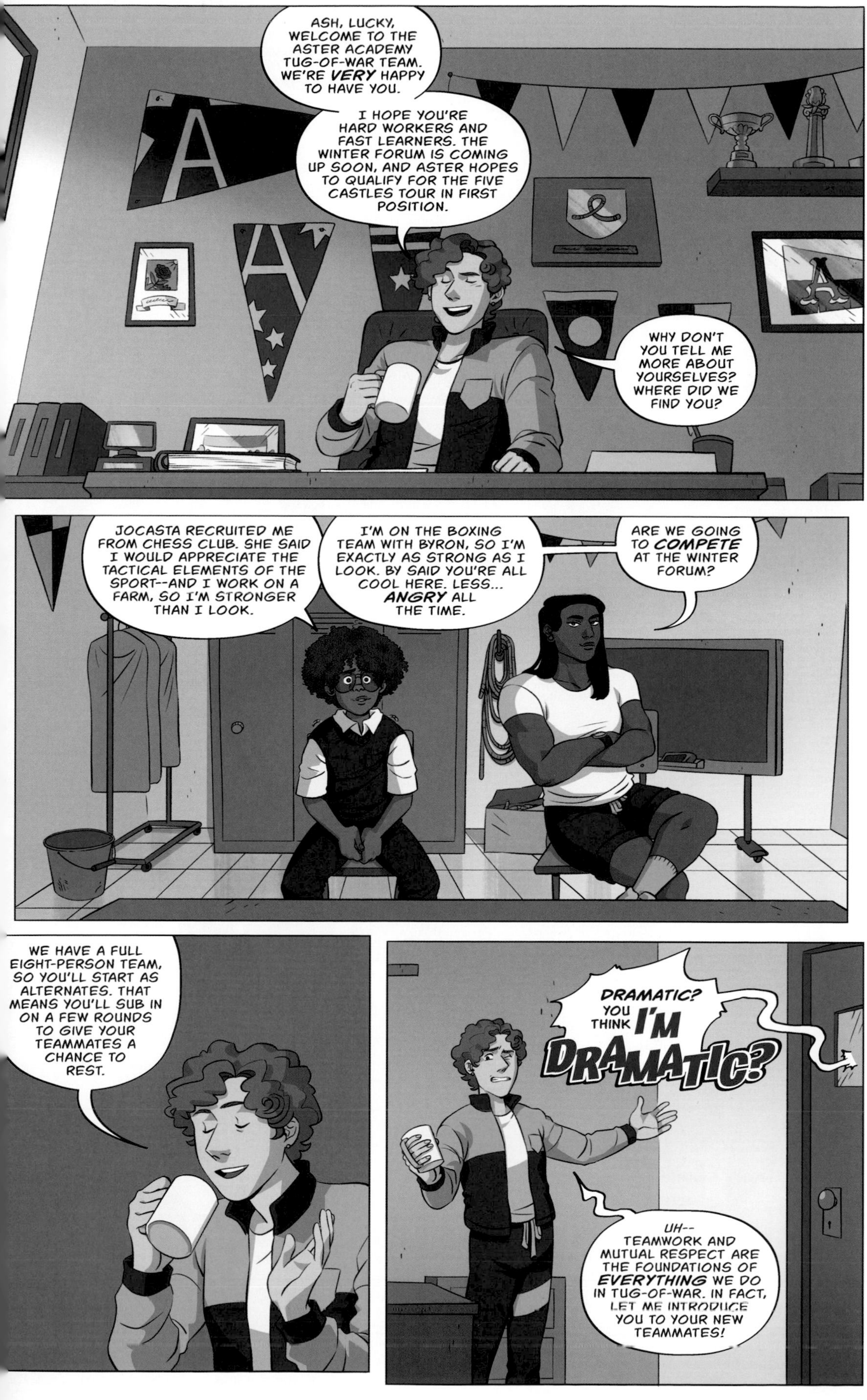
ASH, LUCKY, WELCOME TO THE ASTER ACADEMY TUG-OF-WAR TEAM. WE'RE VERY HAPPY TO HAVE YOU.
I HOPE YOU'RE HARD WORKERS AND FAST LEARNERS. THE WINTER FORUM IS COMING UP SOON, AND ASTER HOPES TO QUALIFY FOR THE FIVE CASTLES TOUR IN FIRST POSITION.
WHY DON'T YOU TELL ME MORE ABOUT YOURSELVES? WHERE DID WE FIND YOU?
JOCASTA RECRUITED ME FROM CHESS CLUB. SHE SAID I WOULD APPRECIATE THE TACTICAL ELEMENTS OF THE SPORT--AND I WORK ON A FARM, SO I'M STRONGER THAN I LOOK.
I'M ON THE BOXING TEAM WITH BYRON, SO I'M EXACTLY AS STRONG AS I LOOK. BY SAID YOU'RE ALL COOL HERE. LESS... ANGRY ALL THE TIME.
ARE WE GOING TO COMPETE AT THE WINTER FORUM?
WE HAVE A FULL EIGHT-PERSON TEAM, SO YOU'LL START AS ALTERNATES. THAT MEANS YOU'LL SUB IN ON A FEW ROUNDS TO GIVE YOUR TEAMMATES A CHANCE TO REST.
DRAMATIC? YOU THINK I'M DRAMATIC?
UH-- TEAMWORK AND MUTUAL RESPECT ARE THE FOUNDATIONS OF EVERYTHING WE DO IN TUG-OF-WAR. IN FACT, LET ME INTRODUCE YOU TO YOUR NEW TEAMMATES!

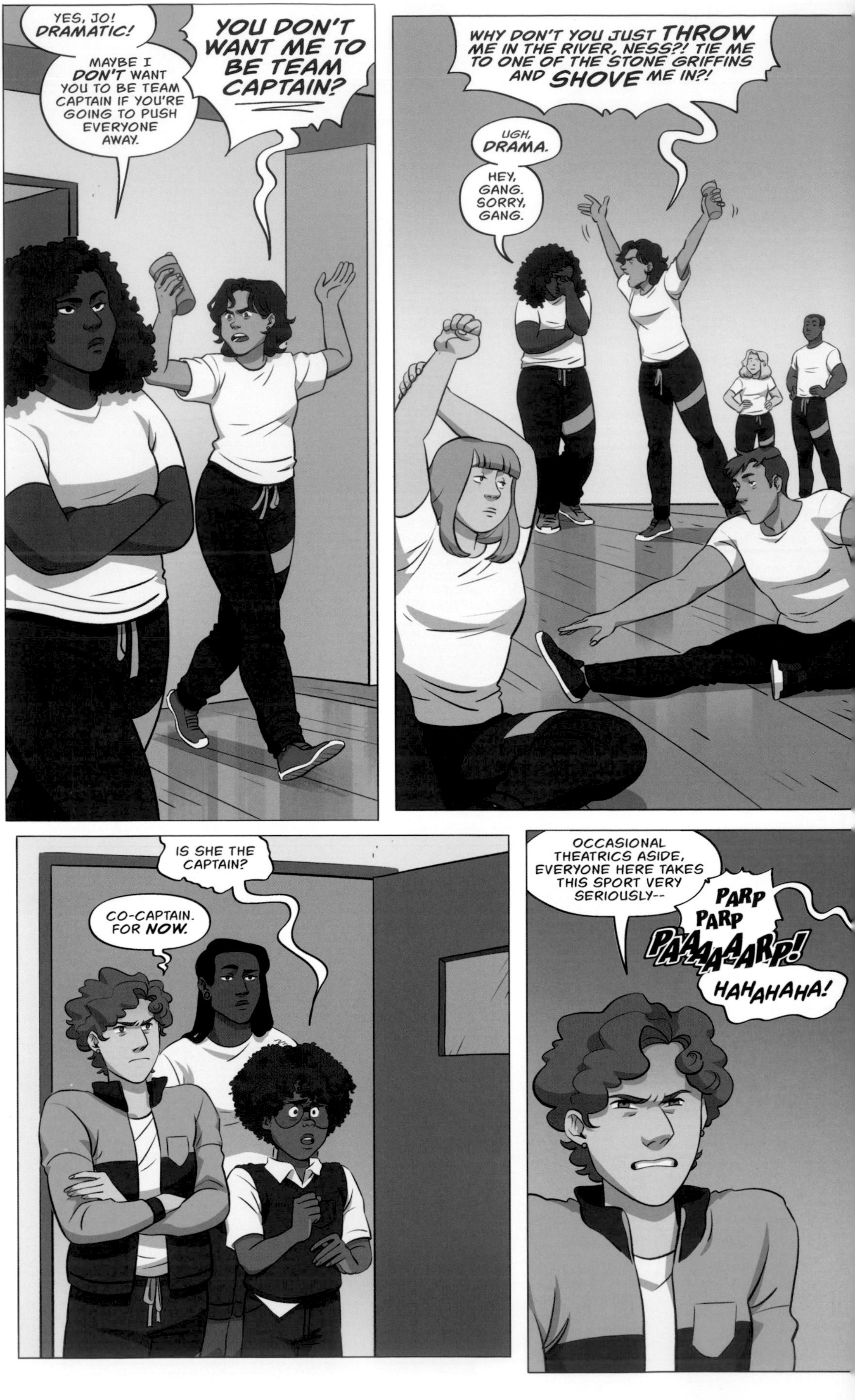
YES, JO! DRAMATIC!
MAYBE I DON'T WANT YOU TO BE TEAM CAPTAIN IF YOU'RE GOING TO PUSH EVERYONE AWAY.
YOU DON'T WANT ME TO BE TEAM CAPTAIN?
WHY DON'T YOU JUST THROW ME IN THE RIVER, NESS?! TIE ME TO ONE OF THE STONE GRIFFINS AND SHOVE ME IN?!
UGH, DRAMA.
HEY, GANG. SORRY, GANG.
IS SHE THE CAPTAIN?
CO-CAPTAIN. FOR NOW.
OCCASIONAL THEATRICS ASIDE, EVERYONE HERE TAKES THIS SPORT VERY SERIOUSLY--
PARP
PARP
PAAAAAARP!
HAHAHAHA!

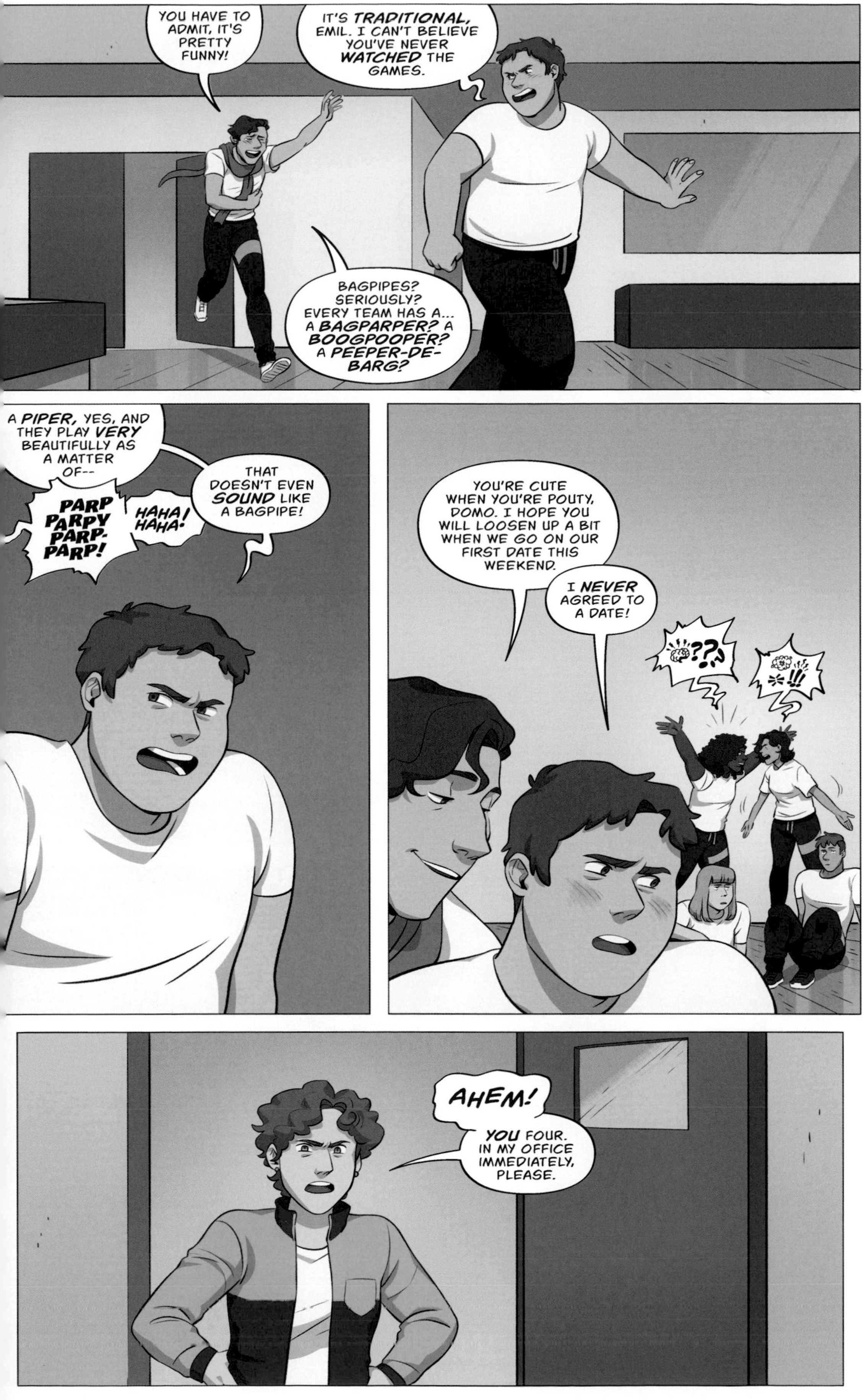
YOU HAVE TO ADMIT, IT'S PRETTY FUNNY!
IT'S TRADITIONAL, EMIL. I CAN'T BELIEVE YOU'VE NEVER WATCHED THE GAMES.
BAGPIPES? SERIOUSLY? EVERY TEAM HAS A... A BAGPARPER? A BOOGPOOPER? A PEEPER-DE-BARG?
A PIPER, YES, AND THEY PLAY VERY BEAUTIFULLY AS A MATTER OF--
PARP PARPY PARP-PARP!
HAHA! HAHA!
THAT DOESN'T EVEN SOUND LIKE A BAGPIPE!
YOU'RE CUTE WHEN YOU'RE POUTY, DOMO. I HOPE YOU WILL LOOSEN UP A BIT WHEN WE GO ON OUR FIRST DATE THIS WEEKEND.
I NEVER AGREED TO A DATE!
AHEM!
YOU FOUR. IN MY OFFICE IMMEDIATELY, PLEASE.

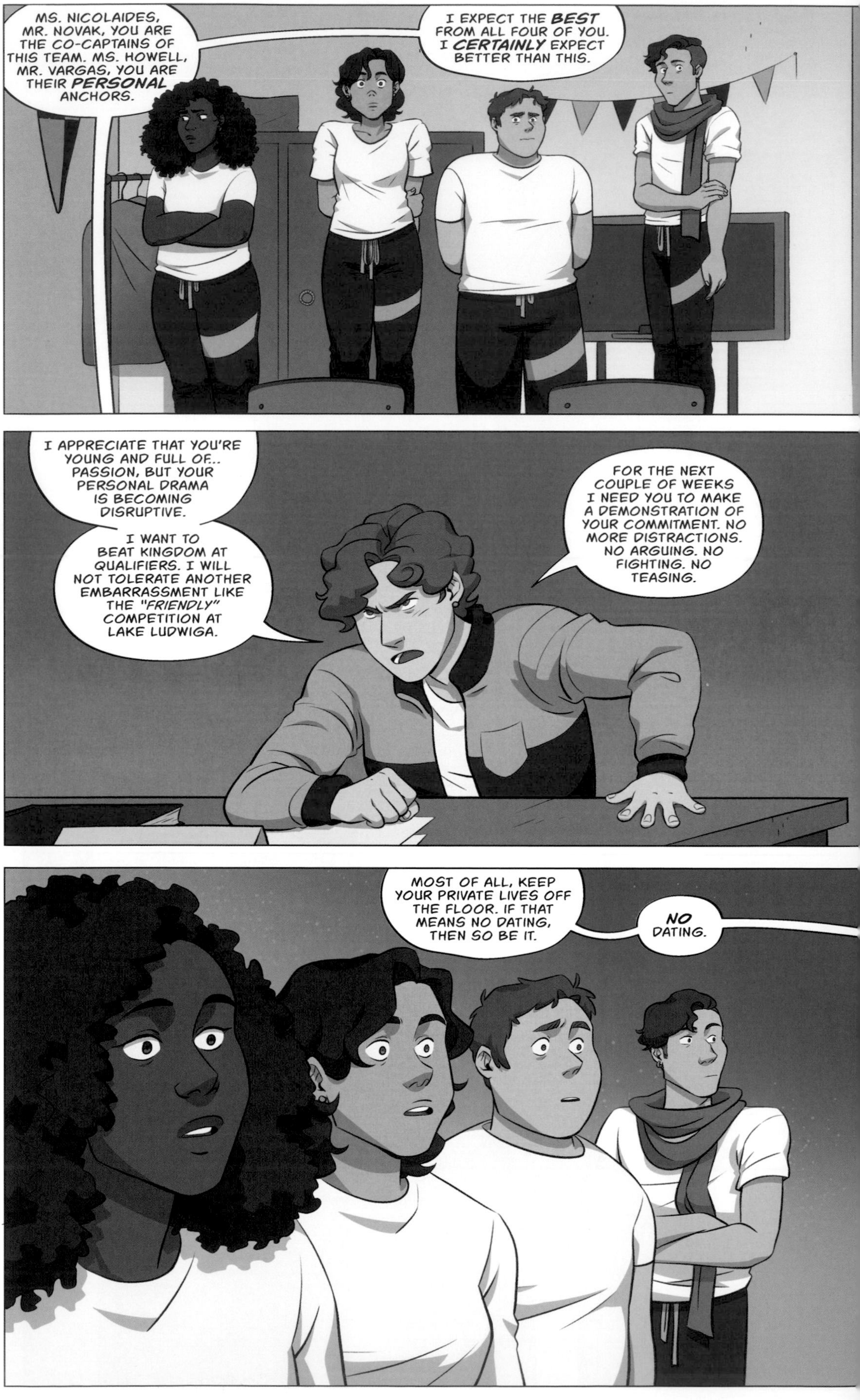
MS. NICOLAIDES, MR. NOVAK, YOU ARE THE CO-CAPTAINS OF THIS TEAM. MS. HOWELL, MR. VARGAS, YOU ARE THEIR PERSONAL ANCHORS.
I EXPECT THE BEST FROM ALL FOUR OF YOU. I CERTAINLY EXPECT BETTER THAN THIS.
I APPRECIATE THAT YOU'RE YOUNG AND FULL OF... PASSION, BUT YOUR PERSONAL DRAMA IS BECOMING DISRUPTIVE.
I WANT TO BEAT KINGDOM AT QUALIFIERS. I WILL NOT TOLERATE ANOTHER EMBARRASSMENT LIKE THE "FRIENDLY" COMPETITION AT LAKE LUDWIGA.
FOR THE NEXT COUPLE OF WEEKS I NEED YOU TO MAKE A DEMONSTRATION OF YOUR COMMITMENT. NO MORE DISTRACTIONS. NO ARGUING. NO FIGHTING. NO TEASING.
MOST OF ALL, KEEP YOUR PRIVATE LIVES OFF THE FLOOR. IF THAT MEANS NO DATING, THEN SO BE IT.
NO DATING.

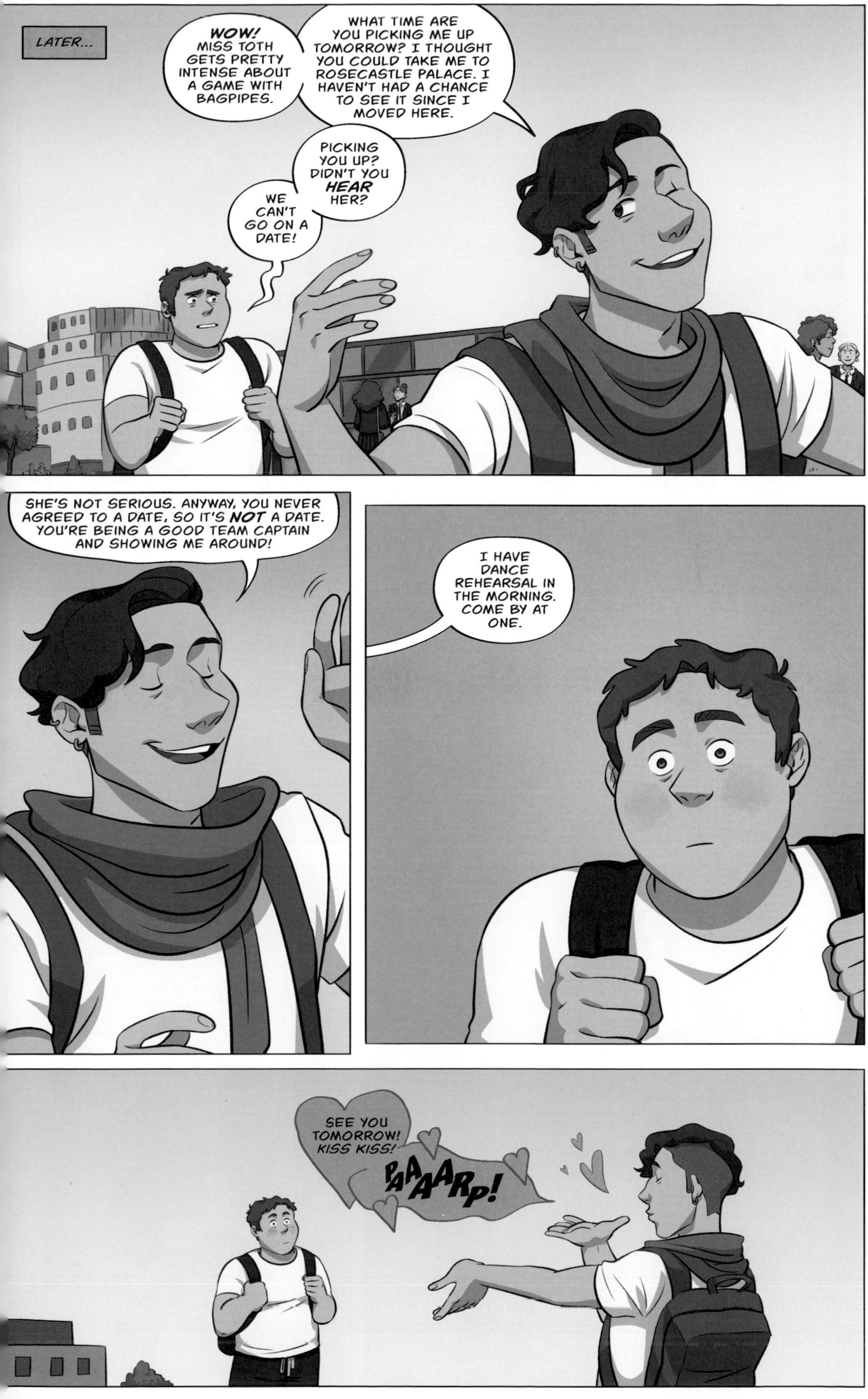
LATER...
WOW! MISS TOTH GETS PRETTY INTENSE ABOUT A GAME WITH BAGPIPES.
WHAT TIME ARE YOU PICKING ME UP TOMORROW? I THOUGHT YOU COULD TAKE ME TO ROSECASTLE PALACE. I HAVEN'T HAD A CHANCE TO SEE IT SINCE I MOVED HERE.
PICKING YOU UP? DIDN'T YOU HEAR HER?
WE CAN'T GO ON A DATE!
SHE'S NOT SERIOUS. ANYWAY, YOU NEVER AGREED TO A DATE, SO IT'S NOT A DATE. YOU'RE BEING A GOOD TEAM CAPTAIN AND SHOWING ME AROUND!
I HAVE DANCE REHEARSAL IN THE MORNING. COME BY AT ONE.
SEE YOU TOMORROW! KISS KISS!
PAAAARP!

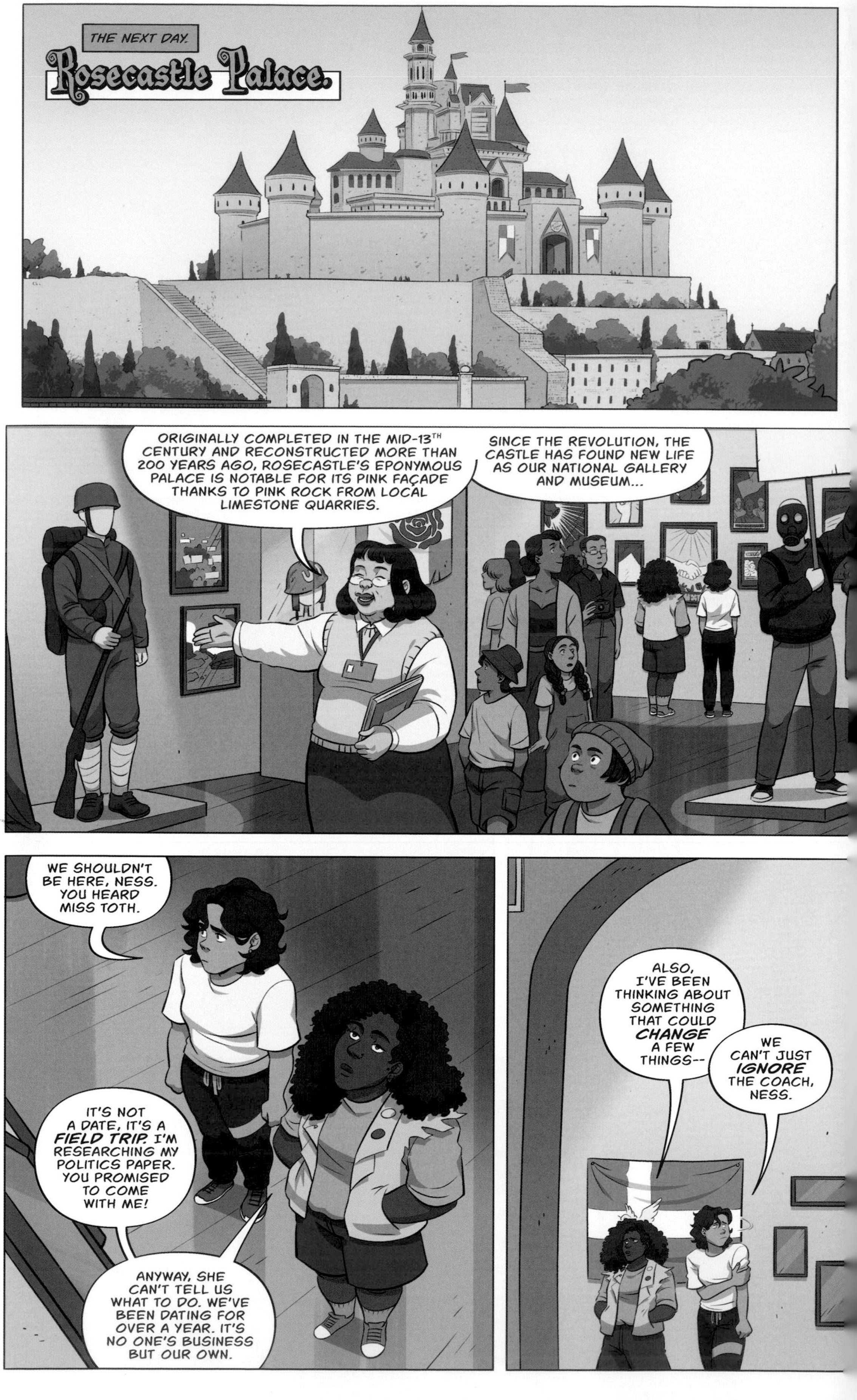
THE NEXT DAY.
Rosecastle Palace.
ORIGINALLY COMPLETED IN THE MID-13TH CENTURY AND RECONSTRUCTED MORE THAN 200 YEARS AGO, ROSECASTLE'S EPONYMOUS PALACE IS NOTABLE FOR ITS PINK FAÇADE THANKS TO PINK ROCK FROM LOCAL LIMESTONE QUARRIES.
SINCE THE REVOLUTION, THE CASTLE HAS FOUND NEW LIFE AS OUR NATIONAL GALLERY AND MUSEUM...
WE SHOULDN'T BE HERE, NESS. YOU HEARD MISS TOTH.
IT'S NOT A DATE, IT'S A FIELD TRIP. I'M RESEARCHING MY POLITICS PAPER. YOU PROMISED TO COME WITH ME!
ANYWAY, SHE CAN'T TELL US WHAT TO DO. WE'VE BEEN DATING FOR OVER A YEAR. IT'S NO ONE'S BUSINESS BUT OUR OWN.
ALSO, I'VE BEEN THINKING ABOUT SOMETHING THAT COULD CHANGE A FEW THINGS--
WE CAN'T JUST IGNORE THE COACH, NESS.

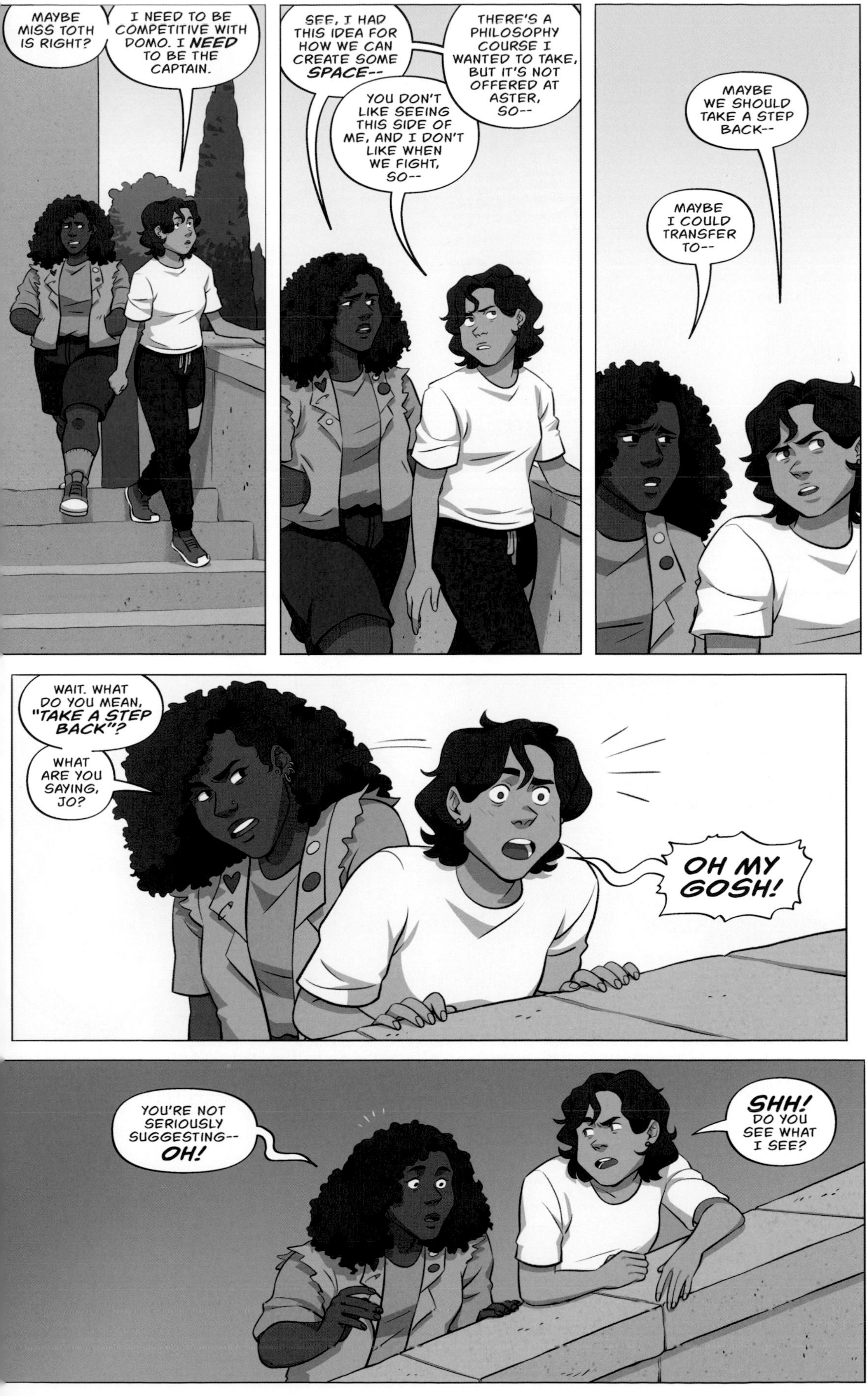
MAYBE MISS TOTH IS RIGHT?
I NEED TO BE COMPETITIVE WITH DOMO. I NEED TO BE THE CAPTAIN.
SEE, I HAD THIS IDEA FOR HOW WE CAN CREATE SOME SPACE--
THERE'S A PHILOSOPHY COURSE I WANTED TO TAKE, BUT IT'S NOT OFFERED AT ASTER, SO--
YOU DON'T LIKE SEEING THIS SIDE OF ME, AND I DON'T LIKE WHEN WE FIGHT, SO--
MAYBE WE SHOULD TAKE A STEP BACK--
MAYBE I COULD TRANSFER TO--
WAIT. WHAT DO YOU MEAN, "TAKE A STEP BACK"?
WHAT ARE YOU SAYING, JO?
OH MY GOSH!
YOU'RE NOT SERIOUSLY SUGGESTING-- OH!
SHH! DO YOU SEE WHAT I SEE?

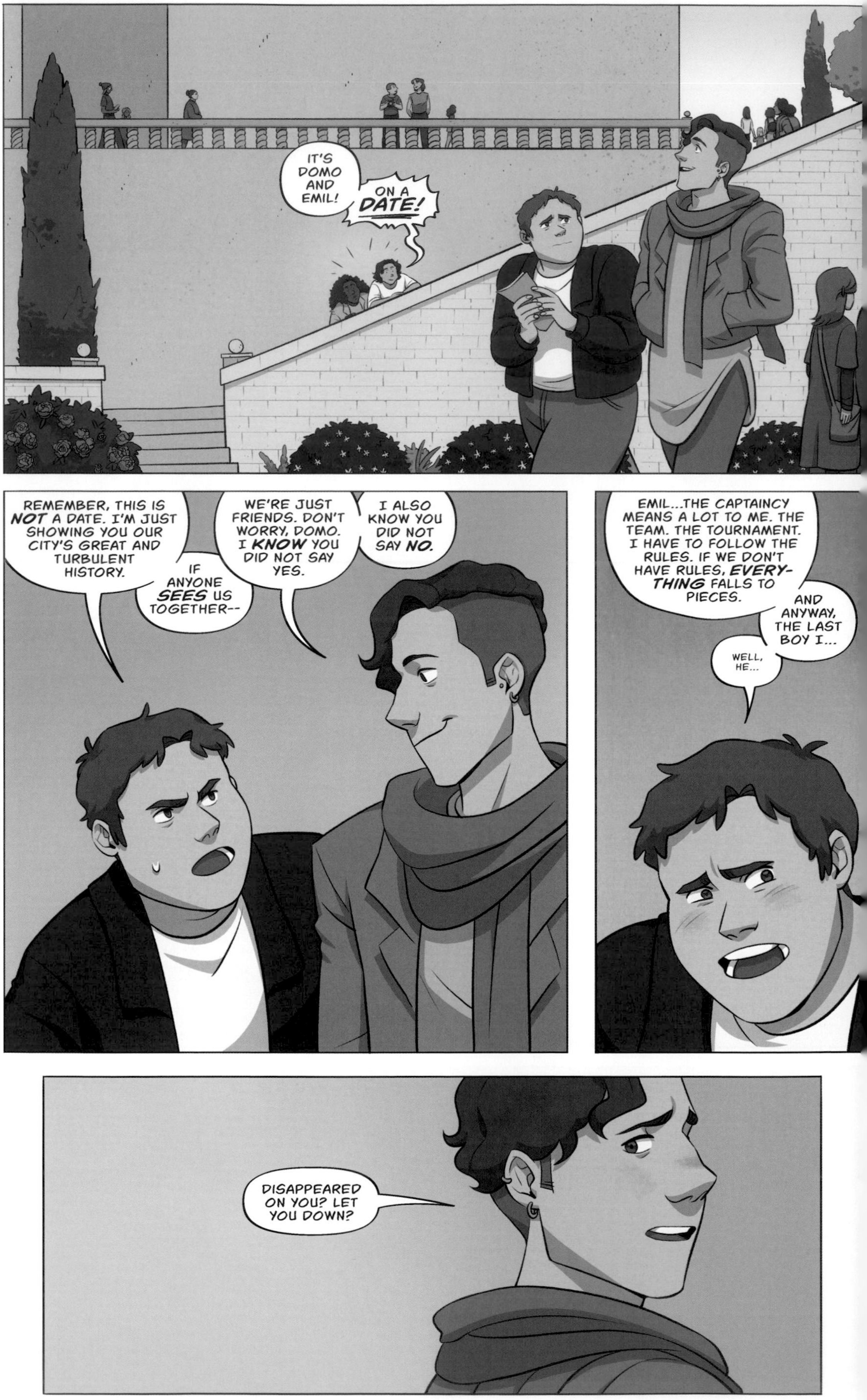
IT'S DOMO AND EMIL!
ON A DATE!
REMEMBER, THIS IS NOT A DATE. I'M JUST SHOWING YOU OUR CITY'S GREAT AND TURBULENT HISTORY.
IF ANYONE SEES US TOGETHER--
WE'RE JUST FRIENDS. DON'T WORRY, DOMO. I KNOW YOU DID NOT SAY YES.
I ALSO KNOW YOU DID NOT SAY NO.
EMIL...THE CAPTAINCY MEANS A LOT TO ME. THE TEAM. THE TOURNAMENT. I HAVE TO FOLLOW THE RULES. IF WE DON'T HAVE RULES, EVERYTHING FALLS TO PIECES.
AND ANYWAY, THE LAST BOY I...
WELL, HE...
DISAPPEARED ON YOU? LET YOU DOWN?

I GET IT. YOU LOOK AT ME, YOU SEE SOMEONE WITH HIS HEAD IN THE CLOUDS. I'M A DANCER, A FREE SPIRIT, I HAVE A SHORT ATTENTION--

WOW, IS THAT VELVET? THAT'S GORGEOUS.

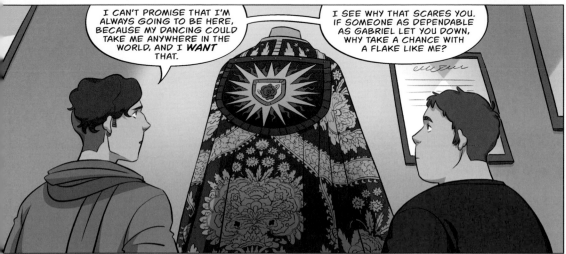

I CAN'T PROMISE THAT I'M ALWAYS GOING TO BE HERE, BECAUSE MY DANCING COULD TAKE ME ANYWHERE IN THE WORLD, AND I **WANT** THAT.

I SEE WHY THAT SCARES YOU. IF SOMEONE AS DEPENDABLE AS GABRIEL LET YOU DOWN, WHY TAKE A CHANCE WITH A FLAKE LIKE ME?

AND MAYBE WE **DO** GO OUT A COUPLE OF TIMES AND WE DON'T CLICK, AND WE REALIZE WE'RE BETTER AS FRIENDS. THAT WOULDN'T BE A DISASTER.

ALL I CAN TELL YOU IS THAT I REALLY LIKE YOU. I THINK YOU'RE SMART, AND CUTE, AND SO, SO SERIOUS.

I NEED SOME OF THAT IN MY LIFE. I NEED SOMEONE WHO CAN GROUND ME. OTHERWISE I MIGHT BLOW AWAY.

SO, DOMO...

...WILL YOU GO OUT WITH ME?

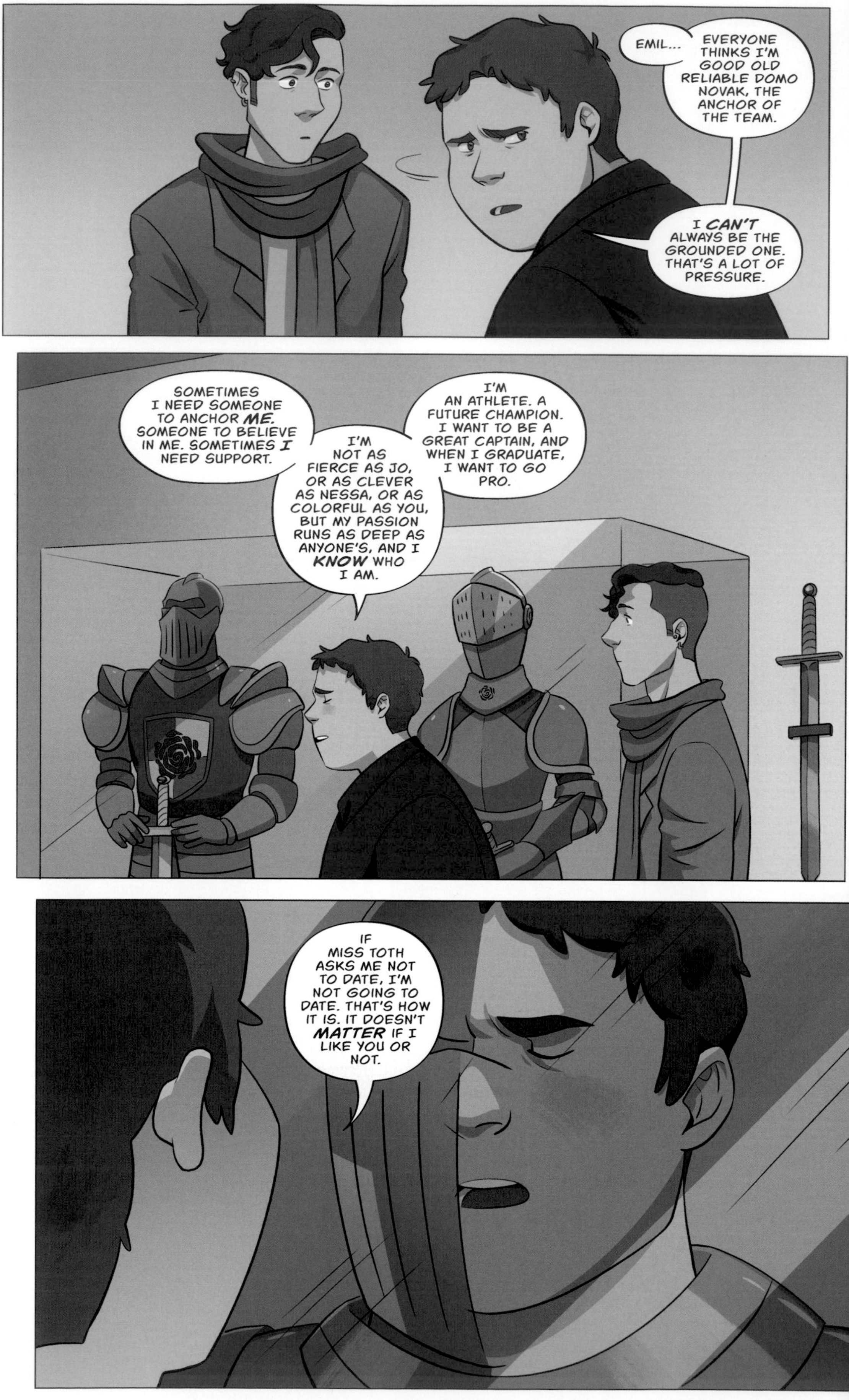
EMIL...
EVERYONE THINKS I'M GOOD OLD RELIABLE DOMO NOVAK, THE ANCHOR OF THE TEAM.
I CAN'T ALWAYS BE THE GROUNDED ONE. THAT'S A LOT OF PRESSURE.
I'M AN ATHLETE. A FUTURE CHAMPION. I WANT TO BE A GREAT CAPTAIN, AND WHEN I GRADUATE, I WANT TO GO PRO.
I'M NOT AS FIERCE AS JO, OR AS CLEVER AS NESSA, OR AS COLORFUL AS YOU, BUT MY PASSION RUNS AS DEEP AS ANYONE'S, AND I KNOW WHO I AM.
SOMETIMES I NEED SOMEONE TO ANCHOR ME. SOMEONE TO BELIEVE IN ME. SOMETIMES I NEED SUPPORT.
IF MISS TOTH ASKS ME NOT TO DATE, I'M NOT GOING TO DATE. THAT'S HOW IT IS. IT DOESN'T MATTER IF I LIKE YOU OR NOT.

YOU DON'T EVEN *CARE* ABOUT TUG-OF-WAR! YOU ONLY JOINED BECAUSE YOU WERE BORED!

I JOINED FOR *YOU!*

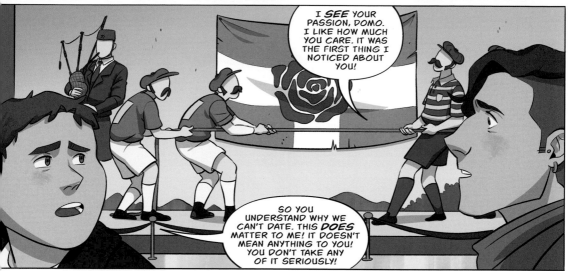

I *SEE* YOUR PASSION, DOMO. I LIKE HOW MUCH YOU CARE. IT WAS THE FIRST THING I NOTICED ABOUT YOU!

SO YOU UNDERSTAND WHY WE CAN'T DATE. THIS *DOES* MATTER TO ME! IT DOESN'T MEAN ANYTHING TO YOU! YOU DON'T TAKE ANY OF IT SERIOUSLY!

YOU THINK IT'S FUNNY THAT WE HAVE PIPERS!

IT *IS* FUNNY THAT YOU HAVE PIPERS!

WE. *WE* HAVE PIPERS.

IF I *AM* GOING TO DATE, IT HAS TO BE *AFTER* THE WINTER FORUM, AND IT HAS TO BE SOMEONE DEDICATED, SOMEONE SENSIBLE, SOMEONE LIKE--

OH NO.

GABE.

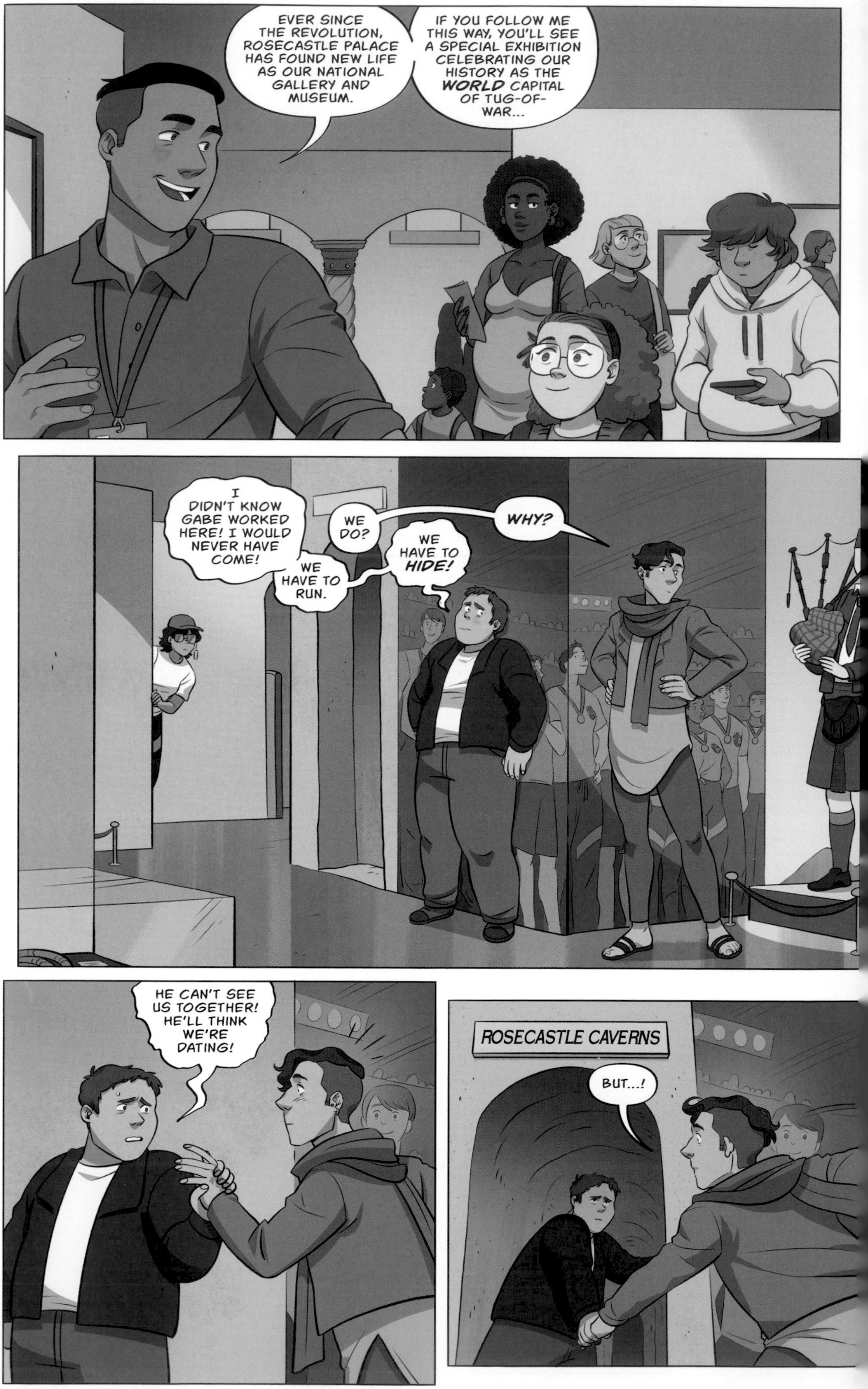
EVER SINCE THE REVOLUTION, ROSECASTLE PALACE HAS FOUND NEW LIFE AS OUR NATIONAL GALLERY AND MUSEUM.
IF YOU FOLLOW ME THIS WAY, YOU'LL SEE A SPECIAL EXHIBITION CELEBRATING OUR HISTORY AS THE WORLD CAPITAL OF TUG-OF-WAR...
I DIDN'T KNOW GABE WORKED HERE! I WOULD NEVER HAVE COME!
WE HAVE TO RUN.
WE DO?
WE HAVE TO HIDE!
WHY?
HE CAN'T SEE US TOGETHER! HE'LL THINK WE'RE DATING!
ROSECASTLE CAVERNS
BUT...!

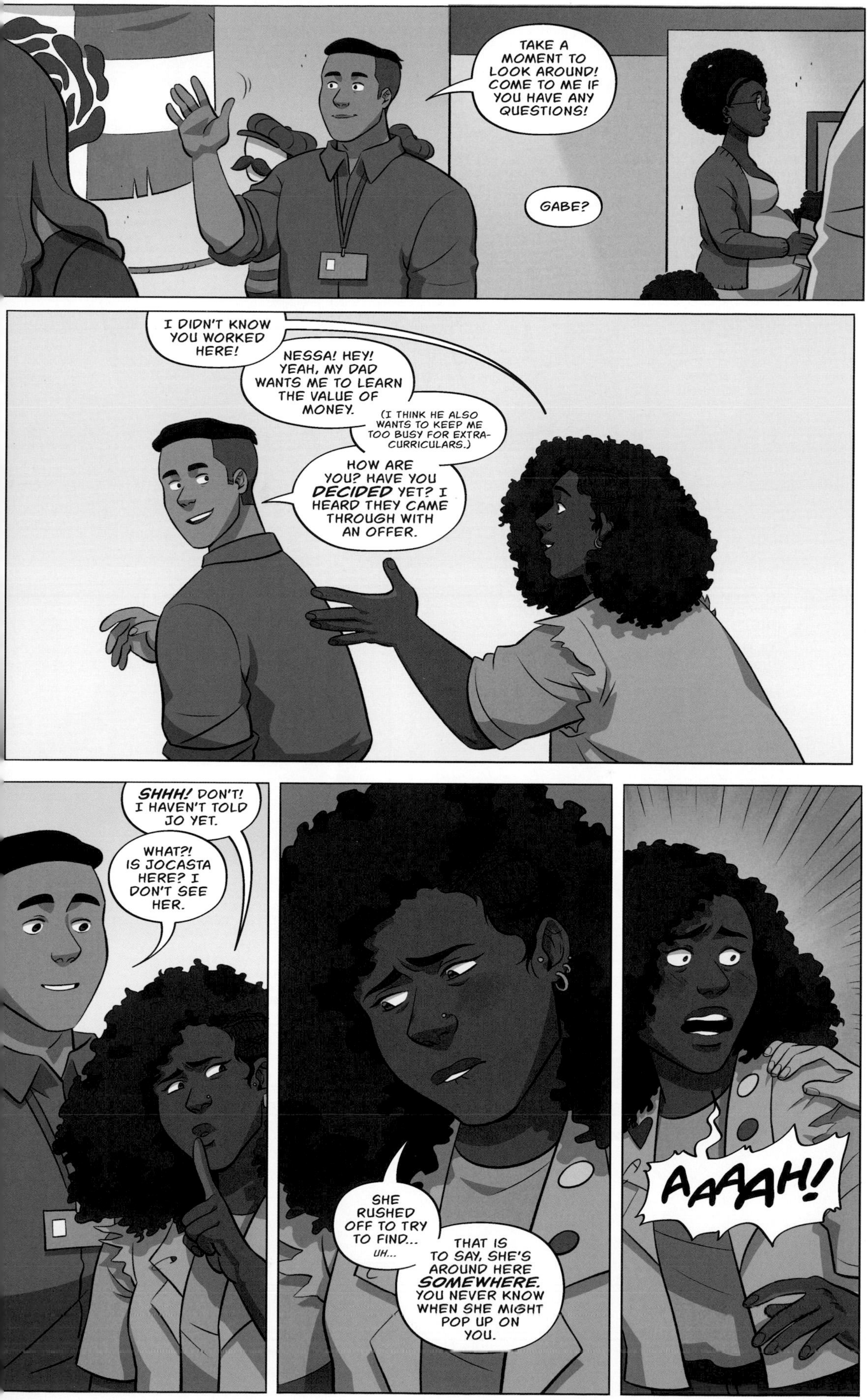
TAKE A MOMENT TO LOOK AROUND! COME TO ME IF YOU HAVE ANY QUESTIONS!
GABE?
I DIDN'T KNOW YOU WORKED HERE!
NESSA! HEY! YEAH, MY DAD WANTS ME TO LEARN THE VALUE OF MONEY.
(I THINK HE ALSO WANTS TO KEEP ME TOO BUSY FOR EXTRA-CURRICULARS.)
HOW ARE YOU? HAVE YOU *DECIDED* YET? I HEARD THEY CAME THROUGH WITH AN OFFER.
SHHH! DON'T! I HAVEN'T TOLD JO YET.
WHAT?! IS JOCASTA HERE? I DON'T SEE HER.
SHE RUSHED OFF TO TRY TO FIND... UH...
THAT IS TO SAY, SHE'S AROUND HERE *SOMEWHERE.* YOU NEVER KNOW WHEN SHE MIGHT POP UP ON YOU.
AAAAH!

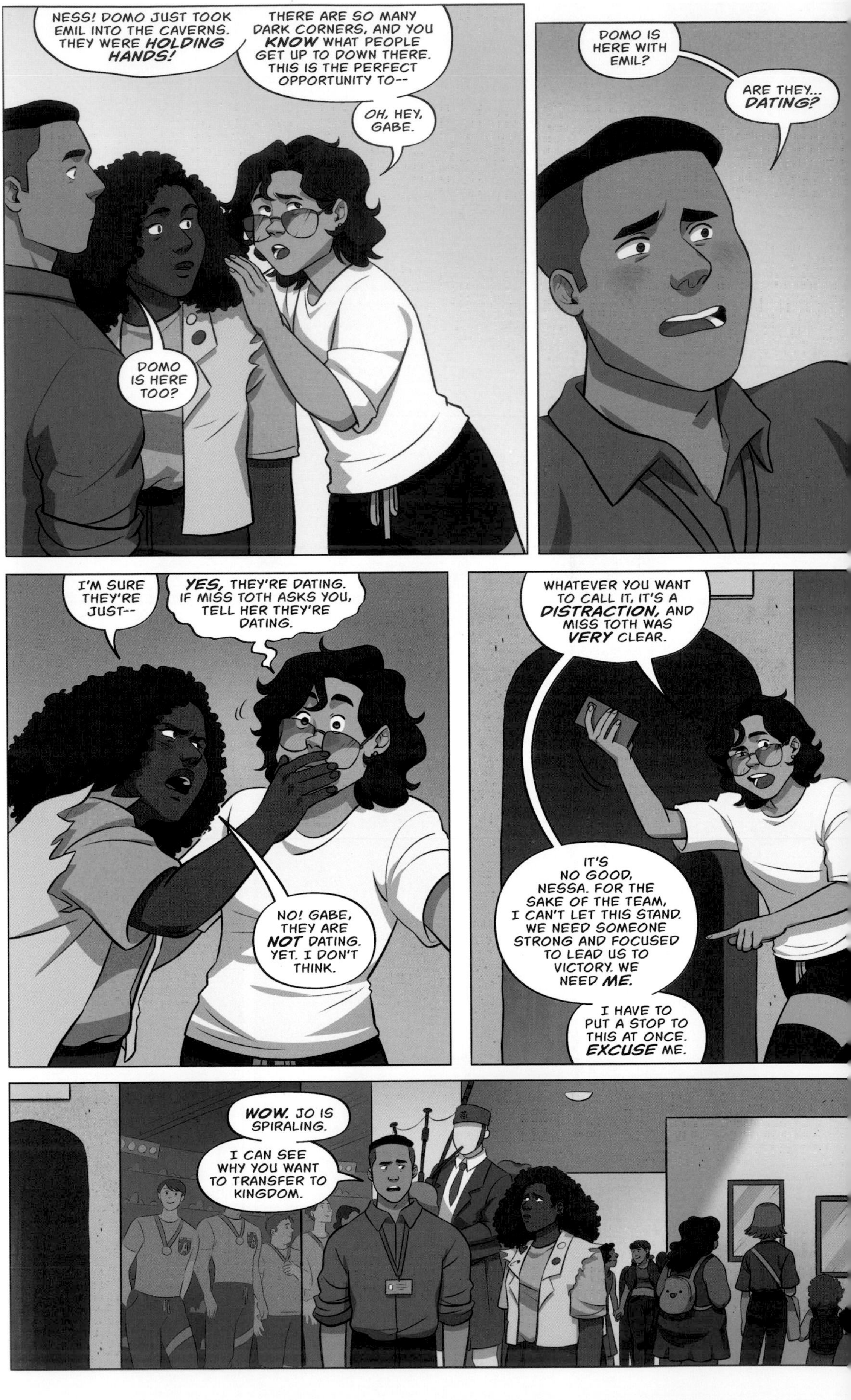
NESS! DOMO JUST TOOK EMIL INTO THE CAVERNS. THEY WERE HOLDING HANDS!
THERE ARE SO MANY DARK CORNERS, AND YOU KNOW WHAT PEOPLE GET UP TO DOWN THERE. THIS IS THE PERFECT OPPORTUNITY TO--
OH, HEY, GABE.
DOMO IS HERE TOO?
DOMO IS HERE WITH EMIL?
ARE THEY... DATING?
I'M SURE THEY'RE JUST--
YES, THEY'RE DATING. IF MISS TOTH ASKS YOU, TELL HER THEY'RE DATING.
NO! GABE, THEY ARE NOT DATING. YET. I DON'T THINK.
WHATEVER YOU WANT TO CALL IT, IT'S A DISTRACTION, AND MISS TOTH WAS VERY CLEAR.
IT'S NO GOOD, NESSA. FOR THE SAKE OF THE TEAM, I CAN'T LET THIS STAND. WE NEED SOMEONE STRONG AND FOCUSED TO LEAD US TO VICTORY. WE NEED ME.
I HAVE TO PUT A STOP TO THIS AT ONCE. EXCUSE ME.
WOW. JO IS SPIRALING.
I CAN SEE WHY YOU WANT TO TRANSFER TO KINGDOM.

INSIDE THE CAVERNS...

DOMO, I HAVE QUESTIONS.

ONE, WHY IS IT SO DARK IN HERE?

TWO, WHY DID WE JUST RUN AWAY FROM YOUR EX?

AND THREE, WHY ARE YOU HOLDING MY HAND?

I CAN LET GO.

NO! PLEASE, DON'T. I'M ACTUALLY KIND OF **TERRIFIED** OF THE DARK.

ALSO, IT'S FREEZING IN HERE, AND YOU'RE VERY WARM.

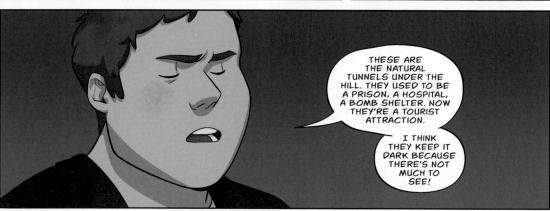

THESE ARE THE NATURAL TUNNELS UNDER THE HILL. THEY USED TO BE A PRISON, A HOSPITAL, A BOMB SHELTER. NOW THEY'RE A TOURIST ATTRACTION.

I THINK THEY KEEP IT DARK BECAUSE THERE'S NOT MUCH TO SEE!

AND I WASN'T RUNNING AWAY, I JUST...

...I'M NOT READY TO MOVE ON.

FROM SOMEONE WHO DOESN'T EVEN CARE ABOUT YOU?

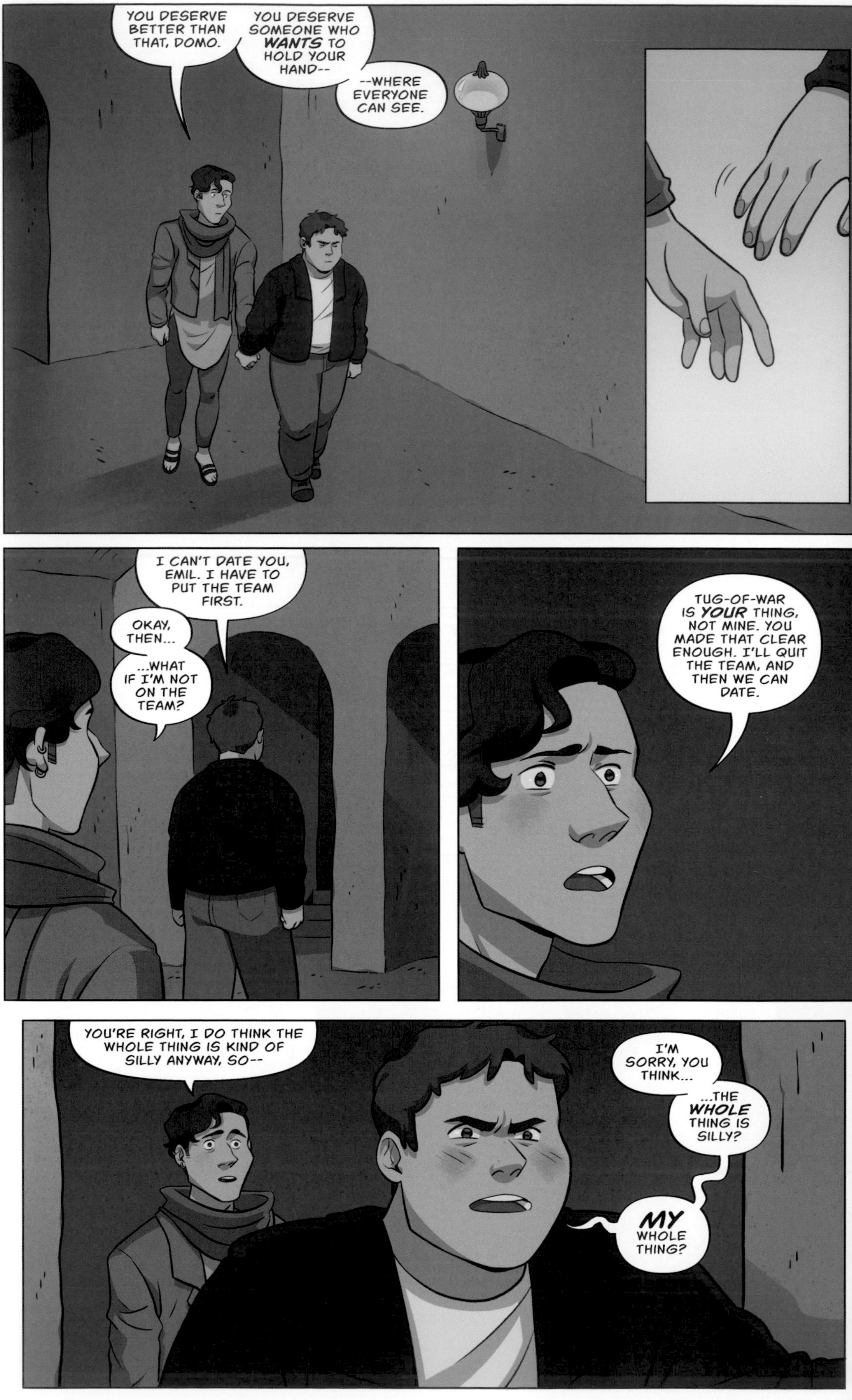
YOU DESERVE BETTER THAN THAT, DOMO.
YOU DESERVE SOMEONE WHO WANTS TO HOLD YOUR HAND--
--WHERE EVERYONE CAN SEE.
I CAN'T DATE YOU, EMIL. I HAVE TO PUT THE TEAM FIRST.
OKAY, THEN...
...WHAT IF I'M NOT ON THE TEAM?
TUG-OF-WAR IS YOUR THING, NOT MINE. YOU MADE THAT CLEAR ENOUGH. I'LL QUIT THE TEAM, AND THEN WE CAN DATE.
YOU'RE RIGHT, I DO THINK THE WHOLE THING IS KIND OF SILLY ANYWAY, SO--
I'M SORRY, YOU THINK...
...THE WHOLE THING IS SILLY?
MY WHOLE THING?

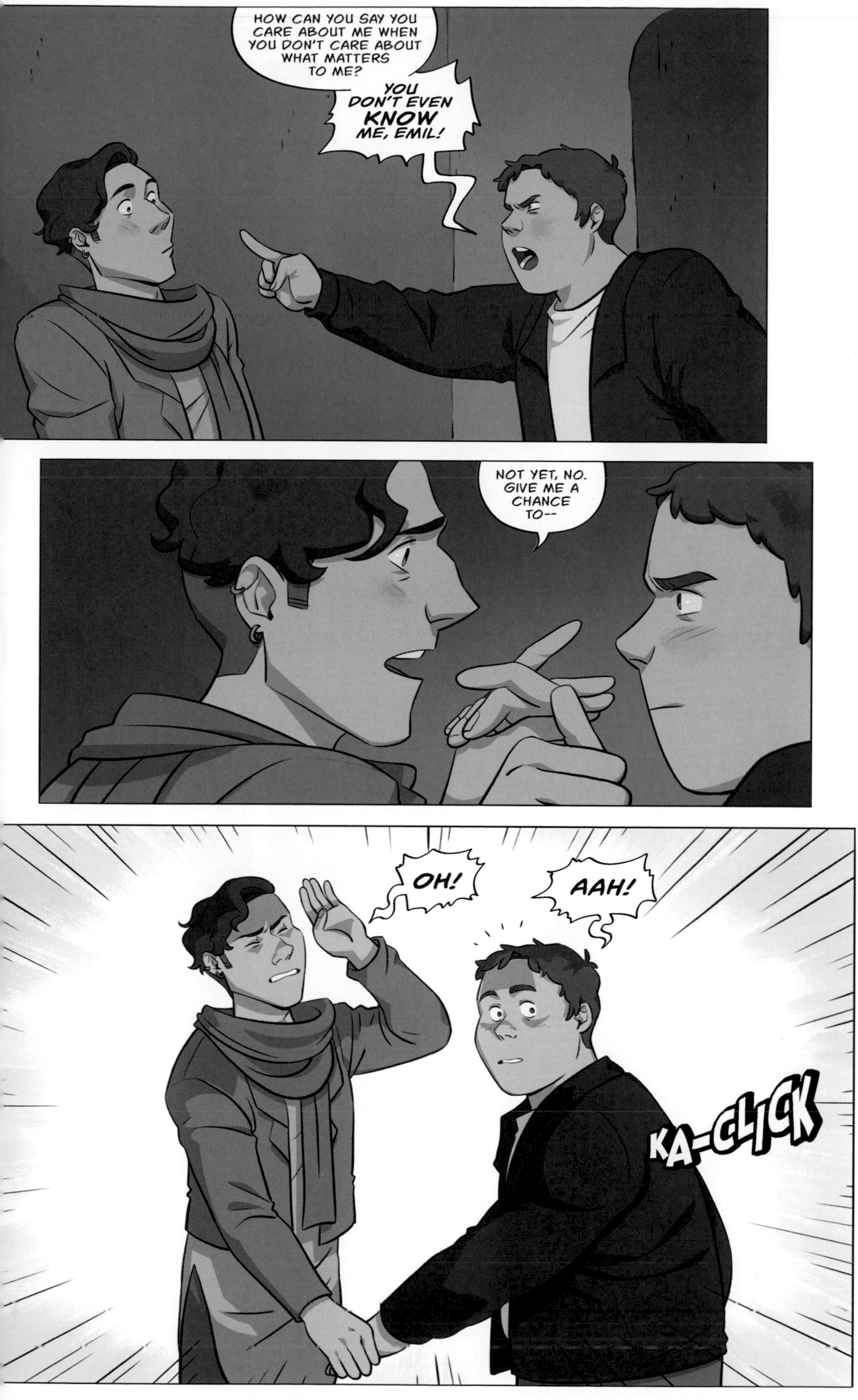
HOW CAN YOU SAY YOU CARE ABOUT ME WHEN YOU DON'T CARE ABOUT WHAT MATTERS TO ME?
YOU DON'T EVEN KNOW ME, EMIL!
NOT YET, NO. GIVE ME A CHANCE TO--
OH!
AAH!
KA-CLICK

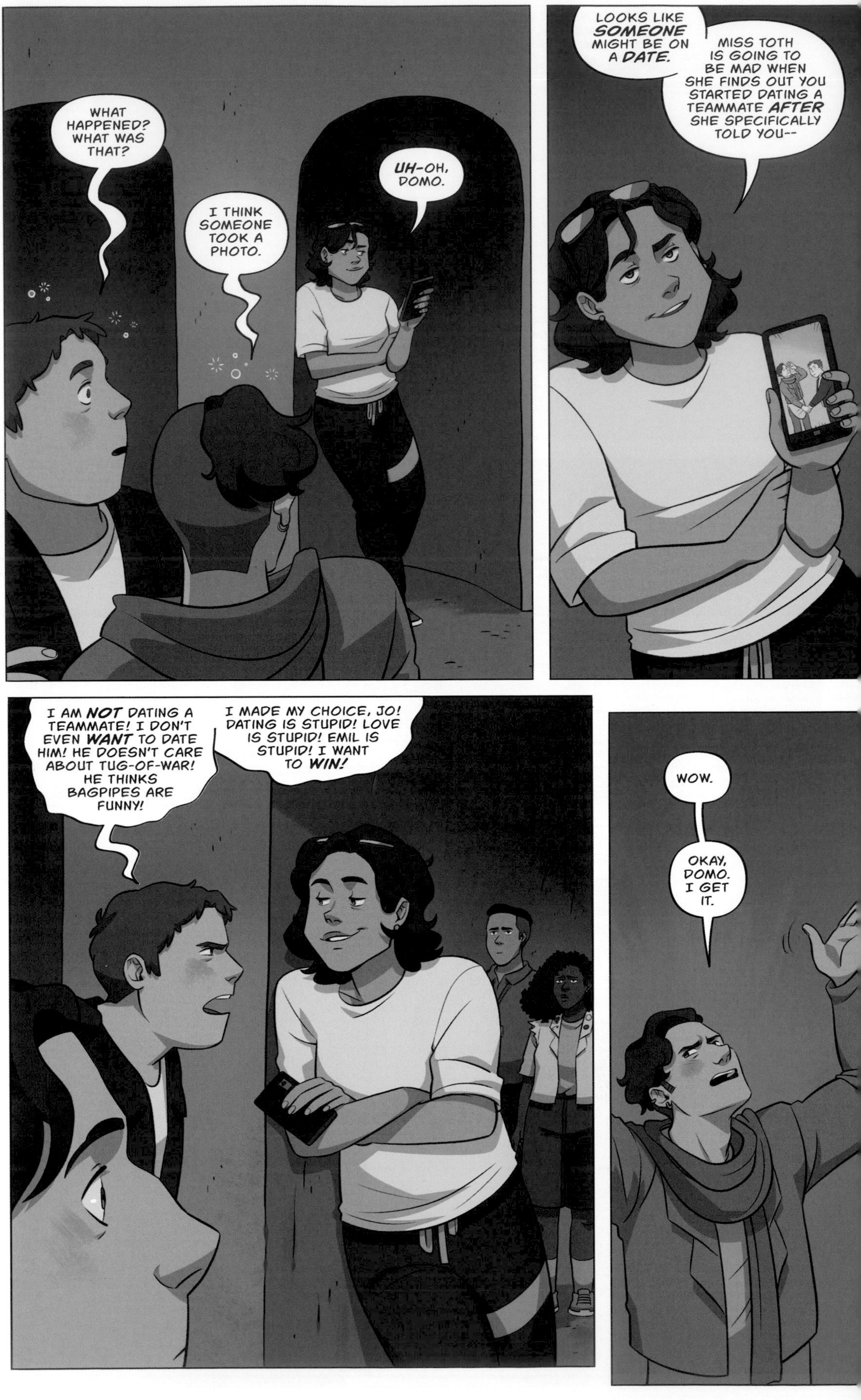
WHAT HAPPENED? WHAT WAS THAT?
I THINK SOMEONE TOOK A PHOTO.
UH-OH, DOMO.
LOOKS LIKE SOMEONE MIGHT BE ON A DATE.
MISS TOTH IS GOING TO BE MAD WHEN SHE FINDS OUT YOU STARTED DATING A TEAMMATE AFTER SHE SPECIFICALLY TOLD YOU--
I AM NOT DATING A TEAMMATE! I DON'T EVEN WANT TO DATE HIM! HE DOESN'T CARE ABOUT TUG-OF-WAR! HE THINKS BAGPIPES ARE FUNNY!
I MADE MY CHOICE, JO! DATING IS STUPID! LOVE IS STUPID! EMIL IS STUPID! I WANT TO WIN!
WOW.
OKAY, DOMO. I GET IT.

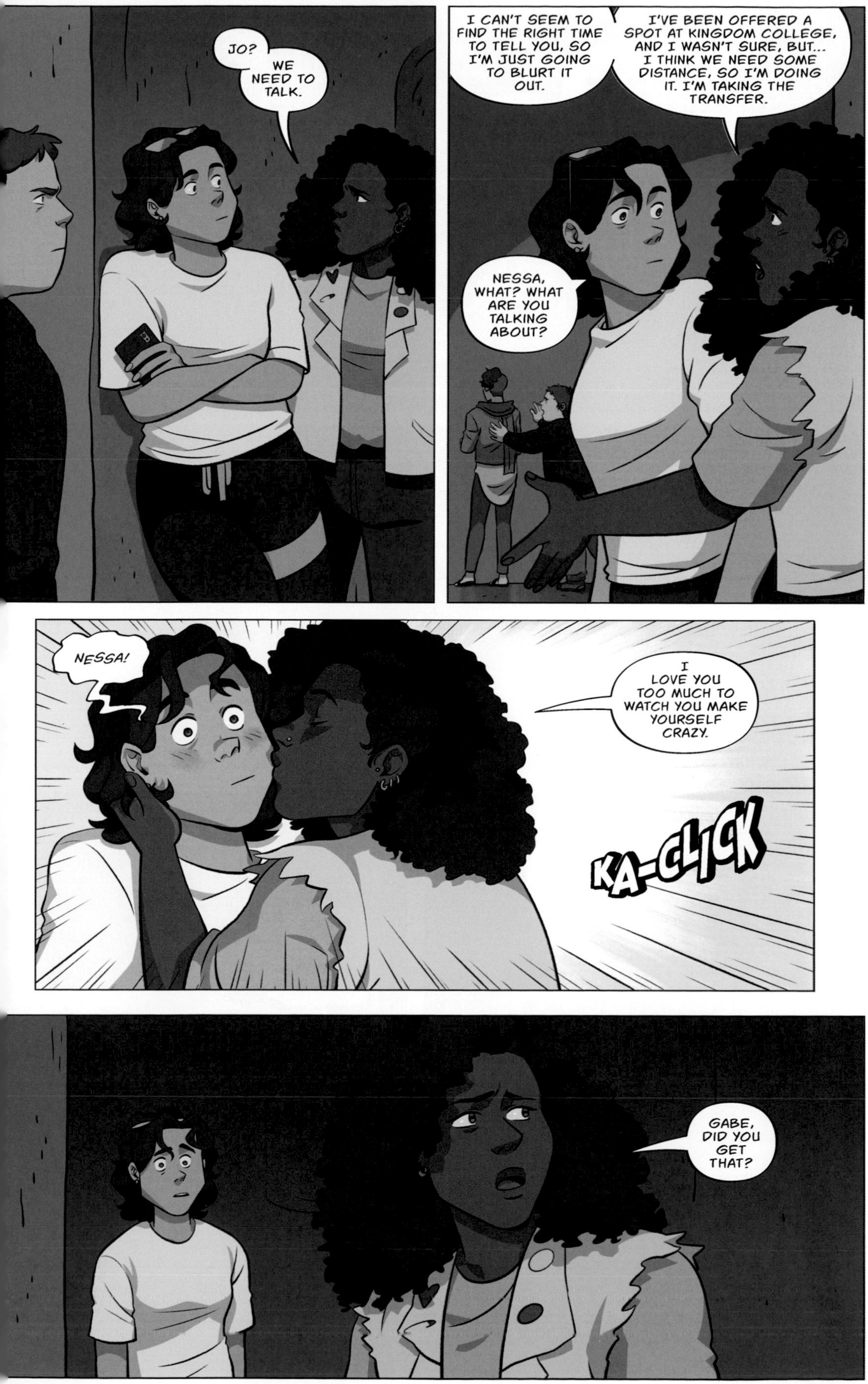
JO?
WE NEED TO TALK.
I CAN'T SEEM TO FIND THE RIGHT TIME TO TELL YOU, SO I'M JUST GOING TO BLURT IT OUT.
I'VE BEEN OFFERED A SPOT AT KINGDOM COLLEGE, AND I WASN'T SURE, BUT... I THINK WE NEED SOME DISTANCE, SO I'M DOING IT. I'M TAKING THE TRANSFER.
NESSA, WHAT? WHAT ARE YOU TALKING ABOUT?
NESSA!
I LOVE YOU TOO MUCH TO WATCH YOU MAKE YOURSELF CRAZY.
KA-CLICK
GABE, DID YOU GET THAT?

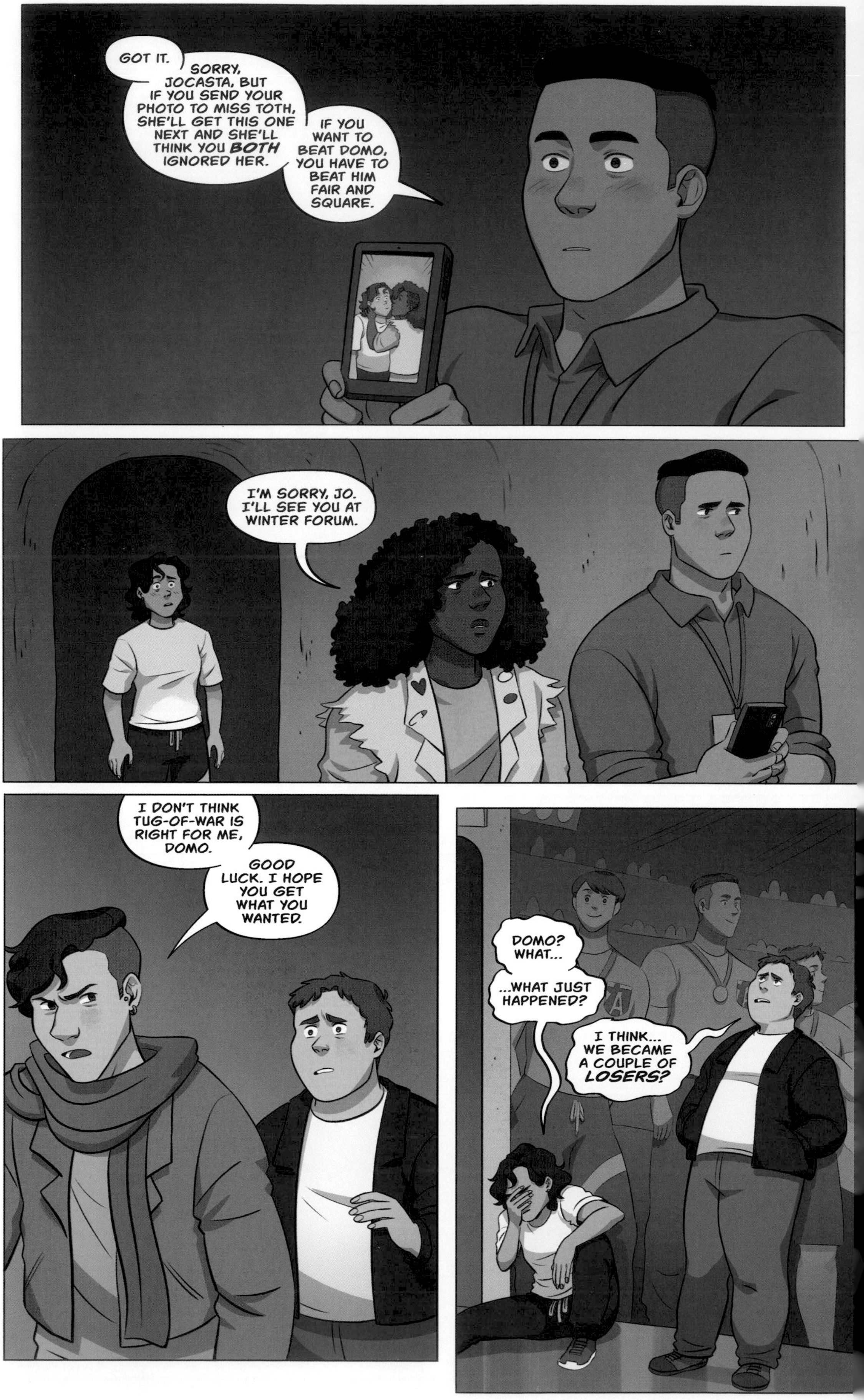
GOT IT.
SORRY, JOCASTA, BUT IF YOU SEND YOUR PHOTO TO MISS TOTH, SHE'LL GET THIS ONE NEXT AND SHE'LL THINK YOU BOTH IGNORED HER.
IF YOU WANT TO BEAT DOMO, YOU HAVE TO BEAT HIM FAIR AND SQUARE.
I'M SORRY, JO. I'LL SEE YOU AT WINTER FORUM.
I DON'T THINK TUG-OF-WAR IS RIGHT FOR ME, DOMO.
GOOD LUCK. I HOPE YOU GET WHAT YOU WANTED.
DOMO? WHAT...
...WHAT JUST HAPPENED?
I THINK... WE BECAME A COUPLE OF LOSERS?

CHAPTER

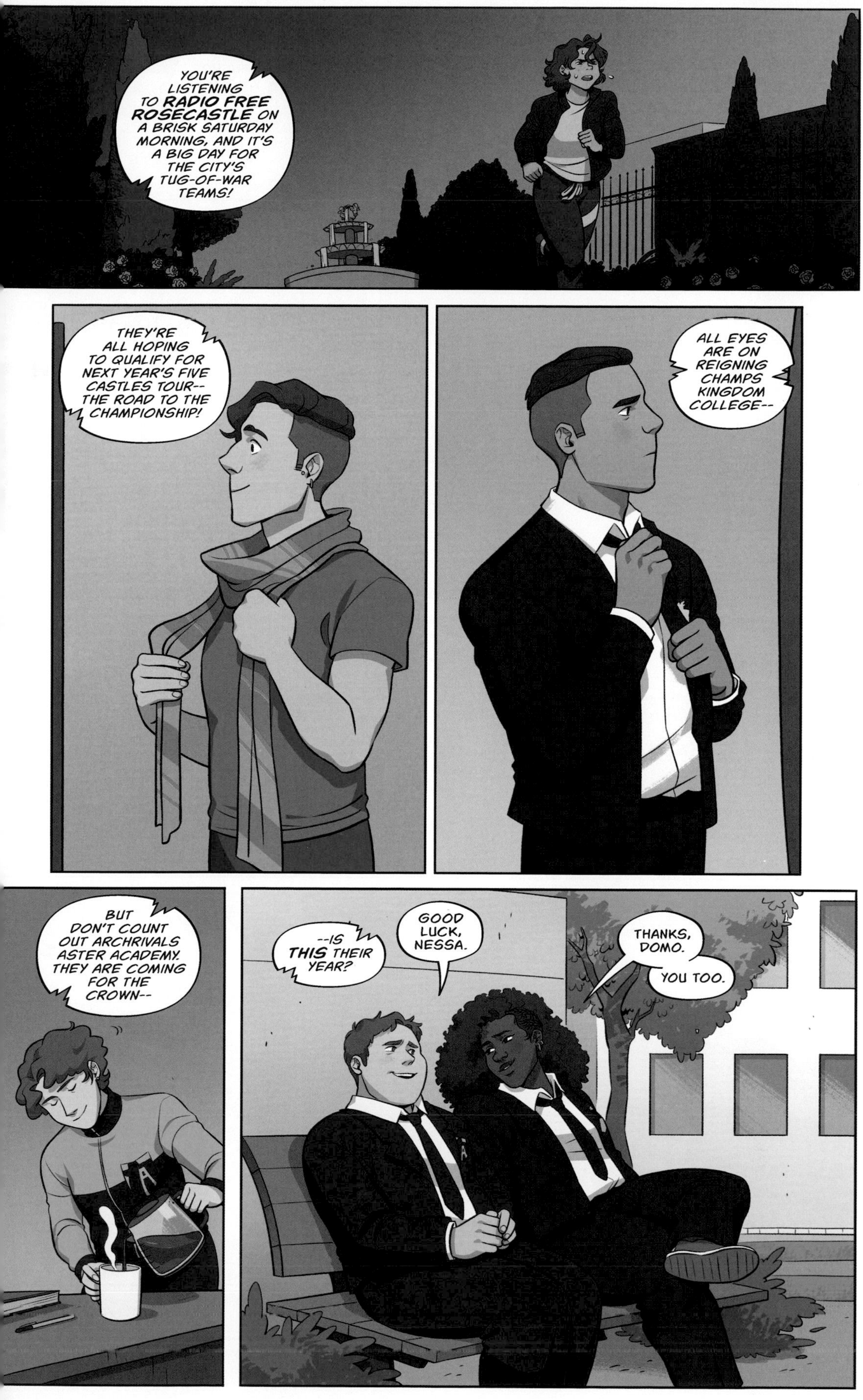
YOU'RE LISTENING TO RADIO FREE ROSECASTLE ON A BRISK SATURDAY MORNING, AND IT'S A BIG DAY FOR THE CITY'S TUG-OF-WAR TEAMS!
THEY'RE ALL HOPING TO QUALIFY FOR NEXT YEAR'S FIVE CASTLES TOUR-- THE ROAD TO THE CHAMPIONSHIP!
ALL EYES ARE ON REIGNING CHAMPS KINGDOM COLLEGE--
BUT DON'T COUNT OUT ARCHRIVALS ASTER ACADEMY. THEY ARE COMING FOR THE CROWN--
--IS THIS THEIR YEAR?
GOOD LUCK, NESSA.
THANKS, DOMO.
YOU TOO.

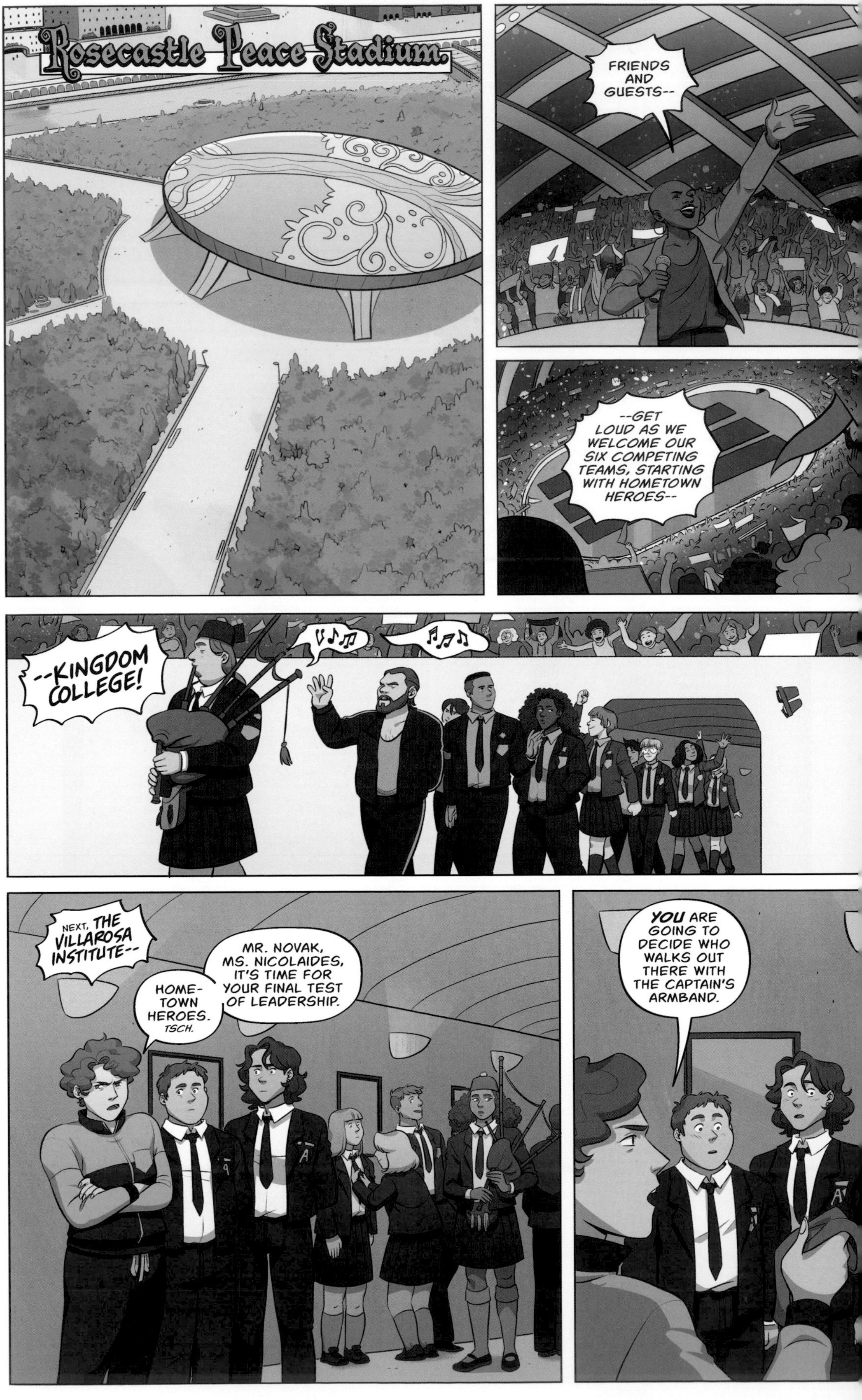
Rosecastle Peace Stadium
FRIENDS AND GUESTS--
--GET LOUD AS WE WELCOME OUR SIX COMPETING TEAMS, STARTING WITH HOMETOWN HEROES--
--KINGDOM COLLEGE!
NEXT, THE VILLAROSA INSTITUTE--
HOME-TOWN HEROES. TSCH.
MR. NOVAK, MS. NICOLAIDES, IT'S TIME FOR YOUR FINAL TEST OF LEADERSHIP.
YOU ARE GOING TO DECIDE WHO WALKS OUT THERE WITH THE CAPTAIN'S ARMBAND.

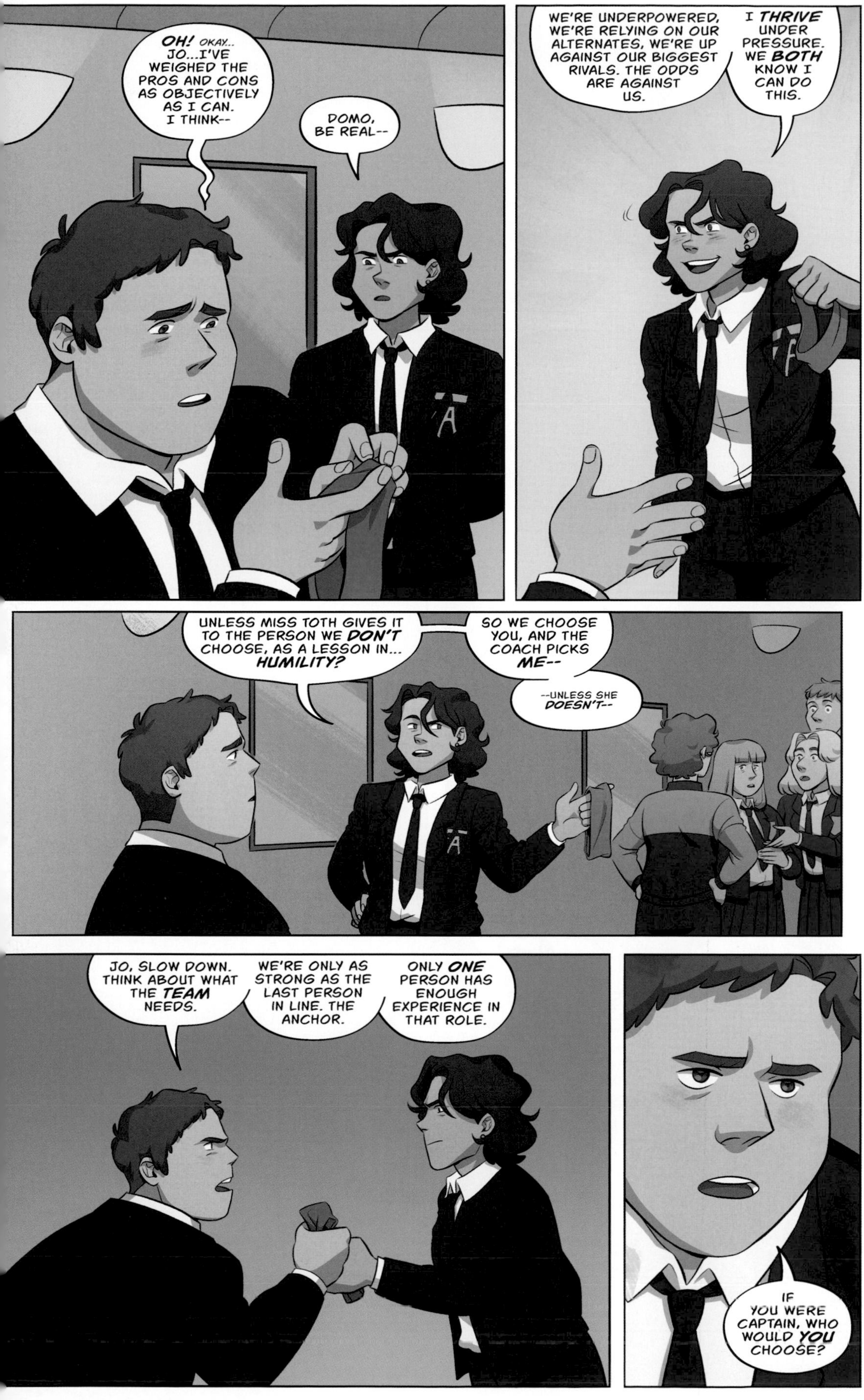
OH! OKAY... JO...I'VE WEIGHED THE PROS AND CONS AS OBJECTIVELY AS I CAN. I THINK--
DOMO, BE REAL--
WE'RE UNDERPOWERED, WE'RE RELYING ON OUR ALTERNATES, WE'RE UP AGAINST OUR BIGGEST RIVALS. THE ODDS ARE AGAINST US.
I THRIVE UNDER PRESSURE. WE BOTH KNOW I CAN DO THIS.
UNLESS MISS TOTH GIVES IT TO THE PERSON WE DON'T CHOOSE, AS A LESSON IN... HUMILITY?
SO WE CHOOSE YOU, AND THE COACH PICKS ME--
--UNLESS SHE DOESN'T--
JO, SLOW DOWN. THINK ABOUT WHAT THE TEAM NEEDS.
WE'RE ONLY AS STRONG AS THE LAST PERSON IN LINE. THE ANCHOR.
ONLY ONE PERSON HAS ENOUGH EXPERIENCE IN THAT ROLE.
IF YOU WERE CAPTAIN, WHO WOULD YOU CHOOSE?

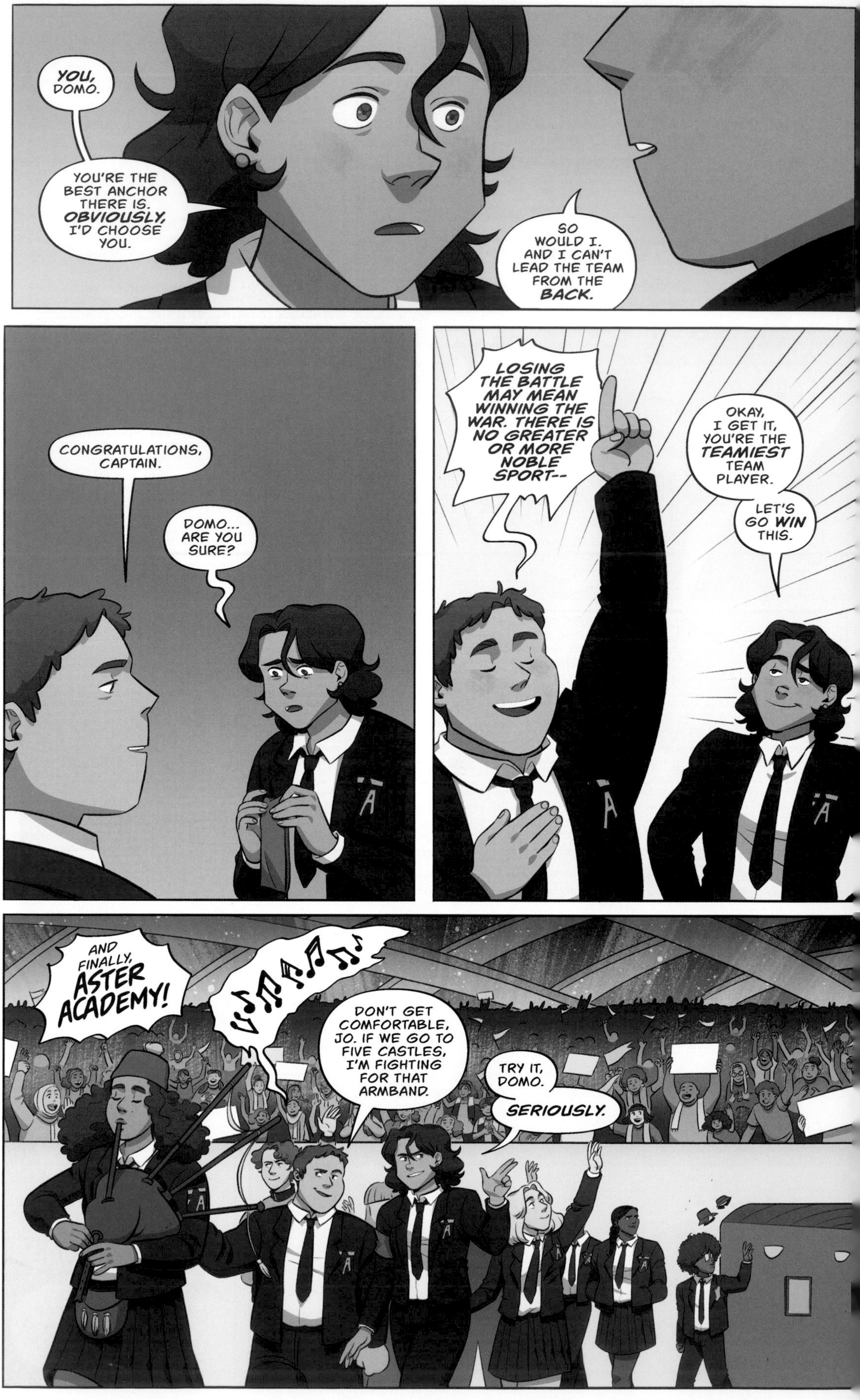
YOU, DOMO.
YOU'RE THE BEST ANCHOR THERE IS. OBVIOUSLY, I'D CHOOSE YOU.
SO WOULD I. AND I CAN'T LEAD THE TEAM FROM THE BACK.
CONGRATULATIONS, CAPTAIN.
DOMO... ARE YOU SURE?
LOSING THE BATTLE MAY MEAN WINNING THE WAR. THERE IS NO GREATER OR MORE NOBLE SPORT--
OKAY, I GET IT, YOU'RE THE TEAMIEST TEAM PLAYER.
LET'S GO WIN THIS.
AND FINALLY, ASTER ACADEMY!
DON'T GET COMFORTABLE, JO. IF WE GO TO FIVE CASTLES, I'M FIGHTING FOR THAT ARMBAND.
TRY IT, DOMO.
SERIOUSLY.

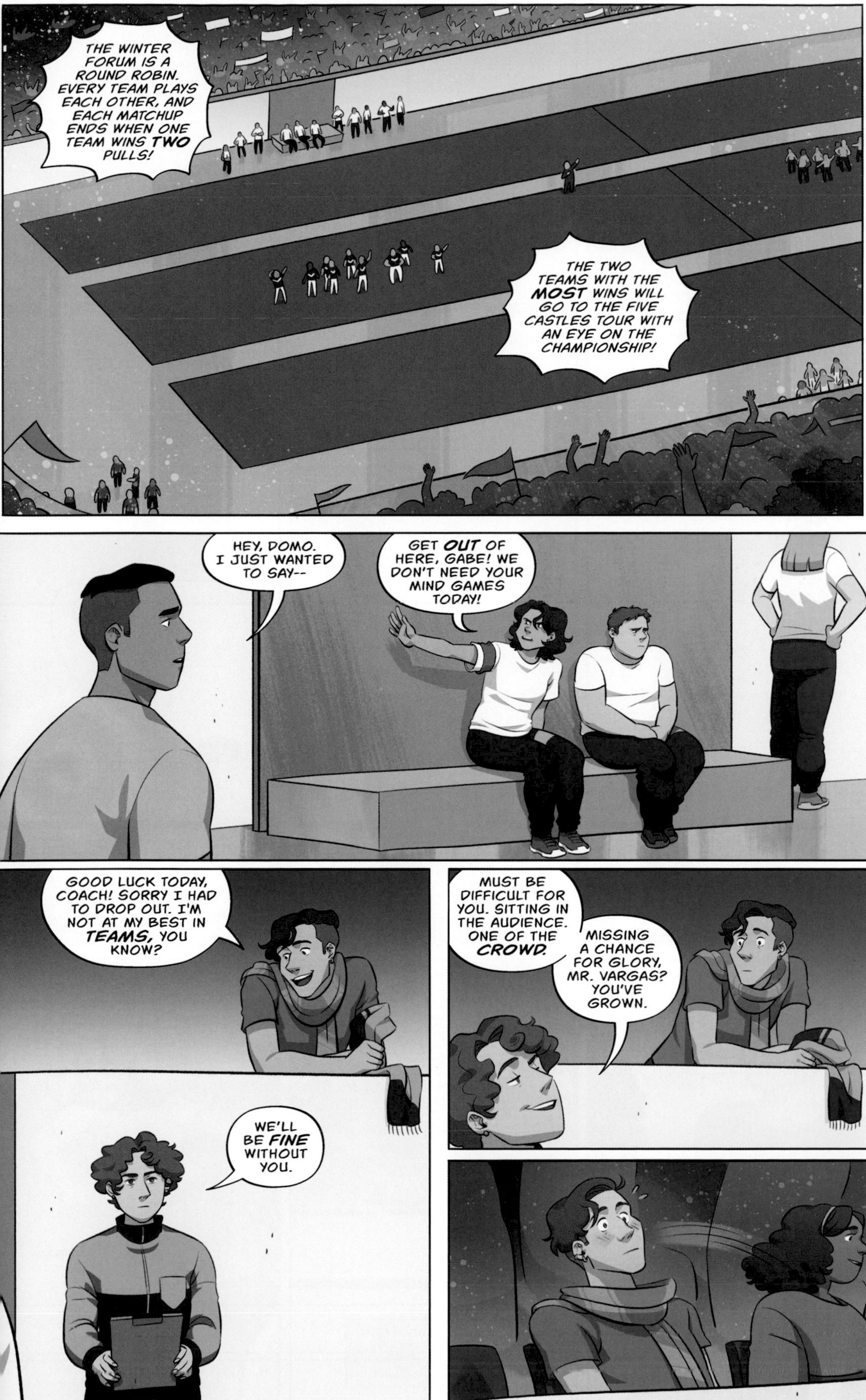
THE WINTER FORUM IS A ROUND ROBIN. EVERY TEAM PLAYS EACH OTHER, AND EACH MATCHUP ENDS WHEN ONE TEAM WINS **TWO** PULLS!
THE TWO TEAMS WITH THE **MOST** WINS WILL GO TO THE FIVE CASTLES TOUR WITH AN EYE ON THE CHAMPIONSHIP!
HEY, DOMO. I JUST WANTED TO SAY--
GET **OUT** OF HERE, GABE! WE DON'T NEED YOUR MIND GAMES TODAY!
GOOD LUCK TODAY, COACH! SORRY I HAD TO DROP OUT. I'M NOT AT MY BEST IN **TEAMS,** YOU KNOW?
WE'LL BE **FINE** WITHOUT YOU.
MUST BE DIFFICULT FOR YOU. SITTING IN THE AUDIENCE. ONE OF THE **CROWD.**
MISSING A CHANCE FOR GLORY, MR. VARGAS? YOU'VE GROWN.

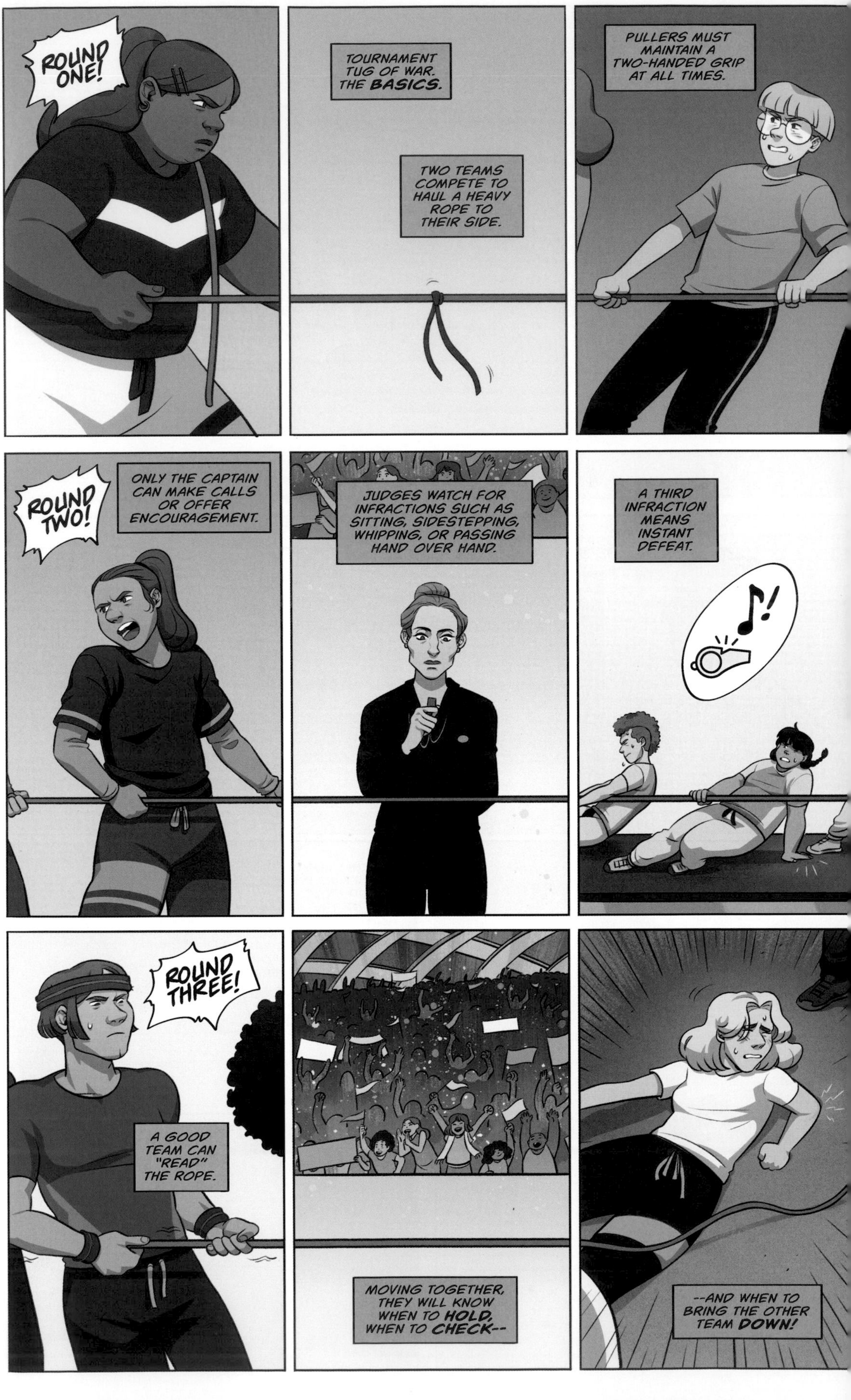
ROUND ONE!
TOURNAMENT TUG OF WAR. THE BASICS.
TWO TEAMS COMPETE TO HAUL A HEAVY ROPE TO THEIR SIDE.
PULLERS MUST MAINTAIN A TWO-HANDED GRIP AT ALL TIMES.
ROUND TWO!
ONLY THE CAPTAIN CAN MAKE CALLS OR OFFER ENCOURAGEMENT.
JUDGES WATCH FOR INFRACTIONS SUCH AS SITTING, SIDESTEPPING, WHIPPING, OR PASSING HAND OVER HAND.
A THIRD INFRACTION MEANS INSTANT DEFEAT.
♪!
ROUND THREE!
A GOOD TEAM CAN "READ" THE ROPE.
MOVING TOGETHER, THEY WILL KNOW WHEN TO HOLD, WHEN TO CHECK--
--AND WHEN TO BRING THE OTHER TEAM DOWN!

A TUMBLE FROM ASTER ACADEMY IN THE THIRD ROUND! THAT LEAVES KINGDOM THE ONLY UNDEFEATED TEAM!

THANKS, DOMO.

KINGDOM AND ASTER WILL MEET IN THE FIFTH ROUND, AND IT SHOULD BE A *CLASH OF TITANS!*

TEAM	PTS
KINGDOM	6
ASTER	5
VILLAROSA	4
MERCER	4
REINGOLD	3
CHEVALIER	I

YOU'RE DOING GREAT, DOMO! YOU WON *FIVE* PULLS!

KINGDOM WON *SIX.*

ARE YOU OKAY? I KNOW SEEING GABE ALWAYS THROWS YOU OFF.

OH--!

YEAH. I GUESS. IT'S KIND OF *STRANGE* BEING BACK HERE.

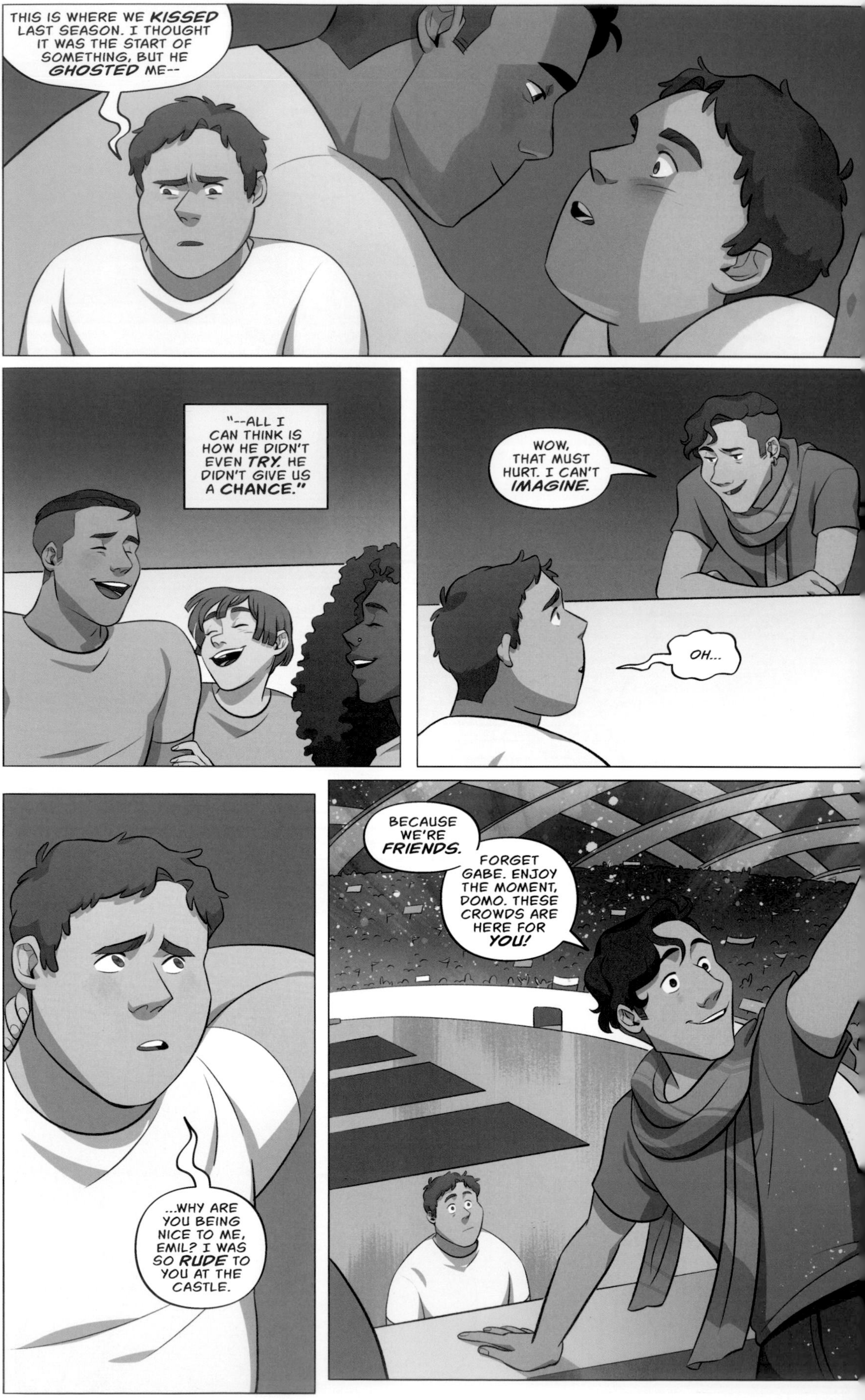
THIS IS WHERE WE KISSED LAST SEASON. I THOUGHT IT WAS THE START OF SOMETHING, BUT HE GHOSTED ME--
"--ALL I CAN THINK IS HOW HE DIDN'T EVEN TRY. HE DIDN'T GIVE US A CHANCE."
WOW, THAT MUST HURT. I CAN'T IMAGINE.
OH...
...WHY ARE YOU BEING NICE TO ME, EMIL? I WAS SO RUDE TO YOU AT THE CASTLE.
BECAUSE WE'RE FRIENDS.
FORGET GABE. ENJOY THE MOMENT, DOMO. THESE CROWDS ARE HERE FOR YOU!

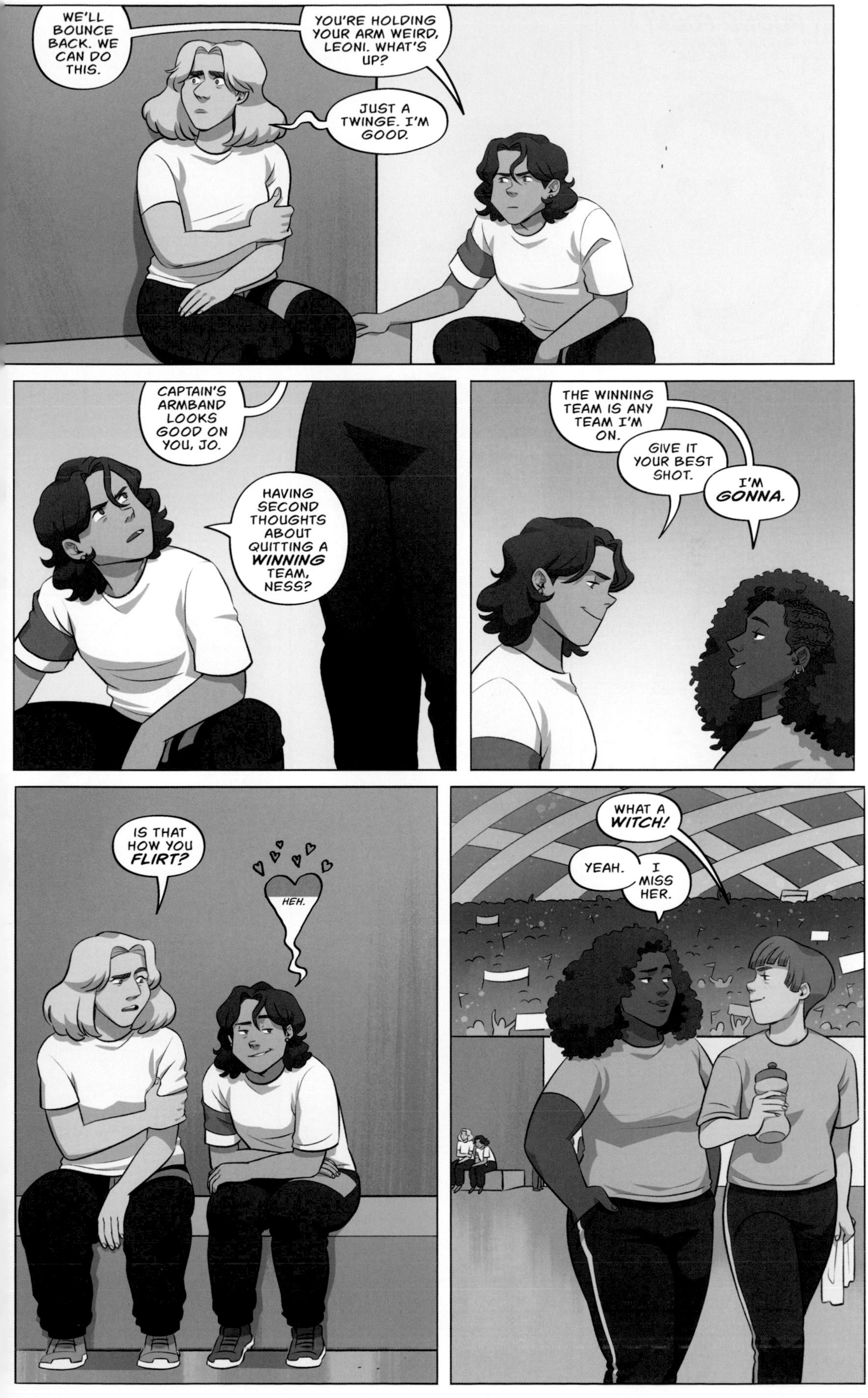
WE'LL BOUNCE BACK. WE CAN DO THIS.
YOU'RE HOLDING YOUR ARM WEIRD, LEONI. WHAT'S UP?
JUST A TWINGE. I'M GOOD.
CAPTAIN'S ARMBAND LOOKS GOOD ON YOU, JO.
HAVING SECOND THOUGHTS ABOUT QUITTING A *WINNING* TEAM, NESS?
THE WINNING TEAM IS ANY TEAM I'M ON.
GIVE IT YOUR BEST SHOT.
I'M *GONNA.*
IS THAT HOW YOU *FLIRT?*
HEH.
WHAT A *WITCH!*
YEAH.
I MISS HER.

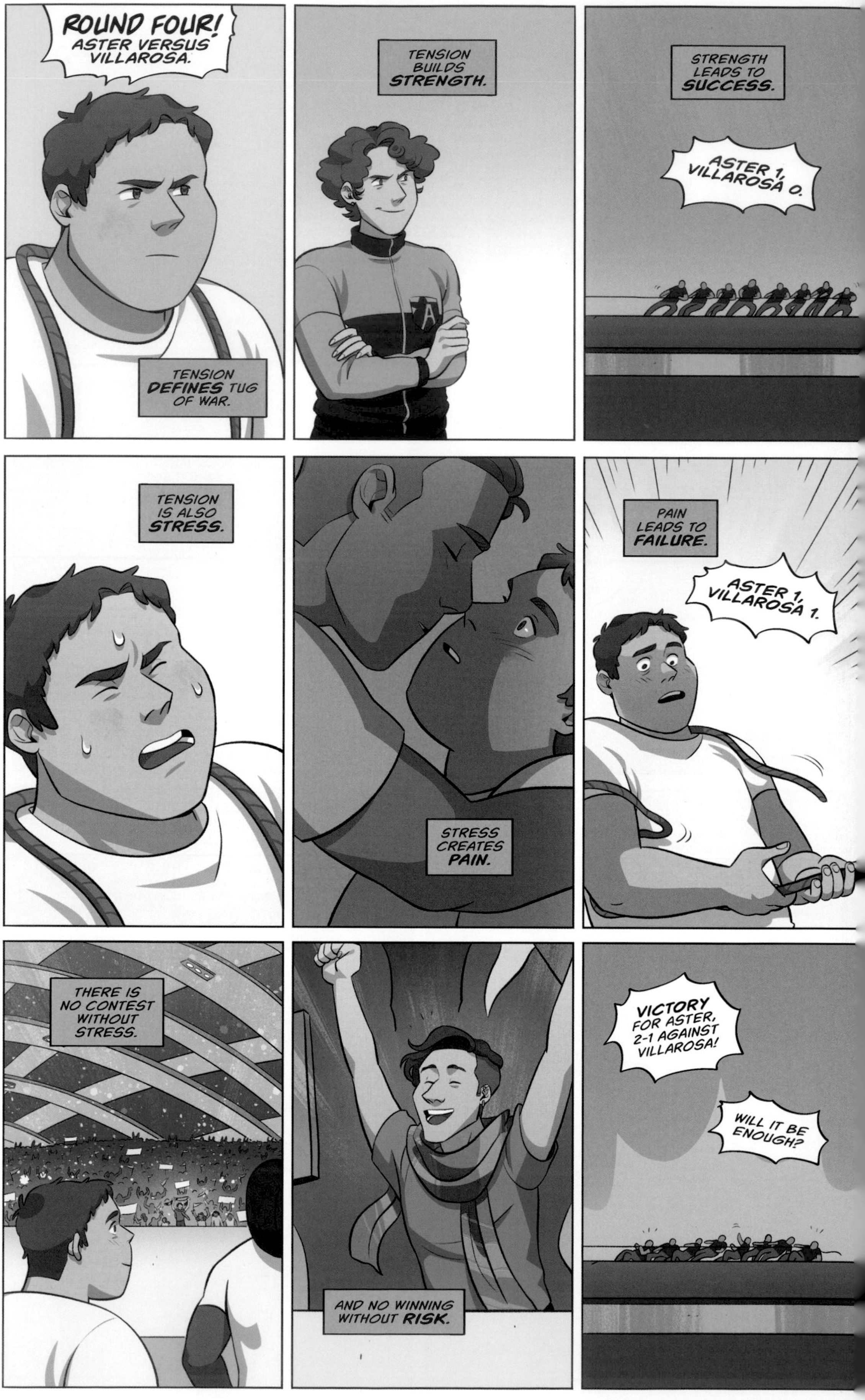
ROUND FOUR! ASTER VERSUS VILLAROSA.
TENSION DEFINES TUG OF WAR.
TENSION BUILDS STRENGTH.
STRENGTH LEADS TO SUCCESS.
ASTER 1, VILLAROSA 0.
TENSION IS ALSO STRESS.
STRESS CREATES PAIN.
PAIN LEADS TO FAILURE.
ASTER 1, VILLAROSA 1.
THERE IS NO CONTEST WITHOUT STRESS.
AND NO WINNING WITHOUT RISK.
VICTORY FOR ASTER, 2-1 AGAINST VILLAROSA!
WILL IT BE ENOUGH?

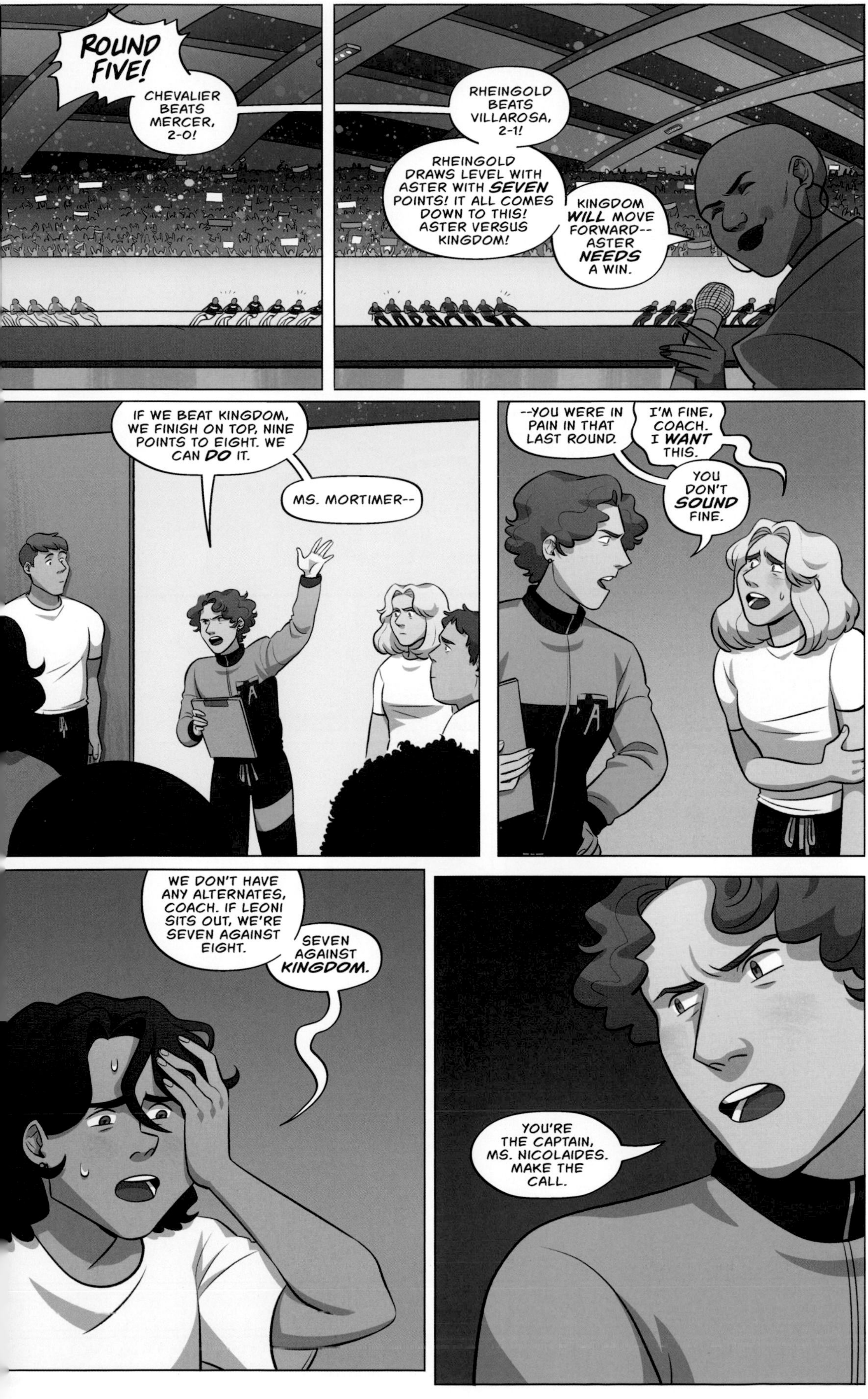
ROUND FIVE!
CHEVALIER BEATS MERCER, 2-0!
RHEINGOLD BEATS VILLAROSA, 2-1!
RHEINGOLD DRAWS LEVEL WITH ASTER WITH SEVEN POINTS! IT ALL COMES DOWN TO THIS! ASTER VERSUS KINGDOM!
KINGDOM WILL MOVE FORWARD-- ASTER NEEDS A WIN.
IF WE BEAT KINGDOM, WE FINISH ON TOP, NINE POINTS TO EIGHT. WE CAN DO IT.
MS. MORTIMER--
--YOU WERE IN PAIN IN THAT LAST ROUND.
I'M FINE, COACH. I WANT THIS.
YOU DON'T SOUND FINE.
WE DON'T HAVE ANY ALTERNATES, COACH. IF LEONI SITS OUT, WE'RE SEVEN AGAINST EIGHT.
SEVEN AGAINST KINGDOM.
YOU'RE THE CAPTAIN, MS. NICOLAIDES. MAKE THE CALL.

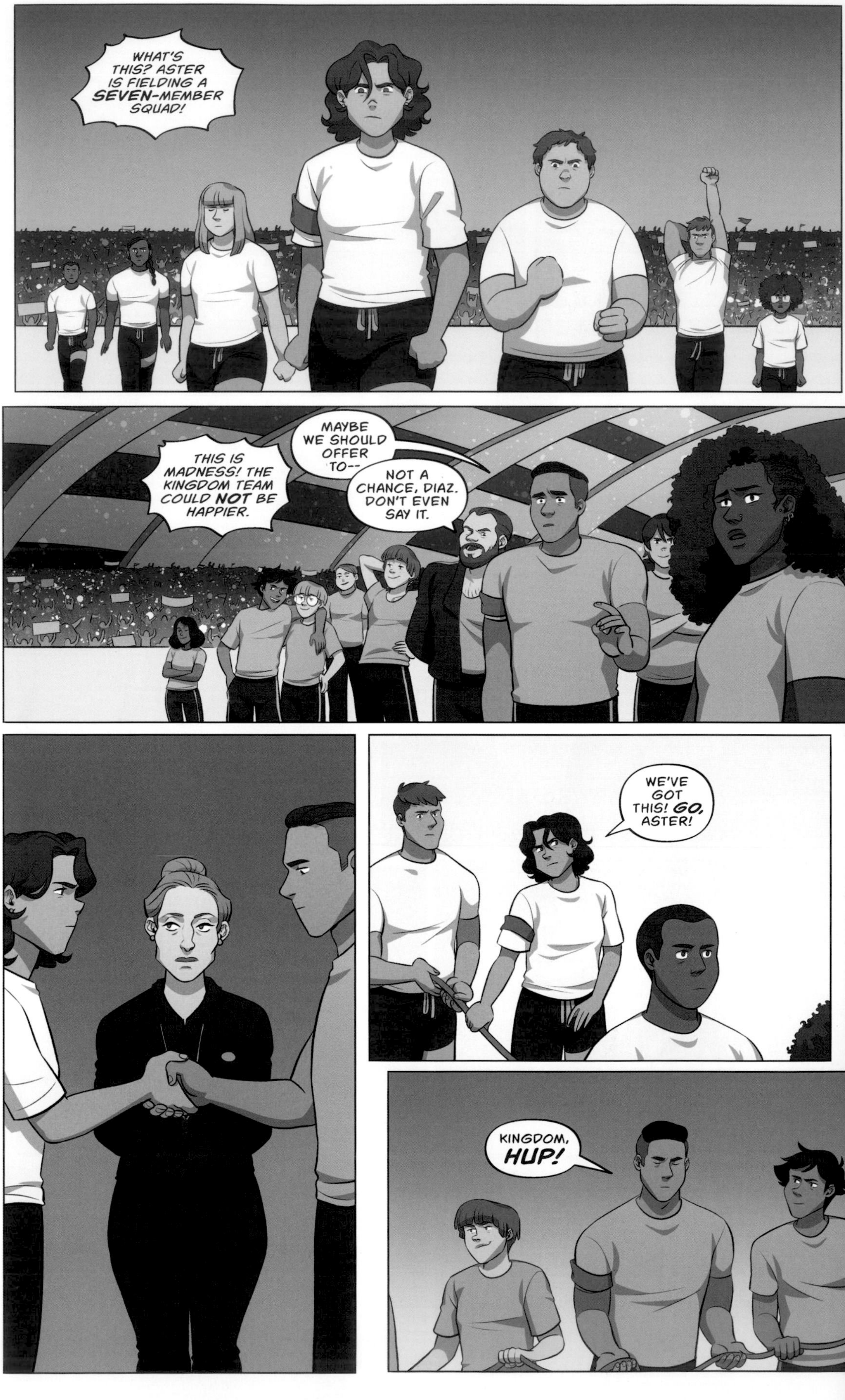
WHAT'S THIS? ASTER IS FIELDING A SEVEN-MEMBER SQUAD!
THIS IS MADNESS! THE KINGDOM TEAM COULD NOT BE HAPPIER.
MAYBE WE SHOULD OFFER TO--
NOT A CHANCE, DIAZ. DON'T EVEN SAY IT.
WE'VE GOT THIS! GO, ASTER!
KINGDOM, HUP!

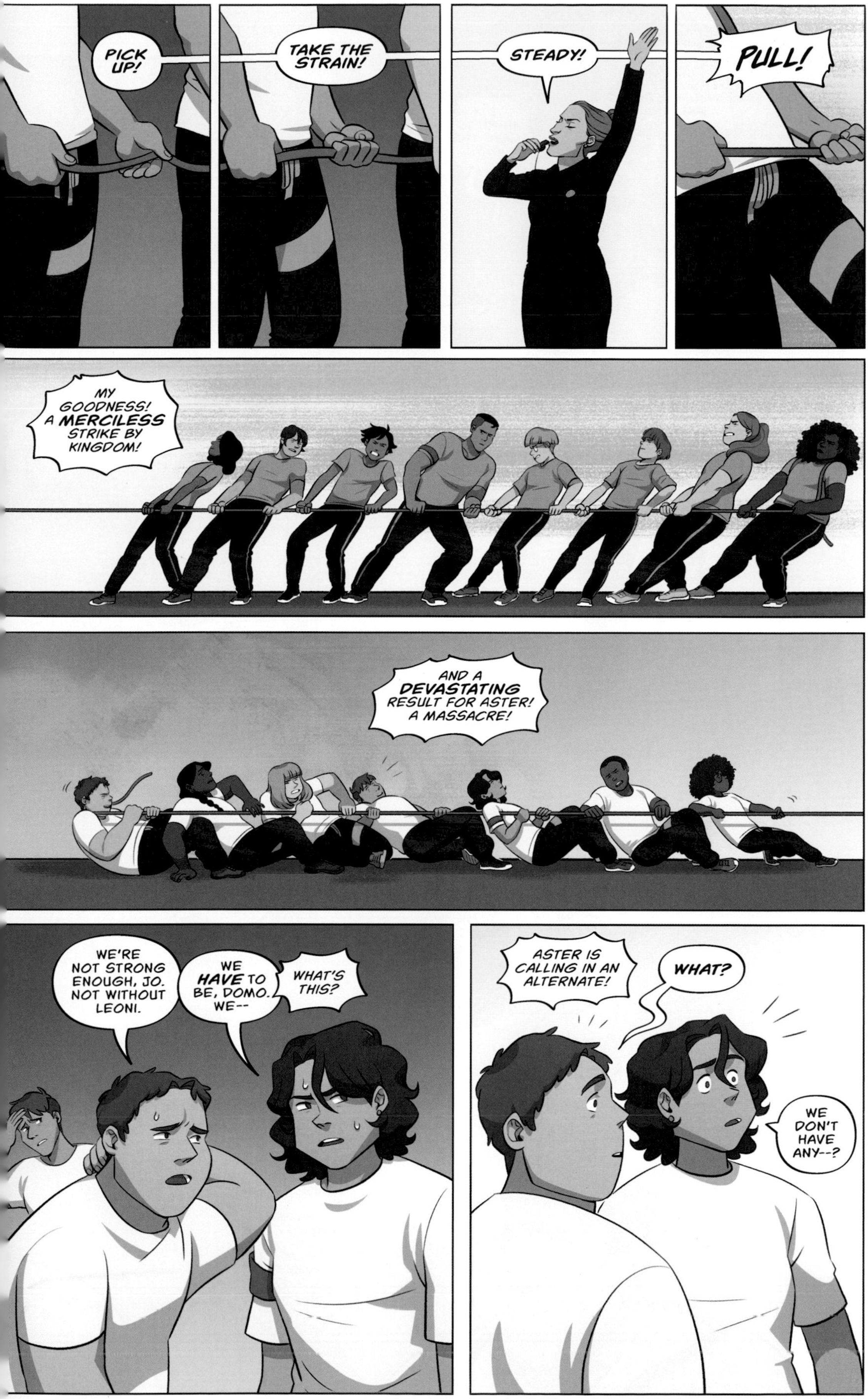
PICK UP!
TAKE THE STRAIN!
STEADY!
PULL!
MY GOODNESS! A MERCILESS STRIKE BY KINGDOM!
AND A DEVASTATING RESULT FOR ASTER! A MASSACRE!
WE'RE NOT STRONG ENOUGH, JO. NOT WITHOUT LEONI.
WE HAVE TO BE, DOMO. WE--
WHAT'S THIS?
ASTER IS CALLING IN AN ALTERNATE!
WHAT?
WE DON'T HAVE ANY--?

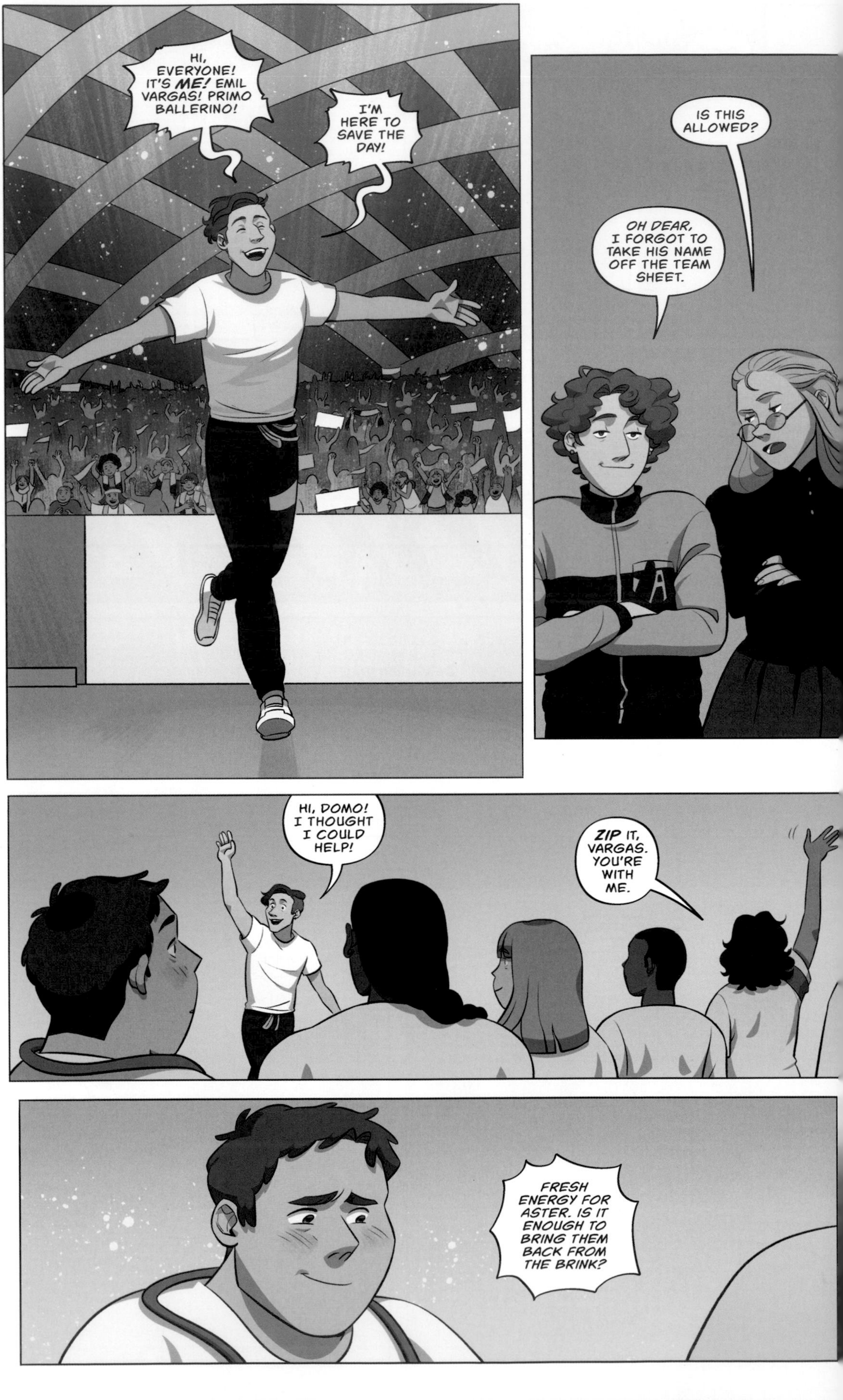
HI, EVERYONE! IT'S ME! EMIL VARGAS! PRIMO BALLERINO!
I'M HERE TO SAVE THE DAY!
IS THIS ALLOWED?
OH DEAR, I FORGOT TO TAKE HIS NAME OFF THE TEAM SHEET.
HI, DOMO! I THOUGHT I COULD HELP!
ZIP IT, VARGAS. YOU'RE WITH ME.
FRESH ENERGY FOR ASTER. IS IT ENOUGH TO BRING THEM BACK FROM THE BRINK?

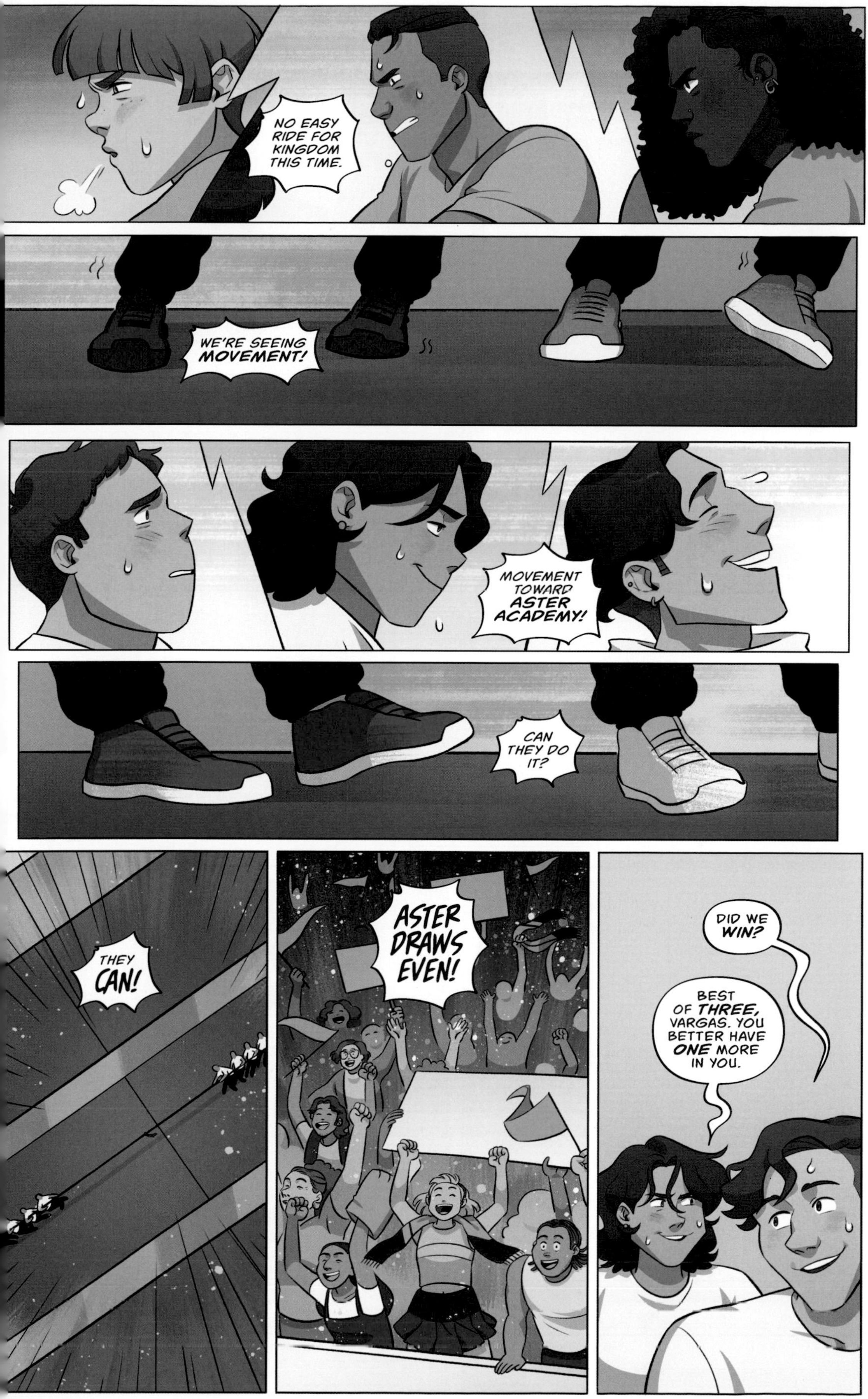
NO EASY RIDE FOR KINGDOM THIS TIME.
WE'RE SEEING MOVEMENT!
MOVEMENT TOWARD ASTER ACADEMY!
CAN THEY DO IT?
THEY CAN!
ASTER DRAWS EVEN!
DID WE WIN?
BEST OF THREE, VARGAS. YOU BETTER HAVE ONE MORE IN YOU.

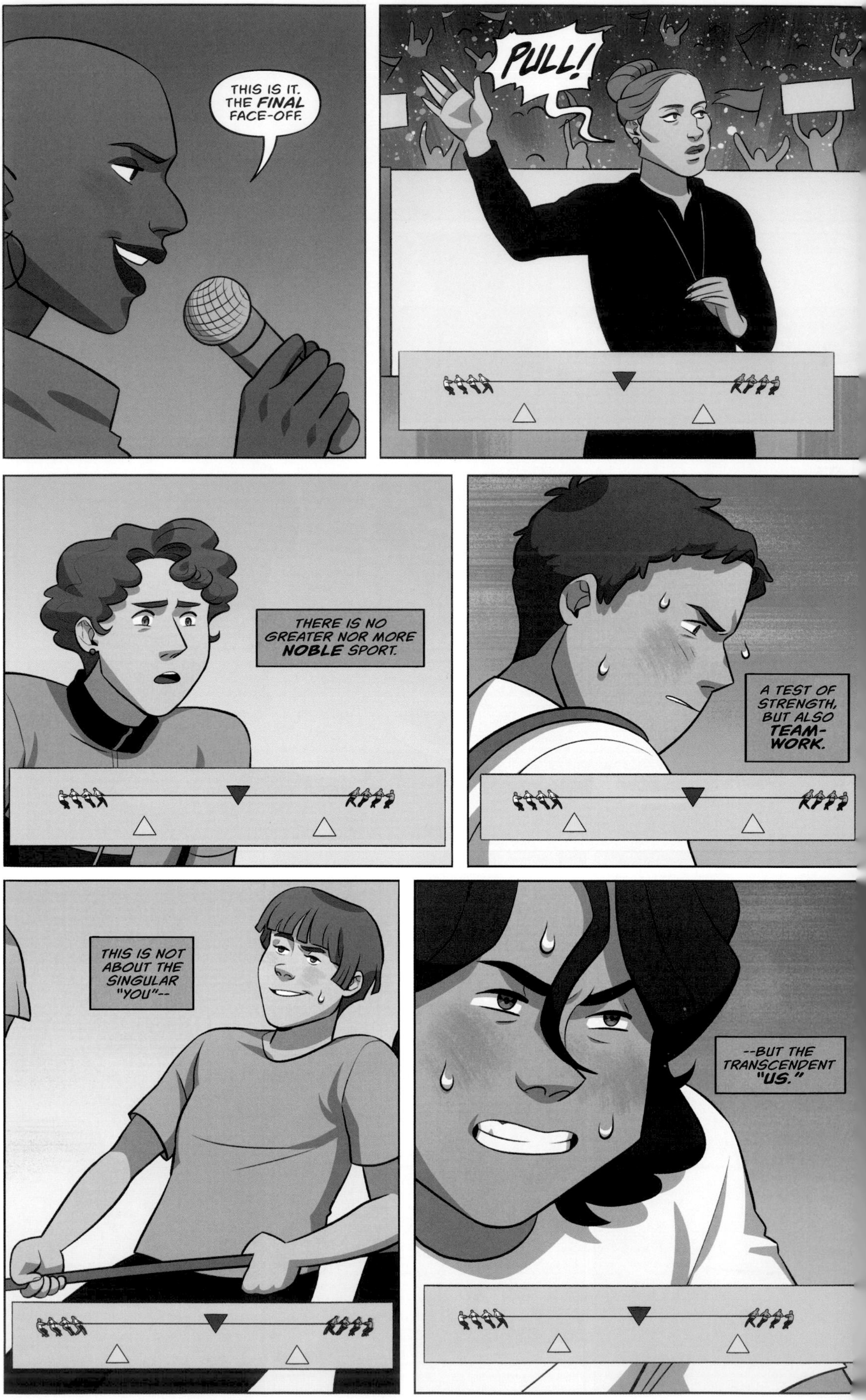
THIS IS IT. THE FINAL FACE-OFF.
PULL!
THERE IS NO GREATER NOR MORE NOBLE SPORT.
A TEST OF STRENGTH, BUT ALSO TEAM-WORK.
THIS IS NOT ABOUT THE SINGULAR "YOU"--
--BUT THE TRANSCENDENT "US."

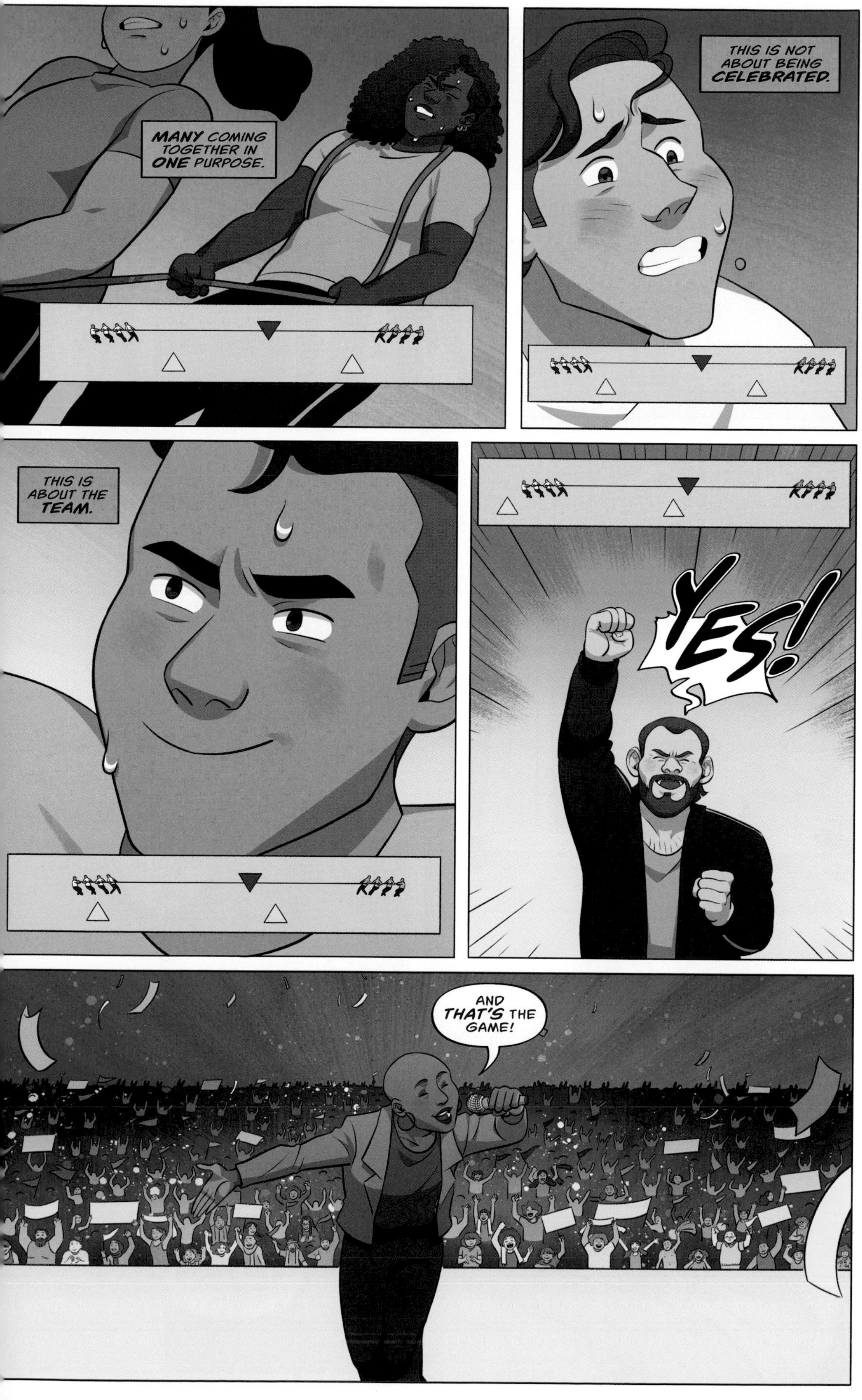
MANY COMING TOGETHER IN ONE PURPOSE.
THIS IS NOT ABOUT BEING CELEBRATED.
THIS IS ABOUT THE TEAM.
YES!
AND THAT'S THE GAME!

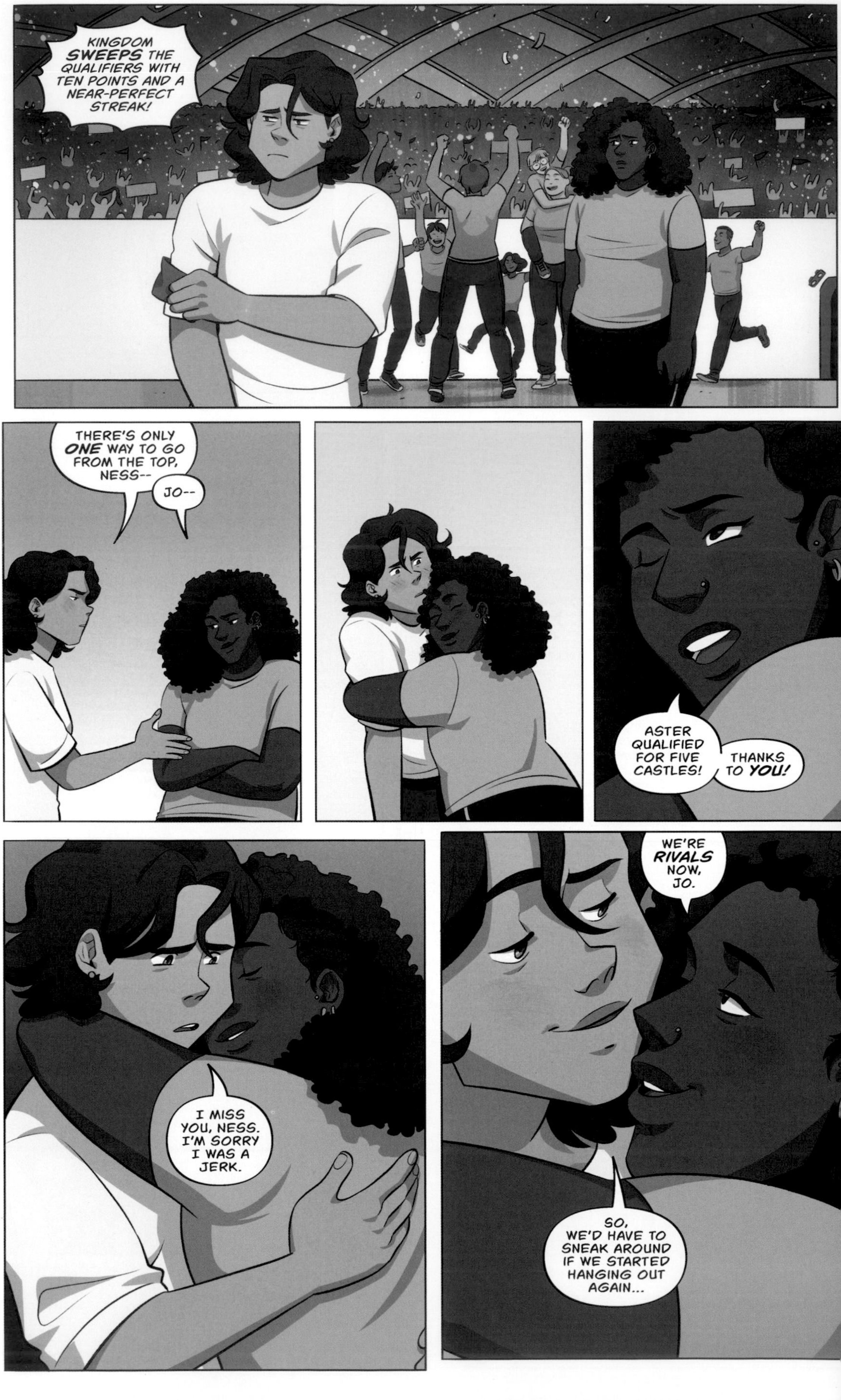
KINGDOM SWEEPS THE QUALIFIERS WITH TEN POINTS AND A NEAR-PERFECT STREAK!
THERE'S ONLY ONE WAY TO GO FROM THE TOP, NESS--
JO--
ASTER QUALIFIED FOR FIVE CASTLES!
THANKS TO YOU!
I MISS YOU, NESS. I'M SORRY I WAS A JERK.
WE'RE RIVALS NOW, JO.
SO, WE'D HAVE TO SNEAK AROUND IF WE STARTED HANGING OUT AGAIN...

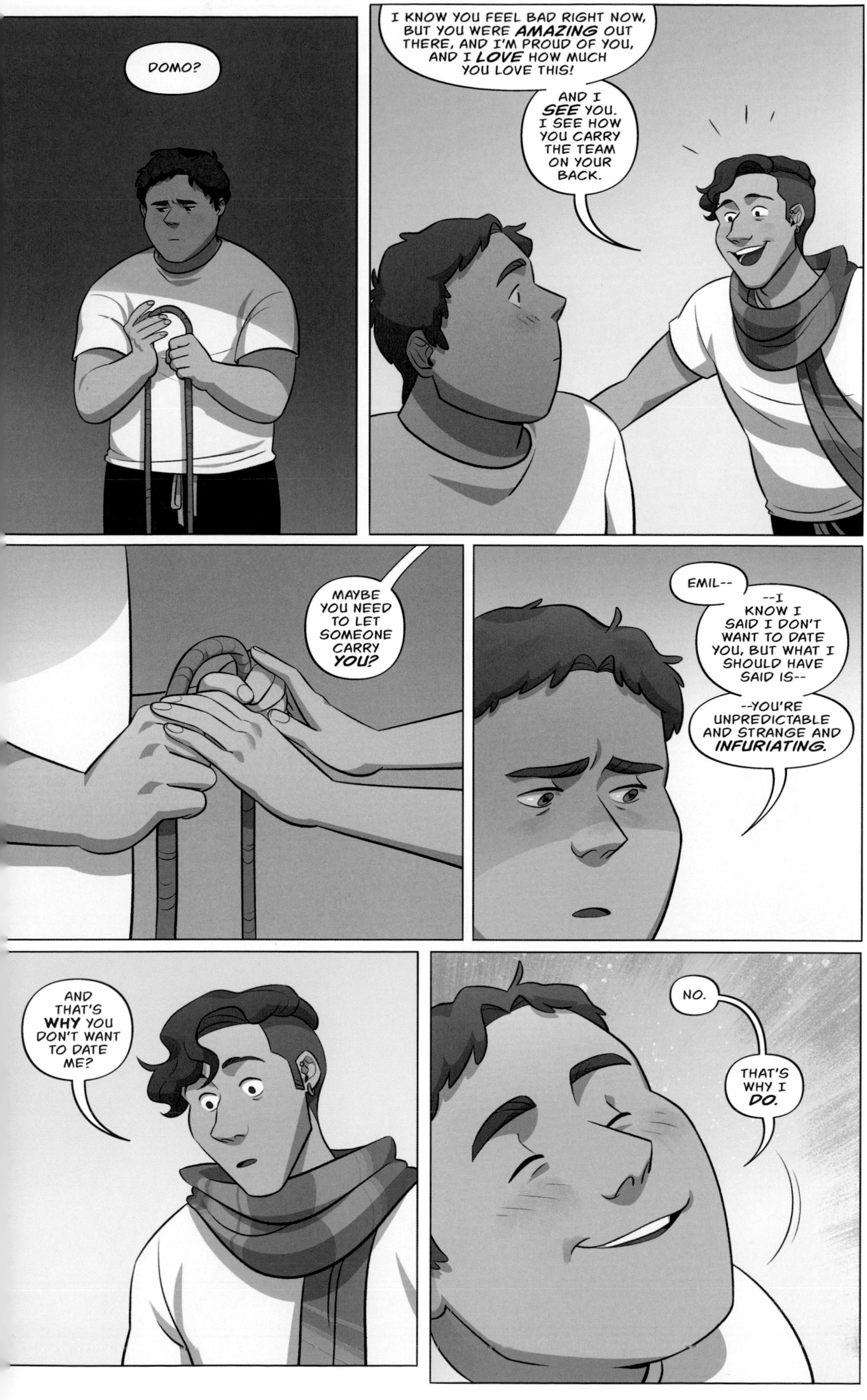
DOMO?
I KNOW YOU FEEL BAD RIGHT NOW, BUT YOU WERE AMAZING OUT THERE, AND I'M PROUD OF YOU, AND I LOVE HOW MUCH YOU LOVE THIS!
AND I SEE YOU. I SEE HOW YOU CARRY THE TEAM ON YOUR BACK.
MAYBE YOU NEED TO LET SOMEONE CARRY YOU?
EMIL--
--I KNOW I SAID I DON'T WANT TO DATE YOU, BUT WHAT I SHOULD HAVE SAID IS--
--YOU'RE UNPREDICTABLE AND STRANGE AND INFURIATING.
AND THAT'S WHY YOU DON'T WANT TO DATE ME?
NO.
THAT'S WHY I DO.

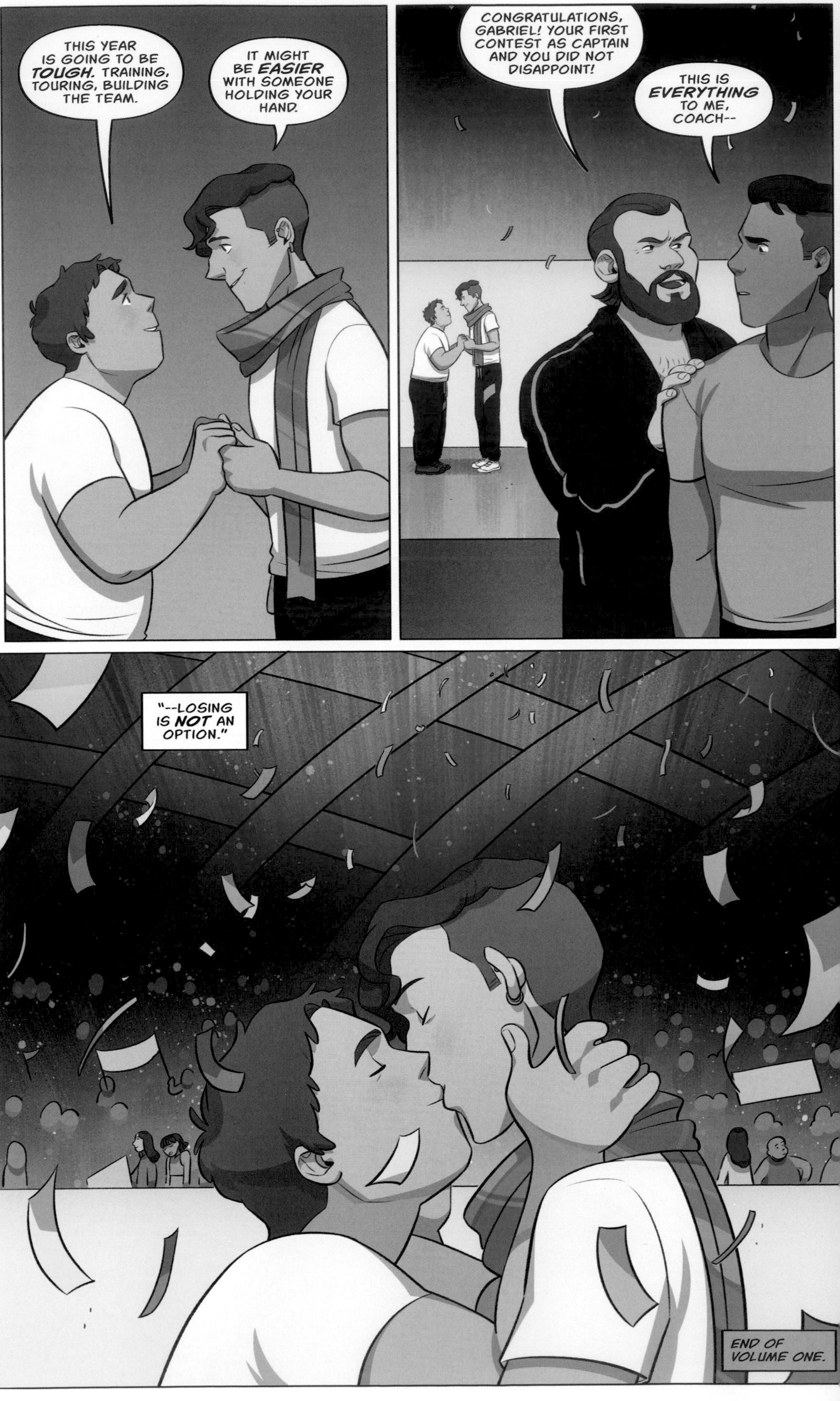
THIS YEAR IS GOING TO BE TOUGH. TRAINING, TOURING, BUILDING THE TEAM.
IT MIGHT BE EASIER WITH SOMEONE HOLDING YOUR HAND.
CONGRATULATIONS, GABRIEL! YOUR FIRST CONTEST AS CAPTAIN AND YOU DID NOT DISAPPOINT!
THIS IS EVERYTHING TO ME, COACH--
"--LOSING IS NOT AN OPTION."
END OF VOLUME ONE.

ISSUE 1 COVER

ART BY GUILLERMO SAAVEDRA COLORS BY C. R. CHUA

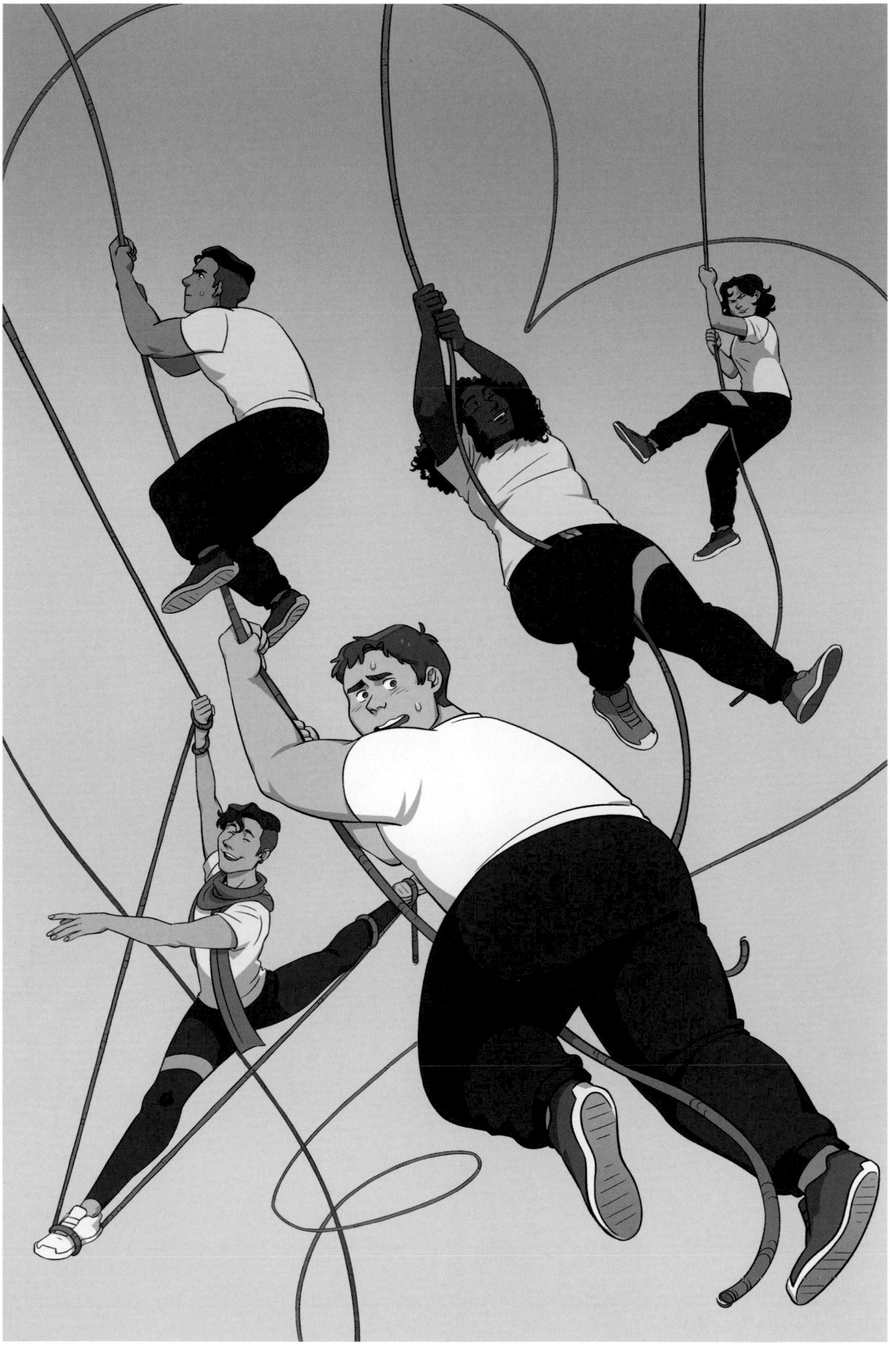

ISSUE 1 COVER VARIANT

ART BY KILLIAN NG COLORS BY C. R. CHUA

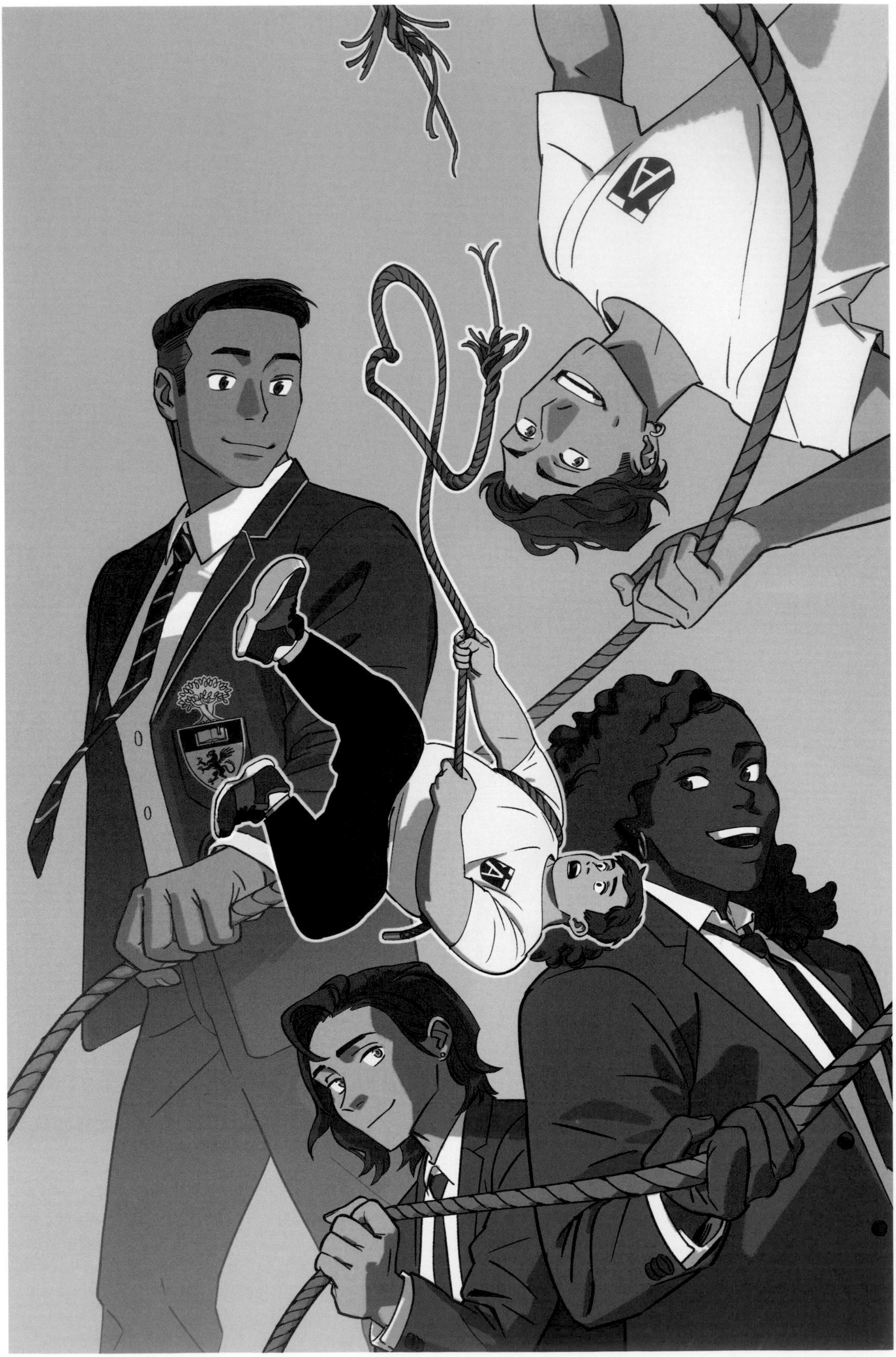

ISSUE 2 COVER

ART BY GUILLERMO SAAVEDRA COLORS BY C. R. CHUA

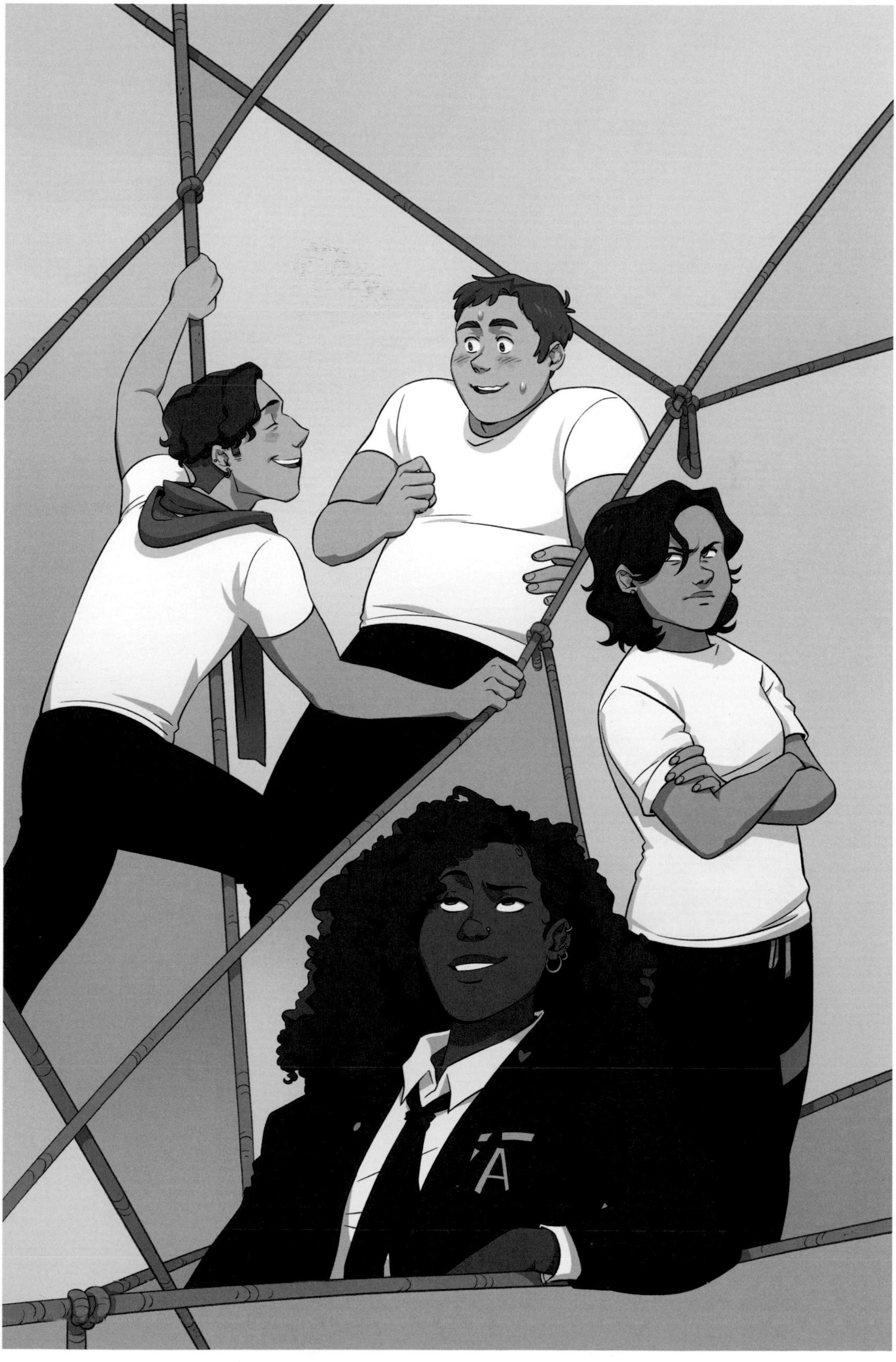

ISSUE 3 COVER

ART BY GUILLERMO SAAVEDRA   COLORS BY C. R. CHUA

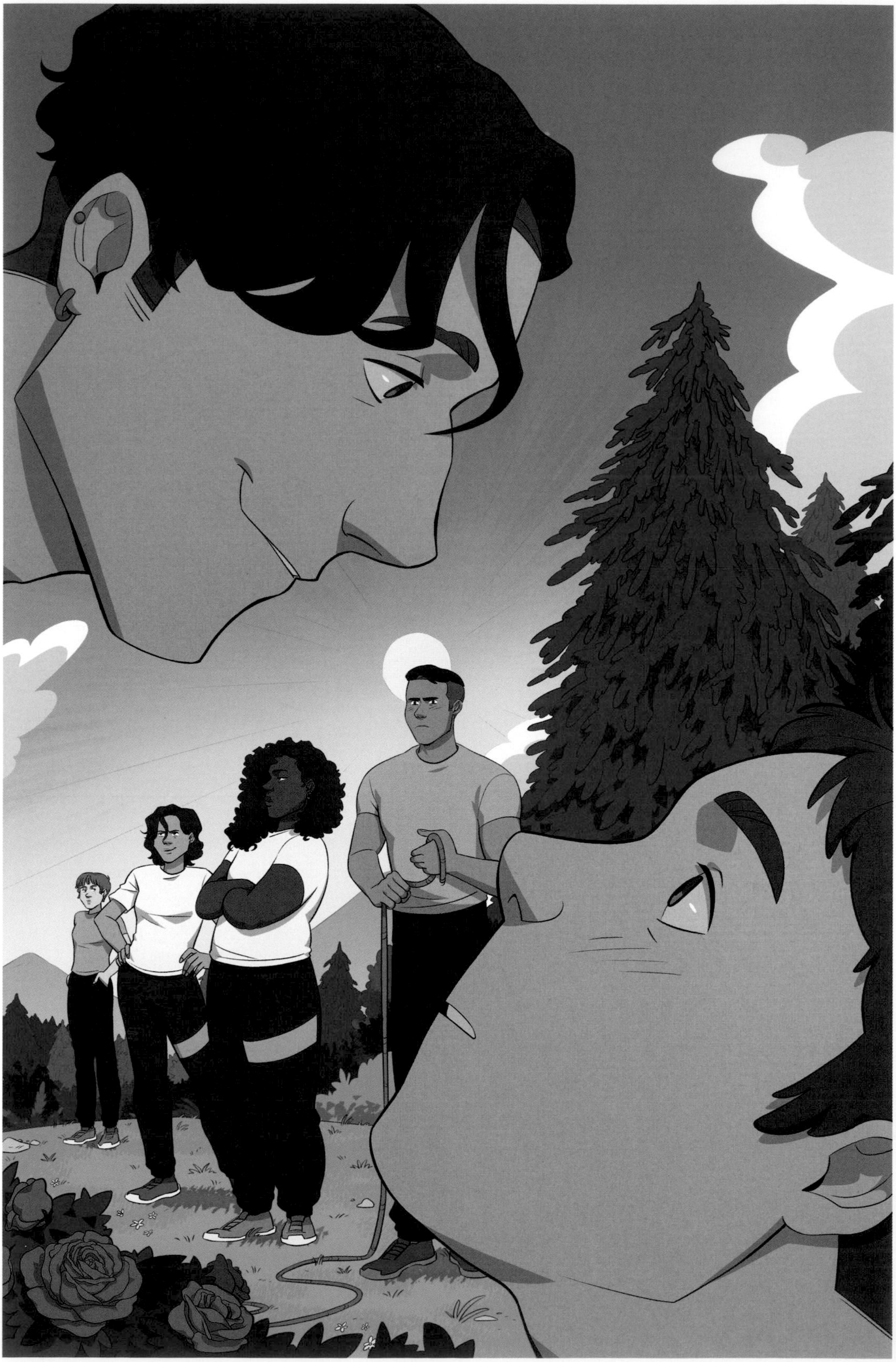

ISSUE 4 COVER

ART BY GUILLERMO SAAVEDRA COLORS BY C. R. CHUA

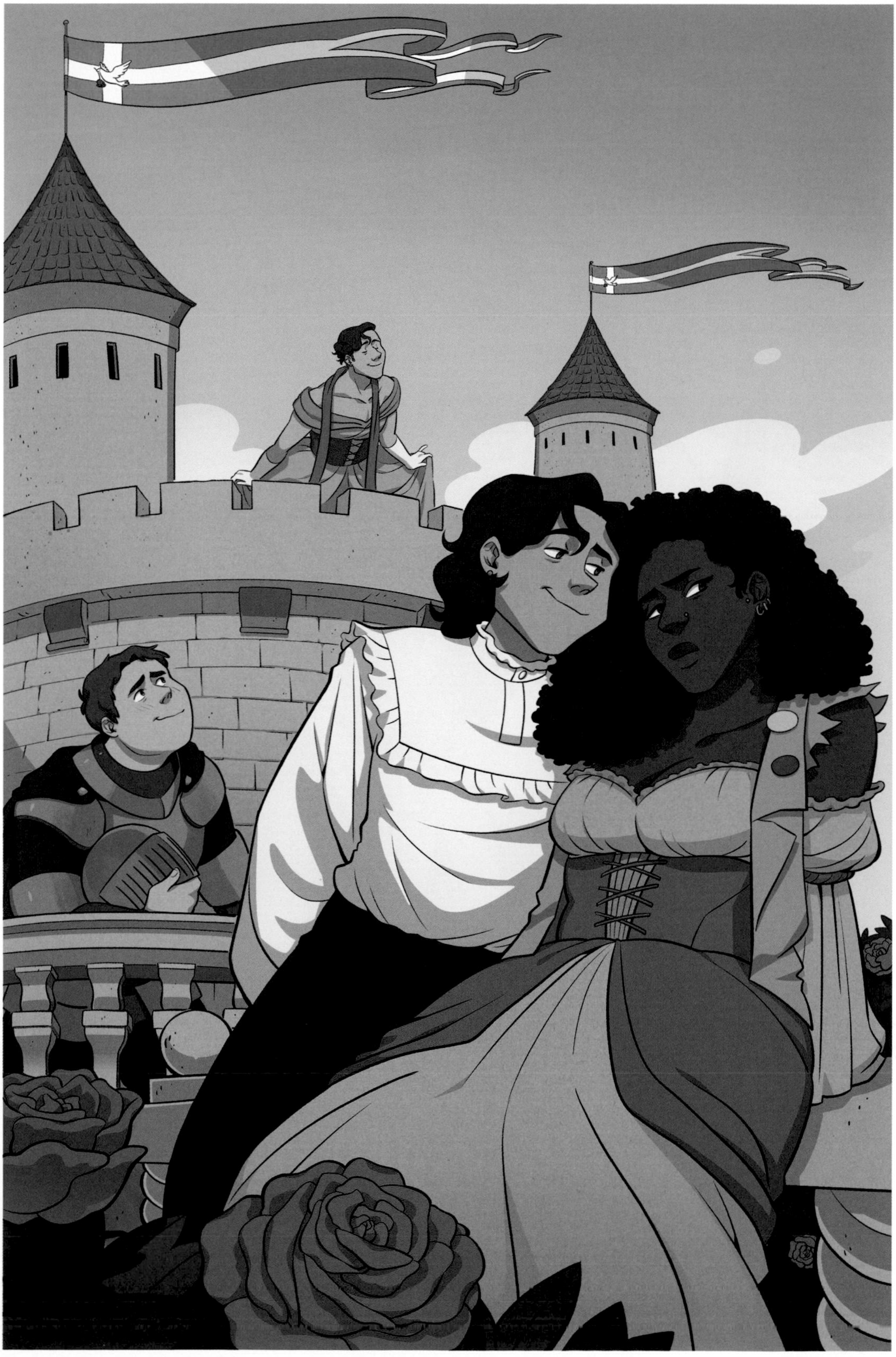

ISSUE 5 COVER

ART BY GUILLERMO SAAVEDRA   COLORS BY C. R. CHUA

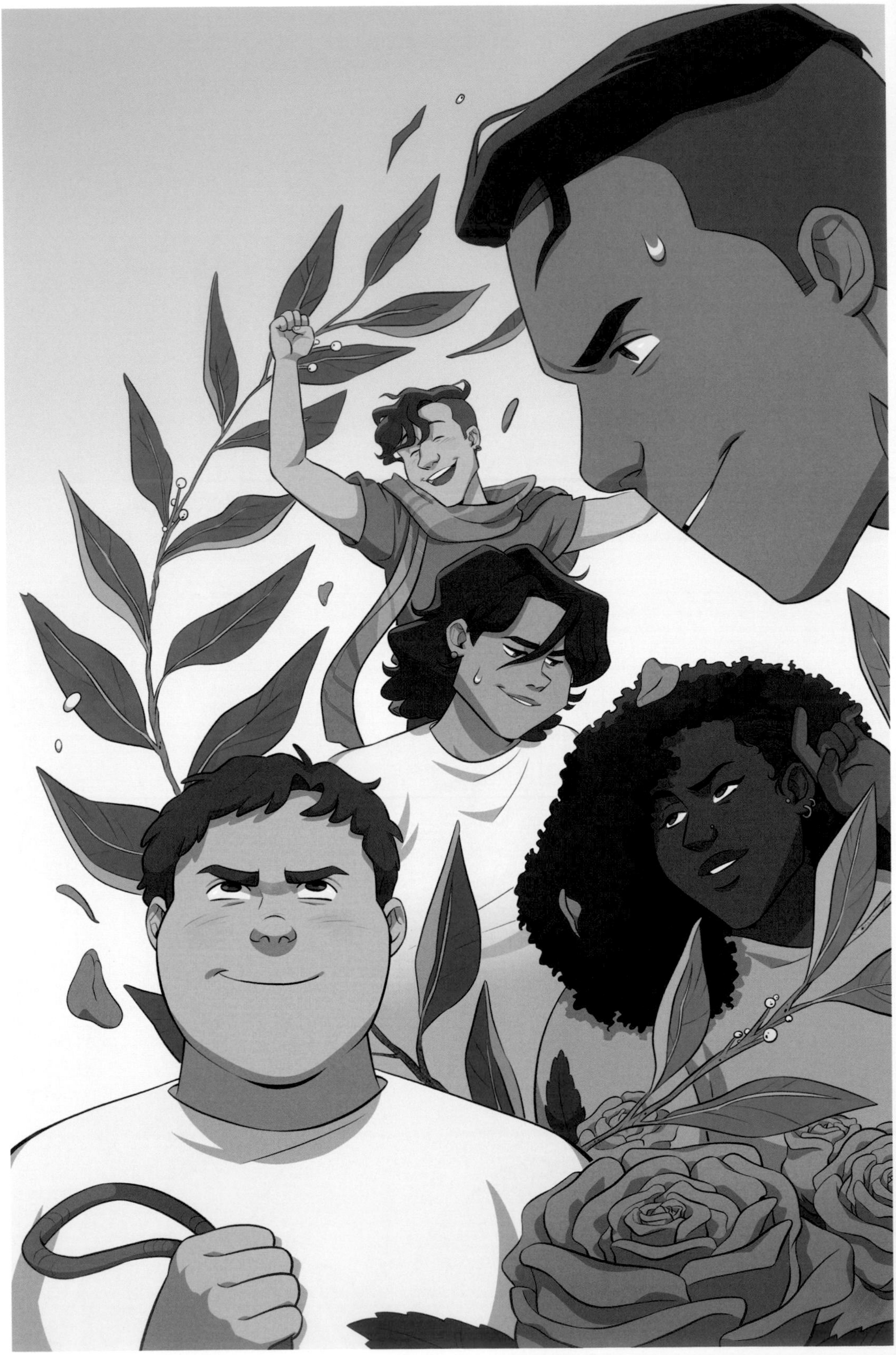

Aster Academy
YEARBOOK

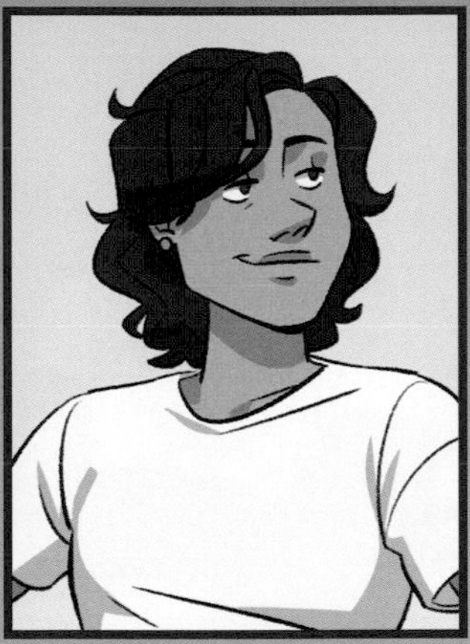

JOCASTA "JO" NICOLAIDES

Studies: Sports performance, coaching, and management.

Clubs: Tug of war.

"Most likely to break a world record."

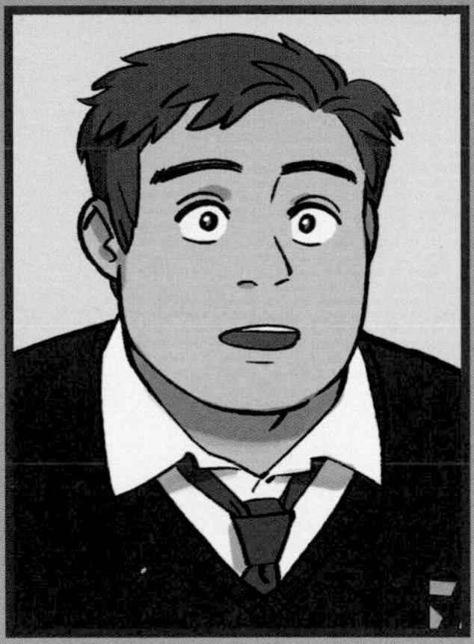

DOMINIC "DOMO" NOVAK

Studies: Sports performance, health sciences.

Clubs: Tug of war.

"Most dependable."

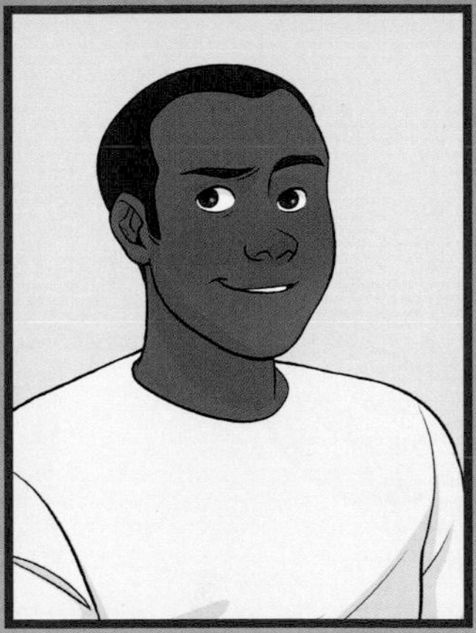

SIMON PATERSON-MOORE

Studies: Health sciences, music.

Clubs: Tug of war, orchestra, anime/manga.

"Best singer."

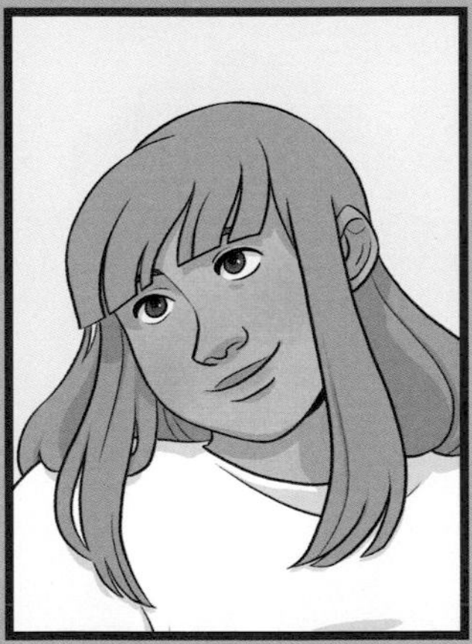

BETHANY MOSS

Studies: Creative writing, health sciences.

Clubs: Tug of war, poetry, wrestling.

"Most likely to travel the world."

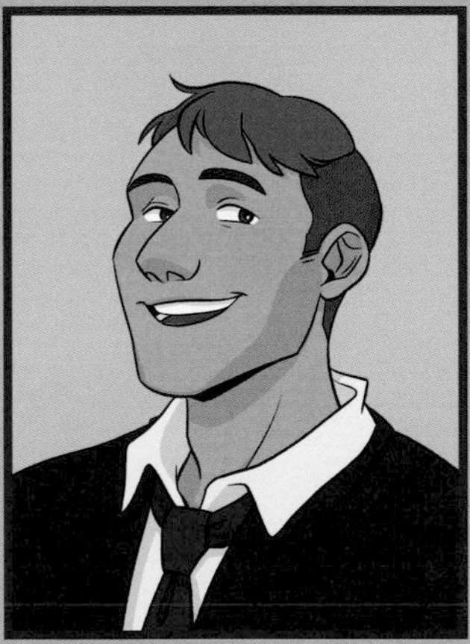

BYRON "BY" KOVACS

Studies: Sports performance, art history.

Clubs: Tug of war, boxing, drama.

"Most likely to come through in a crisis."

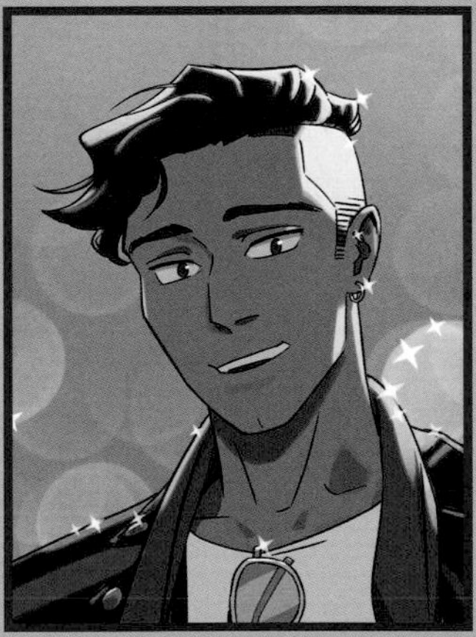

EMIL VARGAS

Studies: General studies.

Clubs: Tug of war, anime/manga.

"Best dressed."

Aster Academy
YEARBOOK

LEONI MORTIMER
Studies: Fine arts, art history.
Clubs: Tug of war, swimming, orchestra, journalism, puppetry, trivia.

"Most talkative."

ASHER "ASH" GABOR
Studies: Mathematics, business management.
Clubs: Tug of war, chess, anime/manga.

"Most likely to make billions."

LUCKY SHAKOOR
Studies: Fashion, psychology.
Clubs: Tug of war, boxing, self-defense.

"Most likely to walk a red carpet."

SZANDRA TOTH, COACH
Two-time world champion.
Olympic silver medalist.
Rosecastle Order of Merit.

GABRIEL "GABE" DIAZ (TRANSFERRED)
Studies: Health sciences, coaching and management.
Clubs: Tug of war poetry.

"Most inspirational."

VANESSA "NESSA" HOWELL (TRANSFERRED)
Studies: Political science, history.
Clubs: Tug of war, debate, student government.

"Most likely to lead a protest."

CHARACTER DESIGNS

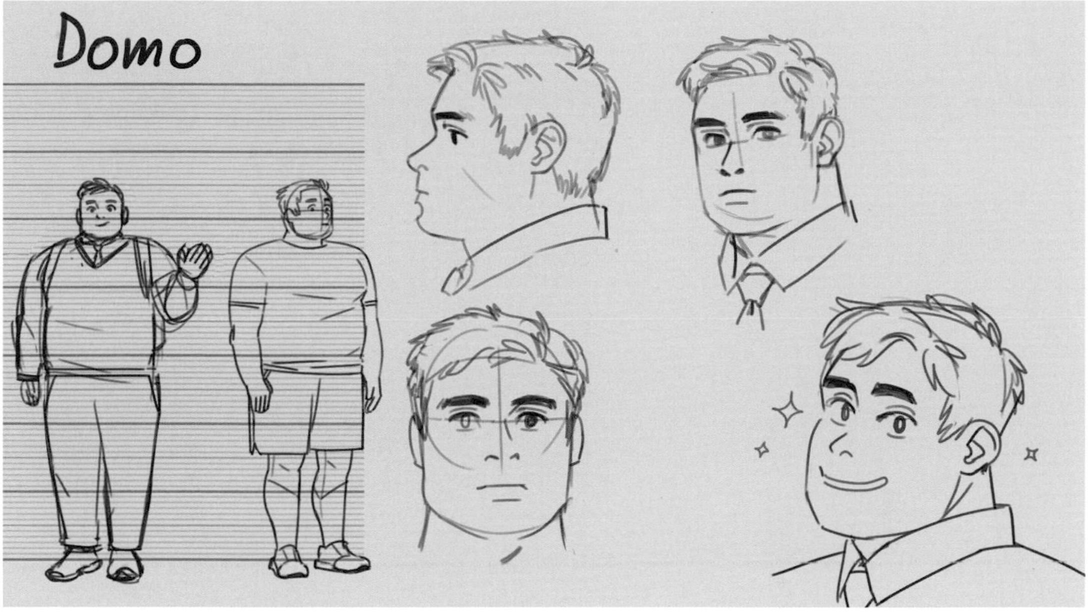
Domo

BY KILLIAN NG

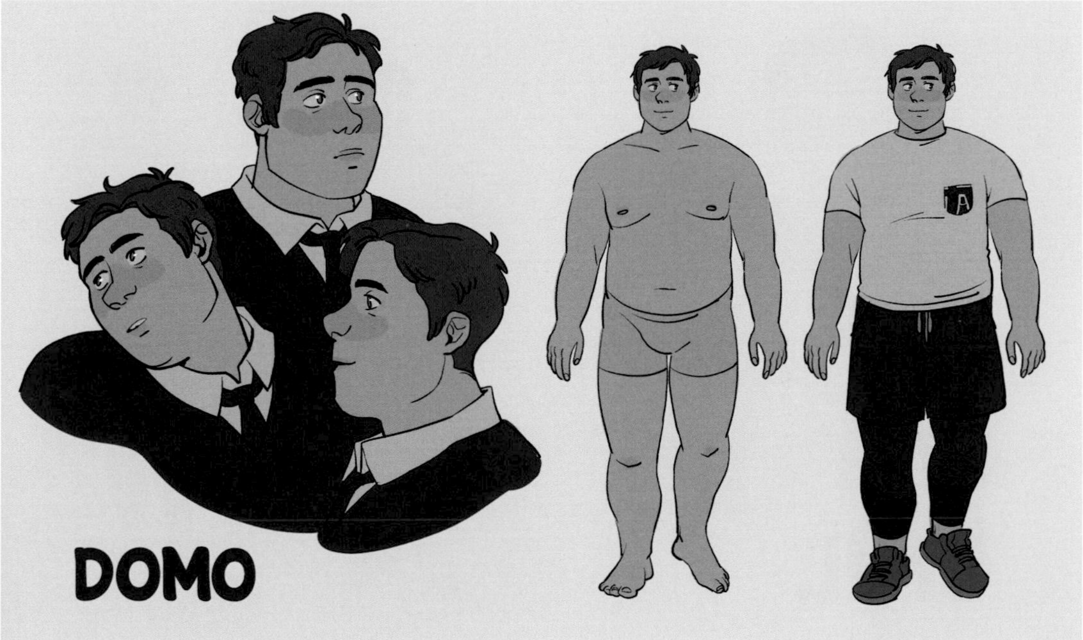
DOMO

BY GUILLERMO SAAVEDRA

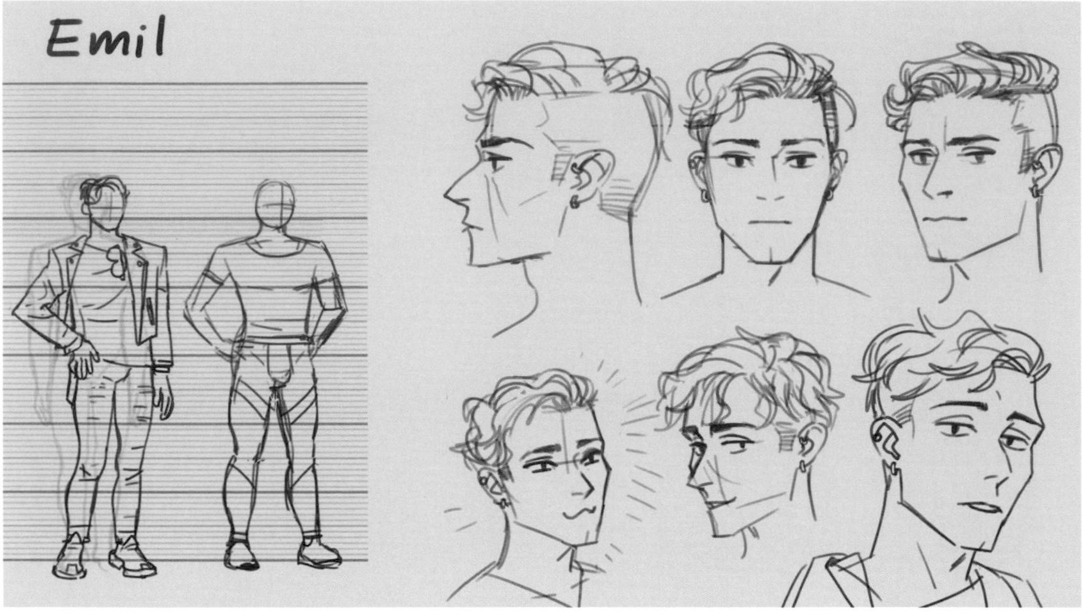
Emil

BY KILLIAN NG

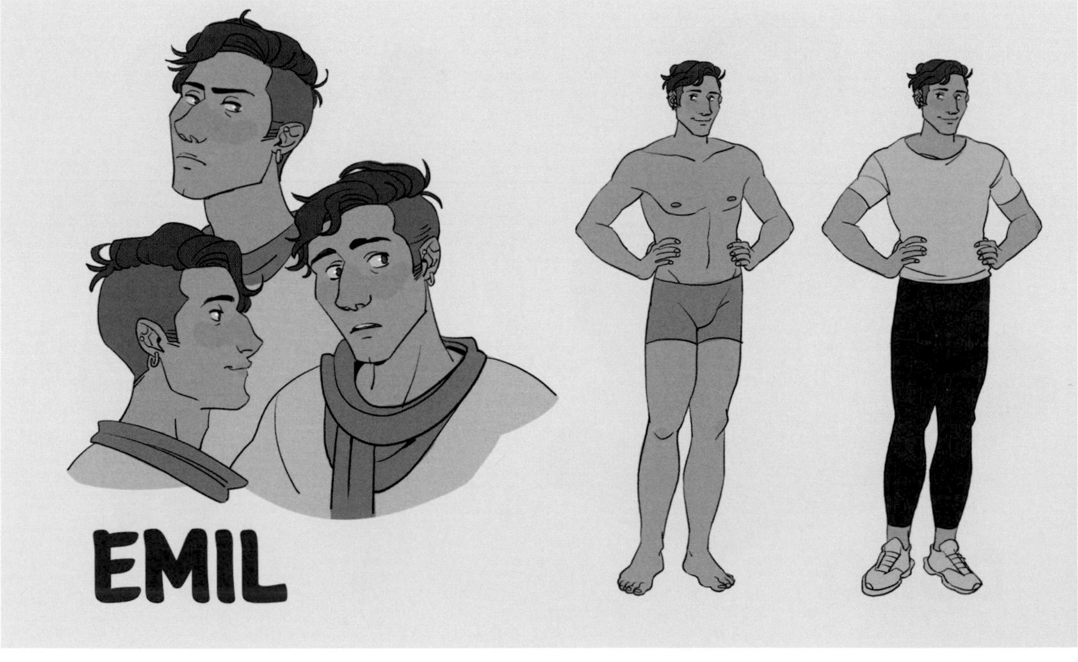
EMIL

BY GUILLERMO SAAVEDRA

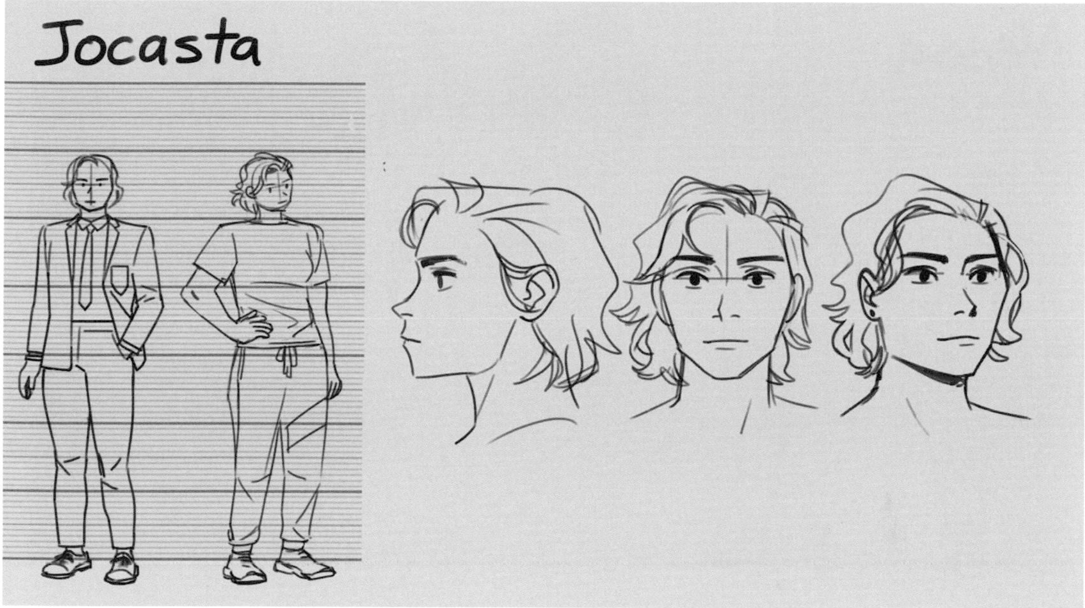
Jocasta

BY KILLIAN NG

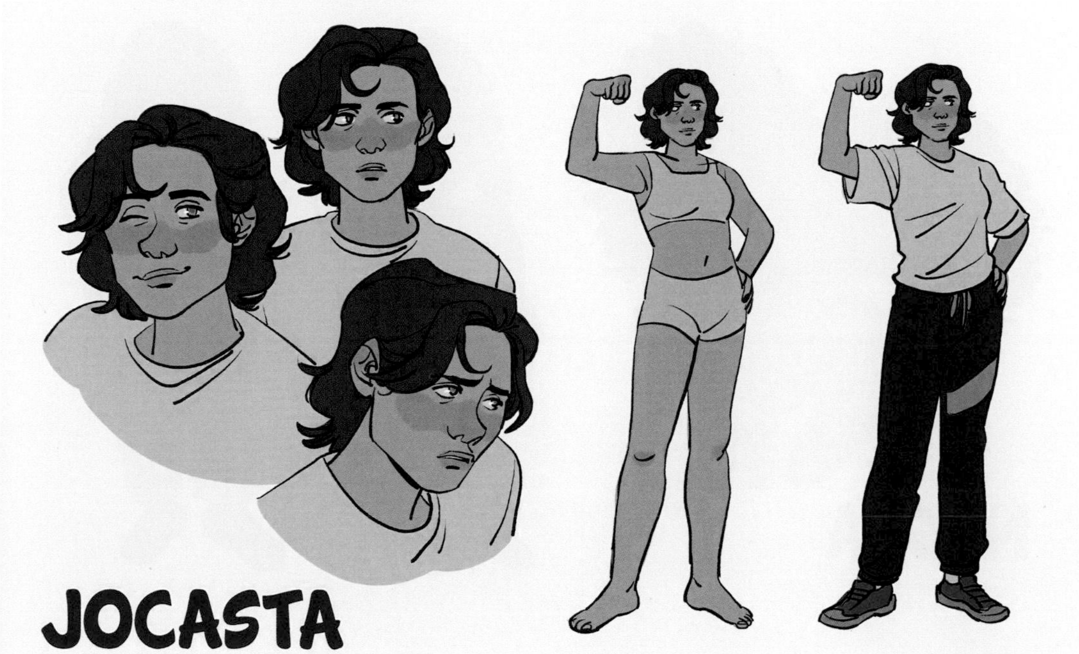
JOCASTA

BY GUILLERMO SAAVEDRA

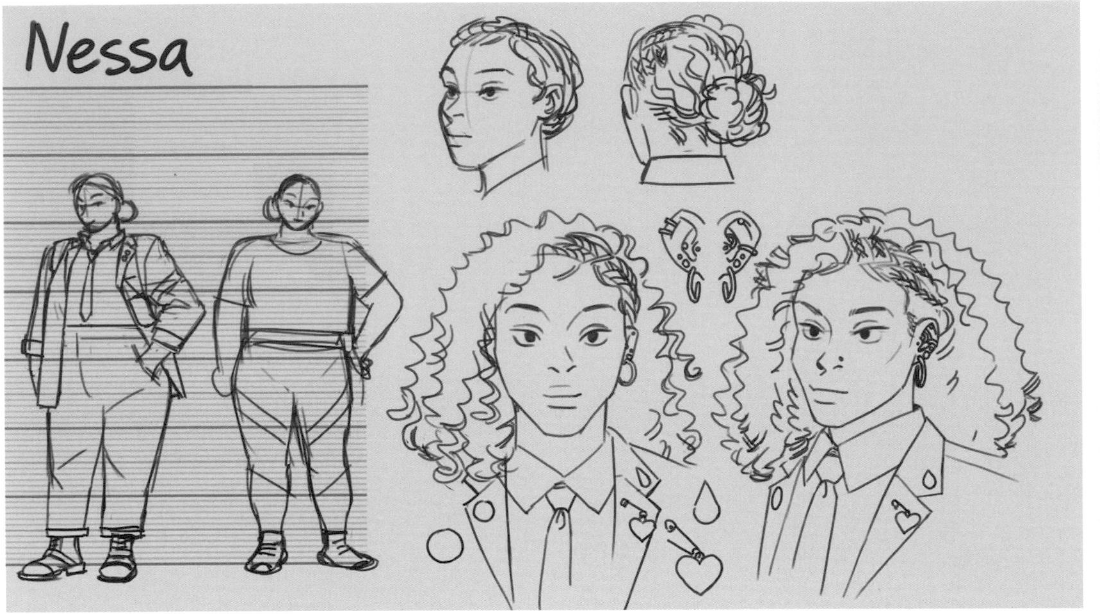
Nessa

BY KILLIAN NG

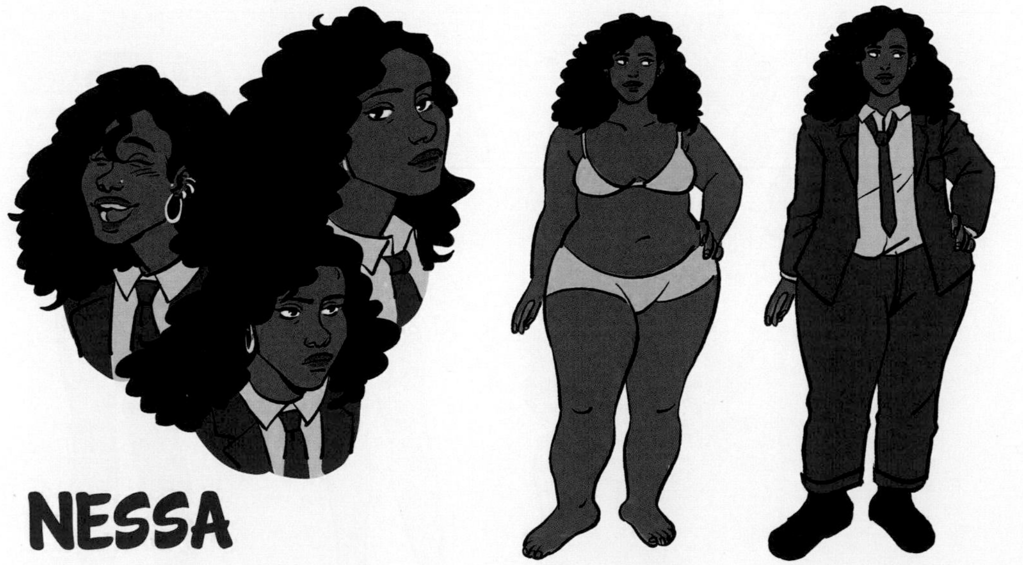
NESSA

BY GUILLERMO SAAVEDRA

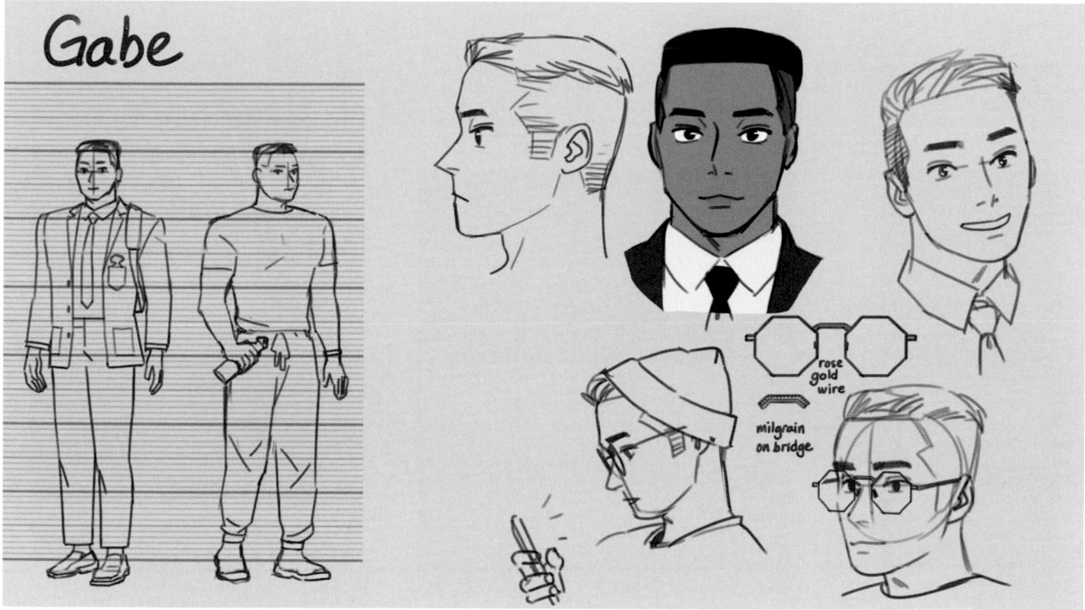
Gabe
rose gold wire
milgrain on bridge

BY KILLIAN NG

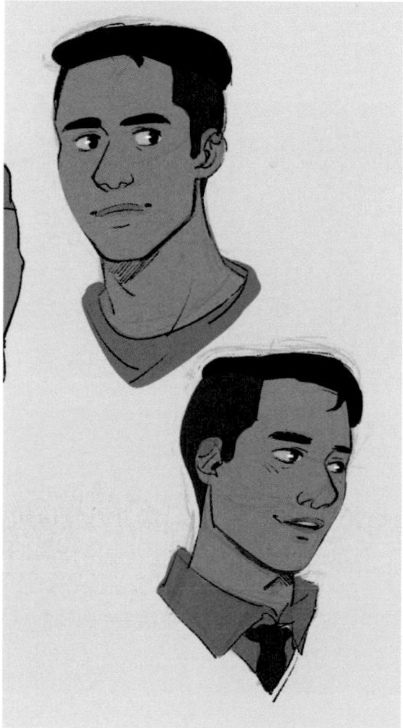

BY GUILLERMO SAAVEDRA

CONCEPT ART Flag designs for Rosecastle

2 shades
of pink
+
white?

pastel
green
maybe?

COMIC PROCESS

THIRTEEN

Panel 1: A butterfly settles on EMIL's finger, and he smiles at it, instantly in love.

1. EMIL	I've been to so many places. Touring with the ballet since I was eight. Never in one place for long.
2. EMIL	All the memories get mixed up in my head.

Panel 2: DOMO looks up at EMIL. He's curious and mildly horrified.

3. DOMO	Since you were <u>eight</u>?
4. DOMO	I don't think I've been away from my own bed for more than a week at a time.
5. DOMO	Don't you miss... <u>home</u>?

Panel 3: On EMIL, a far-off, romantic look on his face.

6. EMIL	I've learned to enjoy where I am, instead of worrying about where I could be.
7. EMIL	You have to take the time to stop and look around and say...

Panel 4: On DOMO, really seeing EMIL for the first time and realizing he's something special. Maybe there's butterflies around his head?

8. EMIL (off)	"Hey, this? Right now?"
9. EMIL (off)	"This is <u>beautiful</u>."

Panel 5: EMIL and DOMO sit side-by-side, facing each other. EMIL is smiling and, reluctantly, so is DOMO.

10. EMIL	I'm going to head back. You coming?

13

LAYOUT BY GUILLERMO SAAVEDRA

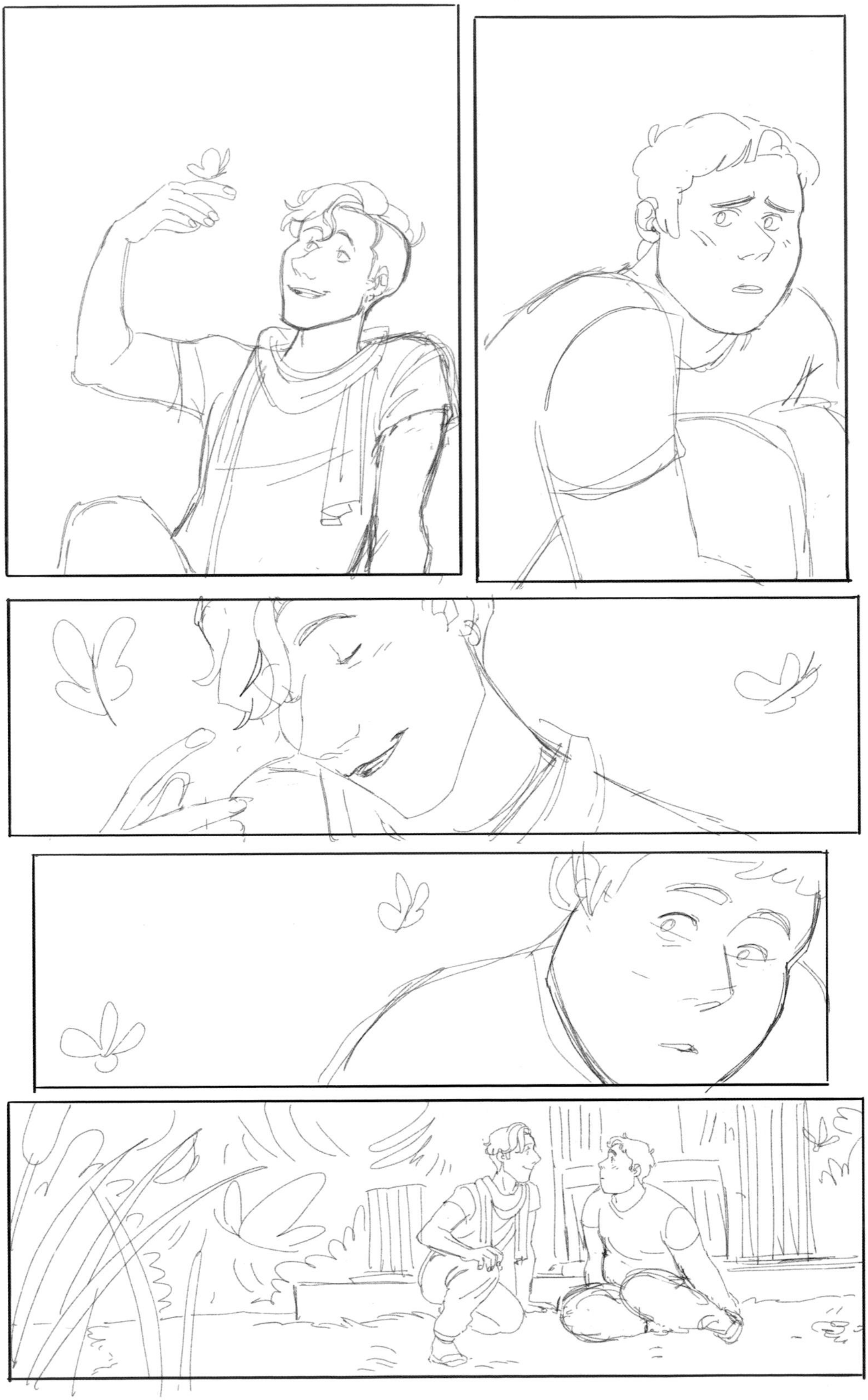

PENCILS BY GUILLERMO SAAVEDRA

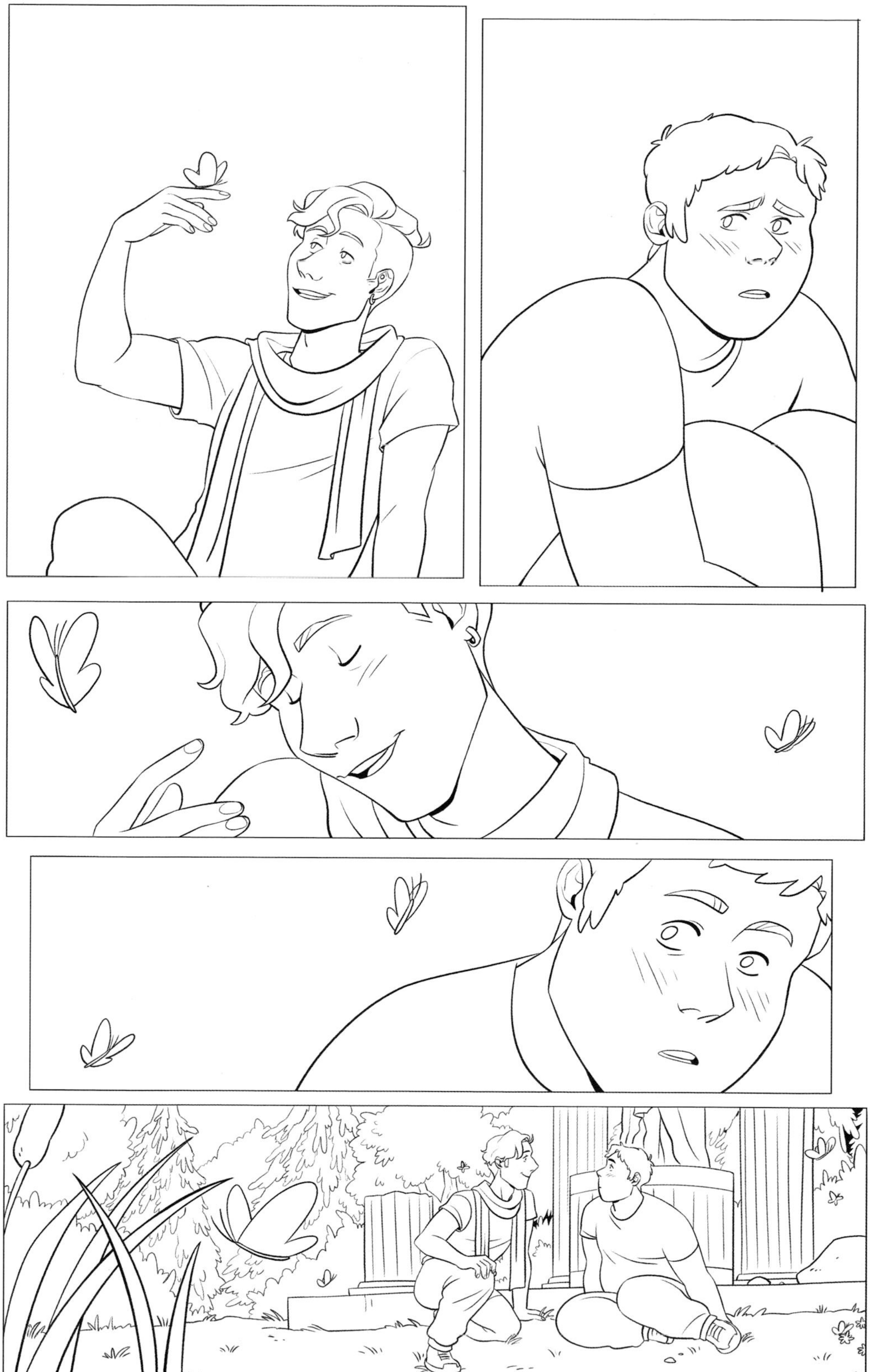

INKS BY GUILLERMO SAAVEDRA

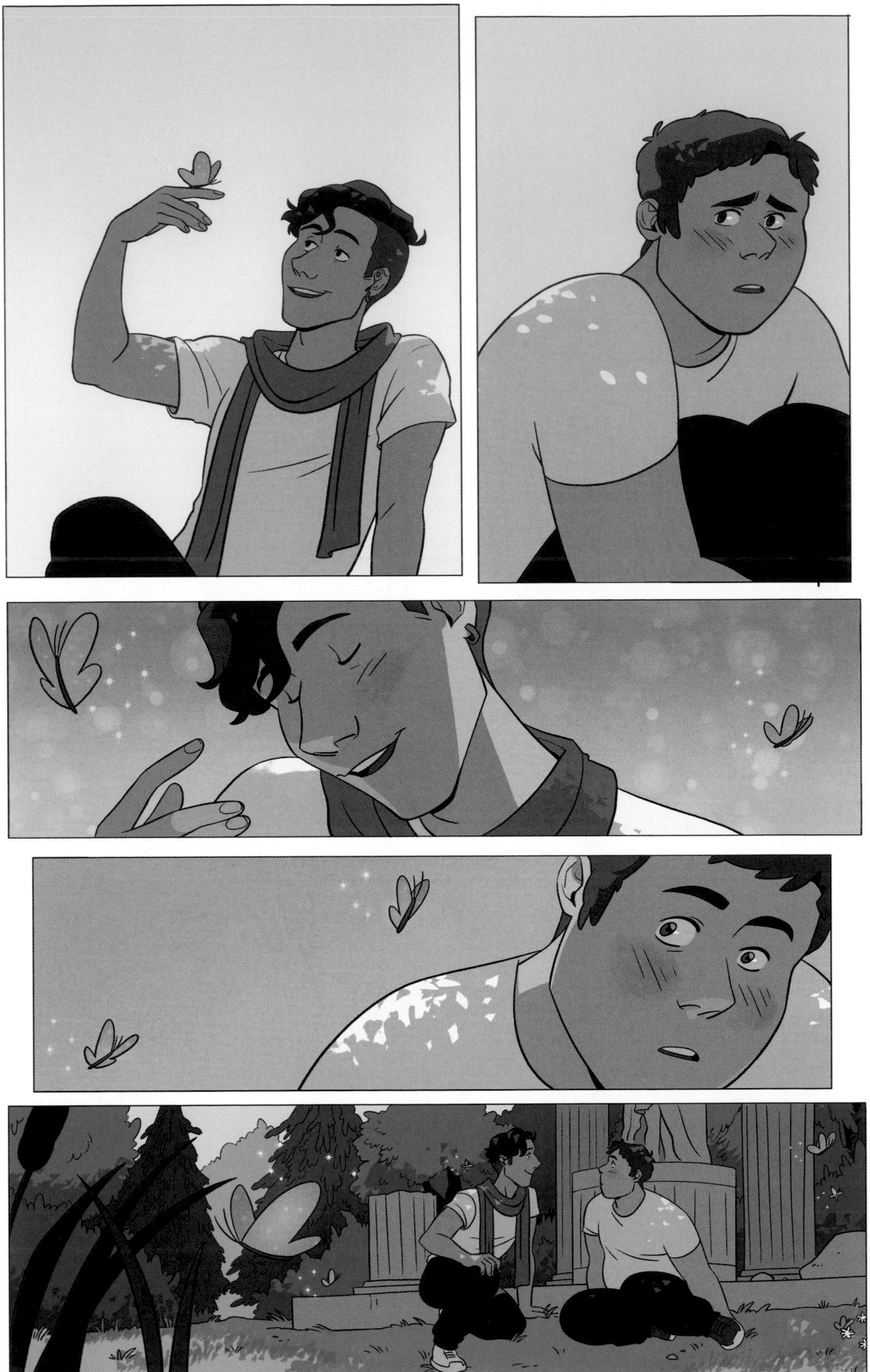

COLORS BY C. R. CHUA

ANDREW WHEELER

Andrew Wheeler is an award-winning Toronto-based writer. His credits include *Wonder Woman: Agent of Peace*, *The Old Guard: Tales through Time*, *Freelance*, *Another Castle*, and the Dungeons & Dragons Young Adventurer's Guides. He's also the editor of the Prism and the Shuster-nominated queer young-adult anthology *Shout Out*.

🐦 @Wheeler

GUILLERMO SAAVEDRA

Guillermo Saavedra is an indie cartoonist from the Canary Islands. His recent publications include *Siembra* from Dibbuks.

🐦 @deathrowromeo_

KILLIAN NG

Killian Ng is a comics artist and background painter working in comics, animation, and games. Past credits include the *Legend of Korra* comic, *Adventure Time with Fionna & Cake: Party Bash Blues Blues*, *Bravery Network Online*, and *We Are OFK*. They are also a proud owner of over one hundred houseplants.

🐦 @KLLiiNNG

C. R. CHUA

C. R. CHUA is a cartoonist and illustrator from Manila who also loves coloring. She coauthored and illustrated *A Sparrow's Roar*, a young adult graphic novel from Boom! Box with Paolo Chikiamco. She really likes dogs and tweets sparingly.

🐦 @ceearrchua

THE TEAM

HASSAN OTSMANE-ELHAOU

Hassan is a British-Algerian letterer who has worked on comics like *X-O Manowar*, *Undone by Blood*, and *Count*. He's also the editor of the Eisner-winning *PanelxPanel* magazine.

🐦 @HassanOE
https://hassanoe.co.uk/

ADITYA BIDIKAR

Aditya Bidikar is a comics letterer and occasional writer based in India. His recent work includes *Blue in Green*, *John Constantine: Hellblazer*, *Coffin Bound*, and *Afterlift*.

🐦 @adityab
http://adityab.net

ALLISON O'TOOLE

Allison O'Toole is a freelance comics editor and dog lover. Her credits include the *Wayward Sisters* anthology, *Afterlift*, *The All-Nighter*, and *Newburn*.

🐦 @allisonmotoole
https://www.allisonotoole.com

CINDY LEONG

Cindy Leong is a graphic designer and illustrator hailing from Canada. She has been involved in the production of a variety of works, including *Freelance*, *The Wellspring Trilogy: The Crystal Key*, and *5lHundred*.

🐦 @deadbeatdearest
heya.im.cindy.@gmail.com

COMIXOLOGY COMES TO DARK HORSE BOOKS

JASON LOO
CHIP ZDARSKY
AFTERLIFT

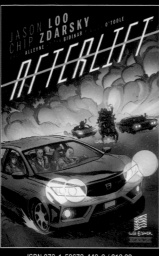

ISBN 978-1-50672-440-9 / $19.99

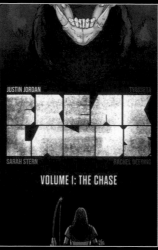

JUSTIN JORDAN
TYASSETA
BREAK LANDS
SARAH STERN
RACHEL DEERING
VOLUME I: THE CHASE

ISBN 978-1-50672-441-6 / $19.99

curt pires
alex diotto
dee cunniffe
micah myers
Youth
Named One of "10 Comics to Celebrate Pride" by the New York Times

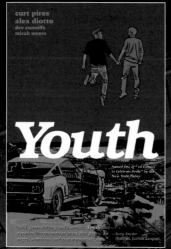

ISBN 978-1-50672-461-4 / $19.99

Named one of the "5 New Comic Book Series for the End of Summer" by the New York Times

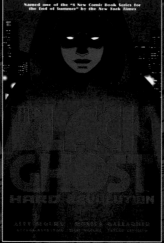

ISBN 978-1-50672-446-1 / $19.99

THE PRIDE
OMNIBUS

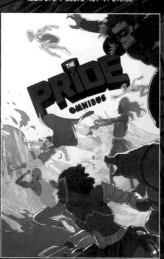

ISBN 978-1-50672-447-8 / $29.99

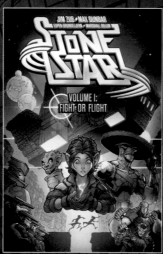

JIM ZUB + MAX DUNBAR
STONE STAR
VOLUME I:
FIGHT OR FLIGHT

ISBN 978-1-50672-458-4 / $19.99

AFTERLIFT

Written by Chip Zdarsky, art by Jason Loo

This Eisner Award–winning series from Chip Zdarsky (*Sex Crimi* Daredevil) and Jason Loo (*The Pitiful Human-Lizard*) features chases, demon bounty hunters, and figuring out your place in world and the next.

BREAKLANDS

Written by Justin Jordan, art by Tyasseta and Sarah Stern

Generations after the end of the civilization, everyone has pow you need them just to survive in the new age. Everyone ex Kasa Fain. Unfortunately, her little brother, who has the potenti reshape the world, is kidnapped by people who intend to do just *Mad Max* meets *Akira* in a genre-mashing, expectation-smas new hit series from Justin Jordan, creator of *Luther Strode*, *Sp* and *Reaver*!

YOUTH

Written by Curt Pires, art by Alex Diotto and Dee Cunniffe

A coming of age story of two queer teenagers who run away their lives in a bigoted small town, and attempt to make their w California. Along the way their car breaks down and they join a g of fellow misfits on the road. travelling the country together in a they party and attempt to find themselves. And then . . . somet happens. The story combines the violence of coming of age wit violence of the superhero narrative—as well as the beauty.

THE BLACK GHOST SEASON ONE: HARD REVOLUT

Written by Alex Segura and Monica Gallagher, art by George Kamab

Meet Lara Dominguez—a troubled Creighton cops reporter obse with the city's debonair vigilante the Black Ghost. With the he a mysterious cyberinformant named LONE, Lara's inched clos uncovering the Ghost's identity. But as she searches for the breakthr story she desperately needs, Lara will have to navigate the corrupti her city, the uncertainties of virtues, and her own personal demons she have the strength to be part of the solution—or will she be the problem?

THE PRIDE OMNIBUS

Joseph Glass, Gavin Mitchell and Cem Iroz

FabMan is sick of being seen as a joke. Tired of the LGBTQ+ comm being seen as inferior to straight heroes, he thinks it's about time he did something about it. Bringing together some of the w greatest LGBTQ+ superheroes, the Pride is born to protect the and fight prejudice, misrepresentation and injustice—not to men pesky supervillain or two.

STONE STAR

Jim Zub and Max Zunbar

The brand-new space-fantasy saga that takes flight on comiX Originals from fan-favorite creators Jim Zub (*Avengers*, *Samurai* and Max Dunbar (*Champions*, *Dungeons & Dragons*)! The nor space station called Stone Star brings gladiatorial entertainme ports across the galaxy. Inside this gargantuan vessel of tournar and temptations, foragers and fighters struggle to survive. A thief named Dail discovers a dark secret in the depths of Ston and must decide his destiny—staying hidden in the shado standing tall in the searing spotlight of the arena. Either way, h and the cosmos itself, will never be the same!

AVAILABLE AT YOUR LOCAL COMICS SHOP OR BOOKSTORE / To find a comics shop near you, visit comicshoplocator.com / For more information or to order direct, visit darkhorse.com

COMIXOLOGY ORIGINALS

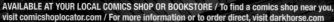

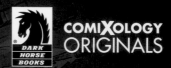